MY SISTER'S SHADOW

ALSO AVAILABLE BY JANUARY GILCHRIST
(WRITING AS AVA JANUARY)

The Mayfair Dagger

My Sister's Shadow

A NOVEL

January Gilchrist

NEW YORK

This is a work of fiction. All of the names, characters, organizations, places and events portrayed in this novel are either products of the author's imagination or are used fictitiously. Any resemblance to real or actual events, locales, or persons, living or dead, is entirely coincidental.

Copyright © 2025 by January Gilchrist

All rights reserved.

Published in the United States by Crooked Lane Books, an imprint of The Quick Brown Fox & Company LLC.

Crooked Lane Books and its logo are trademarks of The Quick Brown Fox & Company LLC.

Library of Congress Catalog-in-Publication data available upon request.

ISBN (hardcover): 979-8-89242-058-7
ISBN (paperback): 979-8-89242-232-1
ISBN (ebook): 979-8-89242-059-4

Cover design by Jocelyn Martinez

Printed in the United States.

www.crookedlanebooks.com

Crooked Lane Books
34 West 27th St., 10th Floor
New York, NY 10001

First Edition: March 2025

10 9 8 7 6 5 4 3 2 1

For all the sisterless sisters

PART 1

CHAPTER 1

Harewood Hall, Gloucester, 1904

I stole through the hall on stockinged feet, creeping through wood-paneled corridors, listening for the slightest noise that would indicate someone else was stalking the same rooms. Cocking my ear toward the dining room, I paused before lifting my skirts and running up the stairs as quietly as I could, avoiding the squeaky third tread that would betray me. Time had gotten away from me in the garden, as it was wont to do, and I daren't risk running into Nanny Jones or, God forbid, Father, who strongly disapproved of me spending time in the garden with the staff. Fraternizing, he called it, with a lifted lip, as if he had been assaulted by a waft of something unpleasant.

But they weren't staff to me. Morris, who tended to the grounds of Harewood Hall as his father had done before him, and now his son Graham (even thinking his name brought a blush to my cheeks) were part of the house. Morris, whom I'd spent more time with than Father, had taught me all the names, Latin and common, of every flower and plant in Harewood's extensive garden, and Graham whose calm and gentle nature and graceful artist's hands always drifted into my poems.

I couldn't—and wouldn't—think of either of them as *staff*. They seemed more family to me than my own father. A portrait of Father frowned down on me as I stole around the corner onto the mezzanine landing, and I offered him an insolent salute before turning swiftly and barreling straight into the man I was hoping to avoid.

"Adelaide." Disapproval made his voice hoarse, so common when he spoke to me that I'd begun to wonder if there was any other tone available to him.

"Good afternoon, sir." I clutched my skirts tighter, hoping to hide the damp stain blooming on them, from where I had been kneeling in the dirt.

His gaze dropped to my hands, and his countenance told me he'd spotted it. His lips were pressed together so tightly they appeared bloodless, and his cheeks took on the ruddy hue that signaled grave displeasure. I took a step out of arm's reach.

"We have important guests." He hissed the final letter of the word.

A muscle below my right eye began to pulse thickly as the grandfather clock in the hallway coughed its hourly chime. Father was hosting a dinner party with important business associates, he had informed us gravely, and they were to be treated as such. A Horton James Henry Gilbraith, fourth Earl of Gymouth, known as Lord Stanley, would be in attendance, all the way from London.

"You are to be on your best behavior," he had warned us heavily. "If you are ever to marry, you must learn to behave as ladies. Keep quiet, no speaking unless asked a question directly, and do not offer your opinion; these men are not here to listen to your inane thoughts. You will comport yourselves in the manner appropriate to young, well-bred ladies. Not"—here he had taken a long swill from the amber liquid in his glass before staring moodily at the fire crackling in the grate—"like *her*."

I didn't know what had disturbed me more, the mention of our mother (forbidden) or the reference to marriage. *We must marry? Says who?* I wondered. I had looked to my sister for reassurance, but her gaze remained fixed on the wall behind Father's head.

"I expressly forbade you to go outside," Father growled, yanking my arm, causing the skirt to fall from my hand, displaying the shameful truth of my exploits, "and yet here you are, as grubby as a street urchin." His fingers bit into the soft flesh of my arm, I tried not to call out in pain as that only seemed to inflame Father, but I couldn't help but wince.

"I'm . . . I'm sorry, sir," I croaked out, disappointed at how thin and helpless my voice sounded.

"You will be on your best behavior tonight." His fingers tightened, tightened, tightened around my arm until I thought I would have to cry out; then suddenly he thrust me from him, sending me stumbling among my skirts. My heart fluttered like a trapped bird as I clutched the smooth wood of the banister. The very banister my mother had toppled over to her death.

"Stop it." The frown on Father's forehead deepened until it appeared to be three thick gazes splitting his face. "Stop it. You leave me no choice."

I righted myself, my hands slick with sweat. Father stared at me with a faraway look, a strange expression, as if he were seeing someone else.

"Father?" My words seemed to bring him back. The forehead creases disappeared, and his eyes refocused on me.

"Make yourself presentable," he bit out. "If you do not conduct yourself appropriately, then I will be forced to make arrangements."

Fear, equal parts frigid and burning hot, flooded me. The alarming threat of *being sent away* was one he had begun to pull out with more regularity. *To some awful distant relative I'd never heard of? A nunnery?* Although he never specified where to, or with whom, the mere mention of it was enough to cause my palms to dampen with fear and a great trembling to overcome me.

I had never wanted to live anywhere else except Harewood House, the family home that had shrouded our secrets for over two hundred years.

This was where I belonged; this was home. Endless, dingy corridors; the smell of damp and mice in every corner; the threat of Father in wafts of tobacco and whiskey.

Harewood lived and breathed for me, and I loved every flower, every blade of grass.

Father wouldn't send me away—I wouldn't allow it. I would haunt the halls of my home long after Father was just another portrait on the wall.

I would do whatever it took, I vowed, I would simper and smile and laugh at these *important* men as they spoke about their *important* things, and Father would see how very well I could play the part of the well-behaved young lady. But only while these important men were here, and Father was watching. Then I could go back to being the real me.

"Yes, sir," I offered to his back, but I had already been dismissed.

* * *

"Adelaide. You're late." The disapproval in Victoria's voice was palpable.

I leaned against the door, breathless from my run to our room.

"Sorry." I brushed my skirts. "Graham and I were planting the tulips. Isn't it amazing the way bulbs sit on the shelf for months, as though they're dead? But they're only sleeping until the right conditions wake them." I forced myself to stop speaking and finally met my sister's gaze.

Gray eyes, large and luminous, were narrowed in our heart-shaped face, our mouth a tight line. A thick plait, as pale as the gardenias that lined the driveway, hung over her shoulder. A gift from our Finnish mother, beyond the grave. *"Uncanny,"* I'd heard Cook say to Nanny once, how much like *her* they look.

MY SISTER'S SHADOW   ☞ 7

I smiled widely, and an expression I couldn't decipher flickered across her face, like a dark cloud scudding across the sun.

"I can assure you, I have no interest in discussing flowers and even less in discussing the gardener's tasks. Lord Stanley has arrived and—" She broke off as her gaze landed on my hands.

I resisted the urge to hide them behind my back, but why should I feel afraid of my sister? Wasn't Father's scolding enough? Then I noticed her dress. She was a vision of pink satin and lace.

"Wasn't I to wear the pink?" I said, confused.

"I changed my mind. The blue suits you better."

Like the two of us, the dresses were replicas of each other, but different only in color. An easy way for the people at tonight's party to tell us apart.

"As you wish," I said as I untied my apron. She had chosen the blue the minute I'd laid my hand on it at the dressmakers, foisting an overly bright pink fabric on me. But I didn't say a word, so used was I to her feckless ways.

"Don't ruin tonight for me, Addy."

Victoria had spun what little information we were given about tonight's party into a web of fantasy and adventure, as she was inclined to do. A lord, all the way from London. She had earmarked him as her ticket away from our childhood home here in the country.

Victoria, long obsessed with female adventurers and rule breakers, yearned to explore the world. To see what waited outside the boundaries of Harewood Hall and its restrictive, antiquated confines. To scrawl her name in a history book somehow.

She'd always made me feel strange and deficient in my contentedness here. For I never wanted to live anywhere else except Harewood House.

But Victoria and I were two halves of the same piece.

If she left Harewood, what would become of me?

My hands trembled as I dipped them in the bowl of bathing water, scrubbing them fiercely. Thoughts like that were pointless.

We hadn't even met the men, let alone left Harewood to marry one of them. I was being foolish. My nerves, often the subject of Victoria's disdain, were getting the better of me. Just another way my attributes, when stacked against Victoria's, were found lacking.

Victoria was putting the final touches on my hair when Nanny Jones—or simply "Jones" as we were supposed to address her since our eighteenth birthday, but didn't unless in jest or pique—appeared in the doorway, her tight gray curls surrounding her round, peach-cheeked face.

"Ladies." Her Welsh accent wavered the vowels of the word into song. "The guests have all arrived. It's time for your grand entrance."

My heart restarted its frantic fluttering, and I swallowed hard.

Victoria turned to Jones, hands curled decorously at her waist. "How do we look?"

"As beautiful as ever, as you well know." Jones shot a wink at me behind Victoria.

"And you, *cariad*," she said to me.

Satisfied, Victoria offered me her elbow. I hooked mine through hers, the warmth of her skin easing the nerves that skittered through me.

It seemed unbelievable now that there was no warning premonition of the chain of events that dinner would unleash. No raven sat on our windowsill, no closed door mysteriously opened on its own, no apparition appeared to warn us of the peril ahead.

So we skipped down that hallway together, clutching each other's arm, breathless in our youth and beauty.

Toward the absolute ruin of it all.

CHAPTER 2

The clamor of the gallery and the dense, acrid aroma of cigar smoke greeted us in the hall. My throat tightened and I clung to Victoria's arm tighter. Small talk was never as effortless for me as it was for her—I preferred the estate's menagerie or the company of our staff to outsiders, but strangers seemed to invigorate Victoria. She flourished under the scrutiny of others, transforming into something luminous. Wherever we went, we caused a hum of disquiet. How similar we looked! Did we think the same thoughts? Could we feel each other's pain? Young children trailed us, watching as we performed our tasks, and men's dark gazes monitored, tracked, and pursued us, the weight of all that attention a heavy cloak I could not bear for long. To be studied like a bug in a case caused me to clench my fists. The gaze of others caused me to wither, a shriveling like the core of an apple left in the sun, shrunken and parched. As Victoria shared her laughter, so much like the delicate chime of tiny silver bells on a velvet ribbon, I became increasingly stilted and reticent, overthinking each word before it left my mouth.

Oh, how I preferred our house silent and still! But Father's threat hung over my head like a guillotine. I must be as charming and vacant as a porcelain doll. Just for one night. Anything could be done for a single night, I reassured myself.

10 ❧   January Gilchrist

Nanny Jones led the way toward the oversized doors that led to the gallery. Her wooden heels echoed off the timber alongside the ancient yet still bright runner. Harrold, standing at strict attention by the door, had discarded his usual butler's uniform for a formal double-breasted waistcoat with gleaming buttons and pleated tails. He cleared his throat, a tell-tale sign of nervousness, and nodded at us twice.

"Behave yourself now," Nanny Jones warned. "Don't be after embarrassing your father."

Her gaze rested for a hummingbird's heartbeat on Victoria, who dipped a shallow curtsey in response. "Yes, ma'am."

Nanny Jones tsked. "Enough of your cheek, pet. Mind yourself. I'll find out sure enough."

Harrold scrutinized us and opened the door to announce us. Wordlessly, we assumed our positions. Arms linked, my left foot slightly turned out at the toe, mirroring Victoria's right foot—the polite, blank expressions people preferred of Nice Young Ladies firmly in place.

"The Honorable Misses Victoria and Adelaide Windlass," he announced.

We stepped over the threshold in unison, freezing in place like the butterflies pinned to their boards in Father's study. Victoria tugged on my arm, prompting me to lift my head to the room.

The hubbub dulled as the guests turned to us. A man stood at the doorway, slightly apart from the other guests, wearing a black dinner suit and an expectant expression. The air around him seemed thicker, darker. A trick of the light perhaps, but still, I shivered.

It wasn't difficult to guess he was Lord Stanley—an air of importance surrounded him. He was tall, and his face was all hard angles and brooding bones, split by a beaklike nose. A well-manicured mustache twitched as he gazed at me through eyes that made me think of the field mice that descended on the stables every May.

My Sister's Shadow   ⌒ 11

Introductions were offered, and greetings exchanged. The mustache prickled through my glove as he pressed it against his lips.

"I say, you're awfully alike. Can you tell them apart yourself, Lord Radcliffe?"

Father huffed a little breath, uncomfortable with the truth—that he often looked up from his ledgers with watery confusion, not entirely certain who stood before him. As if wholly befuddled to find not one, but two young ladies haunting the halls of his ancestral seat, like one of the many specters that walked its dimly lit, echoing rooms.

"Of course," he said, avoiding our gaze. "Since the very day they were born."

Lord Stanley narrowed his eyes, examining us. I entwined my fingers through Victoria's.

"Remarkable," Stanley pronounced after a long pause. "Mirror twins, you said?"

He spoke about us to Father as if we were specimens in a cage. I disliked him already.

Victoria gestured to me. "I am right-handed, and Adelaide is left-handed. We do everything the same but opposite, as if looking into a mirror. Where I am fast, she is slow, and I daresay if you were to look inside, you'd find her heart on the wrong side."

As if a spell had been broken, or cast, Victoria released my hand. I watched her offer it to Lord Stanley but could swear I still felt it in my own.

I stood alone in the middle of the bustling room, cast adrift and hidden from view by the long shadow cast by Victoria.

"But one of us has a tiny mole that the other does not, and if you're very good, I shall share its location with you." Her laugh was the soft ring of silver touched to crystal.

I cringed at her coquettish tone and shot a furtive glance to see which footman was in hearing range. There would be a uproar if Nanny heard about her speaking to a man like that. Good girls were supposed to be beautiful and restrained, and I had promised I was going to be so good that no one, not even Father, who seemed to find wrongdoing in anything I did, could find fault with me.

★ ★ ★

After what felt like an eternity, the dinner gong interrupted the conversational speculations of whether the current weather would hold and the wellness of various parents, aged or otherwise. Although it was a small party of only eight, the air in the room felt soupy, over warm and too thick. Lord Stanley caught my eye and signaled me over with his empty glass. Victoria's mouth pressed into a tight line as I approached.

"Will you do me the honor of both escorting me to dinner?" he said, extending an elbow to Victoria and the other to me.

Victoria glowered. We rarely needed to speak to communicate, and I understood her finely enough now. She did not want to share Lord Stanley, but if I were to obey Father, he needed to see me entertain our guest as he had demanded.

Lord Stanley's eyes flitted between us, studying us intently, as if we were one of Father's curios. "My word, how alike you are."

I smiled tightly. Some held a strange fascination for twins, and clearly Lord Stanley was one. Experience had taught me it was better to get talk of the peculiarities of twinship over quickly with people like him. "As Victoria is the elder of us by one hour and five minutes, she should escort the guest of honor, but"—I swallowed hard and mimicked everything I had ever witnessed Victoria do: shoulders back, chin up, rapidly fluttering eyelids, and a simpering tone that brought bile to my throat—"it would be an absolute delight to escort you."

I tucked my arm through his, resisting the urge to flinch as his scent overcame me. It was equal parts repellant and intriguing. Woody and spicy, with a dark mossy undertone, like the forest floor.

My Sister's Shadow 13

"Ah." It was a small sound, caused by a drop in the jaw and a slight depression on the back of the tongue, but something unknown to me lurked, unuttered, in that one noise.

My breath sank deep and cold.

I thought of this morning's light, how the mist had rolled along the valley below the ridge as I'd ridden my horse, Hera. I unclenched my shoulders and focused on my steps. How I resented strangers at Harewood. Everything was better when things remained as they were. Victoria, Father, and I. Here at Harewood Hall, together, forever. I couldn't wait for this night to be over and for these strangers to be gone.

We moved with barely a sound through the hall and took our places in the line to the dining room.

I looked to Victoria, but her gaze was fixed on Stanley, chin tipped toward him in invitation. She laughed and nodded while he pontificated about the virtues of Florence. "A backward lot, really, and far too many pigeons, but if one wants to expand one's mind, among the art of the greats is the only place to do it."

"Oh, I could weep!" Victoria exclaimed. "I dream of visiting the art galleries of Italy. Did you climb the Fort di Belvedere? I've heard the sunset is exquisite."

"Spectacular, yes. Although it must be said, too many tourists," Stanley said without irony. "And too many Italians."

"The nerve of them. And in their own country too," I said lightly.

Stanley laughed but Victoria frowned, leaning forward to tap me on the arm. "Adelaide, you are a humbug. Lord Stanley is such a grand storyteller that I feel as though I were there myself." Her tone was light, but her eyes were cold iron.

Again, I was to remain silent and seen. The wordless rebuke from Victoria felt like a betrayal. Surely she understood why I was trying to please Father by entertaining our guest? Father leveled his threats at her as often as at me, although they had less effect on her. Sent away? How exciting, how she would love that so!

14 　　　　　　　　　　January Gilchrist

"And you, Miss Adelaide? Do you have interest in seeing the galleries of Italy?" Stanley asked, his dark gaze trained on me.

I decided to settle on honesty. "I'm afraid not, my lord. I must admit that my tastes run a little closer to home." It was hardly charming to admit that one desired to stay home alone, though, so I threw out the first thing that came to mind. "The Royal Ascot is my idea of art."

Victoria and I had recently devoured the papers about it. She for the fashion, me for the horses.

Stanley turned toward me with a half smile. "You have an interest in horses?"

My smile was genuine. "I do indeed, my lord. I am, in fact, an avid rider. I've trained with my horse, Hera, since she was a filly. And she has a lineage almost as long as Harewood Hall."

Victoria threw me a black look as Stanley turned to face me, quite blind to the fact that she was pressed into the shadow of the hallway with his back to her.

I thought of how to draw her into the conversation, but at that moment Harrold threw the doors open with a rarely used panache, and we entered the hazily lit dining room. Footmen descended on us, linen squares at the ready, chairs pulled and replaced, glasses filled with wine as red as blood.

Cook had outdone herself. Dinner was plate after plate of deliciously intricate dishes, most of which I'd never tasted before. It seemed even downstairs had been informed of Lord Stanley's importance. I gazed at him across the table. *Why is he of such importance?* I wondered idly. I had yet to see proof of anything in the least remarkable about him.

I tuned into his conversation with Victoria with little interest.

"Of course, the most exciting place I have visited is New York. In fact, I shall be moving there shortly," Stanley said.

"New York?" Victoria's voice was thick with envy.

"My passage is booked in two months' time." Stanley nodded, a smug curl to his lip. "They want to build a racecourse to

MY SISTER'S SHADOW 15

rival those of Europe. This is a watershed moment for the Americans, but of course, they need the help of an Englishman. They have the ideas and money, certainly, but they need the centuries of knowledge only an Englishman has."

How could a man of Lord Stanley's age carry centuries of knowledge? One of the mysteries of life, I supposed as I rubbed at a smear on my spoon.

"Some of the big money men want to start their own racecourse, but they want to do it the proper way—the English way. They need our help. Got the blunt, but don't have the class. They need an Englishman to consult. Show them the ways." A clot of soup quivered at the edge of his lip.

"The investors have personally handpicked me, you see. Vanderbilts, Wideners, Williamsons. All are investing," Lord Stanley went on, his gaze trained on me. I smiled in a way that I hoped suggested I was interested, very interested—maybe even fascinated.

Victoria huffed a breath, her mouth a perfect O of pleasure. "My, how esteemed you must be," she breathed in an obsequious tone that was not her own.

Victoria was possessed by the sensational. Penny dreadfuls were smuggled from the village on our monthly trips, and she devoured the tales of pirates, princesses, and murder, long into the dark night. She often acted out these stories for me, so effortless in her imitation of others. She could transform herself into anything, anyone, with merely a switch in tone, a flick of her eyelashes.

I looked to Father to find him staring at the papery hydrangeas heaped along the table; his expression was one of distant thought. Was this what made Lord Stanley so important? The racetrack? But what on earth did a racetrack in New York have to do with us here in Gloucester?

Ignoring Victoria's comment, Stanley addressed me. "Miss Adelaide, if I have my way, people will be able to attend events to rival Royal Ascot in New York City itself."

16 ☙ January Gilchrist

I widened my eyes as I'd seen Victoria do. "I'm sure you'll be as busy as the king—perhaps you should ask Lord Churchill to personally vet your members as he does at Ascot?"

Lord Stanley threw his head back and roared with laughter. "Perhaps, Miss Adelaide. Although, the racecourse I intend to build will far surpass Ascot, both in size and status."

My smile became rictus at both his patronizing tone and the well-aimed kick Victoria landed to my shin.

"With the new steamships, the trip to America is a mere ten days," Stanley said to me.

"Tell me," Victoria interjected, "have you met the Williamsons? Or the Vanderbilts? I have heard they throw the most magnificent parties. I would do simply anything to attend one." Victoria questions were asked in a tone I recognized as her cruel rendition of that of our cousin, Deborah, a dough-faced girl whose life ambition was to marry well, and if she could not achieve that, then to simply marry.

Stanley smoothed his mustache with a finger and thrust his chest forward. "I know them all very well. I introduced Alva Vanderbilt to the Duke of Marlborough. Made a most advantageous match with her daughter. If one doesn't mind lowering one's standards for money, of course. Saved his house, but one hopes she doesn't ruin his reputation with her 'new ways.' The American woman doesn't have what our English roses do. A man needs to have a firm hand. They have all sorts of savage ideas. Obsessed with equal rights and independent thinking." His tone conveyed how little he thought of that.

Our eyes met, and I noticed how bleak his were. They appeared to be bottomless, like the old well hidden at the rear of our orchard.

A sense of dread loomed.

I trained my gaze on the painting on the wall hanging behind him—a flattering portrait of a long-dead relative, watching us with a disapproving gaze.

MY SISTER'S SHADOW   ⟋ 17

Allowing the words of the table to descend to mindless mumbles, I drifted off into thoughts of my garden and was once again among the verdant foliage that lined the craggy stone under my bedroom window, my hands in moist soil, in prayer with the earth. Untouched by the talk of new women and firm hands.

CHAPTER 3

"It's dreadfully dull now that our guests have gone," Victoria declared, a refrain that had echoed incessantly since the departure of our visitors three days ago. Yet I knew she spoke only of one guest in particular.

"It's simply impossible to endure tales of America and grand adventures while we're stuck here, in the middle of nowhere, with nothing to do and no one to converse with."

I rolled my eyes. "Thank you ever so much."

"You know precisely what I mean. Siblings hardly count."

Mercifully, Ida, the parlor maid, appeared in the doorway of the drawing room, rescuing me from having to feign agreement. I had found solace in the return to our usual serene existence, and I certainly did not miss the intrusion of strangers.

In her hands, Ida held a vase filled with flowers, their china-white heads drooping as if in remorse.

"Misses, these are for you."

"A bouquet?" Victoria's voice quivered with excitement.

I stared at the flowers—Virgin Bower, my least favorite. I cleared my throat, the air suddenly thick and cloying. The water in the vase had clouded, and the sight of it churned my stomach unpleasantly.

MY SISTER'S SHADOW ⌒ 19

Victoria blushed as she read the linen card attached. When her eyes met mine, they gleamed. "They're from Lord Stanley," she announced.

The room felt stifling, the scent of the posy nauseatingly close. I averted my gaze from the flowers, which seemed to watch me from across the room, and opened the window, closing my eyes against the fresh breeze carrying scents of grass and honeysuckle.

"Addy?" Victoria interrupted my moment.

I looked at her, her eyebrows knitted and mouth pursed in disapproval.

"You live with your head in the clouds. You're always day-dreaming," she said.

Victoria often accused me of not paying her enough attention, being too distracted, spending too much time with my head in the clouds. I never meant to, but losing myself in the depths of a book or spending time among the flowers and creatures of the garden was so enjoyable that it seemed natural for hours to slip away without me noticing.

And who did it hurt? I wondered.

I smiled placatingly. "Yes, my dear?"

"The card." She gestured toward me with it.

I held it gingerly, the linen rough between my fingers.

It read:

To the sisters,

Thank you for your company. I look forward to more of it.

In affection, Lord Stanley

He hadn't even bothered to list us by name. *The sisters*—two words, harmless yet bearing a weight that brought my hand and the card to my side.

Victoria didn't seem to mind, snatching the card and reading it aloud. "'I look forward to more of it.' That's promising, isn't it?"

20 ⬅ January Gilchrist

Promising? It felt like a threat to me.

"Lord Stanley is going to propose, Ida," Victoria declared.

Ida blinked at Victoria and then at the doorway, as if expecting him to appear. "Is he, miss?"

Victoria sighed. "He will. I can just feel it. From the very moment I heard his name, I knew. He will change my life. Have you ever experienced that?" She stared at Ida with an intensity that caused the maid to take a step backward.

"No, miss, I don't think I have," Ida said, eyes wide.

Victoria jumped up, curtseying to her reflection. "Mrs. Astor, how do you do?" Laughing, she twirled and held a hand imperiously toward Ida. "Lady Stanley. Pleased to meet you."

Ida stared at Victoria. "Very good, miss."

"It is very good." Victoria threw herself into the chair across from me. "Once I escape here, I won't be coming back."

"Escape, miss?"

"Yes, escape. Who wants to live in this ancient old house, full of ghosts and stories? It's too full of the past here; the future doesn't have a chance to show its face."

Ida clutched the vase, gazing at Victoria with a terrified expression. "Ghosts, miss?"

"Vivi," I warned, "Stop it. She's talking nonsense, Ida. Thank you. You are dismissed."

Ida's hands trembled as she dropped a small curtsey.

"I wish you wouldn't do that," I said once Ida had departed.

"Do what?"

"Tease Ida like that."

Victoria rolled her eyes. "It isn't my fault she takes everything so literally. She's worked here for four years, and I don't recall seeing her smile once."

I pursed my lips. It was true that Ida was a serious sort who jumped at shadows and had the fanciful superstitions of the lower classes, but Victoria appeared to relish tormenting her in the way that a cat plays with a mouse before it devours it.

My Sister's Shadow   21

Victoria stared past me into the window. The sun had shifted, casting her in shadow. She heaved a sigh that made her shoulders sag, and pressed her face into the bouquet.

"Do you ever feel as if we are just wasting away here? Biding our time until our *real* life begins? There is so much out there for us to see and do, and we are just stuck here, moldering away like lumps of cheese. I need adventure, Addy—fun, excitement. Nothing ever changes. Don't you wish . . . ?"

The rest of her question lingered between us, unvoiced. The curtains billowed as if the house sighed, and outside a crow shrieked, circling in the endless blue sky.

I swallowed my thoughts and remained silent. Because I didn't ever feel like that. All I craved was here—my beloved horse, the garden, books—and if I had a wish, it would be that everything would remain exactly as it was right now.

CHAPTER 4

Three weeks after the dinner party, we lounged in the drawing room, the warmest part of the house. Without warning, the days had begun to shorten and chill, and we chased the feeble sunlight around the room.

A brisk knock at the door brought my gaze from the book I was reading to Victoria, where she lay with her head in my lap on the threadbare chaise. Her face turned to mine, solemn and still.

The book tumbled open on my chest.

Nanny Jones appeared in the doorway, squinting into the dimly lit room.

"*Cariads*, your father wishes to see you in his study. Immediately."

The hairs on the back of my neck stiffened. Victoria and I exchanged a glance. Father never asked to see us unless we were to be berated about some misdeed, imagined or otherwise. My mind flew through the past days. What had I done? Spent too much time in the garden? I'd fancied myself clever, sneaking in and out of the house, using the servants' stairs, avoiding the garden near Father's study.

Victoria scrambled from the chaise and was clutching Nanny Jones's hands before I had even marked my page in the book and put it on the side table. Perhaps I hadn't needed to press the bookmark quite so carefully into the spine or line the book up so perfectly with the edge of the table. My hand trembled as I ran my palm over its cool leather cover.

If only life were like a novel, and you could skip to the end to find out how it all turned out. But if you knew all that lay ahead of you, you would be paralyzed. You'd never love anyone or anything ever again—you wouldn't dare to. You couldn't. Not if you knew what crouched in the shadows, waiting for your next move.

"Did he happen to mention what he wishes to speak to us about?" Victoria asked, inspecting herself in the mirror over the mantle of the ashy fireplace.

"As if his lordship would bother himself to tell lowly old me." Nanny Jones's voice was gruff, but she smiled as she spoke.

When Victoria was satisfied with her hair, she gestured for me to follow, and we stepped into the hall.

A crisp breeze funneled its way down the hallway to greet us, and with it the scent of clematis and freshly cut grass. I dragged my hand along the wall-papered panels as we walked.

Victoria strode ahead, peppering Nanny with questions: What exactly had Father said when he requested the meeting? Had he received a letter? Had there been a seal or a return address on the envelope? Nanny smoothed Victoria's hair back from her face as we reached the door to father's study, clucking her tongue indulgently.

"Impatient *cariad*, ye'll find out soon enough. Never could wait, could you?" Nanny Jones ran her hands along Victoria's arm, her eyes tender. "Always one to spoil the surprise."

As I joined them on the threshold, she opened her arm, including me in her embrace. I leaned against both familiar bodies and allowed the fear to bubble up like a pot of milk left to boil over. For just a moment, I promised myself—then I would lock it away in the precious box where Mama lived, though apart from a flash of color, my memories of her were dim. With a jolt, I realized I had been without Mama for two decades, having only had

24 ⬅

January Gilchrist

her for four short years. How could someone whose time with me had been so brief, leave such a gaping hole in my life? Love could be such a cruel thing. I breathed in the essence of them both: Nanny Jones, peppermint; and Victoria, lavender water.

Nanny Jones pulled away and made a great show of straightening her apron, blinking away the bright sheen in her eyes.

"Come on then, you lot," she said, "Best not to keep your father waiting."

Victoria turned to me, clasping my hand in hers. "This is it. Lord Stanley is proposing. *I can feel it.* I love you, Addy. Nothing will ever change that. Not even when I'm Lady Stanley of New York." She looked delighted. "Do say you'll come with us. It will be an adventure. Just like in the books you love."

I forced a smile. It was she that loved those books, not I.

"It would be an adventure." But not one I wanted. "I love you too, Vivi." An inescapable truth.

Turning to face the dark, heavy door of father's study, she took a deep breath, straightened her shoulders, and dipped her chin.

That image of her that morning has stayed with me forever.

Brave, proud, hopeful: the epitome of a girl who boldly leaped off a precipice into womanhood and believed she was about to receive exactly what it was she deserved.

Father's study was on the ground floor of the house, in an overcrowded room that housed most of Harewood's books and where he spent most of his time. It was considered off limits to anyone, including many of the household staff. He had very particular feelings about how he needed his things displayed. To us, it looked like an unholy mess, but to him, he claimed, it was orderly in a very specific manner. I had once felt that father's 'collections' were born of a shared love of nature and all its creatures, but as I'd aged, I began to see the collections of brightly colored beetles and butterflies pinned mid-flight to boards was more about Father's need to control, to consume, and ultimately to conquer. We were not alike, he and I.

Victoria knocked at the door, and, at his terse reply, we entered. We dutifully stood in front of Father's desk, a little awkwardly, for we rarely entered while he was in attendance. A fair number of books, however, had been often borrowed and put precisely back into place without his knowledge.

He removed his glasses and peered at us sightlessly until his pupils righted themselves, his eyes moving slowly from one to the other. He looked strange without his spectacles, like a mole surprised to find himself above ground.

Clearing his throat, he studied a piece of paper on his desk.

"Lord Stanley has made an offer of marriage and I have accepted his terms," he said without preamble.

His glassy gaze rested on me. I squeezed Victoria's hand, still tightly clasped in mine. Despite the heaviness in my heart, it rather amused me to find that he was still unable to tell us apart.

"The engagement will be announced in *The Times* next Friday, with a date for the wedding set within the month. Then"—he paused and looked down at the paper again—"passage has been booked for America a month thereafter."

His words landed around us, dampening any sound. A small gasp escaped my lips, disappearing into the room like a puff of smoke.

That soon?

But I had to let Victoria forge her own path, live her own life, even if it made me die a little inside.

Victoria pulled me into her arms. I aligned my breath with her heartbeat.

"Sir, will you allow Adelaide to come to America with Lord Stanley and me?"

I pursed my lips but said nothing. It was easier to go along with Victoria when she sank her teeth into something, and I often just played dead until something else caught her attention. She and I were inescapably linked, but Harewood was my home; I could never—would never—leave it.

26 ❧ January Gilchrist

Father tilted his head and raised his eyes to us. The next words he uttered hit me in the throat.

"Adelaide will be going. It is her he's offered for."

His words hung in the air, a swarm of humming, buzzing, stinging phrases. I couldn't grasp their meaning as the ground gave way beneath me.

CHAPTER 5

I awoke on the hard, scratchy surface of the chaise in Father's study.

My mind was blissfully blank for a too-brief moment before what he had said crashed around me like rocks, hard and unforgiving.

The room was still but for the steady tremor of the mantle clock. I stared hard at the inside of my eyelids. It had always been difficult for me to express myself, to tell people what I wanted. All too often I folded to Victoria's forceful personality and allowed her to speak for me, to decide for me, for both of us. Not this time. This time I would explain to Father the mistake that had been made. For surely, it was not me Stanley meant to offer for. Victoria was the one who sparkled and shone, the one who wanted the New York life he offered.

The very moment the carriage containing him had departed, we had held every word, every look, every sound Lord Stanley had made to the light and examined it from every angle. The irrefutable and unanimous decision had been that, like everyone who met her, he found Victoria utterly charming.

I sat upright so quickly my head swayed like the giant beech along the path to the woods that threatened to collapse in every winter storm.

28 ❦ January Gilchrist

Father looked up from his papers, wordlessly. The room was silent, empty. Victoria was gone.

"Sir. There has been an error. It is not me he means to offer for. It is Victoria. He has confused us."

Father's lips pulled down at the corners and shook his head. "He has been explicit in his request."

My head was too full of words, I could barely choose the right one. "I do not wish to marry him. Victoria does. Not I."

Father brought his fingers together and closed his eyes. Suddenly he was a stranger to me, as if I were seeing him for the first time. His hair, graying at the temples, was receding and thinning. The hands steepled at his chin had shrunk, and were now smaller, narrower than I remembered, and covered with loose, spotted skin. Even his suit was unfamiliar, as if he were wearing someone else's clothes.

Gone was the giant who had rampaged through the halls of Harewood, leaving us cowering among his shouts, the fumes of whiskey, the thrown glasses, the broken furniture.

"It is agreed."

I waited a moment before speaking. "Would you have me marry a man I do not wish to?"

Father removed his glasses and rubbed at the bridge of his nose. "Lord Stanley has asked. I have accepted. That is all you need to know on the matter."

A noise escaped my lips. "All I need to know?"

He looked at me sharply. His voice was crisp, emotionless. "Let me be clear. Lord Stanley has asked for your hand in marriage, and as your father, I have accepted. It will be announced in the papers on Friday. He will inform us of further arrangements."

I stood then, drawn to my feet by shock. Somewhere, deep inside, there was a version of myself that was brave enough to rage at him, to scream at him. *How dare you? How dare you ignore me for my entire life and then sell me into a marriage to someone against my will?* I was not a doll to be picked up and moved between rooms when he saw fit.

But I was.

Regardless, everything Father had ever taught us I employed against him now. *"Stand up straight. Look me in the eye. Shoulders back. Watch your tone."* I must retain my composure.

"You would do this to me?" I asked, fighting back the hysteria that rose in my chest.

His mouth moved silently, like a fish on land. Perhaps with the words the other, kinder version of himself wished he could say. I held my breath.

"You will do as you are told. Dismissed."

My mouth opened.

But ever the coward, I turned on my heel and walked from the room.

*   *   *

I stalked the halls, stumbling in my urgency, down into the depths of my beloved Harewood. The steam and clamor of the kitchen increased as I clattered my way along the barren service stairs. I had to find Nanny Jones. There was not a problem in the world that she could not, had not, fixed for me. She would right this, and all would be swiftly forgotten. Somehow.

My fingers trembled. The eyes of our two kitchen maids, both called Mary, taking their tea at the long, scarred kitchen table shot to me, and they scrambled from their seats so quickly that one chair crashed to the floor.

"Nanny?" I asked.

Kitchen Mary pointed to the laundry room, where Nanny sat on the single roughly hewn chair, darning a dress. One of mine. A favorite. Torn along the hem after a ride with Hera among the brambles. I swayed in the doorway while I considered what to say.

"Nanny." My tone sounded pitiful, even to my ears, but to my surprise, she didn't look up. The needle stabbed through the fabric in her hands. Her expression was set, angry almost. I lowered myself to the ground and buried my face in the fabric in her lap.

30 🐦 January Gilchrist

"Get off the dress. You'll ruin it."

I lifted my face, surprised, and she yanked the dress from under me. Her hand hovered above my hair. I felt its heat, but it didn't connect.

"Come now. Up ye get."

"Father has . . ." The words were stuck in my throat. I could not voice them.

"I heard," Nanny said on a sigh.

She stood and my head, so abruptly removed from her lap, almost struck the seat. I pressed my hand to the warm wood.

A warmth began to spread in my chest. She was angry that Father was marrying me off. She would help me.

"I can't . . . I won't marry him."

"Aye, ye will." Nanny Jones addressed the wall as she hung the dress up and ran her practiced eye over another. "It is for the best. You're too much like *her*. He can't manage it. Marry that lord. It won't be as bad as you think. It never is."

Her? What did Mama have to do with this?

"Nanny, you must speak to Father for me, make him see reason. You must!"

She turned to me with wintry eyes. "What are ye complaining about? A life of luxury, the life of a lady. There's no use in complaining about something what thousands would die to have."

She returned her attention to the pile of clothes. My mouth moved wordlessly.

After a moment she spoke again, her voice less cold. "We have no choice," she said, and I felt as if I were being sent to the gallows.

"I . . . Perhaps we could move to the seaside. You, Victoria, and I. Brighton or Cornwall. I have some sort of inheritance, I'm not certain how much, but surely it would be enough for a cottage? It would all be very respectable. You could be our chaperone."

Her eyes were steady on the dress she folded, twisted, and forced into submission, but a bright spot of color appeared high

MY SISTER'S SHADOW ⌒ 31

on her cheek as if she had been slapped. "Harrold and I are planning to take a wee house ourselves. Now you're both grown, it's time."

I fell into the chair she had vacated, my mouth agape. The chair was as hard and unwelcoming as her tone. I couldn't make sense of what was happening. First Father, and now Nanny?

"You won't help me?"

She made a sound then, a rasping, choking kind of noise, and finally turned to me. "Help you? Come now. Stop crying like a *bairn*. You just need time to find your feet."

But I didn't want to find my feet. I liked them perfectly well where they were.

"Perhaps I could come? With you and Harrold, I mean. You could live as man and wife. I wouldn't expect you to work."

I couldn't even feel embarrassed by my pleading tone. I would get on my hands and knees and beg if it helped.

"And who will cook for you? Clean? You don't even know how to boil water." Her laugh was brittle. "You're a grown-up now. It's time for you to have your own place, your own staff. You'll be fine. Better than fine. Get out of here. Too many ghosts. You remind him, every time he looks at you, at Victoria, you remind him of what he's lost. What he did."

She strode from the room, the conversation over.

The truth hit me so hard that had I been standing, I would have surely fallen to the floor again. Father was finally making good on his threats and doing the unthinkable. My worst fear realized.

He was sending me away. For good. And no one would help me.

★　★　★

The light had dimmed around me, the air dampening as it cooled. I sat in the chair Nanny Jones had vacated. The sounds of the kitchen ramping up for dinner jangled outside the door, but the room I was in remained empty save for me. I imagined I could hear the servants whispering about me as they worked.

My greatest fear—being forced to leave Harewood Hall—had been realized, and it was all my own doing. If only I hadn't tried so hard to please Father that I'd given Lord Stanley the impression that I was everything Victoria was. If only I had risked Father's wrath by remaining stilted and silent as I normally did.

Poor little rich girl, complaining about marrying a Lord.

My mind reeled. I had been so certain Jones would help me. Jones, who had stepped into the space left behind when Mama abandoned us. Who had held our hands in the dark as we'd cried and cried. Who'd shepherded us as our fragile selves, shattered by grief, had begun to knit, and we clung to each other more than ever before.

I pressed a hand against my heart and creaked from the seat, as if the blows I had taken had been physical. I breathed those feelings deep down and willed my insides to iron. Shoulders back, spine stiff, my roots deep in the earth below.

I would not leave Harewood Hall. That I might never see it again was like a mouthful of too-hot tea. The owls that kept me company at night; the shattered bird shells along the mossy, sodden floor of the woods; the flowerbeds I sketched and planned with Morris and Graham, the paths worn from my rides with Hera.

I loved it all.

No, I vowed. *He can try,* I told myself fiercely, *but I will not leave.*

The noise of the kitchen ramped up as I stepped over the threshold of the ironing room into its hubbub. Pots and pans still clattered, steam hissed on the iron hob, and chairs scraped against the floor as the seated servants, finishing their evening meal, stood. But what seemed the loudest of all was their eyes, no longer cast respectfully toward the ground, but searching my face. What did they look for? Surely my red-rimmed eyes told them all they needed to know. I raised my chin and moved through the room, step after arduous step. The tip of my left boot had a small scuff at the toe, and I studied it as my skirt churned around it with my steps.

I needed to find Victoria, my mirror image. Where I was weak, she was strong. Where I wavered, she decided, pressed on. She would be hurt, which was always followed by anger with Victoria, but she would fix this. She was implacable, immovable when she wanted something, and I knew she wanted to be Lady Stanley. My heart fluttered as I recalled her face at Father's words.

Harewood was still and solemn as I trod the stairs to our rooms. An invisible thread tugged at me; I always knew where Victoria was, as if I'd left a piece of myself in another place.

I had never knocked on the door of the room we had shared since we had moved downstairs from the nursery, but now I hesitated, my knuckle frozen in the air. I tapped twice, as light as a caress, before entering. Victoria was lying on her bed. Her accusing eyes met mine briefly before she pulled a pillow over her head and rolled to face the wall. I said nothing. I couldn't. Words caught in my throat like a bone.

Our room was chaos. The door to the wardrobe hung drunkenly from its hinges, clothes spilling from it. The mahogany dresser was bare, bottles of tinctures and creams scattered, broken, on the floor beneath it. The smell of the mixed scents in the room was cloying.

Among the confusion and disorder, the glass eyes of my beloved Betsy met mine. Her delicate china head had been wrenched from her body, and one partially lashed eye gazed at me mournfully from the floor. I bent to retrieve her pieces. The skirt of her bridal gown had been torn off, leaving the lace bloomers exposed. One arm hung loosely in the bodice; the other had been rent from her, a jagged bloom of stuffing where her graceful china arm had once been.

"Oh, Vivi," I said sadly, turning the now headless body in my hands.

I placed Betsy on the dresser and sat myself at the end of the bed. I picked up Victoria's feet, placing them on my lap. Her bones were delicate under my palms.

"I have a proposal," I began.

She pulled the pillow off her head to glare at me. "I am well aware, thank you."

I grimaced. "I meant I have a proposal for you."

She thumped the pillow back down on her head. "I am not interested."

I sighed and steeled myself. She was the determined one. I was only ever happy to follow her directions. She was ruthless in her pursuit of gratification, but this time I would have to be the unmoving one. My idea was the only way for us to have what we both so longed for.

"I don't want to marry Lord Stanley, Vivi. You know that."

No reply.

I rubbed her stockinged feet and felt as low as I ever had. "I can't. I don't ever want to leave Harewood Hall. I don't want . . ."

Any of it.

All of it.

"You can't stay here forever." Her voice was thick.

The very idea of it sent a jolt of surprise through me.

Says who?

"That may be the case, but not like this. I have two ideas," I started again. "We can run away."

Her leg stiffened under my hands. Running away to join the circus was a well-visited childhood fantasy. She would be the horse trainer, and I, the trick rider. Or trapeze artists, throwing ourselves fearlessly into the air, with only each other's hands to save us from plummeting to our deaths below.

She lifted the pillow from her face and glared at me. "You are too ridiculous for words."

My Sister's Shadow ✎ 35

"Please don't say anything until I am finished with this one." I shifted my position to protect myself against her feet. "Let us swap. You marry him. As me."

I tensed as the pillow flew off the bed, shifting to avoid her foot as she kicked out at me. Her narrowed gaze pinned me in place. For one heart-stopping second it appeared she was considering it.

"Now you are being *utterly* ridiculous," she retorted.

She thumped at the bed on either side of her, threw her head back, and screamed. I pressed my thumbnail into the back of my hand and watched as my skin whitened and then darkened, the small crescent shape reddening. The silence that followed seemed endless.

It was suddenly shattered by a magpie landing with a crash on the windowsill. The hairs on the back of my neck shivered as it stared at me with its beady black eye.

One for sorrow.

It bobbed its head once, twice, before launching itself at the window, beak and claws flashing. It was my turn to scream, clutching my hands to my heart.

Its beak tapped manically against the window as if it sought to break the glass and gain entry.

I screamed again, longer and louder, but still it thrashed against the glass.

Victoria stood and waved her hand at the window, shooing the magpie away. She rested her hand on the glass as she watched it glide over the forest. She turned to me, but whatever she was going to say died on her lips. Her expression was opaque against the backdrop of the window. Her gaze shifted from my hands at my chest to my face. A pulse hammered at my throat, and a wave of noise washed through my ears. I closed my eyes and pressed my nail against my thumb, over and over again.

"It was just a bird, Addy. Let me fetch you your tonic." Her tone brought the familiar heat of shame to my neck. Silly

36 ⮡   January Gilchrist

Adelaide, disturbed by things that others paid no heed to. My nerves, as she often lamented, got the better of me.

A tumbler of water was thrust into my hands, followed by a spoon full of foul-smelling liquid. My tonic. Objects flickered and doubled as Victoria pressed the spoon to my mouth. My lips parted obediently, and I gulped the sticky tonic first, then chugged at the water deeply to rid myself of its foul taste. How I hated this medicine.

Father's physician, Doctor Fiddelaers had prescribed it for me after Mother's death—apparently, I screamed every night for weeks—and now Victoria urged it on me whenever my feelings too became big, even in a house as large as Harewood, to handle. *"Weak minded, like her mother,"* I'd heard the doctor tell Father. *"Best to control her moods like this, lest she turns out like her."*

"Her name was Florence," I had wanted to yell. No one ever spoke her name.

Hot tears filled my eyes, and I inhaled deeply.

Victoria marrying Stanley as me was the only plan that had any hope of working. She would get to live the glamorous life of a lady in New York, and I could stay here with everything I loved. Father wouldn't notice if I pretended to be Victoria. Nanny Jones was leaving. The servants wouldn't question it; they wouldn't mind, even if they knew. I held the image of Harewood in my mind. The pale blue sky that stretched endlessly over the forest in summer, and the vibrant garden, laid with seeds and bulbs with my own hands, every nook and cranny as familiar as my own face.

I kneeled at her feet, my hands laced together in prayer. "I do not want this."

Victoria remained mute.

"Please. This is your dream. Take it."

I laid my head in her lap in the same way I had with Jones. We knew each other deeply, Victoria and I, often communicating with little more than a twist of a lip or a twitch of a brow. *Please,* I willed her.

Victoria sighed and placed her hand to my head, weaving her fingers through my hair. My scalp prickled as her fingers flexed and tightened. Pain tore through my head, but just as I would have cried out, she released me.

Her hand began to stroke my hair in a slow rhythmic motion, soothing now that she had satisfied her desire to cause me pain.

"I don't want to go to America," I whispered into her skirt. "But you do. Let me live here as you for the rest of my days. You know I cannot go. Please help me."

Her hand stilled.

"Why should I?" she said finally. "He chose you instead of me. He must want someone weak, unintelligent, and dull, and I am not any of those things."

My stomach clenched. That was true: she was not. She was dynamic and forceful and bold and mercurial.

"I don't want to marry a man that wants me to be those things, Addy. No, while you were off coming up with these ridiculous plans, I made my own. You marry him. But I *will* come with you to New York. To take care of you. Your nerves. You're delicate and need someone who understands."

My breath left my mouth as a gasp, as if I had been struck. I had desperately hoped she would see what this meant to me, that for once she would choose to give me what I needed instead of taking what she wanted.

She tapped my head, harder than she needed to, to let me know she wanted me to move. I sat, swaying as the room began to spin.

Victoria projected her voice as if she were on a stage. "You cannot perform the most basic of tasks. Your head is always in the clouds. And then there is the matter of your weak nerves. There will be men aplenty in New York City. Perhaps not lords, but strapping American men with more money that we can imagine."

38 — January Gilchrist

She pursed her lips at me, and my stomach sank. I was a worm on her hook. When she was in a mood like this, it was best to placate her and ignore it until the mood shifted, as the worst of weather eventually did.

"I do not wish to marry him," I whispered again.

I felt as if I were screaming into a void. Why could no one hear me? The memory of his mustache prickling through my glove came to mind. I closed my eyes, fighting against the clench of my stomach.

"I shall refuse him," I stated, working to focus my vision on Victoria. The image of her skipped and danced as the tonic began to take effect. "Father cannot force me to marry him if I do not wish to."

Victoria gave me a disparaging look. "He can, in fact, do exactly that. If you refuse him, he will cut you off. What would you do with yourself?"

She yanked at the crocheted blanket that lay at the end of her bed. It had taken me the entirety of our seventeenth year to make it as a birthday gift for her. She tossed it at me, the corner of it catching my eye on its way to the floor. I blinked against the burning sensation as my eyes began to water.

"You have no skills at all. No, you must marry Lord Stanley. We will all go to America, and if it doesn't suit, we can simply come home." Her tone was flippant, dismissive.

I knew very little about marriage, but even I knew a wife didn't simply board a ship and return home when she felt like it, that men controlled the money and decided what did and didn't happen.

The farthest we'd ever been from Harewood was a week by the seaside with Aunt Petunia. It had taken us days to get to Brighton, and I had found the hard pebbled beach and colorless water underwhelming. There had been a steamer in the distance, as tiny as a toy. We stood on that beach, waving our handkerchiefs to bid them Godspeed on their travels. I never imagined that one day I would be sent away on one myself.

MY SISTER'S SHADOW — 39

"Now I have had time to think about it, I see this is the best thing for us both. I get my adventure without being tied to some"—she curled her lip and swung her eyes along my dress—"unimaginative stick-in-the-mud who values obedience over everything."

She walked from the room, banging the door with a forcefulness that rattled the pictures in their frames.

As if it were I who had set out to ruin her life.

As if it were I who had proposed to Lord Stanley.

I spent that starless evening with my back curled against the wall, shivering and shaking in my cavernous bed. The bedsheets tangled and tied around my legs. My feet were freezing, my hands icy. My optimism had been ripped from me, and no amount of wailing or sobbing had made a difference.

I was utterly and completely lost.

Father's averted eyes as I begged him to reconsider.

Victoria's face as she refused me.

Nanny Jones's voice when she'd said, *"You'll do your duty, and it shan't be as bad as you imagine. Nothing ever is."*

CHAPTER 6

It's an age-old story. Marriage, swiftly followed by catastrophe. Or was it the other way around? In this case, it was marriage itself that was the catastrophe.

Since the night of the wedding, *my* wedding, a buzzing anxiety had gripped me. While there were photos that show I was there, and a newspaper ran an article on the beauty of it all, I couldn't remember a thing about it.

The stiff-shouldered girl on those steps looked like me. Beautiful in the way well-bred girls are—blank faced; dead-eyed; eyebrows lifted slightly, as if dumbfounded to find herself there. The face on that girl is impassive. Untouched.

I no longer knew *that* girl.

The uncertainty had been sharp and pricked at me as wedding preparations were made around me, a piercing sort of panic that held me by the throat and made me sweat. Unknown fears had easily been banished with a ride through Harewood's woodland, with Hera's thick mane in my hand.

Now, however, the sickness about what lay ahead of me was a dull ache, a constant companion. A creeping misery that twirled and twined itself around me like the ivy that wound around the dovecote walls of Harewood. Memories of the wedding bed swirled in my head, jumping out and surprising me at the oddest moments. A waft of cigar on the breeze, a sharply inhaled breath, a gasp, a small shriek, a murmured male voice, spilled red wine. The memory of rough hands snatching at me, thick weight pressed on me, the sound of hot breath in my ear that had made me think of piglets suckling. Violently vivid bruises that bloomed the next day along my pale skin, like violets in February.

My monthly courses had arrived the weeks before the boat's departure, Jones informing me that meant I was without child. I had spent enough time with Harewood menagerie to understand that "rutting," as Morris called it, resulted in offspring, but I had never made the connection between my monthly and children. When I asked Jones how it related, she had simply tutted and moved on with her tasks. It was infuriating how I was treated as such a child, incapable of making a single decision about my own life.

Whatever my girlish fantasies may have been about Graham—or about marriage, had I ever thought about it—it hadn't been this rough, grasping nightmare. There was no escaping the memories, not even in the opulent confines of the *Orient*.

Proclaiming itself the world's fastest and largest passenger ship, it was equal parts fashion parade and fraternity. Ten days reprieve was what it promised me.

It did not feel long enough.

Men clustered together in the dining and smoking rooms. Women promenaded along the halls, their eyes moving swiftly along each outfit, cataloguing, gauging cost, and forming opinions.

I had never seen such outfits. Hats, each bigger than the last, were covered in feathers that reached for the sky, fresh flowers (where they got those on the boat escaped me—had they a special garden dedicated to keeping wealthy women well appointed?),

42 ⮒   January Gilchrist

and fabric bows as big as bustles. One elderly dame, whose voice was as large as her bust, wore a hat with two taxidermied crow wings attached to either side.

My sister and I encountered finely dressed women whose eyes widened as they darted between us and made exclamations about our similarity before demanding our names, dinner table number, and destination. Stanley's letter had informed Father, then me, that he'd used my dowry to purchase a house he had renamed Greycliffe after his family's ancient pile in Dorchester. This house was located in the newly requisite fashionable area, so he said, off Fifth Avenue. Only two houses down from *the* Mrs. Astor. Victoria had squealed at that.

Women would inch closer when Victoria shared this news and my title, as if Stanley's privilege made me shine a little brighter. They would press their gloved hands against my arm, lean close, offer invitations to tea—but at my wooden responses the smiles would stiffen, and they would slide away, throwing circumspect glances that eventually became averted gazes and whispers. Victoria began to speak of the new house and title as though it were her own, enjoying the exhortations to keep in touch and linen cards with postal addresses carefully printed along them.

Victoria would clutch my arm and hiss words that meant nothing to me: *House of Worth, Poiret, Morse-Boughton*. She would analyze and critique every facet of the women's outfits, asking me whether that was an S-bend corset or whether a trim was perhaps Irish crochet rather than lace. Although I never answered, she persisted.

I wove my trembling hands together so tightly that the seams on my gloves pulled away. I picked at the meals, the dining room too full, too noisy, too bright. Victoria glittered in the bright room, shining alongside the polished brass and blindingly white linens.

It wasn't long before our table began to share sidelong looks and place cards were shuffled as we neared. I made no attempt at

MY SISTER'S SHADOW 43

conversation, and the unlucky person who found themself next to me was often gazing over my shoulder, past me, as if I had become invisible. I didn't blame them. I longed for invisibility.

Halfway through our journey, Victoria stood before the small wash basin and mirror in our cabin, pulling tendrils from her carefully arranged chignon.

Her cool gaze met mine in our reflection.

"The captain will be joining our table tonight, according to Mrs. Carmen."

I lay on the narrow bunk bed, my stockinged feet crossed. "Is he?"

"Yes. This is an enormous honor." When I did not say anything, she clicked her tongue. "Addy, you must make an effort this evening. Just for dinner, if you are unable to manage longer."

Effort. Noun. A determined attempt, something done by exertion.

I grunted with disinterest.

Her gaze was trained on mine in the mirror, her jaw set. She was angry. I felt it in every tight smile, averted gaze, and sharp retort. Since the announcement of my engagement, our relationship had soured steadily, like the slow rotting of a fruit.

A moment of taut silence.

"Perhaps tonight you could take a tray in the cabin. Take your tonic and rest. You seem exhausted." Her forced smile was distorted by the mirror, so it appeared to be more a baring of teeth. It was not a request, but an order, as usual. Victoria didn't ask. She demanded, cajoled, and berated, and if that didn't work, she simply took.

The camaraderie we had once shared was gone, and its loss was like a finger pressing against bruised skin. Perhaps in America, we would get it back and be sisters again once she got what she wanted—to meet the people behind the names she diligently studied in the *Town Crier* and copied into a linen-covered notebook.

I cleared my throat. "You're right. I am tired. I'll order a tray."

She nodded once before returning her attention to herself in the mirror. I thought of the crystal ashtray I'd taken from the galley the night before, the silver candlestick on the mantle in our cabin. Small, heavy items that fit easily into pockets of dresses. Not so heavy as to draw attention, but enough, I thought, to pull a lady and her sodden skirts to the bottom of the ocean.

The days blurred into one another. The stewards attempted to mark the time passing with cheerful welcomes and forced jollity. I had begun to take my tonic after dinner each night, falling into a deep, dreamless sleep, the only relief I could find.

Nine days into our journey, the crowd pushed and jostled at the side of the promenade deck, each person vying to be the first to catch a glimpse of land. Victoria stood on tiptoes, hand to her forehead.

"They are saying you can see land," she said with a delighted smile. "America." A sense of girlish excitement carried her toward the edge of the boat, where a small crowd was forming.

I observed it all as if from a great distance, remaining seated in my deck chair, the blanket over my legs doing nothing to warm me, a book open in front of me, one I carried with me like a talisman, although I had yet to turn a single page.

A man in the crisp white uniform of the Oriental Steam Navigation Company strode by, pausing at my feet. "Madam, here she is. America, the land of possibility." He gestured toward the swarm of people at the rail, but my gaze remained fixed on my lap.

"Thank you."

He hovered a moment, perhaps wondering if I hadn't understood. Excited cries floated along the air.

MY SISTER'S SHADOW 45

I tuned out the exuberant voices and breathed in the salty air, which at first had seemed damp and sticky, but after over a week onboard, was refreshing and invigorating, particularly when compared to the smoke-filled parlors. The thick, cloying cigar smoke had seemed to permeate the entire ship, following me everywhere, even seeping into our cabin as we slept.

I sighed and watched gulls swoop and dip in their sky dance above us, as silent as the grave. *Free.*

I leaned my head back, my lids as heavy as bricks. A silhouette fell over me. The light scent of lavender on the breeze told me it was Victoria, even if I hadn't already known.

"Everything looks dead."

I opened my eyes and gazed out at the never-ending expanse of the ocean. The depths of the Atlantic would solve my concerns. My gaze lingered on the hip-high rails. I imagined the icy chill, the nothingness of it enveloping me as thick as a blanket.

Free.

"It is certainly cold enough to assume it all is," she continued.

The cold on the boat deck was unlike anything we had ever experienced. The promenade was nearly unusable due to the frigid wind that swept across the Atlantic. The spray that it carried whipped around our faces like thousands of icy barbs. I sought that wind out, I reveled in the shock and discomfort it inflicted, preferring it to the memories that hounded me.

"Mr. Waters said we are expected to dock in the next day or so." Her voice held a note of excitement but also a question.

I eyed the iron bars that formed the barrier between me and the long dive to the ocean.

"You've missed your chance," she said.

My gaze flew to her face. Victoria gestured as a crowd of people pushed against one another for a look at this remarkable new land, the beginnings of all their hopes and dreams.

She gave me a hard look, and I gave her one in return.

"I wonder," she said, her tone light and conversational as she resumed her place on the deckchair beside me, "if Lord Stanley will be pleased to have married a mute."

My stomach twisted unpleasantly. Did anyone give thought to what women wanted? Who thought to ask the women being forced into marriage with men they did not choose, what would please *them*? Certainly not Father. The men had spoken, and it had been decided. The woman whose life it was had no say in it at all. Stanley received my dowry, and Father managed to offload the daughters who reminded him so painfully of his dead wife, but what did I get? Nothing, as far as I was yet to see. I couldn't move past the unfairness of it all.

The next two days would be the last I would enjoy a freedom of sorts. The rest of my life stretched before me, as vast and empty as the land Victoria had pointed at from the deck.

I shook off the blanket and stood, suddenly desperate to move. "I'm going to stroll."

Victoria's gaze remained fixed on a tall man standing at the bow. Her hand was at her hair, adjusting with a seemingly aimless grace. But nothing about Victoria was aimless.

I pushed open my parasol and strode out from the covered promenade to the exposed length of bleached wood of the deck.

Soot from the funnels floated in the air like strange-colored snow. The wind, wilder at this part of the boat, pulled at my hat and battered my skirts against my legs. I lowered the parasol to avoid it blowing inside out. The shadows of the lifeboats and their ropes loomed along the side, shielding me from the worst of the sleet.

I moved past the saloon, closed now. In the darkened windows I caught sight of a woman, well dressed but lumbering strangely, as if not quite awake.

With a start I realized that woman was me.

I had avoided all looking glasses since boarding the boat, instead seeking my reflection in Victoria's cheerful countenance. The sight of myself was an assault. I opened the parasol and angled it toward the window to avoid meeting my own fraught eye again.

It frightened me, that face. It was the face of a desperate woman.

CHAPTER 7

After days that both dragged but still passed too quickly, there it finally was.

New York, New York.

As the ship docked, the occupants flocked to the railings, waving and calling to the tiny specks signaling and hollering from the shore. Colored streamers fluttered and beckoned, strewn around the dock like party bunting. An army of ant-sized men swarmed: lifting, moving, packing. Women wiped tears and waved their handkerchiefs in the air, their other hand clutching at the man, woman, or child beside them.

My stomach twisted. The unfamiliar smells filled my nose, and I gulped down my fear and the dread, to take in the strange surroundings.

"America. We're actually here. Can you believe it?" Victoria said.

I couldn't. Or rather, didn't want to.

The gangway dipped and twisted beneath my feet, and I clutched the handrails, my legs trembling so hard I feared I might fall. Victoria strode ahead, leaning over to touch the outstretched hands, sharing smiles with complete strangers.

That walk along the gangplank felt as though I were walking to the gallows.

My SISTER'S SHADOW   ☞ 49

My head swam and I grabbed at Victoria's hand. She propelled me forward to a small vestibule. Porters wove in and out, carrying trunks and boxes, calling to one another. A frigid breeze carried the scents of fish, engine oil, and the body odor of the men who teemed around the docks. My clothes suddenly felt frightful: heavy, tight, cumbersome. I pulled at my neckline without relief.

"Taxi?" a man asked, mangling the grimy cap in his hands.

We were the easiest of marks, two bewildered women in a land far from our own. No matter Victoria's bluster, our naivety was surely clear to all.

"No, thank you. Our husband will be along shortly," Victoria replied archly.

Our? But the man didn't notice Victoria's odd use of the plural, moving off quickly to continue his search for customers.

The crowd was a sea of moving hats. A short man stepped forward, advancing toward us with intent.

"Lady Stanley?" He looked from Victoria to me, in question. His face was heavily lined, his skin the color of tanned leather, and his teeth yellowed and sparse. Dark eyes darted between the two of us. He was gloveless and his hands were stained almost black. Where his index finger should have been was a gnarled stump. I rubbed my own hands together, suddenly cold despite my leather gloves.

It was Victoria who responded. "Yes."

"I'm here to deliver ya. For his lordship."

He turned his back on us and pushed and elbowed his way through the crowd, disinterested whether we were following or not. We scrambled to catch up, me clutching my skirts and Victoria's hand. Victoria clamped her hat to her head and, with pealing laughter, hopped over sludge-filled holes, damp newspapers, and flyers. My hair came unpinned and stuck to my cheeks in damp, sticky strands. Wetness sprang from my armpits, and I stumbled on the uneven ground. My scarf tightened around my throat.

50 ⮒   January Gilchrist

I yanked at it, gulping for air as I endeavored to keep up with the strange man.

He stopped at an open carriage, not unlike the one the grocer from the village had used to deliver the monthly order to Harewood. The bright red lacquer of the paint glistened in the sunshine. A hot wave of shame flooded me. It was uncovered. Were we to sit in an open-top trap like sacks of groceries?

Two handsome black horses stood patiently at the front. A sharp pain in my chest shook right through me at the sight of them. It brought back all I had lost. Harewood Hall. The servants, more like family, who had raised me. The comfort of knowing every nook and cranny of the house I had been born in. Not for the first time, nor the last, I wondered *why*. Why no one had listened when I had told them I wanted to choose my own life, why Father was so eager for us to be gone. The cost of my dowry was more than it would have cost to feed and clothe me for the remainder of his days. The truth burned beneath my skin: He merely hated us and wanted us gone from his life. Like Jones said, we were too painful a reminder of Mama. Although the house had been cleared of any image of her, Jones had shared a small tintype of Mama with us. It was like a glimpse into the future. As we aged, we had grown nearer to that mottled reflection of an unsmiling lady, her gaze fixed on something outside the shot. I saw so much of Victoria in that thin sheet of metal that it was uncanny.

A small, shoeless boy held the reins of the horses. As we neared, he spat on the ground, smirking when I visibly startled. The driver kicked out, connecting firmly with the small boy's backside, pushing him away into the crowd.

"Bugger off." He flicked a copper coin in the boy's direction, and the boy scrabbled among the feet of passersby to retrieve it.

"Vivi." I grasped at her arm tightly. "How do we know this man has been sent by Stanley?" Nerves made my hushed voice squeaky.

My Sister's Shadow   51

She raised her eyebrows at me. "We will just have to take our chances."

"Up ya get. I don't have all day," the man called from the carriage.

He leaned back against his seat and spat a mouthful of tobacco to the filthy ground. Victoria let out a tinkle of delighted laughter and, gripping the dark wooden handle with her pristine gloves and with a flash of stockinged ankle, leaped up into the carriage as if she had been doing it her whole life.

I stood, frozen. Images of fleeing flashed through my mind. I saw myself slipping away into the crowd, just as that boy had.

A whistle blew as a constable directed foot traffic, and the sound brought me back to the present. That relentless wind gusted and lifted my hat. I clamped it down onto my head. Victoria sat imperiously in the seat, her skirts artfully arranged around her.

"It's no different from mounting a horse." She held out a hand to assist me, and as I placed my hand in hers, I experienced a wave of dizziness. Victoria tugged and I was flying, just for a moment. My skirts had barely touched the battered seat when the driver—he had never even introduced himself—clicked his tongue, and the horses were moving through the noise and muck of the crowded port.

Crooked, rotten-fronted shops became smarter, cleaner buildings, which then became attached houses with tidy gardens, which in turn became expanses of brown brick buildings that peered regally down on the street through darkened windows.

Vendors hollered words from the sidewalk. I couldn't understand any of them, my mind overloaded with the smell of burning coal, damp, iron, and stone. Half-finished buildings lurched from the ground, and there was construction everywhere. The city where people said anything could happen was birthing itself before our eyes.

Everything about this city seemed hard, unyielding. The air in Manhattan had a different aroma from that at the port. It was indefinable, as if the money and the dreams that were barely contained within its evenly divided streets added a sweetness to it.

I gulped at huge great mouthfuls of air that smelled less of tar and sweat and more like the maple trees that lined the roads. Clouds the color of filthy rags threatened a downpour any moment. I pulled my coat tighter around me and, screwing my eyes shut, focused on the pain in my chest. *Breathe,* I told myself. But my breath wouldn't come. Spots danced behind my eyes, and I swayed on the seat. My stomach roiled. *I'm all right,* I told myself. *It will all be all right in the end.*

But I didn't believe it.

PART 2

CHAPTER 8

I spent the rest of the ride with my eyes shut and didn't open them until the carriage jerked to a stop. Heaving a steadying breath, I cracked an eyelid for the first look at my new home.

The great mansion seemed to be hewn from great gray slabs of limestone and was three stories high. A sharply slanted, tiled roof drew my eye to soot-stained chimneys. A cloud moved, and the sun's light winked along the diamond-shaped windows on the top level of the house.

The driver stared blankly ahead. Were we to scramble from the carriage and hope no one saw our petticoats? Not that there was anyone about to see.

As if I had spoken aloud, Victoria addressed the driver. "Where are the servants?"

He finally turned to look at us, his small, dark eyes mean. He ran a hand along his jaw. "Inside?"

"And Lord Stanley?"

"You'll find *him* at the raceway," he said with a smirk. "Off ya get—I've got things to do."

Victoria let out an incredulous bark of a laugh at his vulgarity and leaped from the carriage. She pretended to doff her hat at me and held out her hand. "M'lady, let me assist you."

A cool breeze flipped my skirts around my ankles as I dismounted. What would Jones have to say about this? Unbidden, her voice shot through my mind. *"No use complaining about what thousands would give anything to have."*

I adjusted my skirts and gazed at the blank-faced house. It reminded me of a death photograph; something about it rang false—the body remained, but the spirit had departed. I gulped. Victoria was right: I spent too much time with my head in the clouds. It was a house, just a house. Not my home. That would forever remain Harewood.

The driver spat and flicked the reins, and the horses moved off, joining the stream of carriages and carts that crowded the road.

Victoria and I looked at each other with raised brows. Every time we had returned home from our annual holiday at Aunt Petunia's house, the servants had lined up along the entrance to welcome us home. Here, my own husband wasn't around to greet me.

"Well," I said. I had aimed for a light tone but failed.

"Well," Victoria returned in a tart tone that flooded me with relief.

As always, she would take hold of the situation. A wave of gratitude overcame me, and I grasped her hand. *I would have been utterly lost without her.*

"Do we knock? Or wait? Or . . ." I trailed off, eyeing the firmly closed door.

A set of steps, well built and well maintained, led to a mosaic-tiled entrance. Light and color flickered, and I rocked and listed as if I were still on the boat. I was overcome with the sensation that this was all merely a dream.

Victoria shook her head. "No, we channel Aunt Petunia. How many times have we heard her say you must set the tone with servants."

My Sister's Shadow ⌐ 57

She raised her chin and glared down her nose at me, and I smiled. She was a wicked imitator and had entertained Deborah and me with her impersonation of Aunt Petunia for years. Straightening her gloves and her spine, she marched up the steps and opened the front door.

"Good afternoon," she called, her voice echoing down the large hall of the house.

A tall, sharp-faced woman wiped her hands on a piece of toweling tucked into the apron at her waist as she strode toward us along the crowded hallway. Her dress, what could be seen of it around the dingy apron, was a drab gray, hewn from a rough-looking, practical fabric. Small hard eyes peered at us, resentment shimmering. Life had been unkind to this woman, and she responded by being unkind in return.

"Yes?" She cocked an eyebrow.

Had no one been expecting us? Stanley had sent tickets for the *Orient* and a brief letter with Greycliffe's address, confirming he would have someone collect and deliver us.

A sharp burst of relief hit me. This must be the wrong address. I almost laughed at the reprieve.

"You are?" Victoria's tone had me taking a trembling step behind her.

"I am Mrs. Washington. The housekeeper here. And *you are?*" Her tone was mocking.

Victoria tugged the fingers of her gloves slowly. "We are the mistresses of the house."

Washington's eyes narrowed as if the idea meant nothing to her. "Both of ya are Lady Stanley?"

My stomach dropped to my boots. This *was* to be our new home. I would be no match for this woman with her coarse manner and her red, chapped hands and disapproving lips.

Victoria slapped the gloves into the palm of her hand. "Yes. Show us to our rooms. We have had a long journey."

I must have sagged or sighed with relief because Washington's sullen gaze rested on me a moment, narrowing further. Turning her head to the side but keeping her gaze firmly fixed on me, she hollered, "Annie, get in here."

"Really, Mrs. Washington. We needn't raise our voices." Victoria scolded.

Mrs. Washington shifted her ratlike gaze to Victoria's disapproving one. She didn't turn her head, instead choosing to bawl almost directly into Victoria's face. "Annie!"

I shuddered, but before Victoria could react, one side of the woman's mouth tilted slightly, as if in satisfaction of a job well done, and she turned and thumped back into the depths of the house. Then, the rushed tapping of heels clanged through the hallway, and a flushed, harassed-looking girl appeared.

"Annie, is it?" Victoria asked. The slack-faced girl nodded. "Show us to our rooms."

The girl startled, as if woken from a daydream, and nodded, looking between us. "You two look exactly the same."

I closed my eyes and took a deep breath through my nose. I did not have the energy for this.

Victoria gasped and thrust a hand to her chest. "We do? No one has ever mentioned that."

I placed my hand on Victoria's arm, hoping to calm her.

Annie missed her tone and continued. "It's made me come over all odd. You all twins?"

Victoria's arm tensed under my hand. "Actually, we just met each other on the boat."

Dumb silence.

Victoria sighed and pinched the bridge of her nose. "Yes, obviously we are twins."

"Can you read each other's thoughts?"

"Yes, we can." Victoria smiled tightly. "We are thinking how very tired we are and how we would like to be shown to our rooms."

MY SISTER'S SHADOW 59

Annie nodded. With a clumsy attempt at a curtsey, she stepped back and led us through to the ante room.

I was sorry for the girl and her confusion, but I had no energy to feel real empathy. It was like I was moving through a dream, stumbling through the house, waiting to wake up any minute. The room was dominated by an imposing staircase fashioned from a dark, dull wood, which swept upward to a half landing, then hugged the walls until it disappeared into the first floor.

The house seemed to loom around us, crowding us with its heavy mix of wood, glass, fabric, and plants. A strange, oppressive silence hung in the air. It seemed just as cold inside the house as it was outside, perhaps colder.

Annie paused in the middle of the room, as if giving us time to take in our surroundings.

Framed certificates hung on the wall, bearing Stanley's name in varied cursive print, too small for me to make any sense of them. Amid it all hung an oversized portrait of Stanley, aloof and watchful. I gazed back at his brooding eyes. The painter had been generous. His mustache was thick and full, his eyes more evenly spaced, the hook of his nose made smaller, less prominent.

Still, it made me shiver to look at it. *This man is my husband.* None of it seemed real.

We continued through the body of the house, on uneven stairs, our footfalls deadened by the faded runner, frayed along the edges. The staircase turned on itself, and seen from above, the room appeared abandoned. Thick layers of dust perched along the tops of the portraits, the wall sconces, the furniture.

When we reached the landing, we were enveloped in a stifling and sour heat. Annie banged doors open as we approached, gesturing inside the rooms proudly. The house was peculiarly ordered; some rooms were completely bare, and others filled to bursting with mismatched and eccentric furniture. Strange creatures with glass eyes watched us from cases strewn along shelves crowded with strange and jarring objects.

60 January Gilchrist

With an air of a magician about to pull a rabbit from a hat, Annie placed her hand on the handle of the door at the dim end of the hallway.

"This will be your room, miss," she said to me, having assumed that Victoria, with her imperious air, was Lady Stanley.

On a table beside the bed sat a vase of Christmas roses, their heads hanging despondently. Their earthy fragrance hung in the still air.

"Brant will bring your luggage up when it arrives. I'll take you through to your room, Lady Stanley."

Victoria reached for me at the same time I turned, and her nail connected painfully with my arm. "Come see my rooms," she said with a quirk of her brow.

We trod the hallway boards to the opposite end. Annie fairly vibrated with excitement as she pushed open the door to Lady Stanley's chambers.

Annie and Victoria entered, but I hesitated at the threshold, as if delaying my entry into the room delayed the truth. *That I am Lady Stanley.* No matter how much I wished that weren't true.

A mammoth bed dominated the room, its thick crimson drapes bound to mahogany posts. A floral, circular armchair, the bottom edged with pleated fabric in the same material as the damask curtains, hovered in the corner of the room.

A slate-colored hawk, mottled wings outstretched in flight, hung from the ceiling, talons clenched, ready to snatch up its prey. I gasped as it swung slowly to me, turning on its nearly invisible string until its beady glass eyes pinned me with its gaze.

Victoria saw my horrified expression and burst into laughter.

Annie stood between us, her expression slowly sliding into one of bewilderment.

"Is something the matter?" The utter confusion in her voice set Victoria laughing again, and this time I couldn't resist either.

"Not at all," Victoria dismissed her. "Draw a bath for us, please."

My Sister's Shadow ☞ 61

Annie bunched the fabric of her dress in her hands, her eyelids fluttering. "Bath day is Monday."

Our laughter stilled in the air.

"I beg your pardon?"

"Bath day is Mondays. Today is Thursday," Annie said slowly.

Silence stretched between us like a rope as Annie strangled the fabric in her hands. "Mrs. Washington likes to stick to the schedule."

"Are you telling me that the lady of the house, after a ten-day journey is not permitted a bath because it does not suit the housekeeper's schedule?" Victoria's voice was as frigid as the air in the room.

I traced a finger along the faded filigree on the wallpaper, my cheeks flaming. Around and around it swirled. The only sound in the room was the rub of my skin against the paper.

I looked up. The young girl's face was wretched, and I felt bad for her. I hated this side of Victoria—and hated myself even more for relying on it so.

"I am certain that Mrs. Washington will amend her schedule, just this once, for us. After all, we have just completed a long journey," I inserted before Victoria could continue.

Victoria stepped sideways, pressing her shoulder against mine in warning. *Keep quiet.* Annie's eyes flicked from mine to Victoria's, and whatever she saw there made her shoulders drop.

"You don't know Washington," Annie murmured.

CHAPTER 9

There had been a standoff about the bath. One that Victoria had won, in a manner of speaking. Eventually, Annie had brought up two boiled towels, which we gratefully accepted.

We were in what was to be Lady Stanley's room. Marginally warmer than the rest of the house, but my fingers were almost numb.

I ran the rapidly cooling towel over the back of Victoria's neck, her hands woven into her hair to keep it off her neck. Her skin was pale where the towel wiped over it.

I had lain on the deck of the boat wishing I was anywhere but there, and now I found I wished myself back. The seemingly never-ending ocean had made it feel as if time had stood still.

"I had rather expected Stanley to meet us from the boat." Victoria's voice held a note of censure.

I nodded, knowing she understood, even though she couldn't see my movement. The bed loomed in the middle of the room, and a buzzing noise took up in my ears. The wedding night had been unpleasant beyond my imagination. How many times would I be expected to repeat it? Until I was with child? I cringed at the very idea of it.

"And that driver." The indignation ramped up. "Not to mention the housekeeper. Talk about Americans and their new

MY SISTER'S SHADOW 63

ways. Is this the sort of behavior we are to expect from our servants?"

I said nothing, knowing that when she was like this, anything I said would only bring further displeasure. The housekeeper's pinched mouth and Annie's unhappy eyes flashed in my mind. I would let Victoria deal with them; she was far more suited to it.

We dressed for dinner, as was the custom at Harewood Hall. In the brief but chaotic entry to the house, I hadn't seen a dinner gong, and we didn't know the routine of the house, so after dressing, we sat in Lady Stanley's room in obedient anticipation.

"Ring the bell and ask that ninny of a girl when dinner will be served," Victoria ordered.

She sat in front of a cloudy mirror at a dung-colored dresser, and I lay on the bed. A tiredness had seeped into my bones, and I felt utterly unable to face the world beyond the door.

"Are you sure we can't just ask for a tray?" I asked into the heavy drapery of the bed.

"On our first night? No." Victoria was firm.

A bell clanged somewhere below us, and I jolted upright.

"Was that the dinner bell?"

Victoria narrowed her eyes and stomped to the bell cord, yanking with a violence that startled me. "Are we to just sit here all night?" she demanded, as if I were to know.

I lifted a shoulder.

The routines of Harewood were imprinted on my soul. My body knew moments before Harold rang the bell that it was dinnertime. Anything I didn't know, Jones had, and her advice had guided me. Until it had really mattered.

I would do whatever it took to return to Harewood, I swore wordlessly to the water-stained ceiling above the bed. I would not rest until I had found a way to return to England. How, I did not know, but surely I could find a way.

64 ∽ January Gilchrist

I studied Victoria as she focused on her reflection in the mirror, pinching her cheeks and adjusting her immaculate hair. She was so much more suited to this than I.

She stood and presented herself to me in the manner we always had before dinner at home, and hot tears burned behind my lids.

"Oh, Addy, don't," she said, frustration sharpening her tone.

I nodded. "I won't." But I couldn't stop.

She opened her arms to gesture me in. We swayed side to side while Victoria hummed the folk song Jones had sung to us as children whenever we had been poorly. I rested my cheek against her delicate collarbone.

"You're too thin," Victoria scolded, running her hands across my shoulders. She pulled away from me and scowled. "I don't like it."

*　*　*

Our walk through the hallway felt deliciously illicit, as if we were children breaking some nonsensical rule, as adults' rules so often were. We paused at the top step of the stairway, heads cocked, listening for any noise that would indicate where we should go. Hearing none, we continued down into the sitting room. There was a frayed, grimy rope hanging among the shell-shaped wall sconces and sketches along the wall, and Victoria pulled it with a mischievous smile. She nodded to a closed door at the back of the sitting room, and we ventured in.

She turned back to me with a peculiar look on her face. I peered around her shoulder, a shocked breath punched from my lungs.

"Oh!"

We spoke on a singular breath.

A statue, carved from black marble, stood. Stretching to the ceiling, it wore nothing but a grass skirt, pendulous breasts hanging to the waistband. Sketches of women in various stages of undress hung along the wall behind it.

MY SISTER'S SHADOW ～ 65

"Vivi, is he"—I could barely whisper the word—"perverted?" I pointed at the statue with a trembling finger.

Victoria's gaze ran along the statue, pausing a moment on the bare breasts.

Her mouth worked as she tried to make sense of it before she simply guffawed, the sound so unlike her that I laughed too.

Our eyes met, and perhaps it was the strangeness of the journey and the peculiarity of the house, but a kind of hysteria came over us. We clutched each other, bent double, made weak by the laughter.

It was like one had set the other on fire with laughter. In the years to come, this too-brief moment would hover in the shadows like a specter.

As our laughter appeared to be petering out, we caught each other's eyes and were set off again. Slowly, hands clinging to each other's elbows, mouths open, cheeks pressed against each other, we sank to the floor. We laughed until my stomach ached, until I was breathless with it.

When the laughter finally subsided, I rolled to my back and gazed up at the elaborately decorated ceiling. Plaster leaves circled in ever decreasing rings toward the center of the room, wrapping around themselves in a complicated pattern my eye could not make sense of.

Victoria sat and pulled me up with her. "The mistress will have a grand time putting her stamp on Greycliffe House."

"If Mrs. Washington will allow it." My stomach clenched.

"Hmph." How could one small sound seem so ominous? "Let's go find dinner," she said.

As we scrambled to our feet and readjusted our dresses, fixing each other's hair, I asked, "Will you be Lady Stanley?" gesturing with my head to the door.

"If you wish," Victoria said, a satisfied light in her eyes.

We followed the smell of boiling meat and passed through the door that Washington and Annie had appeared from this afternoon.

It seemed unbelievable that only this morning we had still been aboard the *Orient*.

A door in the middle of the wall stood open. I saw a table, set with white linen. The windows were filmy, giving the outside a ghostly hue. Apart from the cutlery and tablecloth, the table was quite bare. No flowers. No gleaming glassware or flickering candles. Two places were set across from each other on the long sides of the table. With a growing sense of foreboding, I followed Victoria into the room.

"Do we sit?" I gazed around the room.

Apart from the table and its crimson chairs, a large mahogany sideboard sat against the wall, and a grandfather clock marked the time with incessant ticking. Dusty crimson drapes slumped in the corner of the room, pooling along the floor, as if they had been made for a larger, taller window.

"We sit." Victoria's tone was certain, far more certain than it ought to have been.

We sat across from each other, under the ticking of the large clock. Although the chair was covered in velvet, it grew hard against my legs. I ran a nail along the table, watching as it gashed the aging varnish. I pressed harder and watched as my nail whitened and sank into the wood. The clock shuddered and sang its reminder.

Time is passing. Time is passing.

Victoria stood abruptly. "I am going to—"

But then Annie appeared, carrying two dishes.

She placed a dish of boiled root vegetables on the table. The second bowl contained a casserole. Without another word, Annie left the room.

The odor of the stewed meat made my stomach twist, as did the sight of the globules of sand-colored fat that had congealed on the surface of the watery gravy. I inhaled shallow breaths to still my curdling stomach.

My Sister's Shadow ☞ 67

Victoria and I stared at the food.

Finally, Victoria spoke. "She expects us to serve ourselves?"

I said nothing.

Victoria shoved her chair back and marched to the grimy cord at the door. I didn't need to look to see her ferocity—the room near crackled with it. My shoulders crept toward my ears as she yanked the rope and then threw herself back into her seat.

Annie's head appeared around the doorway with surprising speed. Had she been lurking behind the door?

"Lord Stanley?" Victoria barked.

Annie stared blindly at Victoria, confusion rending her slack jawed.

"Are we to expect Lord Stanley for dinner?" Victoria ground out.

"Colbine is racing, Miss . . . uh . . . Mrs. Lady," Annie stuttered.

"I do not know what that means." Victoria's tone brought my hands to my lap. I pressed the tips of my fingers together.

"It's Thursday?"

I feared for a moment that Victoria would strike the girl.

"Speak English, for goodness sake."

"Colbine is his lordship's horse," the girl stammered. "He's racing tonight. His lordship will be at the racetrack."

Was that why the house was as silent as a tomb? Could we expect it to come alive tomorrow after the race? I couldn't imagine this quiet and queer house alive with the sounds of people.

"So, we are to start without Lord Stanley?"

Annie's tongue worried at a sore at the corner of her mouth, "Yes?"

Victoria closed her eyes and released a deep breath. "Serve us then."

"Serve you?" There was an incredulous silence. "You mean put the food on your plate?"

68 ⮞   January Gilchrist

I almost laughed then. Annie standing there in her maid's uniform, confused and cowed; Victoria, cold and imperial.

The flickering lamplight sent shadows scuttling about the room. The seat rocked beneath me, and the band in my chest began to squeeze again.

"Do you serve Lord Stanley when he dines, Annie?"

Suddenly I was exhausted.

Annie sniffed. Without another word she leaned over Victoria and dug the large metal spoon into the dish. Droplets of gravy splattered around the plate, spreading on the tablecloth.

I bit my lip. Jones had spent our entire lives explaining the importance of eating carefully, to avoid dripping, wiping, or tearing our clothes, but also to always, always watch the dining linens.

It took a lot of people to make a house run, she would tell us. A true lady never takes for granted what other people do for her, and you mustn't disrespect how hard everyone downstairs works. A true lady is seen and not heard. In essence, she folds herself over and over until she is so tiny that no one notices her.

The last she never actually said, but it was implied in every piece of advice she imparted. How to stand, how to speak, how to eat, which body parts should never be exposed, not even in the privacy of a lady's own rooms. There was no freedom in being a lady.

Victoria's nostrils flared and her lips tightened. "And carrots."

Annie slapped a spoonful of the oversoft vegetables onto the plate. "There you go."

"My lady."

My stomach dropped. Victoria was capable of anything in a mood like this.

Victoria raised her chin and glared at Annie.

"Every single time you address me, you use 'my lady.' Or you will find yourself without a position. Understood?"

MY SISTER'S SHADOW ⌒ 69

Annie's face flushed and her hands fisted at her sides. "Yes. My lady." She did not blink. "Is that all?"

"My sister will need dinner too."

A pulse throbbed in Annie's jaw. I followed the spoon as it dipped in and out of the casserole.

"You are dismissed," Victoria said, her voice an iron club.

Annie shot me a dark look as she stalked from the room.

"Oh, Vivi, I wish—"

"Don't," Victoria commanded, holding a hand up in the air between us. "Do not dare lecture me about what I should and shouldn't do when you can't do any of it yourself. We need to set the tone and set it early."

She again repeated our aunt's words, but now her tone was earnest rather than mocking.

I swallowed down my feelings and picked up a fork. Spearing a piece of gristly meat, I chewed vigorously, grateful for something to do. I kept my eyes trained on the meal in front of me, because everywhere else I looked was too strange, too unfamiliar.

Even when I gazed upon Victoria's face, it was if I didn't recognize her, that cold, hard-faced woman.

* * *

After dinner, we walked together up the dimly lit stairs. My feet dragged against the runner. My limbs were heavy and moved as if I were wading through thick mud. We had sat among the dishes until it became clear that no one was coming to clear them and there was no other course. I had fretted about another confrontation and was greatly relieved when Victoria had thrown her napkin on the table and said, "It appears no dessert will be forthcoming, and after this swill I would rather go to bed without."

We paused outside Lady Stanley's room.

"Will you stay with me?" I asked, my voice pitiful, even to my own ears. Victoria and I had shared a bedroom since birth.

Aside from the wedding night, which I had spent with Stanley, at four and twenty, this would be my first time going to bed alone.

Victoria squinted her eyes and looked at the ceiling as if considering my request, but I already knew the answer.

"Just until he comes?" I pleaded.

"You'll be fine," she said, patting my arm like I was an ailing relative.

I watched her as she walked the hallway; how vast it seemed.

Turning the handle slowly, I inched the door open and peered in. Someone, Annie I guessed, had pulled the vermillion curtains closed, and they hung awkwardly.

I tiptoed around that room. How I longed for the familiar comfort of the drafty suites of Harewood. Even the ship's cramped, damp cabin felt more like home than this echoing chamber.

I splashed my face with stale water from the jug and bowl on the nightstand, the floral motif of the crockery the same crimson shade as the curtains. The nightstand on which the jug and basin sat was a dark, poorly made affair. There was little in the way of beauty in any of it.

The mottled mirror gave me a ghostly appearance, and I couldn't bear to look at myself, pulling the pins from my hair with an averted gaze. I thought about tugging the cord to summon Annie to help me out of my dress, but decided against it.

Victoria was separated from me by only two walls. Was she wondering how to unbutton her dress? Where to put her things? Perhaps she was trailing a hand along the items in the room, picking them up and discarding them not quite as they were, as she was wont to do? Not for her the timidity of how I skulked about, a guest in my own rooms.

My house now. I shuddered at the thought.

I placed my hand on the door tentatively and pressed my ear against the crack between the door and its jamb. Listening for what, I couldn't say. But the cool wood was a comfort, and I don't know how long I stood there, allowing the weight of the house to prop me up.

The wind gusted at the windows, causing them to shudder in their frames, and from somewhere under my window, the shrill shriek of a woman in agony ruptured the silence.

The small round knob rattled unevenly as I turned it, and the screech of metal against dry metal rang through the night. I paused again, ear cocked, listening. I could hear thumping . . . footsteps? No, the beating of my heart. Or blood roaring in my ears. I gazed about fearfully. The shadows were still. There was no movement. I flew down the hallway toward Victoria's door, turning the knob, pressing it open, closing it again, and leaning against the closed door in one rapid movement.

She looked up from the bed, and I saw myself through her shocked eyes, my chest heaving, my hair wild, barefoot. Without a word, she resumed running Mama's hairbrush through her hair with her right hand, her mouth moving as she counted the strokes. I tried to think of something to say, when the woman outside wailed again.

Victoria froze, mid-stroke, the hairbrush hanging slackly in her hand. She shook her head at my unspoken exclamation. "It's just an animal."

It didn't sound like an animal. It sounded like a woman in the depths of hell.

"Are you certain?" I asked in a small, weak voice. How very pathetic I was!

Victoria stood and pulled the bell with a casualness that was stunning.

Footsteps pounded along the hall, and Annie appeared, wiping her damp hands along her apron.

"What is it?" Her eyes searched ours, going to and fro between ours like a shuttlecock in a game of badminton. Back and forth they went, looking for answers.

"That sound," Victoria said. "What on earth is it?"

72 January Gilchrist

Annie cocked her head, and we all stared out into the inky evening beyond the window.

"The screaming. It sounded like a woman," I said.

Annie laughed, relieved.

"That? That's just a raccoon. Not a woman. Gawd, you gave me a heart attack." She clutched her hands to her chest.

"Is it in pain? Can you send a man out to find it and tend to it?" I asked, never able to bear the idea of an animal in pain.

She laughed again, almost cruel this time. "You'd better get used to it. This time of year they carry on every night, and there's nothing you can do for it. Except find it and wring its neck."

Her laugh was brittle, sharp.

"A . . . raccoon? Is that a type of bird?"

Annie's laughter died, and she stared at me strangely. "A bird? You don't know what a raccoon is?"

"Clearly not." Victoria's voice was cold.

"It's like a . . . well. It's just a small . . . I guess if you crossed a rat with a cat? Nothing to fear. They only get noisy when they want to rut," Annie said with a laugh as she left the room.

"How charming," Victoria said in a jolly tone. "*That* sound from an animal that is a cross between a rat and a cat. This country—" She didn't finish her sentence, just made a small noise that could have meant anything.

"Here, let me get your buttons." She gestured for me to turn, and I did automatically, without thought, as if I were one of the small wooden people that had glided on a stick in a toy we'd had as children. When the smooth wooden handle was cranked, the people moved in their groove, performing a tiny mechanical show. I was the unthinking lady, spinning in her groove as the hand cranked. I slid seamlessly, silently, blindly back to my room.

My dress slipped to the floor. I stepped from it, leaving it on the floor like a puddle of spilled water, into my cotton chemise. I tied the tiny cotton rope around the neckline, like a noose, before

MY SISTER'S SHADOW   ☞ 73

gliding between the icy and unwelcoming sheets, where I remained, shivering in the dark.

The night grew deeper, blacker. It was as if my head were underwater, my ears full and everything both dulled and too loud. The house seemed to scream its silence; it echoed off the walls, seeped through the cracks, and pinned me to the bed.

Finally, I fell asleep in the heavy darkness to the sound of a rasping breathing that I felt was not my own.

CHAPTER 10

On my third morning in New York, I was awoken by shouts and bangs from below the window.

I stared at the ceiling in the dim light. It was hard to tell what time it was in this monolithic city. The sun was always in shadow.

The room faced an alley that snaked between Greycliffe and the hulking red brick mansion next to it. The alley linked both houses to stables at the back and allowed delivery carts and servants to access the back entrance.

It often rumbled and clattered with deliveries, but these noises had a different tone. Curiosity had me throwing back the covers and moving to the window. I tweaked the curtain aside and peered through the glass for my first glimpse of my husband since arriving in New York. He'd not attended a single dinner, nor appeared at the breakfast table. I'd begun to wonder if I'd imagined him, like a bad dream.

Stanley stood slightly apart from three men attempting to manage a colt as pitch as night. Even at this distance the colt was beautiful, his coat a black so deep it reflected blue in the sun. He kicked and bucked, his front hoof pawing at the ground in frustration as the men worked at the ropes tying him to the back of the carriage, struggling to work the knots.

MY SISTER'S SHADOW   75

The men wore battered workers' hats, designed to offer protection from sun and dust for the eyes of men toiling in the outdoors all day long. The tallest of the men stood at the head of the horse, his back to me. Stanley shouted orders, a riding crop held aloft.

The horse kicked, and the smallest of the men jumped out of its path. His hat toppled to the ground, and I saw it was the man who had delivered us from the boat. Brant, Annie had called him. Watching through narrowed eyes, I willed the horse to break its ropes and make its escape.

"Go," I breathed against the glass, my breath creating a circle of fog. *Go, go, go.*

But even in its glorious fury, the colt was no match for the men. And where in this city could it go to be free?

The horse snorted, spittle flying, eyes rolling, and with one last burst of rage, it kicked out, connecting with the thigh of Brant. He howled and doubled over, clutching his leg.

Stanley lifted the crop high in air and brought it down sharply on the back of the horse's neck.

The sound whistled through the air to me, once, twice. On the third time I stepped back from the window, allowing the curtain to fall back into place and shroud the room in darkness once more. I took my tonic, crawled into bed, pulled the sheet up, and listened to the sound of his riding crop striking, over and over again, until the darkness swallowed me.

★ ★ ★

It was mid-morning by the time I woke again. A desperate lethargy had overtaken me since our arrival. I moved like a sleepwalker, drowsily drifting from bedroom to dining room and back, the unusualness of it all an assault on my overwrought senses.

That morning as I shuffled into the breakfast room, Victoria was speaking to Annie. "My sister is ill. Can you arrange for a doctor?"

76 ⬧ January Gilchrist

Annie's blank face turned to mine as I entered and wordlessly took my place at the table.

Breakfast had been hours ago, but the food had been left on the sideboard, a request from Victoria or simply Annie's laziness I couldn't determine.

"Sister, darling, how are you feeling? You look peaky."

I met Victoria's spirited gaze with a dead one of my own.

Arriving in New York had seemed to invigorate Victoria. She was lively and had made quick work of rearranging the house. She had thrown out demands and commands, and every time I saw her, she had a linen-covered notebook in her hand. The nib of her pen scratched along paper incessantly as she wrote her lists.

It was all I could to drag myself from bed to the water jug on the hearth in my room. I was listless, flat, made stupid by an exhaustion that lapped at my feet endlessly. All I could think about was returning home to England, to Harewood.

I glanced at the sideboard. A square of lace had been thrown over the food. The edges of the ham had darkened, the bread hardened in the air. My plate had a smear of something brown along the rim.

My stomach clenched. I shivered and rubbed my hands together.

"Annie, would you stoke the fire? It's freezing in here." I directed to the hovering figure at my elbow. The mute reluctance lasted only a moment before she moved to the fireplace.

A cup sat in front of Victoria, beside the ever-present notepad. Her pen was discarded and lay on the tablecloth, a drop of ink gathering on the nib. It grew, ever so slowly, and I watched as if outside my body, wondering how full it could get, how much it could take before it dropped off the nib and landed on the crisp linen tablecloth.

"Stanley has returned," I said once Annie had left the room. My voice emerged like the croak of a door stiff through years of unuse.

Victoria gave me a long cool stare before shifting her gaze to the doorway. "Have you seen him?"

I licked my lips. My throat was so dry. Reaching for her almost empty cup, I drained the remainder of the cold tea. It was overly sweet and tainted with a sickly taste. I gagged and inspected the cup. The bottom of it was lined with a dark sticky liquid. I raised it to my nose. Sherry. Like our Aunt Petunia used to drink when she and Cousin Deborah would come to stay.

Her face would redden and gladden the more she drank. Tiny glass after tiny glass she swilled down. "One more won't hurt, will it, girls?" She would giggle, her face flushed, her laughter growing louder, more fervent with each glass.

I stared at the deep brown liquid as it oozed along the lip of the china. Victoria snatched the cup from my hand and replaced it with an empty one from the table, pouring an insipid-looking stream of tea into it. She dashed the milk in, and I watched as it bloomed, twisted.

"Yes, I saw him," I said.

She didn't respond, and I offered nothing further, both lost in our thoughts.

★ ★ ★

Winter in New York was not the magical mists of Harewood Hall.

There were no rambling tramps through sleeping woods, hands shoved deep in the pockets of our macintoshes, mufflers tied tight.

Here winter was a pursuer. It battered at the windows in Arctic gales that sounded like hands hammering at the glass. It killed everything it touched; it turned rain to sleet—sharp icicles that sliced at one's face like knives. It seeped into every room, no matter the strength of the fire, how many linens I tucked underneath the windowsills. Thick banks of snow appeared in the morning, turning the streetscape gray, for the snow might fall white, but once it touched the filthy streets, it swiftly turned to a murky slush.

The house was cold as a morgue.

The only room that seemed to get above freezing was the front room overlooking the street. The feeble sun shone through the window for most of the day, and I would stand at the glass and, momentarily at least, forget about the dim, dull life we lived in Greycliffe.

It was pointless in a manner that our lives in Harewood had never been. The promised adventures of America had come to nothing. The endless lists of Things to Be Done around the house that Victoria wrote, went no further than her notebook. It was up to me to ask, she'd said, but I didn't know who to ask, or how.

Stanley, I supposed, but there never seemed a moment to do so.

Aside from his snatched visits in the dark, where communication was rough hands and the sour smell of long-worn clothes, we spent no time together. I could hardly ask him in the bedroom; the visits were brief, wordless, and once completed, he returned to his own bedroom. Marriage was a strange land. Much like Father's, Stanley's presence in the house was little more than empty coffee cups and the occasional scent of burnt tobacco haunting the halls. He didn't seem interested in the existence of myself, or of Victoria, at all. Why had he bothered with a wife, I wondered, if he preferred the life of a bachelor? My dowry had paid for the purchase of Greycliffe, he had told Father, and he certainly wouldn't be the first (or the last) lord to marry for cash rather than love.

Did the other men make an effort with their wives? Did they spend mealtimes and make conversation at least? Perhaps not. I knew nothing of marriage, and no one who could shed any further light on it.

Nanny Jones had simply informed me the night before the wedding that "your husband will come and put something of his

My Sister's Shadow   ☞ 79

in your private area. Best just lie there quietly, let him do what he likes so he can get on with it." She'd hadn't been wrong, but I wished she had warned me just how painful and unpleasant it was going to be. The searing pain, the need to escape in my mind while he lay on me, how the sticky feeling flashed on me during the day that brought with it an urge to scrub and scrub at my skin.

I relied more and more on my tonic to pass the days, living in a kaleidoscope of fearful dreams—Graham, Morris, Nanny, Father. Hera. Harewood. Stanley on top of me, pinching, hurting. I would wake screaming, drenched in sweat despite the cold. I no longer bothered trying to resist the pull of sleep and wandered the house in a daze, if I made it out of bed at all.

I began to wonder if anything would ever change. Until one day, heavy footsteps sounded outside my door. Too heavy to be Annie's or Victoria's. I was surprised when Stanley thrust open the door. Beside him stood a squat, heavyset man. I sat up in bed and watched as they peered at me through the gloom. Stanley's expression was one of distaste, as if I were something unpleasant he'd stepped in.

"I see," said the short man. Without asking permission, they entered my bedroom, Stanley to the window, throwing aside the curtains and thrusting open the window; the man to my bedside. I let out a squeal as the man yanked the bedcovers from me and pressed his hand to my shoulder, forcing me back onto the bed.

"When was her last menses?" he asked.

Why on earth would he ask that? I wondered in a stupor as the man pressed his hand against my abdomen.

"Nothing since arriving, Doctor," a voice said from the doorway.

I wrestled myself to a sitting position to see who it was— Washington! Whatever did she mean?

The man prodded my belly with a look of mild disgust. Hot shame flooded me at his rough touch.

He looked up to Stanley and shook his head. Stanley nodded, his mouth a tight line.

"Here is the tonic, Doctor." Washington again, sounding all too eager to please, a tone I was yet to hear when she spoke to Victoria or me.

The doctor took my tonic, his gaze flicking from the bottle to my face and back again. "Laudanum." He wrinkled his nose. "Not advisable while trying to conceive."

I sat up again. Conceiving? Is that what lay behind Stanley's nightly visits? If so, shouldn't a husband discuss it with his wife rather than the housekeeper and a complete stranger? I clutched the bedcovers to my chest, unable to make sense of what was happening.

"I sell a tonic, my own concoction, far better suited to encourage fertility. Continue regular attempts. Call on me if the situation hasn't improved next month."

Stanley remained at the window. "And this nerve condition?" He sounded angry, as if he had just discovered he'd been pickpocketed.

The doctor gazed down at me through watery eyes. Perhaps he was going to ask me how I was feeling.

"Begin every morning with burnt red wine, nutmeg, and toast. The uterus can stimmy blood flow if it is not used as it was intended, causing moods and in some cases hysteria. Conception should assist the nerves. No more laudanum."

My pulse flickered like a lightbulb dying. Where was Victoria? Why were they all speaking about me as if I weren't here? I barely understood anything they spoke of, but through my fugue I understood enough to know that something terrible was bearing down on me. I thought of how my mother appeared in my dreams, the look in her eyes the last time I'd seen her, when she'd crept into our bedroom, the silver light of the moon illuminating her in a way that made me think of angels. She had brushed my hair from my face and whispered into the dark, *"Take care of your sister."*

Before throwing herself from the balcony to her death.

The moon shifted from crescent to orb and back again as the house swallowed week after week until the chill thawed and spring arrived.

Without my tonic the days dragged drearily, and most days it felt as if Victoria and I were the only occupants of the house. If there were any servants other than Annie and Mrs. Washington, I had yet to espy them. During daylight hours, Annie scuttled and scurried throughout the house, disturbed air and the sound of doors clicking closed the only signs she existed.

We sat in the warm front room together, me with a book, Victoria with her face pressed against the window, watching the world pass us both by.

Until the night Stanley crashed into the room on a cloud of whiskey fumes.

"We have been invited to a party. Befriend the man's wife. He's an important investor. Or could be. He's as hard to get access to as the King."

His eyes were wild, his tie skewed, and he stank of horse and alcohol.

"This is it," Stanley said, leaning against the doorway. He pointed a finger at me. "I don't care what you have to do. *Befriend. His. Wife.* Befriend them all. Vanderbilts, Carnegies, Belmonts, Williamsons. They're all going to be there." Stanley looked very pleased with himself. "This is my opportunity to get in the pockets of these stupid Americans. Fools and their money are soon parted. Who knows where this will take us?"

He chuckled, a sound that set the hairs on my arm on edge.

CHAPTER 11

My hands trembled as I forced the tiny pearls into their silk eyes.

"Not so tight." Victoria pinched the soft skin at my wrist.

I gentled my touch, but my fingers felt thick, as if they belonged on someone else's hand. Heat bloomed in my wrist, and I longed to rub it but dared not stop wrestling the buttons.

"Stop pawing at me!" Victoria yanked her neck, and the fabric around it, from my hands with an accusing look. "I'll do it myself."

A sigh escaped my lips. Victoria's eyes met mine fiercely in the mirror. My smile flickered and faded once she returned her attention to her reflection and fastened the buttons at her neck. Her pale hair was partially down, loose, and the gentle wave of it belied how many hours she had spent adjusting it. All afternoon she'd threaded snow-white feathers into the crown of her hat. Angling it on her head, she jabbed pins into it with a ferociousness that unnerved me.

I ran my hands along the front of my dress to still their trembling. Tonight was our first foray into New York's society. At last we had a purpose. The weeks in the lead up to the party had been trips to the fabric stores and dressmakers. Victoria had planned our outfits like a battle, she in a romantic green costume (not

MY SISTER'S SHADOW

green, but eau de Nil—the next *big* thing, the salesman had assured us) and me in a beaded dress that rattled unnervingly as I moved. Despite the excitement over the dresses, I couldn't shake the anxiety that bobbed inside me all day.

No longer able to rely on my tonic to soothe my nerves, I had taken to scratching the inside of my elbow with a perseverance that had drawn blood.

"So, there are Winifred, Ethel, Charlotte, and Beatrice Helmsley. Their mother was a Vanderbilt. And a Martha—or is it Marcia?"

I narrowed my eyes in the pretense of consideration, but I neither knew nor cared.

"Martha," she stated, as if agreeing with me. "And then there's the other arm of the family. Barbara, Elizabeth, Katherine, Margaux. Most of the Helmsley girls married Williamsons, who apparently"—Victoria maintained a disinterested expression, but a note of delight crept into her voice—"own most of New York. State *and* city. Or the parts that matter, at any rate."

I raised my eyebrows. I really didn't care.

"There must be an eligible one among them. They can't all have married one another." Victoria laughed, a light, musical sound, and I watched as she angled her face to catch the last languorous light of the dimming sun.

"This is the exact thing I dreamed of. A party with New York high society." She turned to me then with an assessing gaze. "We only have one opportunity for a first impression so . . . if you like, I could act as Lady Stanley?" Her air of casual disinterest did not fool me.

I shook my head, no. "Not with Stanley around."

She turned back to the mirror, her mouth a grim line. It would have suited me just fine for her to pretend to be Lady Stanley on a night like tonight, but it was too risky to try with Stanley around. He was not a man that took slights, perceived or otherwise, easily. Since the doctor had visited, I had tried my very hardest to give him what he wanted. A pliable, amiable wife who did not suffer from *nerves*. If only he were trying as hard to please me himself, but our interactions still consisted only of nightly visits which had blessedly decreased in time spent, if not in frequency.

When Victoria considered herself suitably adorned, we made our way down the stairs, arms linked: Victoria tall and proud, the queen on her way to her coronation. I hunkered along beside her, as if I were the beast to her beauty, not her identical twin.

Stanley leaned against the entrance in a fugue of cigar smoke. The door was thrown open to the street, and an unfamiliar carriage waited at the roadside.

The sky, which had been low and dark all day, began to empty its black clouds with an astonishing lack of notice. No misty, all-day drizzle here. The New York rain was in as much of a rush as everyone who lived there. It dropped in huge, fat droplets that battered you, causing your clothes to stick to you like paste.

It left behind a sickly, decaying scent, not the clean smell of burgeoning greenery and soil, like at Harewood.

A footman appeared between the house and the carriage, taking refuge under an ivory-handled umbrella. Stanley glanced at us, then away, and ground his cigar under his heel. With a nod to the footman, he ducked under the umbrella and into the carriage. Victoria and I echoed his movements noiselessly, wiping our hems with a cloth once we were seated. Already the curls had fallen from Victoria's hair, and the feathers on her hat had wilted miserably.

Something about the way the feathers hung caused my stomach to twist. A night like this, with these kinds of people, was Victoria's purpose, her passion. But all her hard work had been ruined in a matter of moments. She had wanted so badly for tonight to be perfect, and already it had not gone as planned. I squeezed her hand, my heart aching, but my hand fell onto the seat between us as she slipped hers from under mine.

MY SISTER'S SHADOW   85

We traveled in silence through streets sodden with water, pulling to a stop outside a colossal building built from the same brown brick as its neighbors. Across the street a castle that would not have looked out of place in the pages of any nursery book seemed to lurch. How incongruous it appeared among the other buildings in the cityscape.

Stanley cleared his throat.

"Winifred Williamson." He ordered: "Hook her, garner some invitations. I don't care what you must do to make it happen, but make it happen."

His finger was aimed at me like a pistol. "Her mother was a Vanderbilt. Her father is responsible for most of the buildings you see in New York. He's out of it all now but still is highly regarded. Her husband, Walt, has friends in the right places. Governments, industry, society."

There was a gleam in Stanley's eyes that sent gooseflesh scuttering along my skin. His gaze was unfocused, as if he were orating to a crowd rather than in conversation with his wife and sister-in-law.

"Once I get Walt on board, the rest of these dunces will follow. All I need is someone like him to back this project, and it's full steam ahead. Little more than a pack of sheep, this lot are." He gazed out the window. "Keep their gilded doors closed to newcomers, but they're obsessed with old money. And my title is older than their entire country."

He ran his gloved fingers along his mustache and sucked at his teeth. The noise set my nerves on edge. I followed his gaze out the window. Extravagantly dressed couples flowed up the steps of a brownstone, met by liveried servants. The windows of the house were lit up, casting a golden glow on the onlookers who milled about on the street, watching with envious looks the swells exit their carriages and move up the steps. My stomach twisted. Victoria's face was close to mine, watching the scene on the street, shining with delight. I wished I were brave like her and that a night like this would excite me instead of turning my stomach and rendering me almost insensible with fear. A wave of gratitude for her nearly overcame me, and I clutched her knee. Perhaps my touch was too persistent, as she snatched her leg away with a click of irritation.

Stanley leaped from the carriage and strode toward the house without a backward glance. I went next and watched as Victoria alighted with the delicacy of a ballerina, her face turned toward the house and lit with a mix of awe and fervent desire.

What a wife she would have made Stanley. Their interests in this style of life, in the showiness, the splendor, the glamor, the money; their desire to dance among the glittering socialites of upper society. As Lady Stanley, Victoria would have waged a campaign against the unsuspecting people of New York that would have earned Lord and Lady Stanley a place at every table and unlimited generosity with the checkbooks of high society. How I rued my choices that fateful night we'd met Lord Stanley, to act unlike myself in order to please our father. Oh, that I had not spoken at all and let her shine. Stanley would have chosen her, and we all would have been spared the agony of his mistake. Perhaps they would have grown to love each other, Victoria and Stanley. They might have enjoyed a happy marriage, full of children, and been well known and highly regarded in society.

I must try my very best to make it up to Victoria, to Stanley, for deceiving him and depriving her of the life she deserved. I would do my utmost to befriend Winifred Williamson and get Stanley what he wanted. We would attend every party and become acquainted with every influential person in New York so Victoria could meet a man who was a good match for her. Not enough atonement by half, but enough.

Stanley took the stairs ahead of us. His long strides, coupled with our constraining corsets, meant we were still on the second step when he reached the top. He gave our names to the butler and disappeared into the house.

MY SISTER'S SHADOW   87

The butler welcomed us and directed us into the foyer.

"Oh my days," Victoria breathed.

I was speechless.

The reception room was as big as the ballroom at Harewood, which was a vast and cavernous room. Brown marble gleamed along the floor and shimmied along the walls. The room was bathed in the radiant light of what seemed to be thousands of candles. Rainbows of light danced as the crystals in the chandelier reflected the luminous glow. A double staircase, made from the same marble as the floors and walls, loomed over the room. Each side of the staircase hugged the wall before joining at a platform where a life-sized painting of an imperious woman glared down at us.

"Impressive, isn't it," a bejeweled woman drawled beside us. "Your first time to the triple palace, I assume?"

She smiled at our mute nods. "Wiffy usually likes to greet her guests by standing right under her portrait. As if you are seeing her in double vision." She pointed up to the painting. "It's the only time anyone will ever look up to her."

I turned to the speaker. She was a buxom woman with diamonds dripping from her ears, throat, wrists, and somehow giving the impression of a chandelier. Her hair was bundled up on her head, held there by a band of diamonds, a huge sapphire in its center.

Her eyes darted from me to Victoria. "How perfectly charming. There appear to be two of you."

I smiled tightly, but Victoria leaned across me. "The Honorable Victoria Windlass. How do you do."

The woman's gaze flicked to me. "And you?"

I cleared my throat. "Lady Stanley."

Her eyes widened, and the smile, which had dimmed merely moments before, flared a little brighter. "A real-life lady? So pleased to meet you." She dropped into a perfect curtsey. "I am Sally Este Bruce. My husband is Mellon Bruce, of the Bruce Bank, but my daddy is *The Axe*."

88   January Gilchrist

Jones's years of hounding us about manners did not go to waste. Nothing she said had made any sense. We smiled politely, if a little inanely and Victoria spoke for us. "Forgive me, The Axe?"

"Alexander Xavier Easeman. Hydroelectric? The American Tobacco Company? Owns most of Manhattan."

She seemed baffled by our blank faces, but not offended. "Anyhoo, Mellon is rich, but Daddy is richer." She lifted a shoulder and dropped it. "I'm one of the lucky ones that married for love."

We said nothing, shocked into a silence that she would discuss money in such a manner. And to two strangers. Was this what New York society was like?

A footman, so polished and gleaming that he appeared as little more than a blur of color, saved us from finding a response. "Ladies, may I show you to the ballroom?"

"I'm waiting for my husband," Sally said, throwing a rueful glance at the door. "Business before pleasure. Always. I hope to see you in the ballroom, Lady Stanley." She bobbed another curtsey, and we moved toward the stairs.

Victoria clutched at my arm. Her face contorted in a sneer. "How gauche." Her laughter was sharp and brittle. "Fancy! Wealth certainly doesn't account for taste. My word. And all that jewelry." She ran her hand around her face and hair and grimaced again.

"*Mellon is rich, but Daddy is richer,*" she drawled in a striking imitation.

My throat tightened. "Perhaps she was just nervous speaking to strangers, trying to find things to say." I knew I often said the stupidest things when my nerves got the better of me.

Victoria laughed again, and her tone was sardonic when she spoke. "Of course, Lady *Saintly* will always find a pleasant word to say about anyone. Even someone as tasteless as that."

While Mrs. Bruce's casual mention of wealth had taken me by surprise and made me uncomfortable, I hadn't disliked her and

MY SISTER'S SHADOW
89

saw no need to speak ill of her. But it was Victoria I needed to appease. "She was awful, truly tasteless," I agreed, shooting a glance over my shoulder to ensure I wasn't overheard.

Climbing the stairs seemed to take an age, but finally the footman handed us over to another, just as brightly outfitted.

"Ladies Stanley." He announced to the other footman manning the door.

It struck me with the clanging of a bell that these people, for all their wealth and prestige, had little experience with titles and hierarchy. There could only be one Lady Stanley. I waited for Victoria to step in and correct him, but her gaze was focused on the room beyond, and she didn't respond. So I merely nodded and followed Victoria's gaze, my cheeks flaming.

If the room was not full, it certainly gave the illusion of it. Perhaps it was the thick haze of purple smoke that hung in the dim lights, the smell of damp wool, body heat, and laughter.

There seemed to be men everywhere, varying heights and breadths. Impressively tall men; men who loomed larger than life, their shoulders and stomachs straining at the buttons of their jackets; men with tall silk hats, small felt bowlers, and soft-rolled brim hats.

A slight man, dressed in what appeared to be silk pajamas, a pipe hanging from the corner of his mouth, met my gaze and arched one eyebrow.

I was piteously grateful to have someone to rest my gaze on, and the small dark eyes holding mine were warm and friendly. He smiled and in return I pressed my lips together in a semblance of a smile.

Stanley, seeming to remember us at last, hovered near the entrance. As soon as we were announced to the room, the men moved toward Stanley like fish on a hook.

He pumped arms and tapped shoulders, sharing laughter, jovial and thick, while we stood like puppets, awaiting instructions.

It wasn't until the men's eyes slid from Stanley to us, that he offered introductions. And with a hand on my elbow, delivering

90   January Gilchrist

me like an entrée on a silver platter, I was presented. Lips pressed against my glove, and gazes were directed at my breasts, very few bothering to make the journey to my face, but instead moving swiftly to Victoria behind me. Their eyes widened and returned to Stanley, offering colluding, envious looks. Stanley's chest pushed forward, and his chin lifted.

Too quickly we were released into the pack of woman behind the men. My heart fluttered like a bird in a cage at the sight of them.

A barrel-shaped woman, in both height and width, stood in the center. A flock of women stood in a semicircle around her. Barrel lady lifted a cigarette to her lips and met my gaze with a bold and assessing gaze.

I inhaled a sharp breath. A lady smoking! In public! I glanced around but not one other person was perturbed by such brazen behavior.

This woman, around whom all the other women seemed to orbit, extended her cigarette-less hand toward me. Pale flesh dimpled through the lace of her glove.

"You selfsame beauties can only be Lady Stanley and her sister. My word, how alike you are."

I stared at her outstretched hand, nonplussed. Did she expect me to shake it like a man? I settled on awkwardly gripping her fingers. She placed the hand with the cigarette over mine and held it tightly, peering at my face as if all my secrets were written there.

"I'm Wiffy." A beat of silence. "Winifred," she corrected herself with mock sternness.

Mrs. Walter Williamson, née Winifred Helmsley. Society queen. Daughter of a US ambassador, now married to the son of America's richest industrialist. It had given me pause when Victoria had read it from her precious book. A politician's daughter marrying a working man's son, but I saw now that the class system from which we emerged held no ground here. Here, a working man was nothing

MY SISTER'S SHADOW   ~ 91

to be ashamed of. Not when the profits of his work enabled him to build houses such as this. *"Richer than the King,"* Stanley had said about one of them. I saw now that what they lacked in pedigree and family history, they made up for in cold, hard cash.

Winifred Williamson considered me though narrowed lids. I surreptitiously took in her olive woolen dress, in a style so unflattering that she must be too important for her dressmaker to tell her that neither the style nor the fabric suited her. I recognized it from a picture in one of the biennials Victoria loved. It had been worn by a French princess to the opening of the Russian Opera in London and had caused quite the stir because of its dropped waist and narrow skirt.

"We have been dying to meet you, haven't we, girls? When we heard a real-life lady from England were on her way, well, all I can say is, I hope you're ready to answer questions about fashion. None of us have been to Paris since last season."

She still hadn't released my hand, and instead of doing so now, reached for Victoria. With the cigarette still between her fingers, she pulled Victoria into her orbit, creating a neat little triangle.

"You are just so beautiful. I can't get over how alike you are. Let me introduce you to the girls. I warn you, though: watch what you say, as we're all either sisters or cousins."

"Or sisters-in-law." A birdlike, redheaded lady piped up.

"Oh, Juju, you don't count."

There was laughter then, from the ladies standing behind her as well as Victoria. I tried to join in but only managed a jerk of my lips. I was so out of my depth here that I was drowning.

Wiffy offered a whirlwind of strange-sounding words that seemed more code than names: Guppy, Chichi, Bessie, Lottie, Reeny, Gogo.

My eyebrows raised when she stopped at Barbie and Beebah.

"They're Barbara and Beatrice, really. Cousins, but they were so inseparable as little ones, that we called them the twins."

Barbara and Beatrice studied Victoria and me through their small black eyes. They were similar enough to be taken as sisters, although most of that could be attributed to their matching hairstyles, dresses, and sullen expressions.

"They even had their own language for a while, didn't you, girls? That's where the names come from. I suppose we thought it cute once, but now they're stuck with it. I can't imagine they'd answer to anything else now."

The "twins" considered us silently, their gaze roaming across our features as if committing us to memory. My stomach curdled. These women were unlike any I had ever met. Loud, brash. They took up space in the room, demanded people look at them, drew attention to themselves *on purpose*. All of them laughed freely, drank, and when Winifred's husband lit and handed her a cigarette, I feared my jaw was on the floor. She blew long plumes of smoke into the air around us, punctuating her sentences with small jabs of the smoldering stick between her fingers.

A glass was pressed into my hand, and I raised it to my mouth unthinkingly. My face contorted as the sickly sweet liquid caught in my throat. The lights were loud, the air too close, the voices strange, the sharp accents piercing, and I was dizzy and disorientated.

The man in the pajamas I had seen on arrival appeared and gestured to Winifred. Her thick arm pressed around my shoulders as she pulled me in close to her side. The man raised a brown box to his face and the bulb popped and flashed, leaving me blinking into the halos it left in its wake.

"John Carter," Winifred murmured out of the corner of her mouth. "The society pages of the *New York Herald*. A terrible rag, really, but can be counted on when needed."

The man in question ran his eyes along my dress and pressed his card into my hand. "My readers will want to know about this dress, Lady Stanley. What can you tell me about it?"

MY SISTER'S SHADOW ☞ 93

A notebook appeared from the depths of those pajamas, and he licked the nib of a squat pencil, eyes trained on mine. I swallowed against the lump in my throat, and my hand scrabbled for Victoria's. She was not where I had expected her to be.

I was vaguely aware that Winifred was speaking to John Carter on my behalf, but I couldn't concentrate on anything she said, instead searching for Victoria in the hazy room, which was both too bright and too dim.

Finally my gaze landed on my sister, standing apart from the huddle of ladies, the thick air giving her a menacing glow. She narrowed her eyes at me, her mouth a thin and unamused line. The smog of the room distorted her image, and for a frightful moment it appeared as if she were snarling. Winifred jostled my attention back to Mr. Carter. We exchanged words, and when I looked back, Victoria was gone.

★　★　★

The night dragged on in a blur of noise and color. I nodded and smiled in all the right places but didn't listen to a word. Which seemed to make me the most popular woman in the room. People lined up for a moment of my silent time, eager to say they met me, had pressed their hand against mine, studied my costume. One woman pulled a bead from my dress as a keepsake, like I was a curiosity in an exhibition.

My unfamiliarity, my accent, maybe even my reserve appealed to the Americans. Their voices were too loud, too shrill, and the drink in my hand refilled too many times; it wasn't long before I was lightheaded and woozy.

After what felt like a lifetime, Winifred captured me by the arm, her grip firm and steadying. We were at the edge of the room, then on a concrete balcony overlooking the street below. It had felt aimless to me, but as Winifred walked me to the balustrade, I realized it was a summons. I gazed out to the horizon, where a twilight sky ducked and wove between buildings. I had

94　January Gilchrist

never seen so much concrete, steel, or glass. I strained my eyes, imagining I could see the spire of Harewood House in the distance. The same water that had borne me here could bear me back. *Would* bear me back, of that I was certain. I needed to befriend Winifred so her husband would donate, and then this racecourse nonsense would be done, and I could return home. Perhaps not to Harewood, but to England at least.

Like the bulbs I used to plant with Graham in spring, I reminded myself. I was merely hibernating, awaiting the conditions to be right, and I could return to my real life. I closed my eyes and was flying on the back of Hera, the crisp clean Gloucester air in my hair, the woodland birds singing me home.

Winifred squeezed my arm, and I was back on the concrete step overlooking a city in its infancy. Gone was the soothing burble of the stream, the scent of fresh-cut grass and honeysuckle, the cool air of the wood, replaced by rotting rubbish, cigarette smoke, and smut.

The doors to the ballroom were latched against the walls, which created a kind of frame of the people inside. It could have been a painting titled *People at a Party*. They glimmered golden under the lamps, their frocks made of lace, silk, and money; liquid sunshine in their glasses; the whites of their necks exposed as they threw their heads back to bray with laughter. I didn't belong here.

"Picture-perfect, isn't it?" Winifred said. She gestured to the ground below us, "There's hundreds, thousands even, who wish for entrance to parties like these. They'd sell their soul just for one night. But for us, it's just one *more* night. Another night to top the others until the next one does."

I glanced down to the street. A foursome, two young ladies and two young men, strolled arm in arm. Walking in the other direction, two young men in their best suits looked up and caught our eyes. Their words were lost on the breeze, but their intentions showed on their smiling faces. Winifred leaned over the curved iron edge.

"'Evening, boys! Looking fine tonight." Her face was animated as she waved, but when she turned back to me, her face was blank.

"What they don't know"—she gestured to the street below—"is that the corsets tear the skin from your bones, and the shoes pinch until you can't walk for days. You swelter in so many layers, and the drinks are never cold enough. But we are all willing to feign the jollity of it all, in the hopes that the pretense will encourage the real thing."

She looked at me from the corner of her eye. "There's a freedom in seeing it for what it truly is, don't you think?"

I didn't. I didn't see freedom in any of it. It felt murderous in its restrictiveness. Most days I felt as if this life would choke me. But I nodded in what I hoped was a thoughtful manner.

"So, you must understand," she continued casually, "that when something new, something shiny, like yourself, appears, how it invigorates us so."

Another cigarette in her mouth, a pause while she lit it, inhaled, exhaled.

"I expect you look at us like poor cousins, out here where everything is new. But the endless possibilities of New York can bring a person to their knees or raise them to dizzying height. There is power in knowledge, Adelaide. May I call you Adelaide?"

It was couched as question, but there was only one correct answer: *whatever she wanted*. I nodded.

"Lovely, and you must call me Wiffy. I simply won't answer to anything else."

I watched a small black spider dance along the wall. I didn't want to be here. Not just on the concrete balcony or at the party. The city. The country—I wanted to be home in Harewood, lying among the artifacts of my ancestors, breathing the fresh, clean air of my childhood home. I wanted to return so badly I could scream.

"They think they run it all. The men. But it's us, isn't it, really? Oh, I leave the grandstanding to them: let them beat their chests and have at it, but the truth is, without us, without the female machinations behind the scenes, goodness knows where we would end up." She laughed then, not the gentle tinkle of a lady's bell, but a genuine laugh, so loud my eyelids fluttered.

Her smile was that of someone the moment they capture your queen in chess.

"Modernity is where the future lies. New York could be great, truly great. A powerhouse with a beauty to rival any European city. But to get somewhere we have never been before, we need a strong leader who isn't afraid to make bold decisions. And his team needs to be as strong. As committed to his successes, his ideas."

Her eye flicked to mine, searching for something. I tilted the corners of my lips. My head hurt and I longed to lie down.

"So, what do you say? Do we have your support?"

"Absolutely." My answer was swift. It cost me nothing to offer nothing.

"Good girl," she said with a twitch of a strong black brow that bore no resemble to any natural brow I had ever seen. "I just knew we were going to be firm friends."

Conversation over, she recaptured my arm and drew me back into the room. One by one, the ladies looked over, their eyes meeting hers in wordless communication, and then, once finding what it was they looked for, moving to mine. Each offered me their own version of a smile.

A sliver of dread ran through me, quite like you might feel should you suddenly find yourself in water much, much too deep; and upon looking down, realize the water is muddied with sharks.

It's not what you see that you need to fear, but instead the things moving in the water, deep and dark below you, in absolute silence.

CHAPTER 12

Victoria folded the paper back into its creases with sharp movements. My heart lurched at the sight of her face, lips so pinched they were devoid of color. The newspaper hovered above the table. In my mind's eye I saw her stand and hurl the newspaper at the wall, sweep the china from the table, and whirl about the room, pitching and screaming.

Her dark gaze met mine. The newspaper quivered in her hand.

"I am not mentioned. At all."

My hands were in my lap, trembling under the napkin. We had ridden home from the party in thick, tense silence, and she had been alternately curt and cruel to me since.

"Whatever do you mean?" My tone was light, casual, placating.

She lobbed the paper at me. It landed on my plate. I unfolded it and read the piece that had infuriated her so. The butter from my toasted bread left an oily scar along the words.

"It is as if I weren't even in attendance. Or that I was invisible. That rat-faced man doesn't even mention you have a sister! That there is another woman who you are the mirror image of is not even mentioned in passing."

"I . . . I saw him and that man speaking. It's purely business, to raise Stanley's profile. That last piece, about the racetrack and

98 ∽ January Gilchrist

Walter Williamson, that is truly what they—the men that is—want to be made public."

She studied me for a long, fretful moment. There was little placating her when she was in a mood like this.

"I was the one in eau de Nil," she hissed.

I swallowed hard. "It is a lovely day out. I am so looking forward to spending the afternoon with Winifred. Let's put all that behind us and enjoy the day. We've longed to see Central Park since our arrival, and it's finally warm enough. And in a motor, no less."

Wiffy had sent a letter across the day after the party, an invitation to take a drive in her motor and allow her to show us all the sights that 'our blossoming city has to offer.'"

Victoria lifted her lip. "To see the sights? Docks, building sites, slums, and dead trees. How utterly thrilling."

I ran my thumbnail along the length of my index finger. While we hadn't seen much of the city, what we had seen had left us underwhelmed when compared to the vast greenness of Harewood and its surrounds.

"Winifred did mention the city is undertaking a large amount of work, and of course these things take time. Harewood Hall was built before the colonization of America." These were Stanley's words. My tone was cajoling, as if I were speaking to a small child petulantly refusing its dinner.

"Since *colonization*? You don't even know how to spell the word." Her tone was mocking. She pushed her chair back ferociously and stalked to the door. "Tell Washington I wish to take a bath."

I stared at the small half-moons of my nails and sighed. So that was to be my punishment. Battling Washington for a bath.

It wasn't Monday.

★ ★ ★

I checked my reflection in the mirror again, as nervous as a bride on her wedding day. *A bride.* Not as I had been on that day all those months ago.

MY SISTER'S SHADOW ⌐ 99

No, today was how I imagined *real* brides felt on their wedding day, all dry mouth and fluttering stomach.

"Tie my ribbon?" Victoria tilted her head back, showing me the column of her long neck, as smooth and white as marble. A blue vein pulsed under her jaw, and I averted my gaze; the sight of it made me feel woozy. I tied the ribbon as quickly as my fumbling hands could manage.

"I must say, I am so looking forward to this trip. We've barely seen any of New York since arriving," I choked out.

And we hadn't. Apart from the party, we had done nothing but while away endless damp hours in the shadows of Greycliffe's front drawing room. In truth, we hadn't gone anywhere back home either, finding comfort in the familiar sights and activities of Harewood Hall. But there had been what felt like an endless expanse of land to explore, woods filled with ivy-covered trees, the dank floor covered in pine needles that dampened any noise except that of the forest.

Greycliffe was surrounded by damp, gray streets. The road squeaked and rattled and banged, all day and all night.

As the married sister, I was supposed to be Victoria's chaperone, but I had neither the wits nor the fortitude, and we had no money. If we'd ever needed for anything at Harewood, we had simply informed Nanny Jones, who would arrange credit at the stores in the village. Aunt Petunia had been tasked with arranging new dresses during our annual holidays, but here we were trapped.

Stanley had given us a letter of credit to purchase the dresses for the party, but he hadn't mentioned providing me with more, and I wasn't brave enough to ask. What did I need a new dress for, when I barely left the house?

"A Vanderbilt *and* a motor." Victoria raised her eyebrows. "What would Nanny Jones have to say about that?"

A sound cut through the air—a guttural, monstrous whine that set the hairs on the back of my neck alight.

100 ᔣ January Gilchrist

Our wide eyes met each other's before we sprang to our feet and rushed to the window, as excited as children on Christmas morning. There was Wiffy Williamson, pulling to a stop on the roadside in a squat green mechanical monster.

"Oh," we breathed in unison.

We had, of course, seen motorized vehicles before, but never one driven by a woman.

Wiffy wore a straw hat but had pinned it onto her bun in a way so that it sat slightly forward, causing it to shade her eyes and obscure her face. If I hadn't been expecting her, I wouldn't have known who it was. She sat proudly on the right-hand side of the thing, a black leather canopy concertinaed behind her like a fan. She held what looked like a large dinner plate on a pole in her lap, her skirts tucked around her legs, her stockings and boots on full display.

Victoria's face was pressed so close to the glass that her breath had made a small circle of fog. I had a sick moment of worry. This sort of behavior was perfectly fine for the daughter of America's wealthiest man, but I knew Victoria, and this would give her notions.

Notions that wouldn't work for her once we arrived back home. Surely we would return to England as soon as the raceway was complete? I didn't quite understand what it was exactly that Stanley was doing here. Advising, he had said, and yet it appeared he spent all his day and most of his nights at another raceway, a raceway that was already built and presumably did not require his building advice.

The motorcar shuddered to a complete stop with a groan and a stream of steam hissed from its undercarriage.

Victoria had her skirts bunched and was taking the stairs two by two by the time I reached the doorway, her footsteps banging in my ears like a hammer. She threw the front door open, filling the foyer with sunshine and a gust of air that blew into the house, thick with the smells of the street.

MY SISTER'S SHADOW

When I reached the door, Wiffy was already smiling and waving with an energy I found terrifying, and I longed, fleetingly, to feign illness and stay home. The prospect of an afternoon chatting with a near stranger was grueling.

"I can never tell which one of you is Lady Stanley," she called, unwinding her scarf from her neck.

I lifted my hand weakly. Victoria pulled herself to her full height, her expression rigid.

"Are you ready?" Wiffy called. She adjusted her hat, untucked her skirts, and extended a metal step that had been folded up against the lurid green shell of the car.

"There's only room for one I'm afraid." Wiffy was speaking as she moved around the car to unfold the other step. "Victoria, darling, I'll take you out another day."

A hot tension emanated from Victoria. Her back was unnaturally stiff, and although her face was turned from mine, I could see a vivid spot of color high on her cheek.

My fingers clenched and unclenched, and the shaking increased in my chest, moving along my arms until my fingers fairly vibrated.

A marble statue had more life than Victoria did at that moment. It was a strange stillness, the calm before the storm, the silence before the strike.

"Have a pleasant day. I do so hope the weather holds." My sister turned and strode inside. I reached for her hand, but she was moving too fast, so my hand fell into the space left behind.

I wavered in the doorway. Wiffy was standing at the car with an expectant expression.

I inhaled, fortifying myself—she was so *energetic*—and smiled.

She ushered me onto the motor, explaining how to stow the step and the right position for my skirts to stop them blowing in the wind, and showed me a small iron bar in front of the bench seat.

"Hang on to that—we can't have you falling out. Not on your first ride, anyway." She laughed and I clutched the bar so tightly that my gloves strained around the knuckles.

102 January Gilchrist

She cranked the engine, and it roared to life with an unearthly rumble. I clamped my eyes shut as we jerked into motion on the road.

There was no opportunity to speak over the endless noise of the automobile and eventually, without me even noticing, my spine relaxed against the warm, stiff leather, and I started to feel like a lady sitting next to a friend in a motor. As apparently one did in this country.

But goodness, the racket!

And the stares. I was accustomed to being stared at; Victoria and I drew attention wherever we went together, so unusually alike we looked, but it was something I tried to ignore. These stares seemed to energize Wiffy. She greeted each turned head with a jaunty wave, at times even singing out to them. I supposed at first that she knew each and every person, but it soon became apparent that most were strangers.

Wiffy slowed the automobile as we came to a pair of thick, large stone columns that formed a break in the spear-shaped iron fence we had driven beside for some time. The car juddered across the cobblestones, and she pulled it to a complete stop and turned to me with a grin.

"Welcome to Central Park. It's a bit shabby, but it's a wonderful space to ride through in the mornings."

I copied her movements and, lowering my step, climbed out of the motor on unsteady legs. They quivered as if the tremors from the car shook them still, and my ears rang so that I could barely hear Wiffy as she pointed to the parkland.

"Walt is starting up a park commission. They intend to form a committee and elect a commissioner, somebody to oversee the caretaking. Tidy the park up a bit."

I made a small noise that I hoped indicated interest. I followed Wiffy's lead, and we began to stroll along a cobblestone path that led into a shadow created by the rows of trees that lined either side of it.

MY SISTER'S SHADOW   103

"Walt has the idea of creating public playgrounds for the city's children," she continued. "Get them out of the crowded slums and into the fresh air."

"He sounds wonderful."

She turned to me, eyebrows raised. "Walt?"

For a moment I wondered if I had missed part of the conversation, as I sometimes did. I nodded tentatively, my mind racing over her previous words.

She rolled her eyes. "He's all right."

The words may have seemed dismissive, but her tone told me that she believed he was more than all right, and I released my breath as a sense of relief washed over me. *I didn't do or say the wrong thing this time,* my mind sang.

I would pay attention, I vowed. I would hang on every word she said, and she would find me, if not amusing, then pleasant company. She would encourage Walt to donate, and I would be back in England before I knew it. I crossed my fingers, too afraid to hope.

We entered the shadowed part of the path. Despite the bright sunshine around us, the shade was cool, and the cobblestones slightly damp and mossy. My skirts were heavy around my boots, which had begun to pinch at the heel. Wiffy's strides were long and energetic, and I hoped she wasn't intending an earnest turn around the park.

At the end of the shaded corridor, an expanse of manicured green greeted us. Along one side of the park was bare dirt, with large piles of stones stacked at regular intervals. This *park* was nothing compared to the verdant beauty of Harewood.

Winifred gestured to a sunny spot on the grass. "Shall we sit for a spell?"

She had thrown herself to the ground before I could answer. Groups of people sat on the grass around us, some on linen blankets, jackets discarded, shirtsleeves rolled. Women hid under their hats, fanning themselves with their gloves.

I lowered myself gingerly to the ground, unused to conducting myself in such a casual and *common* manner. But if it was good enough for Winifred Williamson, I supposed it would do for me.

We sat in silence, and I listened to the soft drone of the early spring day, the happy murmur of voices on the breeze, the clatter of carriages on the road, the call and cackle of the strange birds that called America home. The breeze was light and warm, and slowly my spine began to loosen.

"Do you like horses?" Winifred broke the stillness. "Of course you do." She answered her own question as she pulled her cigarette case from her handbag and placed a cigarette between her lips. She tilted her head and closed an eye as she lit it. As she discarded the lighter on the ground, I saw the side had been engraved with "Wiffy."

How strange it seemed that a woman should have her own lighter.

At my blank look she said. "Stanley loves horses. Or racing at least. The racetrack is all he ever speaks of. His vision is grand. We wondered, you know"—she paused—"what was the common ground between you."

The silence between us grew full and expectant. I remained quiet. What could I say? There was no common ground between Stanley and me.

Had she and her cousins sat about dissecting and critiquing me? Had I been found lacking or wanting in some way by these brash American ladies? Dark feelings swirled.

I folded my hands in my lap, and perhaps some of my thoughts showed on my face, because she said next, in the manner of a woman used to getting her own way, "Oh, don't be like that. Stanley can be very persuasive when he wants to be. In the small amount of time he's been here, he's nearly managed to convince every Knickerbocker in New York to invest in this racetrack of his. It's just that you are so beautifully English, the quintessential

English rose if you like, and Stanley—well." She guffawed. "Stanley's . . . Stanley. We just wondered what lengths he had gone to, to turn your head."

I did not know what to say. How could I say that I'd had no choice in the matter? I tried to speak, but my lips didn't open.

"Oh, it was like that then, was it? Never mind, you wouldn't be the first, and I daresay you won't be the last." She blew a long plume of smoke into the air around us. It seemed to hang for a moment, much like her words, before dissipating completely.

"My cousin, Consuelo"—her jaw was hard, her voice bitter—"she—well, let's just say her husband was not *her* first choice. Not always anything we can do about that."

She inhaled and exhaled again, and just as quickly as it arrived, the anger was gone. "Do you like it here?"

"Things are different," I started. But I faltered, unsure how to continue. Unsure if I could put into words all the differences.

"How so?" she asked.

I tried to think of things she might find amusing or interesting and gestured to the cigarette. "I'd never seen a woman smoke before you."

She barked an incredulous laugh and peered at the cigarette as if it was now new to her eyes.

"I have seen people smoke, of course, but not a woman of—" I paused. What was she exactly? "Society," I finished.

"Did you find me awfully shocking?" Her expression was eager. She longed to be found shocking, and I found I wanted to please her.

"I did rather." Whenever she smiled, a pulse of pleasure beat through me.

"What else?"

"What else is shocking about you?" I asked.

She nodded and settled down onto her elbow, chin in hand. "The motor surely!"

"Yes, the motor. But mostly you seem . . ." I closed my eyes. Maybe it was the soporific air, the breeze warm enough to make me long to close my eyes and drift into slumber that made me answer so honestly. The air was thick with the calls and laughter of children playing, the rattle and clanging of trams as they urged their passengers on into the bowels of the gloriously young city. The city felt young, as if it was asking us to dance, to shake off our Victorian ideas and shorten our hems.

"So enviably comfortable being yourself," I said.

Wiffy lay on her back, cigarette held aloft. "I suppose I am, rather. I think that's all just a bit jammy, though, isn't it? I mean, Walt's wonderful and we've known each other since I was a girl, so he's always accepted me the way I am." She rolled onto her side to gaze at me, and I was suddenly far too conscious of how correct my posture was, how rigid and unyielding my back. She peered at me through the haze of her cigarette.

"Do you like being a twin?"

The sudden shift in conversation gave me pause. I lifted a shoulder. "I don't know any other life."

"Oh, I hated my sisters when I was younger. Despised the lot of them, but Chichi in particular. The line between love and hate feels so thin with a sister." She laughed as she said it, but I cringed.

How could she laugh when saying such hateful things about her sister? But while her words were hateful, her tone was not. It was rueful and light and loving. Whatever had passed between her and Chichi was water under the bridge. "Cousin Connie was far more like a sister to me," she continued. "I simply adored her. But Chichi—for whatever reason, I couldn't stand sharing my time in the sun with her."

I forced a small smile. I knew there was no sharing. The one standing in the sun must cast a shadow. And it was my lot in life to stand in the shadow.

"What do you enjoy doing?" she asked suddenly.

I stared at the horizon. What did I enjoy doing? I bit my lip; Victoria would have filled this gap with talk of her painting or fashion.

"I'm the quiet one," I said by way of explanation.

She arched a brow. "The quiet one *what*?"

"Well, my sister, she's the one who usually . . ." I waved my hand between us. "I'm not very good at . . . talking."

"Ah."

How to explain that where I was meek, Victoria was bold, and when compared to her, as we always were, it was obvious how dull and uninteresting I was.

Wiffy blew a plume of smoke into the air, and we both turned our heads to watch as it disappeared into the blue sky. "All that sister nonsense, is it?"

"I'm sorry?"

"She's this, therefore you must be that. It's all a lot of rot." She said the last part so forcefully that I was taken aback.

"It's not that . . ." I considered for a moment. The words come tumbling out before I could contain them. "Victoria is the vibrant one. She always knows what to say and when to say it, especially in company. Invariably, I say something stupid and cause offense or embarrass Victoria so horrifically that it's easier to just say nothing."

She narrowed her eyes at me, and a muscle pulsed in her jaw. "It's never easier to just *say nothing*."

"I fear most people who get to know me find me strange."

"I don't find you strange." Her dark tone disappeared so swiftly I wondered if I had imagined it.

"Perhaps you are strange as well, then." I cringed. "Sorry. See? Things just come out and I—"

A blush appeared, heating my face. But Wiffy tipped her head back and roared with laughter. Her laughter was loud, unbidden. There was something wanton about it. Instead of it making me feel peculiar, as it had previously, I found myself smiling. She hadn't taken offense, and I felt a different kind of warmth bloom. I had been an *insider* on the joke this time. She actually liked that I had said what I thought.

"You are funny. I like that. We'll be good friends, you and I. I can just tell." She took another drag on the cigarette and peered at me through the smoke. "Apart from being a sister, what else do you like?"

"I like to ride."

"Horses?"

I blinked. What else could there be?

"Oh, don't look at me like that," Wiffy exclaimed with a laugh. "It could be bicycles, motorcycles even." She waggled her eyebrows suggestively.

"Yes, horses. I had to leave my horse behind in England." My voice creaked at the mention of her. "Hera."

I don't know why I said the next thing; it seemed to find its way out on its own accord. "I haven't felt like myself since."

Wiffy sat and brushed dried grass from her skirts. She took one last deep drag on her cigarette before flicking it with precision onto the cobbled path. "I understand. I've always been mad for horses. Our whole family is mad for them. I'm sure you've heard all about our runners. We bred the last three winners of the Belmont Stakes."

She turned to face me, her face lit with excitement. "I have the perfect fix. Tell Stanley we'll give you one of Queenie's. Jack can collect it."

The idea shocked me. Have a horse, here? But once planted, the idea of riding again began to invigorate me. And if it were one of Wiffy's, I could just give it back when I returned to England. I gazed about us. I couldn't imagine joining the masses of carriages, carts, and motors that converged along the busy streets—where would we ride? No, I stamped on the hope that had begun to bubble in my chest. There was no point.

MY SISTER'S SHADOW   109

I changed the subject. "Jack?"

"You haven't met Jack?"

There was a queer expression on her face, one I couldn't interpret. She was clearly thinking more, but she just stared at the trees. It was one of those rare moments when everything stopped, just for a moment: a lull in the breeze, no motorcars, no birds, no sound at all. It was if the entire world had stopped. Ever so fleetingly.

"Have Stanley get Jack to bring you one of Queenie's foals. He's a magician. Manages them for Stanley. Trains up the geldings that have potential. For the raceway. That kind of stuff. He is the best trainer on the East Coast. It speaks to Stanley's persuasive powers that he managed to lure him away from the Belmont Raceway. Jack has trained three of our winners. Makes his choices based on the horse he gets to work with, rather than remaining in one person's employ. Rather makes him a bit of a catch." She turned back to me with a smile. "I ride through here every morning. There is no better way to start the day. It's settled."

A stableman, I think. So why doesn't she just say that?

"What that man doesn't know about horses is just—" She blinked off into the distance for so long that I turned my own head to see what she was looking at. There was nothing but the trees and their leaves dancing languidly in the breeze.

A slow smile spread across her face. She scrambled to her feet and adjusted her straw boater. "Lunchtime, I think. I'm famished."

I rolled awkwardly onto all fours, pushing against the hard-packed earth to stand. My corset dug into me painfully, and it occurred to me that Wiffy must not be wearing one. The thought shot a bolt of jealousy through me. *How would it feel to be so free?*

She didn't wait for me, but strode across the grass toward a windbreak of trees that seemed to lead down toward a lake. I studied her silhouette as she walked, her hips rolling with a fluidity that confirmed my suspicions of her being corsetless. Her dress dropped from the waist loosely but still followed the bell shape that was so popular. The pink linen of her skirt swished about her boots, and the bright pink petticoat beneath flashed like a beacon. *"Freedom,"* that fabric seemed to whisper. *Freedom.*

"Lunch à la Williamson." Wiffy swept an arm toward an elaborate setup beneath a row of huge elms. There was a table shrouded with a crisp linen cloth, silverware glinted in the sun, and liveried servants stood in the shade.

I was lost for words. How on earth had she gotten a large oak table to the park?

"We had a wonderful nanny—Grace." Wiffy said, around another cigarette. She lit it and closed her lighter with a little snap. A long inhale, an even longer exhale. "More of a parent to us than our own. She'd bring us down here and have the servants set up a table for a picnic like this. I love to recreate it whenever I can."

I thought of Jones. No picnics for us on her watch.

"Nanny was rather unique, I suppose, although at the time none of us knew that. We just knew she was as dedicated to fun as we were, and when Mother and Father went to England, it was just her and us. She tried to swim across the Hudson at night once, for a bet. A fellow had his foot taken off by a shark in the same water not two days later. She never went in the water again. We used to tease her mercilessly on vacation, but she held fast."

I tried to picture it but couldn't. I had never been in water deeper than knee height. On summers days Victoria and I used to sneak away from the house and unroll our stockings, remove our overskirts, and wade in the lake in our bloomers. Until Jones had come searching for us and, scandalized by our behavior, forbade us from ever going near the lake unsupervised again.

The silence went on too long. Searching for something to fill it with, I said, "Your parents lived in England?"

"Oh yes, they were gone for years. Something to do with Father's work. They were gone so long that when Nanny told us they were on their way home, we cried for days. We had assumed they were dead. I don't know if we were crying because they weren't dead or because they were coming home and ruining all our fun." Wiffy laughed again.

I thought of my own mother. How would it feel to have her appear one day, not just in my dreams, but as flesh and blood?

"Grace cared for Martha's wee ones when they came. Chichi's too. They had a frightful row over that one. Both were due to have babies at the same time. Chichi won in the end; said as it was her first and Marcia's fifth, she was owed Grace."

"Will you use her then? For your children?"

A shadow crossed Winifred's face, and she dragged on her cigarette. "There won't be any children for us. Walt had mumps, you see. That's the thing about knowing someone so well; you know what you're getting into and love them anyway."

She grinned at my blank expression. "Darling, a man cannot make children after the mumps."

My cheeks heated at the casual mention of making children. How worldly Wiffy was. What a dolt I must seem. "Do you mind terribly?" I asked, desperate to fill the silence.

"What's there to mind?" she scoffed. "Can't stand the sticky, smelly things." Her voice was as strident as usual, but she blinked rapidly and tipped her face toward the sky, and I could feel the hurt she was hiding.

I hadn't spent my youth in a girly daze, writing lists of potential husband attributes or names of future children as Victoria had. I had assumed I would remain happily husbandless at Harewood Hall. That I would wander the halls alone as we both aged until my body become one with the land that I so loved. What would it be like, to love and to be as loved as Wiffy was? By her numerous sisters, cousins, her *husband*.

For a moment I was breathless with agony that such was not to be my fate. I wasn't sure anyone had loved me in my whole life. Father found me a nuisance, and Mother had chosen to leave,

112 January Gilchrist

unable, it seemed, to manage with the life she'd been given. Perhaps she'd loved me, but apart from flashes of memory, as brief as they were painful, I barely remembered her. Victoria loved me, I supposed, in the way one loves a favorite toy while it holds interest.

As for Stanley . . . there was little affection between us, let alone love. Despite his efforts, and my adherence to doctor's orders, my monthly had arrived like clockwork. Perhaps next month. My hand fluttered to my belly.

Despite the warm air, I shivered.

CHAPTER 13

It had taken me a week to steel my nerves enough to force myself to Stanley's study. I spent the week moving from one room to another, searching for ways to occupy my mind. Victoria refused to come out of her room for the first three days after my outing and had yet to utter a word to me. She would leave the room as I entered, and if I spoke to her, she simply stared into space.

One week of practicing my lines to my fretful reflection in the hazy mirror in my bedroom.

There was absolutely nothing to fear, or so I told myself, as I hovered at the door to Stanley's study. I was perfectly within my rights to ask. If only it didn't matter quite so much.

But it did.

I ran over my lines, trying to find the perfect balance between requesting and begging. Tone light and easy. Not pleading. Never pleading.

A tenant farmer had once found Victoria and me up a tree, an angry mama pig protecting her babies at the bottom of it. It had been, to our eight-year-old eyes, snapping and snarling. Animals can smell your fear, he had said. You had to try your best to remain calm, or they'll know they've gotten the better of you.

One final inhale and I rapped at the door.

"Enter."

114 ᕯ   January Gilchrist

I fumbled with the handle, my hand slippery with sweat. I needed two tries before it turned. Now was the time to channel Victoria, or Washington for that matter, and straighten my spine, lift my chin, replace my heart with stone—but it fluttered in my chest like a trapped bird.

"Good afternoon, Lord Stanley." I was buoyed by the lightness of my voice. It neither shook nor hesitated. "Are you well?"

I stood behind the tall-backed chair at his desk and adjusted my smile until it started to pain.

"I am." A dismissal. He was not interested in conversation. "What can I do for you?"

"I would like to speak with you about the possibility of a horse."

He stared at me, and not for the first time I marveled at the coldness of his gaze. I had never seen him smile spontaneously, in joy. It was always measured, always forced, and never quite met his eyes.

"What for?" he asked.

Brevity was clearly the order of the day.

He had not stood from his chair nor invited me to sit. I rested my hands on the chair back to give myself something to do other than wring them. The movement drew his eyes to them, and they began to tingle as if his gaze was a torch and my hands tinder.

"For . . ." I daren't utter the word *pleasure*. "For Victoria and me. I think it would be helpful. Victoria seems . . . unsettled."

He leaned back in the chair, and the springs of it squealed like a frightened woman. His hands were interlaced behind his head, and my stomach sank at the expression on his face. He was a hunter with a deer in his sight. Lining me up along the barrel of a gun.

I spoke quickly. "Wiffy—that is Winifred Williamson—has kindly offered one of hers. One of Queenie's. She said to send Jack to collect it."

MY SISTER'S SHADOW 115

His expression shifted at the mention of Winifred. It was slight, but I caught it. I had become an expert in reading his expressions, sensing his moods, and ensuring I was out of sight, and reach, when his temper was simmering. A greedy light shone in his eyes. He wanted whatever this horse of Winifred's would bring, this connection with the wealthy Williamsons.

"Fine."

It took me a moment to realize he had agreed. The other parts of my argument died on my lips; I had been so certain they would be required.

But I couldn't help myself. I needed to hear him say it before I gave what I knew would be required in payment. "I may ask Jack to arrange a horse for Victoria and me?"

He tsked in irritation and pushed the chair from the desk. "You may. Now, close the door." Those cold eyes again. "You can do something for me in return."

I took my time to the door, fighting against the bile in my throat. *It's nothing,* I told myself. Nothing that every other wife wasn't required to do. A moment in time that will be forgotten once I am flying on the back of a horse, the wind in my hair, riding so fast, free, somewhere no one can touch me.

"Lock it," he demanded, and my hand stilled on the hard length of the key. It stuck as I turned it, and I had to force it. The sound of the dull click, when it came, sent a thick pulse of dismay through my veins.

*   *   *

I stumbled from that room, reeling, but for the first time since that night in the dining hall of Harewood Hall, there was a lightness.

I stopped to examine myself in the hallway mirror. The woman stared back at me through dead eyes, her bottom lip swollen, a hand-sized mark around her throat.

116 ⬌ January Gilchrist

I couldn't stare at her any longer. She had gotten me what I wanted. I scrubbed at my face with the skirt of my dress, trying to wipe off every trace of him, then smoothed my hair and adjusted my bodice. Wincing slightly, I moved through the hall.

As I pushed through the swing door that led to the kitchen, the smell and heat of the house hit me, and for a brief, too fleeting moment, I was transported to Harewood Hall. Time was suspended, and I closed my eyes, fantasizing that when I opened them, I would look into the laughing eyes of Cook across the aged slab of marble she worked on. The taste of copper brought me back to myself, and I opened my eyes.

Annie started guiltily, with a steaming cup of tea paused halfway to her mouth.

"Miss. My lady?" She still couldn't tell the difference between Victoria and me.

"My lady," I confirmed as I gestured to her cooling cup of tea. "As you were. I'm looking for a Jack?"

"Jack?" She blinked dumbly. What do you want with Jack, my lady?"

I didn't answer her. Only one thought filled my mind: my very own horse. Before Stanley changed his mind.

"Where do I find Jack?"

She jerked her thumb to a dark green door behind her. The door led to the alley that split at the back of the house. One direction led to our neighbor's; and the other, to the back of a squat building. The houses seemed to loom over me as I made my way along the dim, moss-covered earth.

A breeze gusted through the alley, and with it the scent of aging sewage and horse manure. I brought my hand to my nose and hopped down the short set of stairs that led to what I hoped was the stable block.

My steps, so urgent, so confident, faltered when I rounded the corner. Two huge wooden doors were swung open, and Brant was seated on an upturned bucket, his knees comically close to his face, a cigarette burning close to his fingers. His eyes were closed, his face upturned toward the sun, and for the barest of moments—until he opened his eyes and looked at me—he looked like a man who found simple pleasure from the world around him.

His face shuttered when our gaze met, and he was back to the unhappy, unpleasant man I had met on the docks.

"Miss."

"Lady Stanley."

One eyebrow raised as if he doubted my statement, but he didn't correct himself.

My courage departed me, and I stood dumbly before him. A flush began its way up my chest, and I blinked rapidly, breathing in a quest to stave it off.

"His lordship has requested . . . that is . . . I am to have a horse. As my own."

He scratched his neck and squinted into the distance. "Eh? What kind of horse?"

A chestnut mare with a tiny white spot behind her left ear, who loved the crab apples from the back of the orchard, where they were smaller and sweeter. One who craned her neck to meet me, her lips pulling back into what one would swear was a smile.

"I have been told to speak to Jack."

His response: "He ain't here."

I took a breath. I would not be cowed by this man. "Please have Jack attend to Mrs. Walter Williamson to collect a horse for me on his return. She is expecting him."

* * *

A tentative knock at the door wrenched my face from the drawing room window.

The glass was warm, and it wasn't until Annie entered that I realized my face felt heated as well. How long had I stood there simply staring out the window? I pressed my fingertips to my cheeks, hoping some of the chill that never seemed to leave me would cool them. Time had begun to slip from me at times here. I would often wake to myself standing as still as a statue, doing nothing.

Victoria, still cross about my outing with Wiffy, had remained in her room for most of the week. I was being punished. If she deigned to speak to me, it was with the force of an iron door slamming shut. How desperately lonely I was without her. A sister's love can be a cruel thing.

"Miss . . . um . . . your ladyship? Jack's in the kitchen. He says he has your horse. He wants to show it to you. When you're ready."

I blinked at Annie, heart racing. "Now?" Too late I realized it sounded like I was asking permission. She shrugged and I clarified: "What I meant, is this Jack still here?"

She nodded. "He's having coffee with Washington."

There was an expression of repressed laughter on her face, like she was sharing the punch line of a joke I hadn't heard yet.

I followed her through the crowded hallway to the back of the house, which I thought of as Washington's domain. As I suspected Washington did too.

A peal of girly and coquettish laughter rang through the kitchen. When we entered, I saw that laughter had come from Washington herself. She was perched on the edge of the squat table, one leg crossed high over the other, a mug cupped in her hands. How bright her green eyes seemed, almost as if there were a light behind them.

It wasn't until she stood and moved away that I was able to see the man sitting on the timber bench. It was his hands I noticed first. How they made the cup he held appear as tiny as a dollhouse prop. His shirtsleeves were rolled to the elbows, showing a fine dusting of sun-bleached hair on bronzed arms. His eyes were the exact color of the sky I had just been staring into, I thought. No,

MY SISTER'S SHADOW 119

the clear blue of a midsummer sky. He didn't smile when he saw me, but gave me a single nod.

Something in that clear gaze of his held me captive. Anything I had thought to say dissipated like the fog that had rolled in along the valley at Harewood.

As if from a great distance, I heard Washington speak. "This is Jack. He does the horses for his lordship."

He drained his cup and unfolded himself from the bench seat. I craned my neck to keep his gaze—he was taller than I had anticipated.

Have you ever heard the quiet breath of another, inhaled their scent, met their clear gaze for the very first time, but found yourself thinking, *Oh, it's you. There you are.* As if you had known each other a long time ago, and since parting, you'd been searching for them.

Until finally . . . there he was.

"You"—I cleared my throat; my mouth was dry, my head reeling—"have a horse for me?"

"Sure do." His voice was deep, thick, and had the rich timbre of oak rubbing against oak. Like a secret drawer opening after a spell of unuse.

A dusty felted hat sat on the table, and when he put it on, it appeared part of his body. He gazed at me, long and unsmiling, an eyebrow kinked quizzically, as if all my secrets were there to see. My face didn't flame as it usually did under the attentions of others, but my breath was short and shallow, and my heart was beating loudly.

"Shall we?" he asked.

I must have given some sign of affirmation, because he held the door open for me. As I ducked my head to pass under his arm, I smelled him: leather, lemon, coffee, and something else that pricked at my memory. But then I was down the hard step into the weak New York sunshine.

120 January Gilchrist

I pressed myself against the brick wall of the portico, to let him pass. "I don't know where we are going," I said in answer to his questioning brow.

He nodded and gestured to the narrow path that led to the lane to the stables. In truth, I needed a moment to collect myself. The thrill of getting a horse had set me spinning like a top. That was all. *The horse.* That must be all it was. Somehow, I'd imagined that it was he I was reacting to, this person, this man named Jack.

I stepped quickly to catch up to him, his long strides taking him farther and farther from me. He stopped at the small set of steps that led to the stables, and although he reached for me, did not touch me. But where his hand hovered near my elbow, it felt heated, as if he had placed his hand on me.

I was strangely, painfully aware of the nearness of his hip, his thigh, the roll and rhythm of his step.

"Have you ridden much?" Jack asked.

I nodded. "Yes." My voice sounded dry, and I cleared my throat. "Back home. England," I clarified.

He glanced down at me, one corner of his lips lifted. "I could tell home was England."

His tone was laughing, although not mocking, but I blushed anyway. I had forgotten it wasn't just that the New Yorkers sounded strange to me, but that I might sound strange to them too.

"You're on Mrs. Williamson's good side. She's given you a mare from her best. A beautiful girl, but not gonna make it as a runner. Too gentle. Nervous."

"What's her name?"

We had reached the stables now, the dim lighting of the interior making it impossible to see inside.

Jack squinted at me as though trying to bring something in the distance into focus. "Whatever you want to call her."

"She doesn't have a name?"

"Fable."

I nodded.

"Change it to whatever you like. I just thought it fit her, is all."

"You named her?"

He nodded with a dismissiveness that felt too studied, too careful. "Like I said, she's whatever *you* want to call her—makes no difference to me."

We passed through the aisle that led between the half doors, and horses sniffled and snickered in welcome. Jack's entrance energized them. His large hands ran with impossible gentleness along the mane of one, down the neck of another, then gave a scratch between the eyes of the inky black stallion I had seen in the alley. He seemed to know each horse's favorite touch.

We reached the end stall, and the luminous toffee eyes of a chestnut mare greeted us warily. She bobbed her head at Jack, arching her neck to reach him. He rested his forehead against hers, his hands in her mane. I felt like a voyeur, watching this display between the two.

"Fable, girl," he crooned in a voice as soft as honey, "here's your new mistress, Lady Stanley." He stepped away from Fable, one hand still woven in her mane, "Lady Stanley, I'd like to present Fable."

The horse rolled her wide, knowing eyes toward me. I held my hand out, stopping near her nose to share my scent. Her breath grazed my hand in a communication as old as time. With a touch of her muzzle to my open hand, she decided—we were to be friends. I desperately hoped so.

"Good girl," Jack murmured, and for the barest of moments I thrilled as though he were speaking to me.

CHAPTER 14

Victoria wasn't interested in Fable when I spoke about her that night at dinner. My excited words fell like dying petals on the dinner table, and it seemed to me that she hadn't been listening at all.

I spent the afternoon in the stall with Fable, oiling the saddle, brushing her, crooning the song Jones had sung to Victoria and me as children. Gaining her trust simply through my presence.

Jack moved around the stables, alternating between humming to himself and speaking softly to the horses. He had gone about his tasks like I wasn't there. But I felt his presence like water on my skin. I had never been so aware of someone.

So it was with some surprise that the next morning I found Victoria standing at the door of the kitchen, winding a lock of hair around the fingers of her left hand while speaking to Jack. Had they met before? A deep unease rose to the surface, but I swallowed it down.

Her back was to me, but when I got close enough to see her face, my heart stopped.

The way she looked at him. Dazzled? Amazed? It is impossible to name it, even now. It was as if the sky had released a thousand stars, all at once, shooting across a pitch sky.

MY SISTER'S SHADOW ⌒ 123

And as if, like so many other things, she believed that show had been put on earth for her eyes only.

"Jack has ridden in a rodeo," she said to me, her eyes not shifting from him.

"That sounds"—I paused, and all my bitterness poured unchecked into that pause—"fascinating."

They both turned to me.

When he smiled, tiny crinkles formed around his eyes, and his teeth, so white they could have been made from the bleached wood that washed up along the port, flashed.

He nodded, a sparse movement. "'Fascinating' is one word for it."

"I would love to see a rodeo," Victoria said breathlessly, as if the idea hadn't just occurred to her.

My eyelids fluttered against the urge to roll my eyes, wondering if she even knew what a rodeo was.

A corner of Jack's mouth lifted. "I reckon you'd be better off sticking to the city."

"Oh?" Victoria stuck her bottom lip out.

"It's pretty unforgiving out West."

I made a noise and he turned to me. There was a light of invitation in his eyes, and before I knew it, I had said, "It's pretty unforgiving here too."

There was something unnerving about the way he looked at me. As if he were assessing me, examining me like one of his horses. "I wouldn't know about that."

As so often when I spoke, the conversation spluttered and stalled into silence while I waited for someone else to work the bellows to bring it back to life.

No one did this time.

Instead, at Jack's signal we simply walked, without further exchange, toward the stables, Victoria angling her body toward Jack as if he were the sun and she a heavy-headed flower. We made our way down the path, but not together. I trailed behind, eclipsed by Victoria.

"Stop dillydallying—I want to see our new horse," she ordered over her shoulder to me. Her tone was light, but I heard the unspoken command: *"Don't embarrass me."*

Resentment simmered deep within me. That familiar refrain. I had done something wrong without doing anything at all. My mere presence was irritating to Victoria, and as suddenly as a slap it occurred to me that I was tired of it. My outing with Wiffy had opened my eyes to a new possibility. That I wasn't stupid or sullen, and my nerves weren't weak, that Victoria wasn't better or bolder or braver than me. We were simply different. And that maybe some of my differences grew from always being in her shadow, being convinced that that was my place—in the shadow, never in the sunlight.

Fable was *my* horse. Victoria did not like to ride and had never ridden at Harewood. As in so many instances, Victoria was only taking an interest to spite me. I thought of the countless things—ribbons, dresses, books, toys—she had snatched from me as soon as she saw my interest, only to discard them, broken and grubby, once her attention wandered elsewhere. It had always been this way, but for the first time I was aware that I didn't like it.

Jack waited at the top of the steps that led to the stable. Victoria extended her hand toward him. His gaze flickered down to her hand, encased in its fawn-colored glove, before enclosing it in his. My hand tingled while she stepped lightly down the steps.

He remained where he was, and as I neared, held his hand out toward me. I had no gloves on and when our skin touched, the world tilted. I stumbled, and his other hand came to my elbow.

"Careful now."

I nodded. He didn't release my hand or my elbow until I reached the bottom of the steps and when his hand left mine, it felt hot.

My Sister's Shadow · 125

Victoria restarted the conversation as we neared the stables, filling the air with chatter, peppering Jack with questions about his time with Stanley, the raceway, horses.

In the stables, as Fable lifted her brown gaze to mine, I placed my hand on the flat plain of her nose and thrilled when she didn't shy away.

"Oh my." Victoria's words were little more than a breath, but they held a world of wonder—false, I knew, but convincing all the same.

"She's pretty sweet, isn't she?" Jack said, as proud as a new father.

Was that the beginning, I wonder now? That airless day, our feet hot among the sawdust of the stables. The three of us leaning against that low gate, our eyes turned toward the horses, Jack's tanned hand resting on the battered wood of Fable's stall.

It's hard to tell. Beginnings lurk at every corner of the road, ready to spring out when you least expect them.

★ ★ ★

The days passed and life fell into a routine of sorts. For reasons completely unfathomable to me, Wiffy and I had struck up a friendship. Perhaps she saw me as one of her charity projects. A grassroots sort of charity. But I found I didn't mind. She was warm, amusing, and undemanding company. The less she required of me, the easier I found it to speak freely.

Every morning I would dress for riding and meet both Jack and Fable in front of the house. We would stand on the street, reins in one hand, the other absently stroking the soft fur on Fable's neck. Victoria claimed the change of season inflamed her hay fever and opted to stay in bed. That same hay fever didn't seem to bother her while she perched on the gates in the stables, swinging her legs while Jack went about his tasks.

I knew the truth. Like two magnets, their opposing forces repelled each other. Wiffy was in charge, naturally used to getting whatever she wanted. Whereas I was content to go along with Wiffy and, like a leaf on a stream, get swept along by her currents, Victoria resented not being the brightest light in the room.

As expected, Wiffy was as powerful on the horse as she was in life. She would down a cup of coffee from the finest bone china, right there on the street, and spring from her stableman's hand onto her horse, and we would take the streets to the park at an appropriately ladylike pace. But once we reached the privacy of the trees that lined the edge of the park, Wiffy would hunch low on her horse, kick sharply, and let out a shrill, warlike cry, then tear off through the green. We would ride until we were breathless, our hair loose, our cheeks flushed with laughter.

I felt alive for the first time since leaving England.

Then we would perform a lap of the park, backs straight, horses slow, talking to each other about all manner of things, before returning sedately to our homes.

"I'm the perfect lady when it counts. But it won't come at the cost of my actual life." She had said to me one morning early in our riding routine, when I had been too timid to let Fable run. It hadn't occurred to me there could be any other way. That behind closed doors I could do as I pleased.

Wiffy arranged meaningless luncheon after meaningless luncheon for Victoria and me, until one by one until we had met all of Mrs. Astor's infamous four hundred. But at each event, Victoria began as bright and vibrant as she'd always been before drifting into morose silence, glowering at me I tried to introduce her to someone new or include her in our conversations. The quieter she became, the more she drank, and the darker her mood became. She would remain silent at the parties before unleashing on me in the carriage, sometimes railing at me the entire way home, and once squeezing my arm so hard a perfect image of her fingers had bloomed on my skin for a week.

And on it went.

My Sister's Shadow   127

But as the days warmed, and green buds began to unfurl their leaves, something else began to unfold.

I stood on the steps in the bright, crisp morning, enjoying a rare moment of peace in that relentlessly noisy city. It was often said that New York never slept, and I quite believed it.

The rattle of irons drew my attention to the end of the street, and I watched as Jack approached. My whole being tingled in the most delicious way at his welcoming smile, and I lifted my hand in return to his. The golden light of the dawn seemed to cling to his skin, a glow that surrounded him in the cool morning air.

He pulled to a stop and slid from Fable, his hand behind his back, his face creased with delight.

"Look what I found."

I laughed, enchanted, as I took the thick wedge of wisteria from him.

"I saw it and thought of you." His eyebrows knit together. "Although now I wonder if I shouldn't have left it on the tree."

I brought it to my nose and breathed in its familiar peppery scent. It was something to do to hide my flaming cheeks.

"My middle name." I murmured to it.

A beat. "I remember."

One morning while we waited for Wiffy to appear, he had asked me about England, how New York differed. I'd told him about Harewood, how the mists rolled along the never-ending hills into the valley, how the gardens had held me enchanted since my earliest memory. How I missed my hands in commune with the earth, how we had been named for flowers. How passionate my father was about botany, more than about his daughters. It was a simple conversation, but he had remembered.

I closed my eyes and pressed the wisteria to my chest. "There is some in the park, but it hasn't bloomed yet."

"This was just growing wild on the sidewalk in Greenwich."

I smiled, warmed by the idea he had seen it and thought of me.

128   January Gilchrist

"I know the lady who owns the tree—I didn't steal it. She happily gave it. In case you were concerned about its origins. It isn't much," he went on quickly, "but perhaps a small token to remind you of home." He gestured to the concrete around us.

I looked up for the first time in an age. The buildings, gray, brown, or deep red brick, crowded the sky. We stood in shadow, the sun always blocked by man-made monuments. Folly. Ego. Not a green thing in sight. Except this.

Tears pricked my eyes, and I buried my face in the posy again.

"Sorry." His voice was stricken. "Did I get it wrong?"

His image blurred in my tear-filled eyes. He appeared to glimmer and gleam.

I shook my head. "No, you didn't at all. You got it utterly, absolutely right."

We stared at each other; me with wet eyes, he with those endlessly blue, fathomless ones. The look we shared seemed to go on forever, and everything around us blurred until he was the only thing sharply in focus.

I placed my hand on his arm. "Thank you."

His gaze drew down to my hand, but I didn't lift it. I couldn't. It was as if we were magnetized. The energy flow between us like an overfull river we were powerless to stop, but I suddenly found I didn't want to halt its progress.

"Ahoy, fellow travelers." Wiffy's voice boomed like a foghorn through a gloom. Jack took a step back, and my hand fell in the air between us.

"What's that you have?" Wiffy appeared, as she always did, in a cloud of noise and light. Her energy was as thick as molasses, covering all it encountered.

"Wisteria. My namesake. I'm Adelaide Wisteria. Victoria is Lavender. The gardener at Harewood always brought the first bloom to me. Every year for as long as I can remember."

Guilt had me rambling, but guilt over what? I'd done nothing.

She bent her head to my bouquet and breathed deeply. "Gawd," she drawled. "I love wisteria. The west wall at Fairview Court is covered in it. Where did you find this?"

She looked at us both, but we did not reply. The inappropriateness of the situation landed on me like a brick. I blinked blindly at the purple flowers.

"Greenwich Village." Jack answered finally, after a beat too long.

Wiffy didn't seem to notice. "Greenwich? I didn't know you suffered from Bohemia, Jack. Careful, Lady Stanley, that can be contagious." She spoke with a lightness that pulled at something inside me. How I longed to speak so casually with Jack. To tease, as if every word didn't matter. To watch him laugh. To make him laugh. Our conversations were plentiful if shallow, but it was only when we found ourselves otherwise occupied that I was able to truly converse with him.

Wiffy clapped her hands, and my musings were broken. I handed Jack back the wisteria. "Will you take care of it for me until my return?"

He placed the flowers with care on the stoop, straightening up and meeting my gaze. "I will."

There was an undertone to our words, one that perhaps neither of us quite understood.

CHAPTER 15

Among the china and endless cups of tea, talk began of Newport.

"You and Lord Stanley are taking a house, I assume?" Mrs. Griffin-Buttley asked me at a luncheon to raise money for the Settlement House Movement. Although the luncheon was in its third hour, not one conversation had yet been held regarding this Settlement House Movement.

Names like Fairview Court, Breakers, and Beechwood swirled around me.

"I really couldn't say," I replied.

Mrs. Griffin-Buttley squawked, not unlike a parrot, and clutched my arm. "You simply must. Mustn't she, Wiffy?"

"If Mrs. Griffin-Buttley says she must, then she simply must," Wiffy replied drolly.

"I don't know what Newport is," I murmured to Wiffy once the older woman had wandered off to mingle.

Across the room, Victoria held her glass aloft for another refill of champagne. My own was warm in my hand, the bubbles long gone.

"Oh, what an oversight on my part. After Lent, anyone who is anyone heads out to Newport to beat this beastly heat. It's not quite the Riviera, but a change is as good as a holiday. You must

My Sister's Shadow ⌒ 131

come. Say you'll come. We will have the most fun." Wiffy clutched my arm.

"I would have to speak to Stanley. I suspect he'll be busy with the racetrack."

In truth, I had no idea if Stanley would be busy with the planning of the racetrack or, rather, busy gambling *at* the racetrack. I had begun to suspect the latter. Nothing had been said, but the weeks after the evenings when he appeared morose and sullen were cold and spartan, as the regular grocery deliveries stopped. Other nights he appeared in high spirits, alcohol clinging to his breath, adding volume to his words and dulling his vowels. Then, when he joined us for dinner, we ate well: creamy dishes with succulent pieces of meats and sugary desserts freshly made. Although the food was better when he dined with us, at least the nights he returned looking for somewhere to direct his anger were over quickly enough. His dinner-table appearances often went long into the night, and I had found myself stifling yawns well into the early hours of the morning while he explained the intricacies of the racetrack.

Wiffy threw her drink back and gestured to a passing waiter. "Beebah and the Lally Cooler are in Europe—you can take their house." The Lally Cooler was Beebah's husband, I'd learned that no one in Wiffy's life was called by their given name.

I widened my eyes at her. "Wiffy, even you can't offer me someone else's house without asking them first."

"Oh, darling, haven't you learned? I get what I want when I want it, and I have decided I very much want you to come to Newport."

She shot me a sidelong glance. "I should think it will remind you of Mother England. Beebah's house, Fairview Court, is perched on the very top of a cliff overlooking that ocean. Expansive green or blue whichever way you look. You could take Fable along the beach; the horses love it. All that space to roam. The afternoon breeze off the ocean, with a cocktail in hand, is simply

132 ⮌ January Gilchrist

the greatest moment you'll ever experience. There is nothing to do except enjoy all of one's glorious life."

I knew I was being manipulated, but I found I didn't really mind. She had sold me, hook, line, and sinker.

"We all stay the whole summer. It is lawn party after lawn party. You'll simply adore it. There is a freedom in Newport that cannot quite be explained. It feels like just when school was let out."

I had been educated by a governess, year-round, at home, with two days off a year, for Easter and Christmas. I had no idea what school being let out felt like.

"Am I permitted to know what has you so animated, or am I to continue being excluded?" Victoria appeared, her tone sharp.

"Of course, Vivi," I reached for her hand, but she stumbled out of my reach. She was rather unsteady on her feet. My stomach churned. There had been too many instances like this at luncheons we had attended. At Mrs. Gidding's luncheon she had been in the water closet so long that the hostess had a footman take the door off, thinking it was jammed, only to find Victoria curled up asleep on the floor. I had tried to ask her about it but had been rebuffed.

"Wiffy has invited us to Newport," I said, gesturing to the waiter refilling the water glasses, in the hopes of replacing the fizz in Victoria's glass with something less potent.

Victoria closed the space between us. "Newport. How charming. We would simply adore that wouldn't we, Addy?"

Victoria was clearly *au fait* in what this Newport entailed. Not for the first time, I found myself wishing I had listened to her all those nights as she'd read aloud from the *Town Crier* on the boat.

"It isn't our decision, but I will certainly speak to Stanley about it."

I couldn't imagine Stanley would turn down an opportunity to spend time with the upper echelon of New York society. It was

My Sister's Shadow   ⌒ 133

a wonder that he hadn't already mentioned it and ordered me to obtain an invite.

"Leave it with me," Wiffy said. "I'll speak with Beebah and arrange to have the house aired for you. They keep on their staff all year-round, so you wouldn't need to bring many of your own."

I couldn't stop the small smile that emerged at the thought of escaping the oppressive ways of Washington. Despite my dowry and Stanley's talk of the racecourse and all it would eventually achieve, unlike Fairview Court, Greycliffe ran on the skeleton staff of Washington and Annie all year-round. I'd raised the possibility of more staff with Stanley, hoping to hire people who weren't quite so terrifying. His clipped reply, *"No need,"* had left me hesitant to bring it up again.

By the time I'd heard the baker's boy telling Washington there would be no more credit until the last bill had been paid, I'd worked it out for myself. There wasn't as much money as Stanley liked to imply to the outside world. Even less when he lost at the racetrack. I wondered if that was where the rest of my dowry had gone too.

Wiffy misinterpreted my smile as assent and clinked her glass against mine. "That's it—settled then; we'll all spend the summer in Newport."

I tried to catch Victoria's gaze, but she was watching the room with a look of quiet contemplation that sent a shiver along my spine.

*   *   *

"That's it organized." I refolded the letter with a little noise. "And they *are* keeping the house staff on."

"No more Washington?" Victoria whispered.

We shared a look. Relief flooded through me. It often felt like Washington was the mistress of the house, and we her irritating and demanding guests. None of Victoria's requests or ideas had

134 January Gilchrist

been implemented, stalled before even getting out of the gates by Washington. Any small changes Victoria did attempt to make were changed immediately back. We were both exhausted by it. Washington, however, appeared inexhaustible.

"And I am to have Beebah's lady's maid." I pulled an excited face that Victoria did not return.

"And what of me? Am I to do my own toilette?"

"Sorry, I misspoke. *We* are to have a lady's maid."

Her expression was unmoving rock. "You said *you* are to have the lady's maid. Once again, I am discounted, because I don't have the title, so I don't matter. You have forgotten all about me."

I sighed. This had been her refrain for weeks. The smallest supposed slight turned to accusations of overlooking or trying to discard her. "Vivi. Please. I misspoke. *We* are to have a lady's maid."

She stood and fluffed her skirts. "No, *you* are to have a lady's maid. You didn't think of me at all until I questioned you because you no longer care about me. Ever since you've taken up with Wiffy—both of you married women—I am nothing to you."

I stood and reached for her, but she batted my hand away.

"No longer care about you? Vivi, how could I ever?"

"It's Wiffy this, Wiffy that. You never think about me, not even for a moment. I am merely a nuisance. You are selfish and wish to have all the attention on yourself, and I find myself tiring of it."

She turned on her heel and stormed from the room, banging the door so hard that the china on the table rattled. Her footsteps thumped along the hallway and seemed to echo long after she had departed. I slumped into the chair and rubbed my eyes wearily. I should go after her but couldn't summon the energy. Why was it always me placating, appeasing, negotiating?

Victoria had always been difficult, her moods storm clouds that clotted along the horizon, ready to dump a deluge on my head—but lately they were more full-fledged hurricanes that struck with little warning over the smallest slight, both real or imagined.

I had always put Victoria's desires first, catered to her moods and whims and ever-changing needs, to the detriment of myself, but I had done so happily. Because I could not exist without her. Without Mama, Victoria was all I had. I'd felt so certain she felt the same way about me, that sisters loved fiercely, bonded for life.

But her selfishness was beginning to grate, and I was growing tired of her elliptical moods.

Perhaps Newport would be good for us. It sounded idyllic, and with nothing but sunshine and fresh air, perhaps we could become sisters again instead of adversaries.

CHAPTER 16

The carriage turned into a discreet opening in a box hedge. The driveway to Fairview Court was long and winding, hemmed in on both sides by an immaculately trimmed hedge.

Flashes of blue played peekaboo through the shrubbery until finally we turned the corner, and both house and ocean presented themselves. Victoria and I gasped.

Stanley made a noise in his throat. "I say. This is more like it."

He had taken no convincing to depart New York for the summer months, his business at the racecourse apparently evaporating at the very mention of it. I had broached the subject of staying at Beebah's house on the water's edge over a breakfast, and he had almost choked on his egg in his haste to agree.

And now I saw why. In New York it was hard to get a sense of someone's wealth. The houses, while differing in sizes, all shared a similar blank-faced front. Windows were covered with lace, to shield them from prying eyes, and it wasn't until you were inside that you truly got the measure of your host.

Not so in Newport. This house didn't just shout money—it delivered you a bank statement.

The driveway opened to a large expanse of the most verdant manicured lawn I had ever seen. A marble Poseidon, trident held aloft in victory, rose out of the crystal-clear waters of a fountain positioned in the center of the grass. The bottom of the fountain must have been laid with crystal as it shot sparks of light into the air.

The house was exquisite. Three stories of Gothic beauty, made of stone as rough as the wall that marked the lawn from the beach. It was all curves and turrets and twinkling windows. *Fairview Court*. I did not yet know it was the place my life would change entirely.

"Look, Addy." Victoria jostled my arm and pointed to the line of black-suited servants standing at attention along the driveway.

Her smile was broad and free, and for a moment she was the person I remembered all too well.

"The servants," she whispered with a lift of her eyebrows.

I sighed with relief. Washington and Annie were staying on at Greycliffe to maintain the house and provide for Stanley in case of his return to attend to business matters.

The carriage drew to a stop alongside the servants, and four liveried footmen stepped forward.

"I say, old Walt knows how we do things, what?" A greedy light shone in Stanley's eyes as he gazed up at the house.

I thought of the skeleton staff at Greycliffe. This wasn't the way we did things at all. But I had begun to notice it was how Stanley *desired* to do things, his reach never quite meeting his aim. *This*, here, was how the immensely rich and powerful lived, and although Stanley wanted very much to be one of those people, our own lives were sorely lacking. Anything outwardly facing was given attention, but everything else was done on a shoestring. And lately that shoestring become tighter and tighter. Was my role to be the one to open doors to acquiring more wealth?

The footman opened the carriage door. "Welcome, Lord and Lady Stanley, Miss Windlass," he said with a deep bow.

Stanley sucked his teeth and straightened his shirt cuffs, exiting the carriage with a lifted nose.

138   January Gilchrist

My gaze met the footman's as he extended a hand to assist me from the carriage, his face as blank as a slate.

I blinked into the blinding sunshine and inhaled deeply. The breeze carried with it the scent of the ocean, which heaved against the rocks that lined the lawn.

A row of roses nodded their heads along the clifftop leading to the water, scenting the air with their sweet fragrance. Victoria stood behind me and placed her hand on my shoulder, and I rested my cheek against it; it had been some time since she had touched me kindly.

We walked the line of servants, nodding and greeting each one as they were introduced by the starch-shirted butler. Each held a blankly welcoming expression, with no side glances or curled lips. I was so grateful I could have kissed every one of them.

I turned and gazed back over to where the carriage had entered. Through some trick of the hedge, or perhaps the fall of the land, the driveway was visible from here. How clever it was to allow the members of the house to see who was coming but leave the arrivals not knowing they were watched! Everything about the house was opulent luxury: the grounds, the views, the gardens.

We were led into the entrance, a dim portico with air as coolly refreshing as a glass of lemonade on a summer's day. The entry was grand and imposing, thick double doors led into a resplendent expanse of red marble. Two large staircases hewn from that same marble arched back on themselves. A marble angel stood on the landing, her wings stretching from arched staircase to staircase. Her hand was extended to us, eyes both watchful and reproachful.

Maids with averted eyes took us along to our rooms as we moved through, from hallway to hallway I began to fear I would never find my way back. The house felt endless.

"This is your room, your ladyship."

"And my sister's is . . . ?"

MY SISTER'S SHADOW ☞ 139

"She has the mirrored suite across the courtyard, your ladyship." At my blank look, she moved to the window and pulled back the gauze.

The house from the front, appeared to be a square, but was actually U-shaped and my window faced the other, identical wing of the house.

"Fairview Court is like two houses, mirrored, attached in the middle. Makes it easier to get your bearings." Her voice was low and kind.

Mirrored. Reversed. Two halves to make a whole. Like sisters.

I smiled. "Thank you. I just worry I won't be able to find my way about."

"Press the button, miss, and I'll come. I will help you until your own maid arrives." She gestured to the discreet brass button on the wall.

"There is no . . . that is, our staff has stayed on in New York. Lord Stanley may need to return for business . . ." I trailed off, unsure how to ask. "My maid won't be attending. She's staying on in our New York property."

"Very good, your ladyship." She nodded. "I can have Jeanie attend to you during your stay. What time would you like your tray in the morning?"

"My tray?"

"Your breakfast tray. Sorry to assume, your ladyship, but Mrs. Macmillan takes her breakfast in her room. I assumed you would like to as well."

For a moment I wondered who Mrs. Macmillan was, and why how she took her breakfast had anything to do with me. It occurred to me, finally, that Mrs. Macmillan was Wiffy's sister Beebah. I had never heard her called by anything but her nickname.

"Of course. Thank you. Yes, I would love that. What time does Mrs. . . . er . . . Macmillan take hers?"

140 ⚬   January Gilchrist

I was aware I sounded brainless. What kind of person doesn't know what time they like their breakfast? But I had never been asked my preferences before. About anything. I didn't know how to answer.

At Harewood, Victoria and I had been treated as children, chastised and reprimanded freely by the staff. Jones constantly encouraged us to make less work for the servants. And at Greycliffe we were endured under sufferance, as if we were unwelcome interlopers getting underfoot of Washington and Annie's "real" tasks.

"Mrs. Macmillan likes to rise early and takes hers at eight on the dot. Is there anything in particular you would like, your ladyship? Of course, I will bring the week's menu up for you to look over and make changes as you see fit."

I made what I hoped was a noise of assent.

The next question nearly paralyzed me: "Will you be hosting any parties?"

"I . . ." I swallowed hard. "Am I expected to?"

"No, your ladyship. The season is all arranged, but there is the odd night free here or there. We can go over the schedule together tomorrow, if you wish."

A schedule? Wiffy had said it was lawn party after lawn party, but the thought of hosting one had never occurred to me.

"Will there be anything else?" the maid asked.

She was so kind, so accommodating that I fought the fleeting urge to weep.

I didn't hear her leave, so softly she moved. Sound was consumed by the house—by the ceilings that seemed to reach to the sky, the thick, luxurious rugs that stretched from wall to wall.

One wall had a window facing a rose garden that drew the eye all the way to the ocean. An arbor covered with verdant green and pinks was the only thing that broke my view to the ocean.

"You are welcome," the nodding heads of the roses seemed to say.

MY SISTER'S SHADOW   141

This was as far from Greycliffe as the moon was from earth.

Greycliffe. I shivered. I never wanted to step foot in that house again. How I already wanted this summer to stretch on forever.

I sighed with relief and threw myself on the bed. The thick, soft feathers of the blanket embraced me like a hug. A warm feeling spread through me, and I felt energized, electric. The burden I had carried alone for far too long suddenly lightened.

Newport would be life changing, I just knew it.

* * *

The next morning, after breakfast, I searched through the house for Victoria. I found her in the arched doorway of the entrance, half in shadow, half in light.

I studied her profile while she was intent on something I couldn't see. The light was golden here, more radiant, brighter than the dim New York sun that only seemed to throw shadows. It illuminated her. My chest constricted. She was my sister, my shadow. Even though she was a few steps away from me, she felt miles away. My steps rapped out a song across the foyer, my shoes light on the marble, and she stiffened but didn't turn toward me. I placed my hand on her shoulder, but still she didn't turn.

Her gaze was trained on something in the distance. I couldn't see what, but whatever it was had brought a smile to her face. Her smile in turn brought one to my own face. She was often difficult, mercurial, and moody, but who could be unhappy here in Newport, surrounded by such extravagance and beauty? I silently gave thanks for Winifred Williamson and her sister's timely grand tour of Europe.

I rested my head on Victoria's shoulder, closed my eyes, and inhaled deeply. A warm breeze floated through the open door, and with it the sounds and smell of the ocean, that unforgiving Atlantic that had carried me away from all I knew and loved. How gray and cold it had been. That same ocean was now the

142 ☙ January Gilchrist

most startling shade of blue, struck through with threads of silver that danced against the rocks.

Fanciful, but a sign, I fancied, of my luck turning.

The smell of freshly cut grass, of sunshine, summer, and the roses growing along the cliff walk all contributed to a sense of anticipation in the air. Yes, Newport was going to be good for us. We would shake off the lethargy, the cold and damp of Greycliffe. We would be sisters again. I held her hand, overcome with a sense of things righting.

I wouldn't let the distance that had sprung between us increase, I vowed. She was still my sister. Tempestuous and difficult, yes, but she was all that I had.

"I want to stay here forever," she said.

"It's beautiful, isn't it?"

"It isn't just beautiful. It's . . . perfection." She swept her hand through the air, gesturing to it all before us. "It is just perfection. Beyond anything I could have imagined."

Her eyes glittered with a strange light.

"Vivi?"

She turned to me, but I felt she looked right through me.

"The breakfast room is full of flowers. I had a croissant for breakfast. The cook here is French," she whispered in reverent tones.

I nodded. I too had enjoyed a buttery, flaky croissant at breakfast. My tray had been delivered promptly and soundlessly by not one, but two maids—one to hold open the heavy door and the other to wheel the tray in. The platter had been near overflowing with food. Ripe summer fruits, many of which I couldn't even identify. I had tried them all, taking huge bites and letting the juices run down my chin. It wasn't until I had taken at least one bite of everything that I had lain back on the bed until the maid assigned to me had come to help me dress. Cheerful and helpful, Jeanie had regaled me with stories of the recent arrivals and the parties I could expect to attend. It was if we were

My Sister's Shadow   143

Alice down the rabbit hole, how far from Greycliffe this house and its staff were.

"Let's ride," I suggested. "Go exploring."

I didn't want to be inside. I wanted to be along the beach, with Fable, with Vivi, the salt-scented breeze in my hair. I grabbed Victoria's hand and pulled her into the sunshine.

"Let's ride," I called again, the breeze whipping my words into the air around us. I pulled her, laughing, toward the statue of Poseidon, as if I were going to pull her right into it. We sank to the edge of the fountain, laughter spilling into the air like freshly poured champagne.

"What has gotten into you?" she asked lightly, the usual scorn missing from her tone as she tipped her head to the sun.

I was taken back to our time at Harewood, where we had assiduously avoided the sun for fear of unladylike freckles. Had it only been months ago? It felt like a lifetime. What I would have given to go back to that time, when my greatest concern had been sun on skin.

As she exhaled deeply, the breeze caught her sigh, and the unmistakable smell of alcohol reached me. I cracked an eyelid and peered at her. Surely she hadn't been drinking already—we'd barely finished breakfast.

Placing my hand over hers, I lifted it and pressed it to my mouth. *I'm sorry,* I wanted to say. *I'm sorry it went this way. I am going to fix it.* Being here, among the roses, near the ocean, in the sunshine, will fix it all.

But the sweetly fragranced air, sharp with the sea but softened with the scent of blossoming flowers had me closing my eyes instead of saying anything.

Heaven, I thought. *This place is heaven.*

★ ★ ★

We skipped to the stables, an exact replica of the main house, but on a smaller scale, at the back of the property, stopping to pick

144 ❧ January Gilchrist

each other a flower to tuck behind our ears. We were drunk on freedom, perhaps the first we'd ever tasted. Greycliffe had been little more than a damp prison, the streets surrounding it busier than anything either of us had ever experienced, and threatening in its noise, dust, and activity. As a married woman, I was the chaperone, but I hadn't the confidence to leave the house without Wiffy as company.

Fairview Court was idyllic, everything shiny and new. A clean slate.

We rounded the corner to the stables, and our laughter must have announced us, for Jack stood at the door waiting for us, a wide smile across his face. Our eyes met, and something moved between us. Was that smile for me? The way his eyes had lit up, face creased in pleasure. Mine did the same when I saw him.

I knew so little of pleasure. So little of what it meant to be truly seen, but there was a depth in his eyes that unsettled me, brought a hot flush to my face. There was something else between us too, something that reminded me of how I felt about Victoria.

There was something about him that made me feel so safe.

"We are going for a ride," Victoria announced.

Jack nodded. "You've come to the right place." He turned to me. "Fable is dying to get out with you."

I nodded, rendered speechless by his rolled sleeves and tanned forearms.

"What about you, Miss Victoria?" He pretended to consider her with narrowed eyes and pursed lips. "A nice gentle pony? I think we have a sweet old girl here that you might be able to handle."

She laughed and swatted his arm, letting her fingers linger on those tanned forearms. "I want a big brute of a thing. Something strong, to ride hard."

I cleared my throat with a strangled cough.

Victoria pouted and rang that silver bell laugh. "Oops, looks like I'm in trouble. Adelaide wants everyone to be as dull as she is."

MY SISTER'S SHADOW 145

The comment sliced, as sharp as a razor, but I said nothing.

Jack turned away toward the horses, but not before I caught a glimpse of his reddened cheeks. I scowled at Victoria, but she was following Jack into the stables and didn't spare me a glance. She chattered and chirped while Jack saddled a horse for her, a peaceful-looking gray mare.

I ran my hand along Fable's nose, and she snickered in joy at seeing me. My hand in her mane was a deep meditation that I was surprised out of by Jack's voice in my ear.

I opened my eyes, stumbling as I did.

He stepped forward to steady me, his strong hands on my elbows, his eyebrows knit in concern. "Are you all right?"

"I am fine. I was just—"

"Woolgathering." Victoria interrupted. "Adelaide lives in another realm. Always daydreaming."

My face heated. I tried to step out of Jack's hands, but he held tight, ducking his head to keep my gaze. "Are you all right?" he repeated.

His face was so full of concern that my heart began to clamor, wrong footed by his concern.

I nodded. "Yes, I was just lost in a moment with Fable."

Victoria snorted but Jack nodded. "It happens to me all the time with horses." His voice was low and gentle.

That was exactly how it was for me. How lovely it felt to be understood.

Jack saddled up and rode out with us as the groom. He had been to Newport before, he'd said. He was confident in leading the horses from the front of the property along an upward tilting path, and after a short climb we found ourselves at an outlook high over a beach.

A path had been carved along the coastline, winding alongside thick hunks of rocks that seemed to have been designed to keep the sea at bay.

146 ⁓ January Gilchrist

It was breathtaking. An ever-changing, unnamable blue, so clear it was almost green. It glittered, this ocean. Waves twinkled and spun light before us, taking our eye to the horizon.

Houses were dotted along the landscape at intervals, little more than flashes of color and light. I turned back.

Fairview Court was crouched at the point, the very last thing we could see. From here it was all turrets and rock, its welcoming features smudged by the salty ocean air.

The wind was strong and fresh, in the way that air carrying the salty damp of the ocean so often is. With each gust Fable's ears twitched. I leaned forward and kissed her neck.

Victoria and Jack pulled to a stop beside me.

"That's Bailey Beach," Jack said, pointing toward a stretch of sand down the hill.

A vast expanse of green stretched alongside the tawny sand, and an octagonal roof reflected sunlight into the sky.

"What is that?"

Jack squinted into the distance. "The aquarium."

"Will we go?" Victoria asked Jack, and her face reflected what I knew was on mine. A mix of wonder, excitement, and childish glee.

Jack hesitated. "You can do what you please."

Victoria asking him for permission had confused him. To him we had it all: huge houses, staff, dresses, parties, money. But what he didn't know was that we were in a gilded cage. It was all smoke and mirrors. Victoria had asked through habit—we had never done a thing without asking for permission first.

"Well, then, it would please me greatly to go to the aquarium." Victoria smiled and ran her tongue along her lower lip before pulling it between her teeth.

What had gotten into her? The leather of the reins squeaked as my grip tightened around them.

Jack turned to me and inclined his head toward the building. "And you? Would it please you greatly?"

The hairs on my arm trembled, and I glanced away from him. Blinking into the blinding sunshine, I nodded.

"So that sets it. Off to the aquarium we go." Jack slapped his reins and took off down the hill.

Victoria cried out with pleasure and followed suit. The breeze picked up again, bringing the sounds of the beachgoers and promenade walkers. The sun moved behind a cloud, and suddenly the billowing ribbon from Victoria's hat took on a sinister look, like a swirl of blood in a basin of water. I shook my head and took off behind them.

★ ★ ★

The afternoon passed in a blur of colors, strange smells, and laughter. So much laughter. Ours and everyone else's. It was as if time stopped by the ocean. As though no one had any responsibilities, anything else to do except walk the promenade, looking at the stalls and stores. We wandered the rooms of the aquarium, exclaiming over the tanks of brightly colored fish, squealing with childish delight as we were handed slimy starfish from buckets, salty water dripping along our arms.

The sun was sinking low into the horizon when we finally exited. The three of us stood blinking into the golden light, quiet as our eyes adjusted to its still bright glow. While inside the aquarium, the promenade had changed. It seemed we had fallen again through Alice's rabbit hole and now found ourselves in the midst of a raucous tea party. Lights were strung along the shop fronts to the edge of the walkway, zigzagging along the promenade and sending shafts of color cartwheeling along the ground.

A band of brightly dressed men playing fiddles, drums, and accordions beat an energetic tune that held the attention of a large group of people. Some of them danced right there on the path while other clapped, laughed, and whistled along to the music. Some stood against the railing, tapping their feet, drinking mugs of ale or lemonade. Children ducked and wove between the adults, holding balloons, waving streamers, giggling and blowing tin horns. The air was electric with a joy that made me think of the yearly village fete. For a fleeting moment I felt I was home.

Only it was different.

As ladies of the village, we had been required to sit out anything that might have been considered unseemly, of which Jones had a seemingly inexhaustible list. No more than one cup of lemonade, no scones, no toffee apples, and strictly *no*. We had always been whisked away long before the sun had set, Jones muttering dark warnings about the nefarious activities that occurred once night fell.

But Jones wasn't here. I glanced at Victoria, who was looking at the crowd. Her mouth had dropped open, her eyes wide with joyfulness, hands clasped to her chest.

I looked at Jack, who, instead of staring at the band or crowd, was watching me with a small smile that made my chest tingle.

The music suddenly quickened, and the crowd began to cheer and whistle. Their jovial shouts and whoops increased in volume. Men discarded their mugs and led their laughing women into the fray.

I was entranced. The music and excitement of the crowd was infectious. As the music increased in tempo, the crowd grew in volume, louder and louder until it pounded through my head, blocking any thought except how utterly, delightfully wondrous this was and how badly I wanted to be a part of it.

"Would you like to dance?" Jack's voice was soft in my ear.

It wasn't until I felt his warm breath against my skin that I realized I had been holding my own. I released it and shook my head. "No. No. I couldn't. I . . . I don't know the steps."

Jack laughed. "Neither does anyone else."

And he was right. I watched as men, women, and children of all shapes, ages, and styles of dress mingled, arms linked, feet stomping, heads thrown back in laughter. There were no steps to this dance; it was just a pure, unadulterated expression of joy.

MY SISTER'S SHADOW
149

I shook my head again. Not for me, that.

But he must've seen the longing on my face because he reached for my hand, squeezing it firmly, once, in question.

The music pulled at me, and Wiffy's words ringing in my ears—*"It's freedom there"*—I shut my eyes and nodded.

What could it hurt, I remember thinking, *this one dance?* There was no one here to see, to disapprove or chastise.

Jack extended his hand to Victoria who curtsied gracefully as she accepted it with an impish smile.

He pulled us into the center of the seething crowd, and somehow, with his strong hand in mine, I was fearless. We skipped and turned and jumped and hollered, ecstatic noises that mingled tunelessly with music. Boots thumped against the ground, hands slapped thighs and clapped against others while the fiddle sang on and on. A stranger linked his elbow through mine, spinning me around and around, so fast my head began to swim. Laughter burst from me. I had never experienced such freedom. I was free to be myself. No one was looking at me; they were lost in their own joy. The man swung me back toward Victoria, and I linked my elbow with hers and spun her the way the man had spun me. She tipped her head back, eyes closed tightly. I released her elbow and copied her movement. I threw my head back, shut my eyes, and let the music wash over me.

A hand pressed my forearm, and my eyes flew open to meet Jack's deep blue eyes. He was no longer dancing.

"Are you all right?"

My cheeks ached my smile was so wide. I was more than all right. For the first time in my life, I was free. I was myself.

Like most men in the heated crowd, Jack had removed his hat and held it in his hand. His hair fell onto his forehead in a manner that tugged at my insides. A light sheen of sweat glistened along his hairline, and I was overcome with the urge to brush that hair from his forehead. To run my hands along his face. To be held by him.

150 ⤙ January Gilchrist

The music continued its frantic pace, seeping into my blood, heating it, making me think and feel foolish things.

I crooked my elbow at him. "Dance with me," I suggested with a tilt of my chin.

He smiled that slow smile of his and nodded. He slipped his arm into mine, and the noise and heat of the crowd fell away. All that existed was the press of his elbow against mine, the heat of his body mingling with mine. I could hardly breathe as I placed my hand on his arm. His gaze shifted to my hand before moving slowly to meet my eyes. Although my hand was gloved, it felt naked, and burned where it rested on him. I stared into the depth of his eyes, as endlessly blue as Newport's sky and just as unknown to me.

He moved like a ballerina. Graceful, like a person half his size. His large feet never touched mine, and after a beat or two the music was *in* my body. The scent of him was in the air around me, mingling with the beer and sweat. My hand slid along his shoulder, down the length of his arm until it reached his hand. I entwined my fingers with his. They were thick and strong. Capable. I don't know why his hands being strong meant anything to me, but it did.

In that moment, it was everything.

Suddenly the lights were too light, the sounds jarring and off-key. My clothing felt hot and restrictive. I longed to be alone with Jack in way that was completely new to me. My body vibrated with the need to be close to his.

The music rose to a crescendo, and my heart banged painfully. I stumbled one step toward him, then another. His hand rose slowly toward my cheek but hovered in the air as if he longed to touch me but couldn't bear to. I tilted my face, bringing it against his hand. His skin against mine was electric.

Movement. Little more than a shadow, and suddenly his hand was whipped from the air.

Victoria stepped between us. Her back was toward me, her hand gripping his—the hand that had touched me—so tightly her knuckles shone white.

"I'm thirsty. Find me a drink?"

He nodded, eyes blank. He placed his hat back on his head, and he and Victoria moved through the crowd.

When they reached the edge of the dance floor, Victoria turned back, shooting me a look so brief that I might have imagined the dark hatred in her eyes, but for the cold shiver that broke through me.

CHAPTER 17

A hot breeze blew alongside the cool shade of the house. The curved iron table was strewn with cards and paper, my pen discarded on an empty envelope. I was supposed to be writing a long-overdue response to Cousin Deborah in England. Her letters had begun to pile up, my lack of response charitably blamed on an unreliable postal system. But the truth was, Deborah seemed to belong to another time, another place, another person. Somehow, after Newport, without me even realizing, my home had become here, in America.

I watched as a stablehand and Jack stood at the low white fence that housed the runoff. They were turned toward the grazing horses, gesturing at the feed bin and water trough. The battered hat Jack wore shadowed his eyes—all I could make out was the curve of his cheek, the movement of his lips as they talked. He looked up, and although it was surely too far for him to see me in the shadows, our gaze met. I raised my hand from my lap in a wave that instantly flooded my cheeks with heat. How childish I must seem to him. At his lifted hand, the stable hand also turned, lifting and dipping his hat in greeting. His face returned to the horses, but Jack's gaze lingered on mine.

Fine droplets of ocean water clung to the breeze and landed on my cheek, and I closed my eyes, enjoying the cooling

MY SISTER'S SHADOW 153

sensation. Moments of joy like this one had begun to drop into my lap like pebbles into a pond. My life in New York had been so devoid of pleasure that when they arrived, unannounced and fleeting, I clung to them.

Shamelessly, wantonly, and without remorse.

My brow knit as two figures on the edge of the property caught my eye. Victoria stood with a tall, unfamiliar man along the cliff's edge. Her laughter floated to me on the breeze as she pressed her hand on his arm. She gestured toward the house, and her companion shielded his eyes with his hand to stare.

Perhaps he was a tourist looking for directions? But the way she had touched his arm suggested otherwise. I watched with a narrowed gaze as he pressed his cheek against hers. Another peal of laughter as he doffed his hat and set off on the cliff walk. Victoria stood, hands clutched to chest, lifting one to wave when he turned and blew her a kiss.

We both watched his departing back. Once he had disappeared from view, Victoria took the small stone steps to the gravel path that led up the hill toward me. What had she been doing along the cliff walk? And who was the man? I chewed my lip.

Lately, there had been times when she was nowhere to be found. At parties she mysteriously disappeared, reappearing later, cheeks flushed and telling stories of deep conversations in other parts of the house. She'd begun to distance herself from me. Most days she sat in the rose garden overlooking the ocean—drawing, she claimed, but there was an energy about her when she returned that made my heart flutter.

She was halfway up the path before she raised her head, her face flushing as she spotted me under the eaves.

"Hello," I called. I couldn't help the note of suspicion that colored my voice.

"Hello there. I just encountered a friend of Beebah's. He was taking a stroll along the cliff walk and thought he would call in and see if they had arrived for the season."

I nodded. "I see."

"He was most disappointed to find they were not in."

"Would a friend not know they were abroad for the summer?"

She paused, and the shifting of her expression told me everything I needed to know. A masterful liar she might be, but lying to me was like trying to lie to yourself.

"He was away himself until recently." Her gaze tangled with mine, and she offered nothing further.

I studied the layer of earth along the hem of her skirt. "Have you been sitting in the dirt?"

She laughed, a breathless sort of thing. "I couldn't help but get into the stall with Fable earlier. She's something rather special."

Her eyes shone strangely. I didn't believe her but couldn't think of a thing to say in response. She lifted and examined the book of poetry on the table, discarding it carelessly, sending a puff of air that scattered my papers.

"Who are you writing to?" She fingered Deborah's letters, huffing a breath as she read. "It seems like a lifetime ago, doesn't it?" Her voice was solemn as she placed the letters back on the table.

"Hmm," I answered. It was uncanny how often we found ourselves thinking or feeling the same things at the same time.

I studied her as she gazed out to the runoff and the men standing beside it. My chest tightened. She was separate to me, her inner workings unknowable. That was to be expected as we aged and changed, but still, the thought, now realized, burned.

When she turned to me, her expression was hard to read, the sun behind her too bright, giving her look the appearance of pity, or perhaps scorn.

"Nothing stays the same," I said, more for something to say than anything else.

"And thank God," she burst out. "Being here has made me realize how little we had. How little we knew. There is so much

MY SISTER'S SHADOW ～ 155

possibility here. It's like I've stumbled on a peach tree laden with sweet, juicy fruit, and I'm permitted to eat as much as I like."

We stared at each other for a long moment, each caught in the web of our own thoughts.

"Why shouldn't I eat the peaches?" Victoria murmured.

Her tone was like icy fingers along my spine. Before I could ask what she meant, she shook her head, breaking the moment. "Heavens, I'm parched. It's so hot already and not even lunchtime. I'm off to find something cool to drink."

She stalked toward the house, shoulders set. I glanced down toward the runoff, where Jack was now standing alone. The heat shimmered along the grass. His skin seemed to reflect the radiance of the sun. The tuneful melody of a tiny sparrow broke the stillness, and I was alone again.

The taste of peach was in my mouth.

I ran my hand along the soft leather cover of the poetry book and stuffed the letters back into their packets so hastily that both they and my pen fell to the floor. Clutching the papers and book to my chest, I started down the path toward the stables.

Jack remained standing against the low whitewashed fence, and although his gaze was trained on the horses, I couldn't help but think he was aware of my closeness as I neared.

There was something in the way he angled himself ever so slightly toward me.

"She's settling in well," he said when I was close enough to hear. "Fable?"

He nodded. "The ocean air can set some off. Not our Fable girl. It calms her. She needs another ride, though."

I swallowed hard, my mouth suddenly dry. "She does enjoy it. As do I."

There had been little opportunity for us to ride. Wiffy had been truthful when she said it was luncheon party after luncheon party here. They'd all begun to blur into one.

Since the night Jack and I had danced together, it had been all I'd thought of. The way he had moved, how his hand had felt in mine, how much I had longed to touch him.

"I wondered if you would take me again? To the promenade."

His mouth moved like he was chewing the words. "I don't think that's a good idea."

I couldn't stop the small sound of hurt that escaped my lips. "Oh." My cheeks began to heat, and I longed to turn and run, but my legs held me frozen to the spot.

Finally he turned and met my gaze. His blue eyes so bright in the sunshine. "Not because I didn't enjoy it, Adelaide. I just"—he breathed out—"don't want any trouble."

I blinked at him.

That pebble in the pond again. Everyone around me was eating their peaches, seizing pleasure where they found it. *Why shouldn't I?*

Slowly, much like when I greeted Fable the first time, I placed my hand on his, where it rested on the fence. It was as if I watched someone else, a bolder, braver woman, as she stroked her thumb along his long, tanned hand.

Without moving his head, his gaze flicked to our hands and back to the corral. A muscle pulsed at his jaw. Around us the day sizzled; crickets sang, birds called, the wind through the leaves above crashed like the ocean above us.

A long moment passed in which I became certain that I had made the worst kind of fool of myself. Then, wordlessly, he covered my hand with his and placed it against his chest. And all the while his gaze remained fixed on the horses pacing in the corral.

His heartbeat thumped unsteadily against my palm, like a horse breaking free from its reins. As if running for its life.

I was aware of nothing but him and the touch of his flesh against mine, his hand on mine, holding it to his chest. His hand was hard, rough, unbelievably soft at the same time, He swallowed hard, and I suddenly realized what the moment had cost him. That he would risk it all, his station, his position, his wages, for a single touch. My knees began to tremble as the thought clanged through my head like so many bells.

As would I.

He pressed his palm against my hand, trapping it firmly against his chest and then, placed my hand back onto the fence, his gaze fixed on the horses as if nothing had happened. But everything had changed. The rasp of the wood underneath my hand. The heat of the sun on my cheeks. The air that gusted between us. It was all different. I knew now what the poets wrote of when they wrote of love, because I had no doubt that was what moved between us now.

I gazed at him. What was he thinking? The way he held himself made me think of a man bracing for a blow.

Images flicker now when I think back. Maybe I lifted my hand and placed it on his arm, urging him to look at me, to see what shone in his eyes just as much as mine. Maybe I raised myself on tiptoes and pressed my lips against his.

Or maybe I turned and staggered back to the house, soundlessly, listening to the gravel crunch under my feet.

Maybe I found myself standing on the cool marble floor of the entrance hall, turning to find him frozen in the exact spot I'd left him, staring sightlessly into the distance.

CHAPTER 18

"Winifred," a nasal voice called, far too loudly for decorum, across the garden.

Wiffy appeared to freeze, her flaring nostrils the only sign of her displeasure.

A woman, in white brocade of satin and lace and wearing a hat so large that her neck seemed to be struggling to hold up under the weight, gave a cheery wave. A huge diamond bracelet caught the light and sent thousands of sparkles into the air.

Wiffy wiggled her fingers in response. "Nanaline Brownley. Now there's one to watch," she muttered out of the corner of her mouth.

I thought the lady in question looked harmless enough, plump cheeked and plump chested: she was attractive, if a little showy.

"Oh?"

"She has *designs*." Wiffy lowered her voice and raised her eyebrows.

"Designs on what?"

"On this, Adelaide." She twirled her hand to indicate the festivities spilling out across the lawn. "On *this*. Do you not realize?"

I gazed around. It was the day of Wiffy's famous—or infamous as she would have you believe—luncheon. Diamonds and pearls flashed around the throats and wrists of the ladies. Most of the women were terribly pale, as was the fashion, and wore identical expressions of disdain. They were beautiful, unobtainable, intimidating. From the outside it must appear impossibly glamorous, easy. But it was gilded. Scratch the surface and you'd find the same dull iron as anywhere.

The sea of expressionless faces made me think of the paper dolls Victoria and I had cut as children, the same shape over and over, the outfits the only difference. Will this one wear her diamonds at her throat or her wrist? This one will wear both. This one went with the pearls. This one curled her hair. Faces blank, hearts empty.

My thoughts turned me cold, and I shivered despite the warm breeze.

Wiffy studied me as she lit yet another cigarette, then shifted her sharp gaze to Nanaline. "Do you truly not realize? What people will do for an entrée into this world? How the privilege, the money, the diamonds"—she lifted the jewels around her neck—"are like honey to a certain type of bee."

She blew a long, thin plume of smoke into the air and cocked her head at me. "That type of bee will sting you in the back, and you'll never see it coming. Some people will do anything, anything for this kind of life—Nanny!" Wiffy broke off and kissed the air at either side of Nanaline's cheeks.

There was an awkward moment as Nanaline, clearly not expecting the second air kiss, almost collided with Wiffy's cigarette.

"The Europeans do it twice, Nanny. But I forget—you haven't been." She moved swiftly on. "I was just telling my dear friend here, Lady Stanley, about you, wasn't I?"

She shot me a wink, and I smiled despite myself. Whether interacting with bellhop or billionaire, Wiffy had never been anything but impeccably mannered. What was it about this woman that upset her so?

160 ⁀ January Gilchrist

"I do wish you wouldn't call me that, Winifred." The woman turned to me. "Nanaline Brownley. How delighted to meet you. A real-life lady." As if all the other ones she'd met had been fake.

I shook her outstretched hand. Would I ever get used to the brash American way of ladies shaking hands? "How do you do?"

"Oh my." When she smiled, her top lip almost disappeared and showed an unnerving amount of gum. "I just adore that accent, honey."

"Nanny," Wiffy scolded, "you must address her correctly. She is 'your ladyship.'"

Two bright spots appeared on Nanaline's cheeks, and her smile tightened. "Forgive me, your ladyship."

Wiffy turned to me. "You'll have to excuse our gaucheness. What you must think of us, your ladyship. I can assure you that us old knickerbockers understand the rules and regulations, but others—well . . ."

I longed to say something to ease the awkwardness that pulsed in the air, but words stuck in my throat. We stood in silence, my cheeks flaming, Nanaline stony jawed, and Wiffy puffing away on her cigarette, looking content with herself. *What has gotten into her?* I wondered.

I looked about at the party. Liveried footmen buzzed about, holding trays laden with oysters, quail eggs, and strips of meat covered in sticky-looking sauces. The food was declined by the ladies (how could one partake of finger food while wearing satin gloves?), but the men consumed one hors d'oeuvre after another, some barely pausing their conversation while they chewed. The sight of so much meat, the juices being sucked from thick fingers, turned my stomach. The champagne soured on my tongue.

I could not see Stanley, nor Victoria. All I could see were men, all appearing to be the same man from the back, as if a drawing had been repeated over and over. Black suit, bow tie, slick hair. Braying laugh, thick voice.

Nanaline stared at me with unblinking eyes. Suddenly the smell of cigar smoke made me nauseous, and I longed to be elsewhere.

I dabbed at my forehead with my wrist. "The heat is making me poorly. If you will excuse me, I must find a seat."

"Let me find you some shade." Wiffy's elbow linked through mine. "Good show, Ducky," she whispered to me as we departed. "I have no time for social climbers, and let me tell you, I can smell them a mile off."

Luckily Wiffy expected nothing from me, content as she was with the sound of her own voice. Her humorous asides amused her, so I simply nodded.

We wove through the crowd to the seats perched under the beech trees at the perimeter of the party. Away from the crush of the people, the breeze was refreshing.

The tinkle of a silver bell caused me to look to my left. Victoria stood under one of the giant beeches. The lights strung in its branches sent a golden light that flickered around her, as if a glow came from within her.

For a moment I was breathless. She was the most beautiful woman here, but it seemed as if I had never seen her before this moment. Her expression was difficult to read, even to me. She looked calm and happy but as if a tide of emotion swirled within her. I fancied I could see it skitter across her face as she smiled, in the pull of her brow as she turned to another admirer. How could a face so familiar to me appear to be that of a stranger?

She was surrounded by a cluster of men, both young and old, each one captivated as she turned her attention to him, never lingering too long on one. But she didn't seem aware of any of them. Her gaze kept slipping to her left, toward a man and woman standing slightly away from the rest of the crowd. The man's head was bent toward the woman's, hers tilted toward his. There was an intimacy in their pose that made me want to look away.

162 ❮➝ January Gilchrist

A fresh glass was pressed into my hand, and Wiffy maintained her dialogue and dissection of everyone before us.

"Who is that?" I interrupted her. "Beside the fountain?"

Wiffy's gaze slid across the guests until it landed on the couple who had now been joined by a jowl-faced woman covered in sparkling jewels. "*L'homme* is Henry Rothe. *La femme* is Ophelia Quince." She quirked a brow at me. "Debutante of the season. 'Diamond of the first water' as you lot over the pond like to say."

We watched as Henry whispered in Ophelia's ear, making her laugh and bat at his arm lightly.

"Henry is a dish, isn't he?" Wiffy said.

He was, and he was the man I had seen Victoria on the cliffside walk with.

"Terrible flirt, really—best to be avoided," Wiffy went on.

As if the man could sense our eyes on him, he turned and grinned at Wiffy. She lifted her chin and wagged a finger at him like a disapproving nanny. His gaze shifted to me and lingered along my body before coming back to my face. His smile changed. Ever so slightly. I looked away.

"What do you know about him?"

Is he a nice man? I wanted to ask. *A kind man, a loving man? Will he love my sister?* Was he responsible for the anger that burned behind her eyes? For the tightness around her mouth?

"Oh, Ducky, he's *divorced*." Wiffy whispered the last word as if it were a terminal disease.

My mouth dropped open. I had heard whispers of such a thing but had never met anyone who had undergone such a disgrace and still moved within society.

Wiffy laughed. "You looked shocked."

"I am," I admitted. "In England it is a shocking thing. Was his wife mad?" That was the only reason I could that think one would submit oneself to the horror of a divorce.

Wiffy rummaged in her bag for her cigarette case. "Mad? Presumably, when she found him in bed with the *second* nanny."

"Oh."

"When will I stop scandalizing you?" Wiffy laughed around the cigarette in her mouth.

"I meant *mad* as in 'insane,'" I said.

Wiffy narrowed her eyes at Henry. "I know you did. His daddy owns a tobacco company. Big money. The scandal sheets only managed to dig up the bare bones of that story. One doesn't need a highly active imagination, though, once one has seen him in the flesh. Handsome, but utterly unreliable. Like I said, a lovable rogue. But only lovable if you aren't *actually* in love with him, I imagine."

So, not Henry then. For us. Did Victoria know any of this about him? She mustn't or the longing looks she was sending his way would have ceased, surely?

The day stretched on, and the afternoon sun dipped into the ocean. As twilight gleamed, servants lit candles that had been hung in the trees. Just before dinner was served, Henry Rothe tapped his silver knife to his crystal glass, and with every face at the dinner party turned toward him, shattered my sister's heart.

"I am thrilled beyond belief," he announced, slowly meeting every rapt gaze except ours, "that Ophelia has lost her comprehension and agreed to marry this old reprobate."

There was an uproar of delight as Ophelia stood and was taken theatrically into Henry's arms, but it was Victoria I watched. Her face crumpled and her shoulders folded before she pushed back her chair violently. More cheers. Calls of delight. She stood, clutching her glass of wine and stared as Henry and Ophelia were air kissed and back slapped. I held my breath, an ache in my jaw betraying my clenched teeth. What would she do? The wine in her glass began to tremble along with her hand.

It felt as if a wire were tightening around my throat as I watched her press her shoulders back, dip her chin, and with one last hateful look, storm off into the gloaming shadows.

For once I chose myself and did not follow her.

164   January Gilchrist

Dinner was five courses of agony as I watched the hands of the watch pinned to my blouse circle slowly around its face.

Finally, the dinner was over, the chairs pushed back, and the tables removed. Wine flowed freely, voices rose, and the men stood to one corner of the lawn, clouded in a fugue of cigar smoke. No one would miss me.

With a pounding heart I beat a swift retreat along the stone stairs toward the ocean walk. My heart fluttered in my breast like a caged bird.

If someone saw me, found me, followed me—no, I couldn't bear to even consider it.

Despite my fear, it was impossible not to keep moving along the walk toward the stables of Fairview Court, where a flickering light called like a siren's song. Was the light flickering as Jack moved around, performing his tasks?

The thought of him and his unknown chores squeezed at my chest. What did my love do when we were not together? Did he slip into thoughts of me while he did his chores, like I did? Did his body ache with the nearness of our physical selves throughout the day, unable to share even the smallest touch in case it was intercepted? There were times when I stood next to him, longing to scream, overcome with the agony of denying my gaze, my touch.

Every day I sat in the chintzy, overstuffed chairs—so perfectly acceptable for a lady—and watched the long hand of the mantle clock make its agonizingly slow circle around its dull, blank face. The ticking lulled my mind until nothing existed except the time that stood between me and him. I ate; made the right noises; smiled; readied myself for bed; and sat, as still as an owl on a branch, listening for the quiet that told me everyone else was asleep; and then I snuck from the house. Keeping to shadows, as silent as anyone had ever been.

It was a risk, one that could end the life I was living here—I knew it. In the beginning I told myself I wouldn't take the chance, but my body found itself moving toward the stables. Finally, I stopped the pretense. I knew I would go to him. I needed to. It was beyond me. Being with him, near him, in his presence was the only time I felt alive, like I mattered, like I was real. What flowed between us was what should be between a man and his wife, not like the sham I was trapped in with Stanley.

I paused and watched him through the crack in the door.

He moved with a fluid grace that filled me with awe. His strong, muscular body was constrained by linen, denim, canvas but always, it seemed, as a concession. *"Yes,"* he seemed to say, *"I allowed myself to be dressed in these clothes, but should I change my mind, it would me little more than a moment's work to burst them at their seams."*

My chest squeezed so tightly I feared I would never be able to catch my breath again as I watched him tidy the small space. For me. It was basic, primitive almost, and yet I would have traded all the trappings of my luxurious lifestyle for it. The best moments of my entire life had been within these poorly made weatherboards. On the ground on which he stood.

The land that I had cursed from the moment my boots had stepped onto it. Perhaps from the very moment Stanley had spoken the words *New York* in the dining room at Harewood.

Who would have thought I would now be so thankful for the complex series of events that had transpired to lead me to this place. For him and me to stand right here.

How very thankful I was.

I had found for myself a love I couldn't have imagined, not in my wildest dreams. I had resigned myself to an insignificant life, an empty life, waiting, playing small, staying in the shadows.

The man inside paused, his whole body coiled, and a thrill coursed through me. Turning slowly, he moved toward the door on noiseless feet. He knew whom he was expecting at his door, and he knew, too well, that he prayed he would never find me there. For all our sakes.

166 ◦   January Gilchrist

I ran my hand down the rough wood of the door, widening the crack, allowing him to see me.

Our eyes met and all those words nice girls didn't speak, all the things we should never do and would do tonight, flashed through my mind. I stepped into the light, pulling the door closed behind me. He reached behind me to lower the plank of rough-hewn wood that acted as the lock, bringing a tornado of sensations on me as his scent—leather, lemon, horse, fresh sweat—assailed me.

My skin skittered, tingled, fizzed with longing for him. How I loved this man. Almost to the point of madness.

My hands lifted to his face, framing it, his perfect, beautiful face, and I stared deeply at him, trying to catalog every inch of him. The lightened crow's feet that fanned from the corners of his eyes. The flecks of gold in his irises. Long black lashes. Those eyes searched mine, as if questioning my solemn mood.

"How was Wiffy's party? Any scandalous happenings?" he asked.

I swallowed. I didn't want to bring the real world in here with us. Here was sacred. Victoria could wait. "It was fine. Same as every other party."

He widened his eyes in mock horror. "I won't tell Wiffy you said that," he declared with a smile. "She'll be inconsolable." The smile faded as he looked into my eyes. "What is it? What's wrong?"

I had nothing I could tell him with words: a proclamation of love was useless here. No, between these walls love was shown, love was felt, love was in the tenderness of his strong, work-roughened hands, in how he looked at me, touched me, spoke to me.

Love was shown in the way I sobbed his name into his shoulder as stars crashed around us, setting the world ablaze.

I pressed my toes into the earth, raising my lips to his. There was moment of hesitation, as if he too couldn't believe this was real, before he crushed his lips to mine.

But it was real. It was the realest thing in my life.

MY SISTER'S SHADOW ⌖ 167

His hands were in my hair, his mouth against mine, but in my mind, all I heard was the cool, dark voice of the real world, never quite out of sight.

"This will end badly," it whispered. The only way this could end was badly. I rested my head on Jack's shoulder and listened to him breathe. A solitary tear seeped from the corner of my eye, dampening his shirt. Our breath matched each other's perfectly, his chest rising and falling in time with mine.

And then, as I always seemed to, I ruined our perfect moment. "I love you."

He said nothing. He didn't need to. His whole body tensed, as if to ward off a blow. My hand stilled on his chest as his breath caught somewhere deep.

The clock on the wall ticked out the minutes of my life as we lay there in silence. The damp air wrapped around me in the dying light.

I could hear the wind, the crash of waves against the rocks outside, the rasp of his breath.

I could not hear his returned words, because there were none.

I spoke again. 'You mightn't like it when I say that, but it's true. I do.'

He stepped away from me, My heart felt like it was caught in a trap. A snap I hadn't been expecting and a searing agony that no movement could still.

The words hung in the air around us, and I longed to take them back.

'You think I don't like it when you say that?' he asked. 'I like it too much. There is nothing better than hearing you say those words. I savor those words. To keep me company when this all ends.'

Heat burned behind my eyelids.

'What if it didn't have to end?' My mouth was dry.

Jack shook his head. 'I have nothing to offer you. That dress you wear costs more than I make in a month. Maybe in a year. What do I have to offer you?'

What of love? Of laughter? Safety? Did that not matter? Was that nothing? Perhaps to some, but it was everything to me.

I ran my hand along my arms to ward of the chill that had overcome me.

"I don't need anything but you," I managed to say.

He laughed but it was an awful choking sound. "And when we can't pay the bills? Or it's bread for dinner *again*. What then?"

"I have jewelry. Dresses. Things I can sell. It would keep us."

He shook his head. "It isn't enough. You don't know how hard it is. This is . . ." He shook his head again, and I closed my eyes. My heart had risen in my chest, too full, too high for me to speak.

A minute passed, then maybe two. I thought of how I had pleaded with Jones all those months ago. "You could work with horses on a ranch. Somewhere they'll never find us. New names. New lives. I'll cook, clean, sew, *anything*. I don't care what I do as long as I'm with you."

"You think them in there are just going to let you go?" He jerked his head toward the house.

No. *Them in there* would never let me go. That much I knew. I knew very little of what a real life required, but I knew anything was better than this half life of hiding and denial.

"You deserve better than what I can give you." He didn't meet my gaze. "You deserve silks and expensive dresses, breakfast in bed. Not working your fingers red, worrying about where the next meal is coming from and how you're going to make it last. This life isn't easy."

Tears prickled behind my eyes, hot and fast. I had expensive dresses and silks and carts, and I didn't want any of it.

I slid my palms along the smooth, flat planes of his back and pressed my lips to the hollow at his neck. 'I deserve this. Please take me away from here,' I murmured against his skin.

How beautiful his gaze made me feel, the truth in his touch, the honesty in the way our bodies moved together; how safe when his strong hands touched me, hands that could smash, wrench, and break me, but instead caressed as lightly as a butterfly on a flower, as if he could memorize every part of me through his palms.

He turned to me then, his eyes blazing with something I had no name for.

'What am I supposed to do? When you talk like that, kiss me like that?' he asked. There was a tilt to his lips, but his eyes were dark.

I smiled widely. I didn't know much, but I knew the answer to that question. 'Kiss me.'

And he did.

CHAPTER 19

The dining room was silent when I entered. I had been summoned for luncheon with my husband. He'd left for New York on urgent business three weeks ago, leaving and returning without word. My heart lurched unpleasantly when I noticed him sitting at one end of the vast table. His absence had made it easy to pretend he'd been nothing but a dream. But he was not, and he was back. One leg was crossed over the other, and his shoe caught the light as he jiggled his foot. Nothing except his hands was visible, the rest of him hidden behind the newspaper. He didn't move the paper to see who entered. Perhaps he already knew it was me. It was more likely he didn't care.

I touched a tender spot on my wrist. "Good morning, Lord Stanley."

He grunted a response from behind the newspaper.

I helped myself to the sliced fruit laid on the sideboard, overturned pot lids covering them to save them from the ever-present flies. The air in the room was stifling and thick already, and regardless of the early hour, the fruit was already overripe, its scent sickly.

I sat in the chair across from Stanley, with the best view out to the garden. A swallow dipped and dived in the sky, utterly free to do as it pleased. More and more lately, it was all I noticed. The

MY SISTER'S SHADOW ☞ 171

freedom around me. Stanley's absence had sharpened the blade that pressed against me, and I glimpsed flashes of a life I could lead were I brave enough.

Stanley flipped the top of the newspaper down and stared at me, his small eyes hard and dark in the light room.

"Did you fall down twelve steps at the Malibu?"

I blinked. My mind cranked like a piece of rusted machinery starting up, turning over lie after lie. Had I been anywhere near the Malibu? Had I been anywhere that someone could have seen me and reported back to Stanley?

"It's an easy answer." Stanley barked. "Yes or no."

I shook my head. My shoulders crept up, but I tried to smile. "No. What a peculiar question, Stanley. Whyever would you ask me such a thing?"

He rustled the paper. "There is an article." The paper moved again, and his face was hidden. I released my breath.

Any relaxation I may have enjoyed was decimated when he began to read aloud.

"Poor Mrs. Rex Leeper, whose charity luncheon to raise money for the education of the Indigenous population, was disturbed by a lady causing a commotion at the stairs at the Malibu, where Mrs. Leeper, who is kinder than most, felt it was perhaps the heat that caused our English rose to wilt and fall down the steps. This isn't the first sighting of strange behavior from this lady. Perhaps she should go easy on those highballs."

Stanley folded the paper along its crease, placing it with measured care on the table next to his plate. My eyelids fluttered. There was something barely restrained about his movements, an anger he was working to repress. I calculated the distance between us, my gaze darting to the door. Where were all the servants? Why was the house, usually so full of activity, as silent as a tomb now?

172 ☙ January Gilchrist

Laying the neat parcel of paper on the table next to his plate, he reached into his pocket and pulled out a cigar. He tapped it against the table twice, holding my gaze before striking a march and lighting it, right there at the table. An act of such aggressive incivility that I took it exactly as it was meant.

First shot fired.

"It sounds to me like someone is accusing my wife of being intoxicated. Does it sound like that to you?" His tone was as hard as his gaze.

The words that followed in the aftermath—I think about these words even now. Had I spoken with more care, had I chosen a different path, where would we have ended up? Why didn't I say, "That wasn't me, Stanley; it was Victoria." All useless thoughts, of course.

I dabbed at my mouth with the soft-as-silk napkin and moved it to my lap, out of view, where I wrung it like it had done me wrong.

"Stanley." His name caught in my throat, and I paused to clear it. "I am worried about Victoria. She is not adjusting to America as well as we had hoped."

He stared at me, terrifying in his silence.

"What are you trying to say?"

I strangled the napkin in my lap. "I think it may be time to send her home. Back to England."

I had thought then that I was canny. That I'd be free to leave Stanley if I sent Victoria home. Since Wiffy's party and Henry's engagement announcement, Victoria had become a ghost. I had expected fury, but there was a stillness to her that unnerved me. She had rebuffed any attempt to discuss Henry with a brittle laugh and mocking insults. How dull and unimaginative I was to imagine she cared one jot for Henry Rothe. *"Pathetic,"* she'd said. It was unclear whom that barb was aimed at, perhaps both Henry and me. But the air around her was electric, unnerving, like the crackle of energy before a storm.

MY SISTER'S SHADOW   173

Stanley said nothing, just stared at me for a long moment. I returned my gaze to the browning fruit on my plate, considering what inane comment to make next.

An exhalation of air was thrust from me as his fist connected with the side of my face. A hot stab of pain shot down my neck as my head jolted. Swirling bright lights flashed in my vision. I cradled my hot cheek, my breath tearing from me in ragged gusts. The taste of metal in my mouth. I blinked at my plate, not daring to move.

"Don't you dare embarrass me."

We sat without speaking for the remainder of the meal. Not a companionable, easy silence, but one where hatred swelled and swirled between us, thickening the air until any words we might have said were swallowed whole. I had never hated Stanley as much as I did in that moment. I needed to be free of him. No matter what it cost me, I would be, I vowed.

* * *

I went straight to the stables after Stanley hit me, stumbling as if I were drunk. The shock held me together, but as soon as I saw Jack, I collapsed on the ground. That, more than any of my pleading and begging, was enough to make the decision for him.

We *would* leave together. As soon as we could.

I had bought Victoria a return ticket to England, and once she was safe and gone, I would leave Stanley and start my new life with Jack.

I entered my ensuite bathroom, rubbing the soft bar of soap across my hands, I thought of the earlier conversation I'd had with Jack about the train we were going to take across the country to California, where he would find a ranch, and we would live together as man and wife.

The click of a door sounded. I cocked my head. Tell-tale sounds of movement came from the other room.

"Hello?"

174 January Gilchrist

Still no answer. I rushed to the door and pulled it open.

I let out a shriek at the sight of Victoria standing at my desk. "Vivi, you gave me a fright."

She didn't reply. The curtains of the window behind the desk were parted, and through the crack the boat ticket bearing her name glowed with a malevolent light. Her face was gray, and her jaw was set in a way that caused me to shiver.

Blood roared in my ears, sounding just like a river.

"Let me explain," I started.

She rounded on me, her gaze black with fury, and I rushed to speak.

"Jack. Jack and I. Stanley is . . . he isn't . . ."

"You make me sick."

I recoiled at the venom in her voice. "Vivi?"

"I know what you were doing down there. In the stables. With Jack."

"Vivi." I licked my lips. Her anger was fearsome. "We're in love. I'm leaving Stanley with—*for*—Jack. And Stanley . . ." I shook my head.

I closed my eyes, unable to bear the feeling of speaking the words aloud. To dream was one thing, to say it aloud made it real. "He is a bully and a tyrant. Being married to him is like living in manacles that slowly tighten."

I am a dreamer—I've heard that from her too many times to count. And I dreamed again now. In this dream, I told my sister that I was afraid, that I needed her help, that I needed someone to look out for me, and for once she put her feelings aside and gave me what I needed.

When I opened my eyes, it was clear my dream would remain exactly that: a fantasy.

Victoria stood with her arms crossed tightly across her chest, the familiar cruel lift to her lip.

"Stanley will kill you both when I tell him." A humorless satisfaction sharpened her tone.

My Sister's Shadow ⬠ 175

When she told him.

"Why should you get everything you want, Adelaide?" she hissed. A spray of spittle landed on my cheek.

A sound of disbelief shot from my lips. Get everything I want? I had nothing. I had given up everything—no, I had been forced to leave everything I had ever loved behind. I had done what I was told and married a man who had uprooted me from my life without a moment's discussion, and who, like my father, ignored me.

From birth, my entire life had revolved around keeping Victoria happy, but she in turn had never considered my feelings.

"You are selfish. Always taking things from me. I cannot even have my own birthday! You must share in that too."

As if these were things I had designed?

"I share my birthday with you too," I said weakly, but Victoria didn't hear me.

"It is *I* who should be Lady Stanley, not you. The party invitations should have *my* name on them. Instead, I am relegated to a plus one, not even named most of the time. I have become invisible."

Invisible like the storming wind as it lifts roof tiles and topples trees, I think.

"You disgust me. Jack? How the mighty fall. From lady to stableman's mistress."

I smiled joylessly. The thing about a sister, about a twin, is that you know exactly where her soft spot is. On which to lay your head or sink your blade. Sisterhood too often felt like a flurry of blows followed by lips to brow.

Not this time.

Suddenly I could envision myself lunging for her. Grabbing at her hair and forcing her to the floor. We hadn't fought much as children, but when we had, Victoria had always emerged triumphant. Always more willing than I to truly cause pain. Even in a lake of anger my love for her had shimmered at the bottom, catching the sun's rays and reflecting it back to me.

176 ⮌   January Gilchrist

But for a moment my fingertips tingled with the urge to reach for her, to hurt her in all the ways she hurt me.

"Yes, Jack," I spit out. "The man you want for yourself. But he doesn't want you. Just like Henry doesn't."

Her face contorted, and for a moment I was truly frightened and regretted my words. But she didn't lunge for me.

"You cannot leave me," Victoria warned.

A noise I didn't recognize came from me. A hollow, bitter laugh. "You no longer can tell me what to do, sister."

Victoria's eyes narrowed, her lip curled. She adjusted her chin slightly and stared at me as if lining me up down the barrel of a gun. "You belong to me."

For the first time I saw her for what she truly was: a spoiled, selfish child. "No. I belong to myself. As much as it pains us both, I am Lady Stanley. And I believe it is time for you to return home to England. I have concerns you are not coping with the change of climate."

Her forehead furrowed, and emotions flitted across her face. I watched carefully for the tell-tale sign that a victory, no matter how small, was mine.

Victoria turned on me then, her eyes flashing. "Because the pious and well-mannered Lady Stanley says so? Well, I am sick and tired of living in the shadow of your perfect self-righteousness. I am tired of always been held up against you and being found lacking."

It was so like Victoria to twist things, to make herself the victim. I had offered her the chance to have this life, to take my place as Stanley's wife, to let me remain in England, but she had refused. She was the one who had decided to follow along, who had said I needed her, that I couldn't make it without her.

A hot molten liquid swirled inside me, but I swallowed it down. Perhaps it wasn't too late for us, if only she understood what this meant for me. Surely she would give me what I needed. We had loved each other, after all, and certainly we still did.

MY SISTER'S SHADOW ⟡ 177

"Please," I urged, "I have spent a lifetime staying silent, being gentle, denying myself. Over and over again until there was barely anything left of me. "My voice cracked as it rose. "Don't I deserve happiness?"

"What would you know of unhappiness?" Her tone was scornful, mocking.

That hurt more than any of her cruelty. That my unhappiness, my sacrifices had gone completely unnoticed. None of it touched her.

Or if it had, it was only in the manner that related to her life. Her selfishness was such an ugly thing that I wondered how I'd never seen it before. She only knew how to take.

If I were loved in return, I thought, *I might have been able to keep walking this path, treading carefully, picking my way through the dust and debris left behind Victoria and her reckless, thoughtless actions.* I could have remained dutiful to Stanley when he demanded and seized and snatched and hurt. I would have done it all if I had believed that for a moment, I was loved back as much as I had loved.

I wanted to howl with the unfairness of it all. "Please. I am leaving, Vivi. But I can't leave with you here. With *him.*"

"You are abandoning me?"

"I am going with Jack. I can't stay here. Living this empty, half life. Please, take the ticket and go home. Back to Harewood."

She snatched the ticket from the desk and tore it in two. A frightening madness hovered around the edges of her, and in that moment she was a stranger.

Once, we hadn't needed words to speak. A raised brow, a widened eye, a tic, a twitch. I understood all of her feelings, sometimes before she knew them herself. But looking at her now, she was a someone I did not know.

Or perhaps I finally saw the truth of her.

And it horrified me.

CHAPTER 20

I stepped outside into the sunshine and made my way down to the stables. The day was already so bright it hurt my eyes. The ocean was a shifting blanket of teal and aqua, but I spared it little more than a glance. There was one thought in my mind only. The stables. Jack. Fable. This was to be my last morning with her. Jack had booked the tickets, and tomorrow morning the suitcase hidden under my bed would be sent on to Newport Station on the grocery cart. Jack and I would follow mid-morning, separately. We were leaving. Together.

The gravel was loud under my feet, and the roses nodded their heads in the light breeze as if in encouragement. *"Go on,"* they said. *"Faster. Today is a day of wonder."*

He was shoveling hay from a barrow into the stalls when I arrived. He turned to me as soon as I appeared around the door.

"How do you do that?" I asked.

He leaned against his shovel and wiped the sleeve of his shirt across his forehead. "What's that?"

"You seem to know I'm coming before I appear."

We stared at each other a long moment. My heart was in my throat. How I loved this man. Finally he smiled, "My soul knows where you are. Every moment of the day."

My Sister's Shadow   179

I closed the gap between us and stood so close that only the finest piece of gossamer would fit between us.

"Does it?"

"Yes." His hand cupped the back of my neck, and he pulled me against him. "My body vibrates whenever you get near," he murmured against my lips. "Like a tremor before an earthquake."

My legs turned to liquid, and I was grateful he was holding me because I was certain to fall.

His lips were so close to mine, but not close enough. I crushed my mouth against his, kissing him with a ferocity that used to surprise me. But not anymore. Now I knew to expect the surge of feeling that almost washes me off my feet the very moment he touches me, how to clutch at his shirt to keep myself upright, how my skin will sing as he caresses it. How completely undone I am when his tongue meets mine; how time seems to still, then stop, only restarting once I leave his company. Hours were lost while in this man's orbit, and I would stumble from the stables, punch-drunk on love.

I am amazed that no one warned me what a man's hands can do.

★ ★ ★

My boots tapped a steady rhythm along the marble of the entrance to Fairview Court. My thighs groaned as I pulled myself up the stairs. Jack and I had said goodbye to Fable with a ride alongside the cliff top that had taken us all the way to Easton Beach. We had galloped; the wind in our hair, happy in our knowledge that this was to be our last ride. There hadn't been hours of tears as there had been with Hera. This time I was leaving for somewhere I wanted to be. And Fable would go back to Wiffy, my friend Wiffy, whom I could not say goodbye to, but who would, I think, understand. Instead of a thick dread lapping at my feet, it felt as if springs had been installed in my heels. I wanted to run, to spin, to

180 January Gilchrist

sing at the top of my voice. The muscles of my face ached from working to keep the smile from my face. For the first time in my life, I had made a decision based on what *I* wanted.

The house was still, as if it too were dozing in the soporific heat. I felt both as parched as a desert and strangely liquid. My body ached with the exertion of the day, and although I was exhausted, I was exhilarated too. My heels echoed through the hall, but I saw no one as I made my way through the house to my rooms.

My stomach growled. I would call up immediately for a cold luncheon in my room. I hadn't seen Victoria since our argument, and the anger caused by it still burned within me. She had torn up the ticket, but I would purchase another once I'd sold my wedding band, and post it to her. She would see sense. She had to. It was time for us both to stand on our own feet.

As I reached for the door handle I caught sight of my hands. They were covered in a thick dust, and angry red stripes marked my wrists from gripping the reins for so long.

But here, in Newport, I was free to bathe when I deemed fit, and the idea of filling a bath with cool, rose-scented water was enough to override my hunger. Here, brass taps pumped freshly heated water on demand. There was no need to wait or request, and the unimaginable freedom of simply turning on a tap and enjoying a bath was mine. I couldn't resist.

The windows of the bedroom had been thrown open to the ocean, and the sheer curtains billowed in welcome as I entered. I stopped for a moment, my hand pressed to my breast, breathless with gratitude. This view was as awe-inspiring to me as it had been on the first day. To leave here would be a heartache, but what lay ahead of me promised far greater joy.

Brushing a smear of dirt from my cheek, I turned on the tap and ran my hands under the steady stream, listening to the thunks and groans of the waking pipes. The water spat, as if angry to have been woken, and was clouded with a sickly yellow tinge. I

MY SISTER'S SHADOW ⟜ 181

waited as it slowly cleared itself. Taking my time, I languidly dipped my wrists, letting the cool water refresh my aching hands.

A bar of fragrant soap sat on a tray beside the sink. It had dried and cracked along the sides, perhaps because of the heat. I doused it under the stream of water to refresh it and rubbed it between my hands vigorously. I thought idly about lunch. Should I call for it before my bath and have Jeanie leave it for me in my room.

Suddenly, a hot piercing pain shot through my palms. The room spun. Someone cried out. Noise roared in my ears. As if watching a picture reel, I saw a red-streaked bar of soap drop into the sink, and pink bubbles circle the drain.

So much blood. Where was it coming from?

As soon as the water sluiced it away, more of it appeared. I lifted my hands. Rivers of blood ran along my wrists, pooling into my elbows. Two slashes of bright red flesh appeared on my palms. My breath, frozen, restarted in a grating wheeze.

My mind couldn't make sense of what it saw.

A narrow sliver of light glinted in the sunlight that crept through the frosted window. I leaned closer.

There was a shard of glass in my soap.

My vision swam and my mouth began to water. There were two shards of glass on either side of the soap, pushed deep, the edges of them glimmering ominously. This was no accident.

I leaned into the bath and, with a wrenching of my guts, vomited.

Agony arrived so violently that I howled, an animalistic noise torn from deep within me.

Thousands of stars flickered in my gaze. The roaring noise in my head began to swell and push at me. I swayed like I was back on the *Orient*. Like I was standing at the bow, looking down into the foamy waves crashing against the gargantuan iron boat.

It was a long drop to the gray ocean below.

Too far in the end.

I collapsed onto the floor.

CHAPTER 21

There was a droning sound in my ears, a senseless humming, tuneless but melodic at the same time. I wasn't woken by it, but rather nudged into that delicious cloudy interval between awake and asleep. The space where your dreams were as close as reality.

I floated like a leaf on a lake. The noise grew louder and became more discordant. I sucked in a breath, and a wave of nausea hit me. It choked me, and I sat, gagging on the pain that crawled through my hands.

I was in the formal sitting room on the west side of the house, with its uninterrupted view of the ocean, designed to awe and impress visitors. I was on a stiff-backed chaise lounge. There were people speaking behind me, Victoria and a man whose voice I didn't recognize. Not Stanley.

My hands felt thick and heavy, and ached. Oh, how they ached. I looked down, horrified to find they were swaddled in bandages and looked like a pugilist's gloves.

I struggled to sit, and Victoria appeared in my view. Wordlessly, she pressed a hand to my shoulder and urged me back into a prone position.

A black-suited and stony-faced man walked into view. "Can you hear me?"

I nodded, confused. What a strange question. It was my hands that hurt, not my head.

"You've had a rather nasty"—he hesitated, as if searching for the correct word—"accident. I've given you something to alleviate the pain. You've hurt your hands—do you understand?" He was speaking loudly, slowly.

My throat was so dry that I couldn't swallow. My jaw was working, but the dryness remained.

"The pain relief should help make you more comfortable and keep you calm." He frowned at me over the rim of his glasses. My thoughts were thick and cloudy, and there was some trouble with my eyes. They kept rolling back into my head, closing no matter how desperately I tried to keep them open. I widened my lids, trying to force my eyes to focus, but it didn't work. I gave up and left my eyes closed. My stomach rolled, and I sucked in deep breaths to stave off the vomit that was rising.

I could hear them all speaking, but the words sounded muffled, as though they were spoken furtively and from far away.

"I will leave this bottle here with you, but you must keep it out of reach. One spoonful and only when the pain is too bad to manage."

"Thank you, Doctor." The gray fog moved in around me. "What if she tries again?"

The mist rolled over me, and I slipped into unconsciousness.

* * *

"Addy." Victoria's voice was at my ear. "Addy."

A hand on my shoulder jostled me awake.

My eyes met hers. She smiled and despite the pain, I smiled too.

She has forgiven me; my sister has returned to me.

"Addy, what on earth? You have taken years from me with the terror. Jeanie was screaming the house down, and when I walked into that bathroom and saw you on the floor like that, I don't mind telling you, I feared you dead."

My hands were throbbing balls of agony. They burned as if the bandages were fire.

Victoria peered at me. "What happened? Do you remember?"

Images flashed in my mind. Crimson foam, a trail of blood. The glint of the thin edge of glass.

The soap!

I sat upright and reached out to Victoria with monstrously misshapen hands. A look of disgust flickered across her face. Fleeting, but I still caught it.

The room was empty save for the two of us. The curtains billowed out and drifted down rhythmically, as if we were in the lungs of the house.

My breath came in short sharp bursts, and hot beads of sweat dampened my face. Who had done this to me?

"Vivi." My voice was a low rasp, my throat still dry. "Someone put glass in my soap."

Her face was expressionless, and for a moment I wondered if she didn't hear me. I had expected her to jump up, demand to see it, scream for answers, but she stared at me with a carefully blank expression.

"Vivi? Did you hear me?"

Her brow knit and she frowned. But it was all wrong. It was the frown of an indulgent nanny, disinterested friend, a doubting sister.

"I think the pain relief Dr. Mortimer gave you has made you muddled."

She was up and bustling across the room before I could say more, talking, talking incessantly. She reappeared with a spoon of foul-smelling liquid.

"You're in pain. Confused. This will help."

I opened my mouth to recount what I remembered, and she slid the spoon between my open lips. Her other hand came to my

MY SISTER'S SHADOW ⟶ 185

face, her fingers digging into the soft space where my jaw met my ears. Her hand was strong and forced my head back until I swallowed that liquid on her spoon.

"That will make you feel better." She drew the blanket up to my chin. It felt heavy on my throat, and I reached for it, but my hands were too clunky. The blanket felt as if it was tightening, constricting my already labored breathing. My mouth worked, but all that came out was a garbled noise.

"There, there, sleep now."

A warmth flooded my body, starting at my throat and following the path of the medicine. It unfurled its tentacles out, out, out until I was overcome with the desire to sleep.

But I mustn't. There was something I needed to tell Victoria. The idea faded, dipping in and out, and the urgency seeped from me. I worked to keep it in my mind. It was important. I couldn't remember what it was. I forced my eyes open to search for her. Her eyes were small gray pools which reminded me of the lake at Harewood in the dead of winter. The surface reflected the dim winter light, but the depths shrouded the unknown horrors we believed lurked below the water's edge.

I shuddered, closed my eyes, and slept.

* * *

When I woke again, the pain had caught up with me. It pulsed through my hands. My throat was dry, and my head pounded with a ferocity that made me wonder if it too had been damaged. I was drenched in sweat and overheated. The blinds were open, and the afternoon sun cast an eerie glow into the room. I pressed my face to the balding velveteen to remind myself I was awake.

There was a hushed, shuffling sound behind me, and I called out. "Vivi?"

"It's just me, my lady. Jeanie." Jeanie's large eyes appeared in my vision, but she danced and swayed. Why wouldn't the girl stand still?

186 January Gilchrist

Her face again. A tiny furrow between her brows. "Are you feeling well?" She darted a glance at the door and then back to me. "They're saying . . . It's too awful for words. You wouldn't, would you, my lady?"

I struggled to understand. I wouldn't what? Who was 'they'?

"What do you mean?" I managed to croak out.

"They're saying you were seen digging the flower beds and yelling at passersby at Brenton Park before coming home and cutting yourself. But I know it weren't you. It can't have been."

She straightened. "I'll fetch her for you," she said, as though we were mid-conversation. "Oh, look. Here she is. She's just waking now, miss. I was just coming to fetch you."

Jeanie rushed through her speech, dipped into a small curtsey, and then was gone, replaced by the face of my sister. "How are you feeling?" Her cool hand stroked my hair, tested my forehead, her eyes probing.

"Thirsty."

She handed me a glass of water from the table, and it wasn't until I reached for it with my bandaged hands that we both realized I could not hold it. A burst of laughter erupted between us, and the pressure in my chest eased. Victoria had been angry, but she was still my sister. She would take care of me.

While Victoria held the glass against my lips, I tilted my head, and the liquid washed away the rancid taste that coated my mouth.

I struggled to sit against the stiff arm of the couch while Victoria placed the cup back on the table. "Vivi."

"Hmm." She didn't turn around.

"What happened?" I asked her.

She kept her back to me. "You don't remember?"

I didn't really. My head felt stuffed with down. The medicine she was feeding me left me feeling dizzy and queer.

I shook my head, and she peered at me. "No one knows. Jeanie found you passed out in the bathroom, covered in blood."

It came rushing back to me with a force that took my breath away. "Vivi, there was something in the soap. Someone put something in the soap. Glass."

Her expression was painfully indulgent. "Who would do such a thing?"

Silence. Images of the crimson liquid circling the drain flashed through my mind, and I lay back, woozy.

"There was a shard of glass in the soap. Send someone up to look," I said again, weaker this time.

"I had the servants search the bathroom."

"And?"

She fussed with the pillows behind my back, tucked the blanket around my legs firmly before finally meeting my eyes.

"There was a shard of glass. But it was on the side of the basin. Not in the soap."

How could she respond so casually? Someone had hurt me, badly, with intent.

"Vivi, you believe me, don't you? How else could this have happened?"

She heaved a great sigh and sat on the couch. I felt as if I was on the little wooden sailboat we used to float along the surface of the lake at Harewood, and she had just launched me off. Alone.

"If you say that is what happened then, of course, I believe you. But, Addy, tell me honestly. Are you well? In yourself. You've been behaving so unlike yourself lately. That ugliness about returning to England. And now this."

She folded my padded hand into hers. "Let us get you into your suites, and you can have a proper rest."

Victoria whipped the blanket from my legs and had her shoulder under my arm, hoisting me from the couch before I had a chance to get my bearings. Her strength was discomforting. Her touch, once as familiar to me as my own, was now a stranger's. We limped up the stairs like some strange, three-legged monster. We paused, as we always did, when we reached the spot on the landing whereby some trick, the setting sun was visible from every window, washing the landing with golden light. With just as much heat as at midday, the sun took an age to sink low into the Atlantic. The breeze was soft and warm, and as soon as we reached the door, it was like all that had happened downstairs was little more than a bad dream. The floor rocked and tipped beneath me, and I barely made it to the bed before my legs collapsed under me.

Victoria started to croon the folklore song that Jones used to sing to us. The words, foreign and nonsensical, washed over me as my lids dragged closed.

Sleep, child, there's nothing here,
Nothing to give you fright.

I wrenched my eyes open, fighting against the dreamless sleep of the drugged, and there was Victoria, standing over my bed with eyes as pitch as night, a strange half smile on her face, and for a moment I felt a fear so strong I began to shake.

Then the world went black.

* * *

A whine cut through my dreamless half slumber. I was awake but not quite, alive but also not quite. The dull ache in my lower back told me I had been lying in the same position for quite some time, but moving seemed an impossible feat. My arms and legs were leaden. The heat from my hands radiated along my arms, not pain—the drugs had taken care of that—but a buzzing kind of energy.

The whine grew louder and louder, twanging a string of my memory. A tractor perhaps, tilling the grounds. The breeze that skated along my skin was warm enough. But no, I wasn't at Harewood. The scent of the room came to me, a sharp, acidic tang on the breeze.

The rasp of breath razored through the air. I paused, listening. Was someone in the room with me? I fought my way through the fugue, but it was like crawling through molasses such was the effort required.

A door banged somewhere in the house; footsteps followed. The whine ceased. The sound of gravel. It was a car. The fog lifted and memories swarmed over me.

My hands. Newport. Victoria.

My eyes sprang open. The red and gold damask fabric above my bed came into focus. I was still in Newport, in the room overlooking the ocean and the driveway, with its gravel turning circle. There was someone here. In a car.

"Hello." A disembodied voice floated through my window.

Wiffy.

Images fell like dominoes: cold hands forcing my mouth open, spoonful after spoonful of the bitter medicine I had come to dread, the occasional word from Victoria, but those eyes, that look, the last time I had seen her. Something was terribly wrong.

I needed to get to Wiffy before Victoria did. I needed Wiffy to look at this situation and tell me in that direct way of hers what on earth was going on.

I imagined I could see her peering at me though the blue cigarette haze that followed her everywhere. She inhaled and tsked as she stared at me. "Oh, completely crackers, Ducky. You've lost it, as they say."

I rolled to my side with a groan, and my back screamed. How long had I been in bed?

Panting hard, with beads of sweat breaking out along my hairline, I scrambled out from under the bed covers. They twisted and coiled around my legs; my hands fought against them uselessly. They were nothing more than batons on the end of my arms. The bandages were wound so tight I couldn't move a finger. Pain shot through my hands as I used them to lever myself from the bed. A shriek, little more than a squeak, cut through my dry, peeling lips. I needed to get to Wiffy.

The floor was hard and cold under my bare feet. I could hear the murmur of voices below, not loud enough to make out any of the words, but loud enough to tell there were two voices.

I would recognize one of them underwater.

Victoria.

I lurched toward the door, my feet stumbling along the rug, my legs trembling from disuse, and I fell to the door. I pressed down on the handle with my elbow. It didn't budge. I bent and pushed harder, putting all my weight into the lever. Nothing happened.

"Hello," I called through the crack of the door.

Panic blinding me to any pain it might cause, I banged against the door. "Hello?"

I pressed my ear against the wood but heard nothing.

"Can anyone hear me?"

I thumped again on the door, pain hammering through my hands. The house was gargantuan but teeming with servants. Where was everyone? Surely someone would hear me and let me out. Why wouldn't the door open? I jiggled the handle.

It was locked. Someone had locked the door. The drugs had rendered me slow, but once the thought appeared, I couldn't shake it.

Had I been locked in, or had someone been locked out?

I leaned my elbow against the servants' bell, the metal biting into my skin painfully, but there was no familiar click or whirr that told me the bell was ringing. I pressed harder. Still no sound.

It had been disconnected.

The drone of Wiffy's car restarting sliced through the afternoon air.

No.

I sucked in air as my heart thundered. I had to get to her before she left. The exertion of moving after so many days lying

My Sister's Shadow

invalid overcame me, and the floor began to buck wildly under my feet. Darkness blurred the edges of my vision. I dropped to my knees and fought against the blackness that began to close around me. The noise of the motor whirred as I lay my cheek against the cool floor.

It was the last thing I heard before I surrendered to the dark.

* * *

Jeanie's scream woke me. Actually, the sound of glass shattering on the floor woke me. When she'd opened to door to find me lying in the center of the room, she had dropped on the floor the tray of medicine and glass of water she was carrying. It wasn't until I groaned that she had screamed.

Her eyes were wild and terrible, and she was turned toward the door as if moments away from taking flight.

"Help me," I croaked.

She rushed toward me, kneeling without regard among the debris on the floor.

"I thought you were dead," she exclaimed.

"Not quite yet," I managed with a rueful smile.

Her hands were warm on my skin as she tried to lift me to a sitting position. A terrible fear rose in me, and I began to tremble.

"I need you to send a message to Jack. In the stables." My words rushed out in a jumble.

Her eyes were wide, and she nodded insistently.

"You must only give this message to Jack. No one else. Promise me." I tried to clutch at her, but the bandages wouldn't allow it. There had to be no doubt as to the urgency of this message.

"Yes. I will. I promise. Only, my lady, I don't know who Jack is."

You'll know him, I wanted to say. Sunshine sparks from his skin. To look at his eyes, as blue as the sky that stretches forever across the Atlantic, was to look into the future. His smile held all the secrets of the universe.

192   January Gilchrist

"Tall," I croaked. "He's tall."

Her head bobbed again, like she was a marionette controlled by a shaking master.

"He came with us. From New York. He'll be at the stables."

"Yes, yes. I'll find him."

"Tell him—"

The door banged against the wall with a shudder. "What on earth is going on in here?"

I held Jeanie's gaze. "It's still on. No matter what, it's all still on."

"What's that?" Victoria's face appeared over Jeanie's shoulder.

She elbowed Jeanie out of the way and took her place at my side. Her hand was cool when it pressed my forehead.

"You're burning up. Get the medicine and get this mess cleaned up," Victoria ordered.

Jeanie hovered at Victoria's shoulder. I daren't meet her gaze. If Victoria suspected I had given her a message, she would not stop until she had squeezed it out of her.

I knew how relentless Victoria was when she wanted something.

Leaning heavily against her, I closed my eyes. I had done all I could. All that remained now was hope Jeanie understood the message and could get it to Jack. There was no way Jack could come to me—I knew that. But I needed him to know that although I was missing, I was not gone.

They couldn't keep me locked in here forever. As soon as my hands healed, I would take my bag, and we would leave together.

I groaned and rolled my eyes.

Victoria turned on Jeanie. "Now."

She scuttled from the room.

"What happened here?" Victoria held my face between her palms and peered at me. "What are you doing on the floor? I told you, ring the bell if you need something."

"I did. No one came," I said, meek and mild like she wanted me to be.

Her eyes narrowed. "I didn't hear it."

Because you were outside sending Wiffy away.

She hoisted me from the floor, and a wave of unease shot through me at her strength and my weakness.

"Was that Wiffy I heard here earlier?"

Her face shuttered, and her eyes widened in the manner I recognized so well. The spinneret began to turn, turning her sticky silk.

"Wiffy? No. No one but us has been here for days."

She shoved me onto the bed, placed my arms under the blanket, and pulled it to my chin, tucking it tightly around me.

"Don't you worry yourself about our lack of visitors. You need your medicine and to sleep."

I struggled to sit. "I'm feeling better. I don't want any medicine."

Her eyebrows knit. "Nonsense. The doctor said you must take the medicine he prescribed until it is all gone. Otherwise, you might overdo it and reopen your wounds."

"Victoria."

She stilled. I never called her that.

"The door was locked. Why?" I asked.

"What door?"

I didn't answer. She knew what door I referred to.

There was a shuffling sound, and a different maid appeared with a tray. The amber bottle of medicine seemed to pulse with an ominous glow.

Victoria poured it out with an exacting air and when she turned to me, it seemed her eyes had taken on that ominous glow.

I felt as if I were going mad. This was my sister. My other half. The person I could rely on most in life.

But as she neared, that spoon held aloft, I wondered.

Was she?

CHAPTER 22

"I need some fresh air. If I don't get out of this room, I will go crazy. My hands are better now. Look." I held my hands out for inspection.

Since the day Jeanie had found me on the floor, Victoria's presence had been as constant as the sun at the window. Endlessly I drifted in and out of consciousness, and whenever I woke, she was there, ready with that jar of medicine.

Even when I woke in darkness, I could feel her.

She remained mute, her jaw set. But two of us could play that game.

"I need you. Will you help me? Come with me, just to the garden. To sit in the sun for a spell." My tone was weak and wheedling.

The arbor in the rose garden could be seen from nearly every spot on the property. Jack would see me. He would know I was well. Jeanie had not returned to my rooms. Instead, Victoria met the maid at the door with whatever had been brought up. No one was permitted in. For my own good, she'd said.

"Is Stanley still in Newport?" I asked. I lay propped up by pillows, and she sat at the window, the ever-present notebook in her lap.

Her head jerked toward me. "Stanley? Yes. Why?"

I lifted a shoulder. "He hasn't called on me. I thought he might be concerned about his wife."

He had never been concerned about his wife, and I didn't expect him to start now, but I needed to know if he was still in Newport. As soon as I could, I was leaving here. He was the only one I feared could stop me.

I smiled guilelessly at Victoria. Her gaze shifted from my right eye to my left, like she was searching for something. "He's letting you rest, I expect."

"Yes," I murmured. "That must be it."

The argument about the boat ticket hung heavily between us, but I wouldn't broach it again with her. Although my hands had healed, the drugs she continued to press on me left me lethargic and woozy. My thoughts were scattered, and it was impossible to determine how long I had been in the room. For my hands to have healed would have taken weeks, but still she bore that spoon and its liquid toward me.

"Please, Vivi. Take me outside. I need sunshine and fresh air."

She pursed her lips. "If you tire, you must return straight to your bed."

"Of course," I demurred. "I want to recover as much as you want me to improve."

Her mouth twitched. "Fine."

Victoria shot out of her seat and yanked me from the bed so forcefully my head spun. But I refused to show her any weakness. It suddenly felt like the most important thing I could do was to hide myself from her. My sister, my other half.

My enemy? Surely not. I couldn't believe it of her. Jealous, mercurial, controlling, demanding, yes, but my enemy? Once time and space were between us, she would see that leaving had been my only option. She loved me as I loved her.

Victoria hovered in the doorway of the bathroom as I performed my toilette, her eyes as sharp as a fork in my back. My legs were unsteady, and I gripped the vanity counter to still the swaying that rocked me to and fro. I had grown weak from lying in the bed so long. There must be something I could do to stop Victoria and that bottle of medicine. While she had me under its influence, I was powerless.

On our walk through the house, I leaned on Victoria, feigning faintness and lethargy, but with each step I felt my balance restore.

She saw Jack first. I could tell by the way she tensed and abruptly changed direction. It would be safest to pretend I hadn't noticed him, but I couldn't help turning toward him like a flower turns its head to the sun. He led one of the horses around the corral, not Fable.

He paused, as if sensing my gaze on him, and lifted a hand to his forehead as he stared up the hill toward us. He stilled, studying us and, after an eternity, lifted that hand from his head into the air. There was a watchfulness about his stance, much like how he had hovered at the horse's side while I mounted. Ready to catch me, should he be required to.

The idea that Victoria had sent him away or had had Stanley do it had buzzed around endlessly in my mind like a fly against a window. I heaved a sigh of relief to see he was still here, unhurt, unchanged. She hadn't betrayed me, hadn't told Stanley what she now knew lay between Jack and me.

The sight of him invigorated me, and regardless of Victoria standing sentry beside me, I raised my hand in return.

"You'll have to put an end to it. You know that, don't you?" Victoria snatched my hand out of the air and held it roughly by our sides.

I lifted my chin and held her gaze, emboldened by Jack's proximity. "According to whom?"

She narrowed her eye. Things had shifted since the argument, and while my illness had paused it, like a butterfly trapped by a wax strip in a case, it hadn't erased it.

My Sister's Shadow   197

Victoria took a step back. "Stanley will kill you. Or him. Perhaps both of you."

"Undoubtedly."

She gave me a hard look that I returned. "And you would risk it all? All this?" She gestured to the house.

My gaze drifted back to the stables. "Undoubtedly."

* * *

I ambled from the stables to the gravel path along the cliff top, unable to smell the scent of the roses, deaf to the sound of the waves crashing, I was so full of him. His scent. His noise. His voice. His love.

A sense of unutterable joy overcame me. We would leave tomorrow.

Two weeks had passed since my first outing under Victoria's watchful gaze, and as my strength returned I had begun to resist the medicine Victoria thrust on me. Unhappy but unable to physically force me to take it, she had taken to lingering in my room. I faked tiredness, and kept conversation to a minimum, and eventually she would lose interest and leave. Then I would press Jeanie to deliver messages to Jack, arranged packages containing the items I wished to take to be stored at the post office, all in the name of organizing our departure. Today had been the first day I'd managed to leave the house without Victoria trailing me, and we had spent a precious hour in the dim boat shed at the farthest end of the property, where no one would find us, not wanting to risk meeting at the stables.

Jack would collect his final pay envelope tomorrow morning. I was to leave my suitcase at the back door tonight for him to collect. In the morning, I would request a carriage to Newport, claiming a desire to visit the stores, and he would meet me there with my suitcase and his. It had all been planned. Even if Victoria demanded to come into Newport with me, she could not physically stop me from leaving with Jack once he arrived.

January Gilchrist

I stood at the cliff's edge and watched as birds circled above, and matched my breath to the inhale and exhale of the ocean. I closed my eyes and inched toward the edge, my arms raised.

She was behind me, speaking, before I was even aware I was not alone.

"Where were you?"

I jolted at her voice, my heel skidding in the loose dirt at the cliff edge. A piece of sod tumbled down the precipice, smashing into tiny pieces as it ricocheted onto the rocks below. One of the birds shrieked as another plunged toward it, and I gasped at the sound of the collision of their fragile bodies. The hawk circled back, priming to take another dive.

I pressed my hand to my chest and watched as the gull tried desperately to shake its pursuer.

"Addy, what are you doing?"

"Hmm?" I turned to Victoria, shaking my head to clear the image of the birds. "Pardon?"

"Where were you? I was looking for you."

"Oh." I stared out to sea, thinking of how to answer. Did it matter anymore? I shook my head again and gestured to the ocean. "There was a bird. Attacking another."

She gazed out toward the horizon. The birds were gone. There was nothing but the ocean. The sun had shifted, and the soft pink sky had discolored and was now gray, as if we were viewing it through grimy glass.

I restarted along the path, my serenity shattered. Victoria fell into step alongside me. It was curious that I no longer sensed when she was near. Instead, she popped out at the strangest moments, like a morbid jack-in-the-box that wouldn't stay locked away, no matter how tightly I closed the lid.

"Where were you?" she repeated.

"The rose garden, here, walking, enjoying the fresh air."

"I came looking for you earlier. You weren't here."

MY SISTER'S SHADOW   199

There was a loaded pause, thick. The cicadas stopped playing their tune as we walked by. Suddenly the rose arbor felt oppressive, the scent of the warm flowers overpowering and cloying.

I turned and met her gaze, pausing on the path. "What do you want?"

I kept my face expressionless. She continued to stare at me. She fingered a rose, snapping its stem sharply and bringing it to her nose. When she looked back at me, her eyes were dark, unreadable.

"We worry, Stanley and I." A beat. "Your hands. Your *nerves*."

"Stanley and I." I shivered.

I smiled. "Worry? There is nothing for you to worry about, dearest." I held my hands up, palms toward her. "See how well I am healed."

She smiled back ominously, her gaze never shifting to my hands. I know they are red, swollen, misshapen. Jack had kissed along the puckered skin this afternoon, breathing healing energy, he had promised me with a laugh. It had indeed been healing to run those hands along his skin.

Dropping the rose to the ground between us, Victoria ground it with her heel before walking off back to the house alone.

Tomorrow, I reminded myself. *We leave tomorrow.*

I released the air that was trapped in my chest.

Tomorrow I would be free.

CHAPTER 23

The grocer's cart had departed some time ago, in a clatter of hooves and the jangling of bits and tack, and like any other summer morning, the usual post-dawn calm descended on Fairview Court. But something rather unusual was afoot.

Two curtains twitched.

One, facing the rose garden and ocean; and the other, on the wing directly opposite, at the window that faced its twin.

A face appeared at the window, briefly, and the curtain dropped back into place.

Sometime later, a maid came into sight from behind the house, a letter in her hand, and made her way, head down, along the driveway.

* * *

It's inconceivable how things seem to you when you believe it is the last time you will see them. The colors of my bedroom had an added vibrancy, the breeze coming from the open window was extra sweet, extra scented. Newport had been an incredible journey, and while I was sad to leave the opulence of Fairview Court, there was an excitement that tingled along my skin and created a sense of urgency. I longed to run, screaming, from the house to the stables, into Jack's arms. Instead, I forced myself to eat the

MY SISTER'S SHADOW   201

fruit on my breakfast tray, attended to my toilette, and stood as still as a statue as Jeanie worked the myriad buttons on my dress. I'd chosen a serviceable green poplin that wouldn't crush too badly on our journey and had packed a button hook. I would need to master that once my hands healed.

"I'm going to take a wander along the cliff walk," I announced.

"Very good, my lady. Would you like to me fetch your sister?" she asked, meeting my gaze in the mirror.

I pretended to consider. "No, I would prefer solitude today."

"Very good, my lady."

"Thank you, Jeanie."

Perhaps there was something in my tone, for she looked up at me with surprised eyes. "You're welcome, my lady."

"For everything. You've really been such a help."

She nodded, her eyes dark and uneasy. The staff had treated me with a gentle wariness since my "illness," as everyone referred to it. They had all been told the same thing, I assumed: that I was unwell and had harmed myself. I could see it in the way they spoke in hushed tones around me, their watchful eyes following my every move in the house.

I looked out the window. "It's a beautiful day for a walk at any rate."

And it was. The sky was cloudless and full of promise.

I ran my fingers along the gleaming banister as I tripped lightly down the stairs, my footfalls muffled by the opulent carpets. "Goodbye house," I whispered, blowing a kiss to the portrait of Beebah and her beloved Pomeranian that hung on the wall beside the Magna Carta windows.

A smile to a maid and a nod to the butler, and then I was outside in the sunshine. I sucked in a scented breath of air. My insides fizzed and popped like a freshly uncorked bottle of champagne.

"Adelaide."

My heart sank. She must've been watching from her rooms or, more likely, had asked the staff to inform her if I left mine.

202   January Gilchrist

I schooled my face and turned to her. Victoria stood in the arch of the vestibule, dressed as if for company. Her hair was elaborately styled, tidier than I had seen in an age, her face smooth, creamy, and blank. The dress was unfamiliar to me, and I wondered, briefly, where and when she'd had it made. Had she arranged credit in my (Stanley's) name? We had not been to the dressmaker together since before we left for Newport. I was not aware of any trips to town.

"Yes?" One foot was over the threshold of my new life, and the other hung in the air, paused, ready to take that step. It was already in motion; there was little a conversation with her now would do to change it.

"Where are you going?"

"Am I required to inform you of my every movement?"

She moved out from the shadow of the entrance, gliding down the steps toward me. I took a step backward, wanting to remain out of her reach.

"You are not." She gave me a strange half smile. "However, we are expecting someone, and you must be here when they arrive."

My heart was suddenly in my throat. There was an air about her, one I recognized only too well. But I no longer had to fear her. I was leaving, I reminded myself.

My palms dampened, and I ran them along the seams of my skirt. "I'm going for a walk. If your visitor is still here upon my return, then I will call in."

She brushed the backs of her pristine gloves. "That's not possible, dearest. As I said, you'll need to stay for this visitor."

The thump of horses' hooves and the jangling of chains and bits cut through the air. Victoria and I both turned to the driveway. The dark shape of a carriage appeared through the hedgerow.

For a fleeting moment, I thought about lifting my skirts and taking flight. Through the stables, across the back of the

MY SISTER'S SHADOW ~ 203

property, over the low brick wall that led to the ocean walk and the township. Jack's hand in mine. My heart raced as if I had, but my feet remained resolutely fixed to the spot where they stood, on the bone-dry and thirsty ground. Silly. I had nothing to fear.

The unfamiliar coach bore down on us. Through barred windows I saw the hatless faces of the doctors who had attended to me when my hands had first been cut.

I turned to Victoria and her strange half smile.

There was a moment of perfect stillness.

"Vivi?" I didn't know then what the question was, only that it was swirling, gaining momentum just before it crushed me.

The doctors remained seated in the carriage, their dark gazes trained on the front door. I turned just as Stanley appeared. His eyes were shiny pebbles and never landed on me, as though I were invisible. Victoria shifted her weight, and her stance reminded me of the painting *Boadicea Haranguing the Britons* that hung in Father's study.

The taller man stepped from the carriage, smoothing his hair before pressing his hat atop it. He gave a little bow to Victoria.

"Miss Windlass, good afternoon."

Victoria smiled and nodded regally in return to him.

He turned to me. "Lady Stanley, you remember me, I trust? Doctor Tombes." He spoke in a low soothing voice, his eyes kind, reassuring.

I swallowed hard, roaring in my ears. Fear crept along my arms, leaving goose bumps in their wake. The sight of the doctors had unnerved me. I glanced at Stanley. He seemed neither angry nor vengeful. Instead, a stoic kind of energy emanated from him.

"Vivi? Stanley? What's going on?" I asked.

He turned to me then, his brows lowered, his face blank. My husband was a stranger to me; and, it appeared, I to him.

From somewhere on the grounds a dog barked, and a sudden gust of breeze blew my hair across my face.

204   January Gilchrist

I turned again to Victoria. She was looking down at her gloved hands, her lip between her teeth. But when she finally looked up, there was a satisfied gleam in her eyes.

"Gentleman." Stanley nodded once. It was a small movement that brought the other men into motion.

Tombes moved closer, his presence no longer reassuring, but compelling. I straightened, some sixth sense simmering.

The other doctor stood by the carriage, his hand on the door, holding it open. Past him I saw iron chains attached to a scratched iron bar that ran the length of the bench. Doctor Tombes held his hand out toward me.

"Lady Stanley, we are going on a little journey."

My head was light, my legs weak. I stumbled and a hand reached out for me. Only it wasn't supporting, but gripped me painfully.

I struggled against the doctor's viselike hold, but his pressure only increased. He yanked once, hard, and a pain shot through my shoulder. I stilled.

"What has she done?" I cried.

"Come now. You are unwell, and we are going to make you better. But you must not fight us." His voice held a warning; this kindness, such as it was, would not last.

I looked at Victoria, and suddenly, heartbreakingly I understood it all.

I screamed then. I howled and shrieked and wailed. The noise overflowed from the deepest caverns of my soul, where for so long I had kept the lid on all my longing and anger.

"You liar!' I screamed. The words set fire to everything, but no one seemed to notice. They stood, unmoving, unmoved. "Can't you see what she has done?"

I tried to point at my traitorous shadow, but Tombes forced my arm to my side. His eyes burned with pleasure. He wanted me to fight, wanted to use his strength against me. I turned back to Victoria.

Head ducked demurely, she had taken a step toward Stanley and now rested her hand, encased in that unspoiled cotton, on his shoulder. My gloves. My palms were still red and angry looking.

"You have it wrong. I am not mad—she is." But even I could hear the words were too unsteady to ring true.

They didn't have it wrong at all; they had it exactly as they had been told. That I was crazy, weak, an attempted self-murderer. Their hands clasped around my upper arms like heavy iron cuffs.

"Wait," I urged, frantic. "Victoria. You tell them the truth right now. Tell them!"

The silence that followed was louder than anything she could have said.

Stanley cleared his throat. "Do not make this harder than it needs to be. These men are going to take you somewhere to rest for a while. So you can start to feel better. That is all we want for you."

Hypocrite. Liar.

Maybe I yelled the words, perhaps I merely thought them, but they seemed to be the signal to the men that it was time. They pulled at me, and when my legs finally gave way, they didn't stop, but just dragged me toward the waiting carriage with its unforgiving iron bars over the windows. I twisted in their arms, staring back toward the house. The sun was beginning to dip toward the ocean, casting lavender streaks in the sky. Still bright enough to blind, the heat of the sun burned Victoria's silhouette onto my lids.

A vignette that would haunt me every time I closed my eyes.

I watched as Stanley raised his hand and rested it on Victoria's, which was still resting lightly on his shoulder.

Her face was closed as tightly as a fist.

PART 3

PART 3

CHAPTER 24

The room was as cold as a morgue.

Wherever I'd gone in Newport, I had been welcomed with smiles; pleasing but empty words; and endless cups of tea or, after lunch, the most recent signature cocktail. Not now. Everything I had taken for granted was withheld from me. Water, food, kindness.

I was left to sit on a thin iron bench, my wrists bound in thick leather straps, which were attached to the wall beside me.

The cold of the metal beneath me seeped through my already damp skirts, and the cold, unhappy concrete seeped its misery into my muddied and torn stockings. I must have looked a fright. But however awful I looked, no one gave me a passing glance. My shoes had been taken from me, and my right toe had torn through the wool of my stocking. I thought of Jones and her constant reminding how important it was for us to take care of our clothes, how some tears were irreparable.

Irreparable. I turned the word around in my mouth, enjoying its sharp edges.

Irreparable. Irrevocable. Incomprehensible.

Victoria's betrayal had still not yet sunk in. A large part of me—the largest part, the foolish part, the hopeful part—still believed that any minute she, Stanley, *anyone*, would appear,

lecturing, chastising, shaming. I would nod and agree and vow I
had learned my lesson.

Then I would leave. Forever.

The noise of my shoes rapping across the marble of Beebah's
foyer rang through my head, the leather handle of my suitcase
slick in my hand. I would walk right out the front door, head
high, and I would not look back.

Jack and I would do as we had planned: leave Newport and
begin our new lives on the West Coast, where it was all endless
sky to endless sea.

I held that picture in my mind as if I were gazing at a daguerre-
otype. I would leave. As soon as they released me, I would leave.
Scandal be damned, I would divorce Stanley. Let the papers print
what they may. No longer would I allow anyone to keep me from
my life.

The clanging noise of keys striking metal sounded, followed
by the swift footsteps of Dr. Mortimer. I didn't need to look up
when he entered. I could tell it was him. His presence was threatening and watchful, and his scent, cigar and carbolic soap, had
permeated my nostrils on our drive here.

When I finally looked up, I was surprised to find his mouth
moving. The words thrummed in the air around us, but I couldn't
make sense of any of them . . . holding cell . . . Meadowleigh
Insane Asylum . . .

The words pummeled me, but I felt nothing.

Images fell upon each other in my mind, one after another.
Victoria appearing for dinner, late, disheveled. The endless glasses
of wine, champagne, the cups soaked with sherry. The bright
laughter, as sharp as broken glass. The hard glances. How had I
missed it all? I had been so besotted with Jack, so focused on
myself that I had missed it all happening under my nose.

Stanley has had me committed to an asylum.

Victoria has betrayed me.

My Sister's Shadow ☞ 211

And oh, how she betrayed me. I had been deeply, horrifically betrayed by the hand that held mine before we even left the womb. By one whose milky breath had mingled with mine, whose downy arm had been my comfort.

It must have been her that put the glass in the soap, keeping me trapped inside that room, feeding me morphine, isolating me from anyone who might have helped. Images of her sitting with Stanley, encouraging him to call the doctors on me, feigning worry. Did he know the truth? Had they plotted it together, or had Victoria placed ideas in his head, leading him to this gruesome plan?

I sucked in a loud, shuddering breath. I had no idea how long I had been sitting on the cold, hard bench. The numbness of my feet had moved up my legs, and now they felt like lead. I was so very cold, but at the same time felt absolutely nothing. None of it seemed real.

A wave of shame and guilt washed over me. I was so stupid. I dropped my head between my knees and retched it all up. On and on I retched until nothing but bile remained. My throat stung, my stomach clenched, but I didn't raise my head. Just let my forehead rest on my arms, folded on top of my knees.

One would assume a man of medicine would be of a strong constitution, but Dr. Mortimor leaped about, yelling orders, scrambling in his efforts to escape the contents of my stomach and the horrors it held.

Such horrors. Such impossible horrors that this all must be a dream. Perhaps I was still on that crimson couch, the sticky amber medicine doing its work.

A hard hand yanked me from the chair, and the pain was a stark reminder that this was no dream. My wet feet slid on the stone floor as I was moved from one cold empty room to another.

Victoria wanted to teach me a lesson. That I understood. But surely even she wouldn't go this far? Wouldn't let them hold me here against my will. Someone would be coming shortly to take me home.

I was conscious of the sharp sound of iron on iron as the door closed, the screech of the key turning in the lock. There was a droning sound that wouldn't stop. I shook my head.

The image of Jack's strong forearms appeared in my mind, sun-bleached hairs covering bronzed skin. How his large, square hands looked like they could inflict a punishing hit but instead slid along the length of my body, impossibly slow, as if he were memorizing me through our touch.

It gave me strength.

He would come; he would come save me.

I straightened my spine and crossed my left ankle over my right, as good girls do. The prong of my wedding ring scratched at the skin of my fingers as I curled my hands in my lap. I fixed my eye on a damp spot on the bottom of the wall and breathed in deeply and performed my very best trick.

A good girl sits quietly, takes what is given to her.

Don't blink, don't speak, don't make a sound. Don't even breathe too loudly, in case you call attention to yourself, and they remember you're here. No noises, no matter what they do.

Shallow, hushed breaths. Unfixed, blank gaze. Lifeless limbs.

I am nothing. I am nowhere. I am no one.

CHAPTER 25

The dark brick building crouched like an animal awaiting its prey. The windows watched as I was driven through an archway into a vaulted holding area. The iron gate clanged shut. Men called and joked to one another as they locked that terrible gate behind me. Tasks done, their curious eyes turned to the carriage. I stared back, peering through the window.

What would they find in here? A mad woman. Insane, the doctors had declared, and no one had questioned it.

The bolt of the carriage door scraped along the metal. I longed to bury my head in my hands. The preceding days were something of a haze. Despite my belief that this was merely a tactic designed to keep me in my place, that someone would burst through the door at any moment and take me home, that my twin would have a change of heart, it didn't happen. The more minutes that ticked past, the harder it was to hold on to the belief that I would be rescued.

Instead, despite all my prayers, I had been accused of insanity and delivered to Meadowleigh Insane Asylum.

I lumbered out of the carriage in a daze.

A woman in a nurse's uniform was waiting for me, a bundle of coarse-looking linen in her arms.

214 ⬒   January Gilchrist

"Watch your hands with this one, Matron. She might bite," one of the men said.

The men laughed, but the matron eyed me meanly. "She won't dare try with me, or she'll find out right quick where that will lead her."

My hands shook. What was to become of me? The matron gestured for me to follow her into a barren courtyard. We walked a gravel-lined path to a door and entered a dim, pleasureless room. I stood while she tossed out words that sounded like curses and jotted them down in a book that looked menacing.

Lines of similar-looking words covered the pages.

Name. Eye color. Weight.

The sum of all my parts. I had been reduced to a list.

She asked nothing of me, but simply read the words aloud, ran her eyes over me to ascertain the answer, and replied to herself before writing it down.

Did she not trust she would get the truth from me had she asked?

She was right to. I no longer knew what the truth was.

There was a tin tub in the middle of the courtyard, and in it, an inch of stagnant water. She undressed me with her unlovely hands and compelled me into the tin, dumping a foul-smelling concoction over my head. It stung my eyes and filled my nose.

The bristles of the stiff brush tore and scratched as she dragged it along my skin.

"Up." Her nails dug into the soft flesh under my arm as she yanked me to my feet.

I stood, naked and exposed. Tears burned at my eyes, but I did not weep. A rough gray dress was pulled over my head. It caught against my damp skin, and she yanked at it to get it on.

The matron made a bundle of my clothes and handed it to the small, rat-faced girl that stood beside her. The girl rubbed the fabric of my petticoat between her fingers, her face drawn in covert glee. She pressed the fabric against her nose. Our eyes met

MY SISTER'S SHADOW ⌒ 215

and hers darted away, the bundle of fabric—the entirety of my belongings—lowered carelessly onto the ground.

"Sit." The matron pointed at a bare chair that was incongruously positioned in the center of the barren courtyard.

There was something about it that set me trembling. I lowered myself gingerly onto its hard surface.

A metallic rasping noise cut through the air, but it wasn't until the sharp blades were pressed against my neck that I realized what was happening.

I cried out as my hair fell as silently as snow into my lap, but still I did not weep. Matron's hands yanked at swaths of hair as the scissors snipped relentlessly. Cool air tickled unpleasantly at my now naked nape. I fingered a lock of the pale hair that lay in hanks at my feet, strange and foreign looking. Not my hair, lying so limp and lifeless on the ground, surely.

A bonnet was slapped onto my head.

"Tie it." Matron ordered, watching me with suspicious eyes. My fingers trembled so badly that it took three attempts for me to make the bow.

"This way." The matron gestured to a gate with her thumb.

We crossed the wasteland that led to the main building. The courtyard was bare except for dead brown grass. A huddle of women watched as I was led into their fold. I averted my gaze from their curious eyes.

Four leaden steps led into the shadowy doorway.

The door was twice the height of me and thick, with an iron bolt on the outside only. The side that faced inside was covered with a filthy canvas, padded with straw, sticks of it poking through holes along it. The walls had been whitewashed, and a monstrous set of iron stairs stood in the middle of the room. Matron prodded me into motion toward them. They trembled ominously as we clattered up them. The treads were little more than a crisscross of metal, and my stomach flipped as we rose, the floor hovering unevenly below me. I clutched at the handrail, my vision blurring.

216 ☙ January Gilchrist

The matron noticed me looking at the net, strung between the stairs and the landings. "That's to stop anyone falling. We wouldn't want you to hurt yourselves, now would we?"

I eyed her. No, it was she who wanted to do the hurting.

As we climbed those mean stairs, I looked through to the floor. What horrors went on here that the idea of throwing yourself to the mercy of the concrete floor below was preferable to staying?

The matron spoke. "You will be confined to your room from six until six. It has all the modern facilities you are sure to be used to." She pronounced the word *fack-ill-tees*. "You make a fuss, and we put you in the darks."

"The darks?" I croaked.

"A room in the basement. That's where we put the uncooperative wards. No light. No air. It makes this look like a palace."

She stopped so abruptly that I bumped into her. Lowering her head, she gave me a look that chilled my blood.

"I don't ask things twice. If you don't follow orders, you're in the darks. No warnings. No second chances. You hear? I am queen of all we survey here."

The dread that had sat in my chest had moved to my head, filling it so I couldn't hear a word. The way your head underwater in the bath made everything dulled, deadened. I chewed my lip and nodded.

She paused at an open door to a small, dark cell. "Home, sweet home."

An unpleasant smell wafted from it. Something rotten, rotting. She pushed me into the center of the room, and I looked around in a sickened daze.

The floor was covered with oil cloth. A meager metal cot was against a wall under a square of light—a window, too high to reach and covered with bars. A thin gray blanket lay across the end of the bed. A tin pot in the corner. Thick brown streaks covered the walls. I was careful to breathe through my mouth.

My Sister's Shadow 217

I thought of the room at Fairview Court, the furniture stuffed with feathers and covered in velvet. My room there had been luxury beyond comprehension, but everywhere I looked here held misery.

The matron left, pulling the door shut with a thud that jolted me as if I had been poked with a cattle prod.

The back of the iron door was covered in a river of scrapes and scratches, letters and lines. I placed my hand over them, thinking of all the women who had stood here before me.

Still, I did not weep.

I had thought that my wedding day was the worst day of my life. Any day on the boat to New York, a close second. At the time, I couldn't have imagined anything worse than when we'd left Harewood Hall. The wet faces of the servants as they formed a line along the pebbled driveway.

But I would sell my soul to relive any one of those days. I would live them over and over, every last one of them, to avoid the horror of my arrival here.

To think that Victoria had done this was impossible. My head ached every time I thought of it—on every inhale, word rang in my ears: *betrayed, betrayed, betrayed.*

I sat on the edge of the hard bed and clutched myself. What could I do?

The matron had mentioned a doctor. I needed to meet with him and explain what had happened. I would calmly explain the situation, and the doctor would believe me—he must!

At first light, I would request a pen and paper and send a letter to Father, who would surely demand my immediate release. Then, another letter to Wiffy, explaining what Victoria and Stanley had done.

Finally, one to Jack.

The thoughts calmed me.

Father, regardless of how he felt about me would not let this happen to me.

Wiffy was a powerful woman from a powerful family that would use its influence to have me freed.

And Jack.

Jack would flip every stone from New York to the West Coast to find me—that much I knew.

Yes, I would speak to the doctor, and he would see the error. The lie. The doctor would understand it once I had explained it. A man of medicine must be educated, rational, reasonable. He would see through it all.

With a whoosh of air, I lay on that bed and finally wept. I wept until the stingy light moved from filthy wall to water-stained roof.

And then I wept some more.

CHAPTER 26

I lay awake that first night, on the straw-filled thing they called a mattress. I listened to the faint clicking of lice, the din of the other women calling and singing incessantly.

The thick brick of the wall muffled the sounds of the other women, but their cries and calls floated in all night. The wind whistled through the open space above me. Foxes screeched and screamed outside. Carriages clattered by, reminding me that the world, unbelievably, was still turning.

The door rattled and the matron appeared in the doorway. The light shone from behind her, throwing her face into horrifying shadows. I recoiled and she grinned.

I was perched on the edge of the pallet and had attempted to fix my hair myself. Without pins or a comb, I had settled for running my fingers through it and licking my palms to smooth it around my face. There was salt on my skin, dust in my eyes, dirt under my nails. I knew that my protestations of being sane hinged on how I looked, as it so often does with women, so I schooled my face and set my shoulders. My hands turned the bonnet over in my lap like a lucky coin.

There was a look in Matron's eyes. A wariness. As if she were dealing with a wild animal that could snap at any time.

"Bring your tin. Breakfast ain't served in your room."

220 January Gilchrist

I stood. Head up, shoulders back. Deep breath. "I require a meeting with the doctor this morning. And the warden."

The matron raised her eyebrows and turned the corners of her lips downward. "That's nice." Her voice was mild, but her eyes were hard.

"I need to explain that there has been a . . ." What? A mistake? An error? *Betrayal.* ". . . misunderstanding. I should like very much to meet with the doctor, who will find it very easy to ascertain my sanity."

"Should you just?" She mimicked my accent cruelly.

I took a breath. "Yes, there has been a mistake—"

She cut me off. "Enough. If I were to listen to all the nonsense that gets spouted here, then I would be as mad as the rest of you. Get downstairs."

She and her shadow left my doorway, the conversation evidently over.

A breeze, thick with rotting refuse, excrement, and tar crept along the hallway and stroked my cheek. In time those smells would become familiar, but that morning they brought shocked tears to my eyes.

I picked up my bed pan, hot with embarrassment. There was nothing to cover it with, so I carried it out, hiding it behind my skirts as best I could.

"Hurry up." The matron called from below.

I peered over the edge of the iron railing. Women in the same starched, drab, ill-fitting gray dress that I wore were queuing at the exit. Each held a tin bucket in their right hands. Long brimmed bonnets hid their faces from me.

"Stanley," the matron yelled. His name on her lips was a slap in the face. "Every minute you keep me waiting, these girls lose a spoonful of soup."

One by one the white caps tilted toward me at the top of the stairs.

A hand pressed between my shoulders roughly. "Get going. We ain't missin' out on breakfast for you," a voice muttered in my ear.

I stumbled, worried about the stairs and my bucket full of unmentionables. The railing was cool and sticky under my hand as I clutched it.

My face flamed as I made my way down the stairs under the gaze of so many strangers, their stares cold and assessing. They weren't terribly dissimilar to the society faces I had encountered in the ballrooms across New York and Newport. Curious, sharp enough to slice. I had managed the ladies of society; I could manage this.

I took my place behind a woman who was as small as a child. The tip of her cap barely reached my chin. She turned as I took my place behind her, studying me with narrowed eyes and an upturned lip. The look in her eye gave me a chill.

We moved across the yard in a line, stopping to empty our tins into a pit. My feelings of shame were quickly replaced by disgust as bucket after bucket of excrement and urine was flung into the pit. The air was thick with the smell of it. My throat worked, and the harder I tried not to breathe in the putrid scent, the harder it was to hold the vomit back. Tears streamed from my eyes. I pressed the heel of my hand against my mouth, finally allowing the bile to flow out onto the ground at my feet. I was numbly aware of the sound of raucous cheering and mocking laughter.

Someone knocked me sideways.

"Oi, watch my feet." The person I had stumbled into shoved me back the opposite direction.

I staggered, falling heavily on my knee, frantically working to hold the bucket upright. The air was thick with jeers and jibes.

"Quiet," the matron demanded, and the women did so immediately.

222 ᥫ᭡ January Gilchrist

"That will do," she said to me, as if I had been carrying on for attention. "You'll be cleaning that up."

Averting my gaze from the malodorous mess, I lurched to my feet. My lip trembled. These women wanted to see me shamed, to see me brought low, but I would not give them the satisfaction. I had been brought lower than I had ever imagined possible— there was nowhere else for me to fall.

"Certainly." I responded. The fabric of my dress was rough as I wiped my hands along it. "Do you have something for me to mop it up with?"

The line erupted again into jeers and mocking calls of "Ooh, certainly."

"A mop! A mop!" One woman screamed, over and over.

"Shut it," the matron roared among the noise, and once again the women fell silent at her command.

She narrowed her eyes at me. "Don't start with me. You will lose."

I set my jaw. Her rudeness would not go unmentioned when I met with the warden.

We were led across the grounds to a round copper tub and stood in line as one by one the women lathered up a soiled bar of yolk-colored soap onto a square of cloth and wiped their faces and hands. Some lifted their skirts and wiped beneath. It was performed soundlessly and swiftly, each woman performing the same action, like automatons. Rinsing the cloth in the tub of water, lathering it on the soap, and rubbing the cloth over their skin.

I shuddered when it too quickly became my turn. I plunged the rough flannel through the film of gray filth into the ice-cold water. Water gathered in my mouth again. A layer of sludge as thick as gravy clung to my hand as I removed it. My stomach twisted and I coughed.

"We don't have all day." The matron clicked her tongue.

MY SISTER'S SHADOW 223

Keeping my gaze fixed to a spot on the ground, I sucked in a breath and swiftly ran the flannel over my arms and back of my neck before dropping it back into the murky water.

The matron gave me a knowing look. She was new to me, but not I to her. She'd seen it all before. "Let's see you wash your face then."

My tongue felt too big for my mouth. Bile burned the back of my throat.

"Rules of the house. All the parts we can see must be washed every day."

It was Jack I thought of then, and how the spot between his ear and shoulder smelled just like gingerbread. I screwed my eyes shut and ran the flannel across my face, as quickly as I could. When I opened my eyes, I met the matron's smirking gaze. There was a light in her eyes that reminded me too much of Victoria, and it sparked that rage that had begun to simmer. I was so tired of that hateful gaze, that knowing smirk.

Lifting my chin, I dug back into the filthy water and pulled out the dripping flannel. Water ran down arm and chest as I ran it over my face.

The matron's eyelids flickered.

Rage scorched through my veins. I was done with being told what to do.

The flannel dropped into the bucket of slop with a satisfying plop. I took my place at the end of the queue, holding my breath against the stench that clung to my skin.

* * *

The next stop for the gray-clad women was breakfast. We trudged in line, like an unwieldy troop of silent soldiers toward the block of buildings that housed the kitchen and laundry.

Matron stood at the entrance to the dim room and barked orders. As we entered, she caught my eye but glanced away quickly.

224 ⁓   January Gilchrist

The line shuffled toward a large, battered dining table, where a large woman was ladling thin colorless soup into bowls and handing half a loaf of bread to each woman.

I followed the woman ahead of me, collected my bowl, and cradled it between both hands. The boat-breasted woman met my gaze as she held the bread toward me. It was as heavy as a rock.

"That there's ya lunch. Hold on to it." She was older than I had first thought, her size giving her face a plump youthfulness. Her face was very tan, a spiderweb scar marring one side of her face. Her eyes were kind as she filled my bowl with the gruel. I followed the ladies to the large table where they all sat, and placed my bowl on the table.

But I didn't sit. Instead, I sought Matron out.

"Matron, if you please. I need to speak to the doctor or the warden as a matter of urgency."

Matron yawned. A grotesque stretching of her face that she didn't bother to hide. A puff of sour air hit my face, and I tried not flinch.

"Everyone's here 'cause of a mistake. Just ask any of that lot there." She jerked her chin to the table, where all eyes were on us.

"My sister has lied, played an awful trick. My husband is Lord Stanley. He's . . . he's . . . important."

Matron pushed off the wall. "I know that. He's the one that got you sent here, ain't he? Sit down and eat your breakfast. The doctor is due around lunchtime." She held a black-tipped finger to my face. "One thing you better learn is we don't dance to your tune."

Her mouth twisted in a way that reminded me painfully of Washington, of the pleasure being unkind to others brought to a woman like her.

I moved back toward the table of women, who now sat with their heads bowed toward their bowls.

MY SISTER'S SHADOW 225

"Smith, put your hands where I can see them," Matron barked behind me. "And cut the chatter. This ain't Sunday school."

A dark-haired lady with her back to Matron met my gaze viciously. She looked as if she wanted to hit me if she could.

It was strange to think that a room so full of women could be so quiet. There was no sound inside the building save for the clinking and scraping of our cutlery. The spoon was light in my hand. The face of it was scratched and stained. Using the nail of my thumb, I scraped a brown residue from the tip of it.

The gruel was a temperature that curled my stomach. Neither warm nor cool, its tasteless texture reminded me of the bile I had emptied my stomach of earlier.

But I forced myself to eat. I would do as they asked of me this morning, all the better to make a case of it with the doctor when he arrived. Matron would be able to vouch for my gentle nature, my willingness to abide by her rules. I would explain what had happened, and he would release me.

The other women shoveled the gruel into their mouths. Unseeing, untasting, they moved the spoons from bowl to mouth, eyes fixed on the table. All except the dark-eyed woman across from me. Her spoon moved in unison with the others', but her narrowed gaze remained fixed on me. As if I were some strange beast in a zoo cage.

A bell cut through the air, and chairs were pushed back, fingers scraping the last of the gruel from bowls, and the woman made their way to a bucket on a bench. They dipped their cutlery and bowls in the bucket of water, wiped them with a stained rag, and stacked them on a ledge beside the bench.

As I neared the bucket, I looked for something in which to empty my leftovers; I hadn't managed more than two mouthfuls.

I hovered uncertainly.

The woman standing at the side of the table flicked her eyes to my bowl and back to me.

"Not good enough for you?"

226 ⮒   January Gilchrist

I didn't reply. She took the bowl from my hands and upended it into her mouth. Wiping the back of her hand across her mouth, she smiled at me, showing me a mouth full of twisted teeth. "Waste not, want not."

She pressed the bowl back into my hands.

"What's taking you so long?" Matron called across the room.

"I ain't doin' ya dishes." The woman beside me scowled, jerking her chin toward the bucket.

I dipped the bowl into the sludge of the bucket, drying it off and placing it next to the others on the ledge.

There were murmurs behind me and a cackle of cruel laughter. My cheeks began to burn. But I had nothing to be ashamed of. What these women thought of me mattered not one jot. As soon as I had met with the doctor, I would be released, and the night I had spent here would be nothing more than a nightmare. I would relegate it to the darkest depths of my memory.

Since the wedding night with Stanley, I had become skilled in banishing unpleasant memories.

Resuming my place behind the young girl, I clasped my hands together to stop their trembling. Matron led us across the courtyard, where we stood in line, not speaking. She, of course, had entered the cool rooms of the building that housed her office.

The girl in the line turned back, watching me with her round eyes.

"You're not mad," she stated.

"I'm not?"

"No." Her gaze bored into mine. "You're not. I can tell. They say I am too. Only I think I might be."

Although Matron was inside her rooms, I didn't answer, fearful she would see us. I couldn't afford to get reprimanded so close to my visit with the doctor.

"Most of us aren't. Not really." She squinted into the sun. "But if you aren't mad before you enter, you will be before you leave."

I wondered how long these women had been here. Their dresses were worn and stained, and everyone else seemed to have a clear understanding of what was expected of them. I was the only one fumbling my way through the rules and regulations.

"I'm Bosie." She gestured to a round girl. "That's Rose Saltonstall. One of the Boston Brahmins." She leaned in close to me and whispered, "Fell in love with an Irishman and got herself in the family way."

The bonnets made it hard to make out any defining features, which was clearly the intention behind the long brims, but the girl looked young, healthy, and enormously sad.

"And that there"—she gestured with her bonnet to a tall, broad girl standing close to another—"Dorothea Appleton."

We watched the other ladies for a moment.

"She likes girls. Refuses to denounce it. Will probably die in here. They're not letting her out any time soon."

Dorothea leaned in close to the shorter woman next to her, pressing her mouth to her ear. The other woman lifted her hand to Dorothea's neck. I glanced away.

"And you?" I asked.

"Me?" she snorted.

"How did you end up in here?"

She rolled her eyes and leaned back on her heels. I thought if she had a cigarette, she would have lit it with panache, relishing the tension such a pause created, much like Wiffy did when she wanted to make an impact. Instead, she gave me a wry smile. "I like absinthe and men too much."

A pause. That imaginary cigarette was inhaled and exhaled. "My father is the Colonel."

I widened my eyes and she nodded ruefully. The Colonel, as he was known, was a shipping magnate and recluse, and according to rumor, currently the wealthiest man in the world. His sons had been at many a party arranged by Wiffy, who was related to them in some manner.

228 ⮂ January Gilchrist

"B-b-but how? Why?" I gestured weakly around us.

"I got conned by a brute I met in Europe. Told me he was a prince, and like a fool I believed him. He swept me off my feet and we got married. Turns out he had known who I was, what my trust fund looked like, and he had plans for it. He almost drove me dry. When father found out, instead of copping the scandal a divorce would entail, he had me committed here. Paid my husband off. Made him disappear, like he did me."

My mind whirred. Surely someone missed her? Worried about where she was? Knew her well enough to stand up for her? Did even wealthy women have no rights?

"When will you be let out?"

She heaved a great sigh. "When my father decides to call for me. I've brought shame on the family of a very proud man. He may never forgive me."

"But your family? Surely some of them—"

"He holds the purse strings. They do as he says. If I'm dead to him, I'm dead to them."

"The doctor then. Did you explain this to the doctor?"

Her lip lifted, as if she pitied me.

I placed my hand on her arm. "I'm being released today. Give me the name of someone I can contact. I know people. I will help you get out," I whispered urgently.

She shrugged her arm away from my touch. "Maybe you are mad after all." She met my gaze, and hers was so bleak that I recoiled. "You're not going anywhere."

* * *

We stood in the sun for what felt like an eternity. My neck burned and my face heated. Other woman swished their skirts or waved their hands at their faces to create some breeze. Sweat beaded and slid along my back. When a woman at the head of the queue raised her arms to fan her face I saw big patches of sweat

MY SISTER'S SHADOW 229

blooming along her dress. I looked down at my own with dismay. I was damp with perspiration, and my clothes and hair—what was left of it—stuck unpleasantly to me. Certainly not the image I had been hoping to present to the doctor.

Finally, there was a stir in the doorway of the rooms, and a tall, white-haired man with a thick beard appeared. His head was bent over a large leather-bound book of some sort, perhaps a note from Matron regarding my urgent need to speak to him.

But it wasn't my name he called. He did not look up from the book as he called "Mary Smith."

He reentered his room without checking to see if she was following.

I jolted. Why hadn't he called my name? I had made it clear to Matron I needed to speak with him urgently.

One by one he called the other women in. It was the longest wait of my life. My legs trembled when it was finally my turn to move to the head of the line. Freedom was so close. I could almost taste the cool glass of water I would drink, the long luxurious bath I would take, and the clean, soft touch of a new lawn dress.

The doctor no longer bothered to walk past his doorway, instead simply raising his voice from the cool shade of the chamber.

His gaze flicked up from the book and rested on me. "Adelaide Gilbraith." My married name. So careful not to use my title lest I garner the least bit of social power from it. Not that there was anyone left to hear. I was the last woman waiting. I staggered after him into his room.

The room was pleasantly cool and dim after the blinding light of the courtyard, and I hovered in the doorway, blinking. The chill of the room showed me how overheated I had become, and I swayed, reaching out to the wall to steady myself. My hand missed the doorjamb, and I stumbled slightly. Spots swam in my vision, and I blinked to clear it.

The doctor sat behind a large, poorly made desk. A long bare bench crouched along the back wall. I glanced at it, unsure whether to sit or continue to stand.

"Good afternoon," I said in my most society tone.

He did not reply, his eyes darting left to right as he read his ledger. I wondered what it said and who had written it.

I stood in silence until he lifted his gaze. He stood suddenly and lurched toward me, grabbing at my wrist. I started rather violently.

"Your pulse is rapid." He peered at my face. "How are you feeling?"

"I . . . I am a little overheated, I think." To my shame tears sprang to my eyes.

Disappointment and panic warred inside me. I needed to be calm in front of this man, not collapse in a heap. I felt as though I had performed a great feat, walked for miles up a mountain only to fall to my knees once the summit was in sight.

He moved back to his desk, completely unmoved by my tears. The nib of his pencil scratched on the page. He was too far for me to read the words he etched there. How reasonable I seemed? His reasons for releasing me?

"There has been a mistake," I began, as he paced toward me.

A shadow fell over the doorway. It was the warden—his belly was in the room, while the rest of him leaned against the doorjamb.

The doctor nodded at the warden, who nodded in return.

"Warden. Adelaide here was just telling me that there has been a mistake. She shouldn't be here. Someone must be called. Is that correct?"

The warden made a nasty noise. "Ah, someone must always be called. Always such a mistake."

I longed to tear the vile smirk from his face. The doctor grasped my face in his hands and pressed against the tender join of my jaw, forcing my mouth open. His fingers roamed over my teeth, his hand forcing my jaw so wide it hurt. The hair of his knuckles brushed against my tongue, and I gagged.

"Prone to fits." The warden spoke from the doorway. "Long periods of time unaccounted for. Delusions. Self-harm."

I fought the rising bile in my throat. "No, that's not true. There *has* been a mistake."

"Violent fits?" The doctor spoke to the warden over my head.

He grasped the back of my head and dragged it so close to his I could feel his fetid breath on my face. I stiffened and tried to pull away from him, but he increased his pressure. He pried my eyelids apart roughly with the thumb and forefinger of his other hand. His breath was hot and sour against my cheek.

"Unfortunately so, although we are yet to see them here. You won't want to try it, Missy."

Shock brought a small noise from me. "Violent? That's not true! That's what I'm trying to tell you—"

"I don't see any need to medicate her yet, but I shall provide Matron with some pills. She can dispense as required." The men spoke about me over my head, as if I weren't even in the room.

Pills?

"Listen, please, this is all a great mistake." My voice had risen, desperation giving it a sharp edge. I must try and regain my composure. To lose it now would be to confirm everything they'd been told about me.

The doctor moved back to his desk and wrote something on the great ledger again. Not, as I had so hopefully suspected, anything to do with my release.

"I shall return in two days' time, and we can review the situation."

My head twisted between the two men. It was as if the patient they spoke of was a specter, and I, merely wallpaper. Less than wallpaper, which once, in the choosing of it at least, had proved to be of interest.

"Doctor." I was pleased when my voice did not shake. I twisted my hands together to still their awful trembling. His gaze fell on them before lifting, finally, to my eyes.

"There has been a misunderstanding. I can assure you I am perfectly sane. My sister and husband have conspired to put me in here. She is a difficult personality. Demanding. Obsessive."

He shook his head and narrowed his eyes. "A conspiracy? Now, I wonder why they should go to all the bother of that?"

I opened my mouth and then closed it again with a huff of breath. Why indeed. Money, jealousy, Victoria's ever constant need to be in control, Stanley's selfishness, his gambling?

My heart ached at the thought of speaking those unspeakable truths, an ache so deep it stole the breath from me.

"Lady Stanley?"

I opened my eyes. I hadn't even realized I had closed them. How must I have appeared to them, standing in the middle of the room with my eyes closed, swaying like a drunkard. My nose pricked unpleasantly, and I bit hard on my quivering lower lip.

A feeling of such utter exhaustion, such desolation came over me that I couldn't think of a single thing to say.

The doctor nodded again at the warden, who tugged me from the room. His fingers dug into the soft flesh of my underarm, and I stumbled at the sudden jerk.

"Wait! Wait!" I cried.

The matron dashed over. "That's enough."

"If you cannot control yourself, then we will be forced to medicate you," the warden warned, his voice low and hot in my ear. "You don't want that. Money means nothing here. I am the one in charge."

Matron seized my other arm, and the three of us swayed like mad dancers.

"Please, just listen to me," I called to the doctor, aware that I was not behaving as I should, but unable to stop myself. I couldn't

MY SISTER'S SHADOW 233

bear the thought of spending another night trapped in this filthy hovel. Away from everything I'd ever known and loved.

Jack.

His name was like a bucket of frigid water had been dashed over me. What had they done to him? Stanley would kill him if Victoria told him, that much I knew. My knees gave way under me, and I fell onto the hard-packed earth. The warden released my arm, but the matron hung on, her fingers gripping painfully as she yanked me upright.

"There now, you behave yourself. You'll set the other girls off."

"Careful, she's prone to fits."

That word again. Hadn't I spent my entire life being obliging and demure? Hadn't I always done exactly what everyone had told me I should? Marrying Stanley, moving to New York, attending the endless empty parties, doing everything and anything asked of me?

I had denied myself over and over again, and yet here I was.

I longed to collapse onto the dirt and wail. What kind of terrible plot had Victoria concocted with Stanley? And to what end? How long would they leave me here?

Matron yanked me to my feet, and I suppose I truly must have looked every inch the mad woman. She ducked her head and peered into my eyes.

"Do we need to put her in the darks?" the warden asked her.

Her hard eyes, as shiny as pebbles, met mine, and finally I saw just what I was up against. The awful realization made my knees tremble again, but I straightened and cast my eyes to the ground. I had a lifetime of pretending to be something I was not. That familiar panic began to flutter in my chest again.

"Forgive me, Matron, I think it was the heat. I should like very much to sit down. I shan't disturb you any further."

She gazed at me, a suspicious slant to her eyes.

234 January Gilchrist

"You can tell him, her . . . you can tell my husband, my sister, that they win. They win. They can have whatever they want. Tell them, please," I reached for her arm, but she shrugged me off like I was a bug. "Tell them," I implored.

That was the only way they would let me out. As soon as Victoria felt herself the victor, this would be over.

Matron shook her head at the warden, sparing me from God only knew what.

But she couldn't spare me from the rest of it.

CHAPTER 27

Two days later—two days of the same awful routine, the night bucket emptying, the pretense at washing, the vile food, the wails at night—the doctor was back, and this time I had a clear plan. After we performed our tasks, we stood in the courtyard awaiting our turn as we had before. Matron watched me with a pointed gaze as I neared the front. My hands shook with excitement, for this was surely the moment he would set the wheels in motion that would release me.

"The doctor doesn't have time for your nonsense. No fuss today. I'm warning you."

I nodded and folded my hands together at my waist.

"Lady Stanley, how are you?" the doctor asked after the matron had closed the door behind her. He was seated again, looking over his ledger at me.

I sat on the hard bench, my posture painfully correct. "I am feeling much better, Doctor. Much clearer in my head."

His gaze slid to the clock on the wall. "Splendid."

I dipped my head and lifted my eyes to him, staring without speaking until he glanced up at me. I told him how I had seen the error of my ways and was feeling as I should and would very much like to go home.

The doctor nodded in all the right places, summing and aah-ing in a distracted way, the way one might agree with an elderly relative who would not stop talking. With impossible slowness he laid his pen down and moved around the desk to sit beside me on the small hard bench. I flinched away. The smell of his body, the heat of him, it was all too close.

"I'm afraid that is impossible. I am under orders." He placed a finger under my chin and forced me to look at him. His eyes were shot through with blood, and his breath was pungent. A sour taste crept from my stomach to my mouth. His nearness made my flesh crawl.

"You see, I have been charged by Lord Stanley himself to establish the cause of your disease, keeping you here as long as required until we can do so, to ensure I can cure you, once and for all, of your delusions."

"Here? But why? Why not attend to me at my house, where I am comfortable?"

The doctor paused, a moment of hesitation so brief that one might have dismissed it as nothing more than a man finding his words. But there was something in that pause, followed so closely to Stanley's name, that chilled my blood.

"I am researching disorders of the mind. Delusion, fancies. You see, I believe these things start in the body." He finally looked at me, his piggish eyes narrowed as they moved along my breasts. His tongue darted across his lips under the neatly trimmed mustache.

"While I desire to cure you, of course, my life's calling is to understand how these types of delusions begin, so I can pull them out by the root. Then, and only then, will you be fit to return to civilized society.

I could not speak. My whole body began to shake. A hot flush rushed along my chest and neck until it reached my face, where it burned, burned, burned. The doctor peered along his nose at me.

MY SISTER'S SHADOW   ☙ 237

"Ah yes, here it comes." That tongue again, tracing his lips as if savoring a delicious meal. "You see, Lady Stanley this is not just grotesque curiosity, nor is it idle interest. It is my calling."

The repetition rendered his words falser rather than truer as was clearly his intention.

"Do you know where you are? Do you understand?" He moved back to his desk, reaching for his precious ledger and pencil without taking his eyes from me.

I shook my head. The words stuck in my throat like a bone. "Yes," I croaked. "I'm quite in my right mind."

His face tightened, as if slapped. "But how you quiver. I see your body quake."

As if following an order, my body began its devilish shaking again.

"Do you wish to strike me? Strike yourself?"

The pencil was poised over his stupid ledger with its orderly lines filled with spidery writing that must make up his nonsense. It was he that suffered from delusions. All that talk of callings and cures. I didn't believe a word of it.

Lurching from the bench, I stepped backward until my back was against the wall. My hands pressed against it, and I was grateful for the solid weight. My chest heaved as I gasped for breath, and the doctor's eyes fixed on it.

"I am quite in my right mind, Doctor. I simply wish . . ." I trailed off. There was little point in repeating my earlier requests. "Tell me, Doctor. What did you mean earlier when you said you have orders. Ordered by whom? The police? Stanley? My sister?"

His eyes slid away. "Your diagnosing doctors, of course."

Those crooks hired by Stanley. "But surely you are fit to make your own diagnosis? You are skilled enough to see that I am perfectly in my right mind? Fit to leave?"

His gaze returned to his ledger. My calmness disinterested him: he wanted the panic and fear in my eyes; he wanted the heaving chest, the sweaty palms, the labored breathing.

238 ❧ January Gilchrist

"I wish to write to my father," I say. "Lord Radcliffe."

His pencil scratched along the page. "I am afraid that is impossible."

"My husband, then?"

"He will be receiving a monthly report."

My chest tightened. *Monthly.* "From whom?"

"I will provide the warden with my feedback, and he will pass it on to Lord Stanley."

"You will discuss my medical treatment with my husband? The man who has landed me here is the one to whom I must prove I am recovered? From how many miles away?"

"I have agreed to keep his lordship abreast of your treatments, to allow him to make his decisions."

"What treatments are they to be?"

He finally looked up from his ledger. A slow smile spread across his face. "I don't expect you would understand the medical terms. But rest assured, I have been chosen for this position because of my knowledge and interest in cutting-edge medical procedures."

Cutting-edge. What a choice of words.

"Chosen for the position? Why, Doctor, I had assumed you were simply the only one available."

I stumbled blindly to the door.

"Lady Stanley?"

I paused in the doorway. How it pained me to respond to that name.

"You are free to leave. The very moment your husband signs you out. But his opinion will be based on my feedback."

It was a threat. Of course.

My hands fisted at my sides. I straightened my spine and walked from the room into the blinding sunshine.

I made my way to Matron. "What are the rules regarding sending communications and receiving visitors?" I asked her.

MY SISTER'S SHADOW ⌒ 239

"Visitors?" She barked a laugh. "Expecting someone?"

I held her stare. Anger flowed through me, but I kept it tamped down. "The rules?" I repeated.

Her small brown eyes held mine, and I began to sweat. I was a fly, wrapped tightly in the silk of a spider. There was no escape, and the more I wriggled, the tighter the rope bound me.

"You are free to receive any visitors who come *within* the official designated hours." Her lip curled and she narrowed her eyes. "If any of your upper-crust friends would dare lower themselves. One letter can be sent and received every week."

She turned to the line of ladies watching our exchange with gleeful interest. "What are you gawking at?" she barked.

The ladies swung their heads back to the front of the queue, except Bosie.

"They have to let you see anyone who comes for you," she whispered from the side of her mouth as I took my place behind her. "Those are the rules." She didn't glance at me when she spoke, and I gave no sign of having heard.

For I had learned that rules did not apply here.

I was well and truly on my own.

* * *

Later that evening, I lingered over supper, rising only when Bosie stood to make her way to the bucket of putrid water.

"Listen," I hissed to the back of her neck. "I must get out of here. As quickly as I can. I have money. I can send it to you once I get back to New York. I have powerful friends who will get you out. You must know of a way?"

Her back stiffened over the bucket. She took her time with her dish, running her fingers over the lip of the plate, scratching at a stubborn spot with a jagged fingernail.

"I'll tell you how, all right. You do your time and wait for whoever put you in to decide to let you out." She turned to me

240 ◜ January Gilchrist

then, her eyes dark and cool. "Just like the rest of us. They have all the power, and you have none. There isn't anything you can do except wait."

I thought of all the waiting I had done. My whole life I had waited. Like a good girl, I had done as I was told. What good had it done me?

I was done with waiting.

* * *

"I should like to send a letter," I said to Matron.

"Should you now?"

We were standing in the courtyard, and her gaze remained fixed on some distant spot on the horizon. She was not looking at anything—of that I was certain. This was little more than a power game. But I had played power games with people far more powerful than she.

"My father. He is aging and has been in poor health. I worry he has no way of contacting me, to know that I am well, to inform me if he is well. You told me I am entitled to a letter a week, but I've yet to send one."

This hellhole had been my home for three long weeks, and it was becoming harder to hold on to my belief that I would be freed any day. The nighttime was the worst, when the lonely sounds of the prison were the only company. I lay on the bed, so hard and itchy, and stared up at the night sky through the window, imagining that the wind could take my thoughts to Jack, that wherever he was, he would feel the caress of the breeze along his skin and know it was me.

The monotony of the days, the lack of stimulation, the lack of freedom. If I stayed, I knew I would go mad. How could I not?

Our every movement was controlled and monitored, and the matron was not afraid to lash out when she felt challenged. No

MY SISTER'S SHADOW 241

one was coming to save me—that much had become clear. I had to do something.

I slopped my tin, took my place in the queue, ate the watery gruel, rinsed my bowl, rubbed the same filthy square of cloth over myself as the first day. The doctor came to visit twice a week, and on the days he did not, we were led to the square of strawlike grass that the ladies laughingly called "the garden," where we chased the meager shade until the bell for lunch rang, returning after eating to sit silently, awaiting dinner.

* * *

The arrival of winter began, so slightly that if I had had another way to occupy my hands, eyes, and heart, I would not have noticed the air begin to cool. The wind began to whisper a little stronger, and the leaves from the trees beyond our walls colored and dropped.

With no point of reference, the days blurred into one putrid ball of squabbles and petty arguments. Each day moved at the same speed, in the same direction—to the dining room, standing over plates of graying meats and soggy, colorless vegetables. The only break from the monotony was on Sunday afternoons, when Matron read seemingly never-ending passages from the Bible until we longed for the quietude of the week. Who chose the passages I don't know; they were all about punishing wicked women. Where were the verses about retribution? An eye for an eye and so forth. But no. We were left with Jezebel and her dogs.

Then, on the eighth or ninth Sunday, it hit me. My legs began to shake. Women were allowed their post every Sunday afternoon.

I should have received a message by now. Of any sort.

My foot tapped an unsteady rhythm on the floor while Matron's voice buzzed in the air around me, like the incessant

242 January Gilchrist

flies. But none landed. All I could think about was getting to her and asking for my letters. She had to be keeping them back from me. Jack would have written. He would have. Father must have received my missives by now and returned one to me. Shame burned hot within my chest. What Father must have thought when he received my letter explaining what Victoria had done.

How foolish, how petty this would all seem to him. He would have me out with the mere stroke of his pen. Perhaps the warden was holding them back from me. I would demand to see them, because surely they were the key to my release.

"Matron." I pushed my way through the drowsy ladies and stood in front of her, my hands on my hips.

Her eyes flicked from my hands to my face, and her own face twisted. "What now? I've had it with your jabbering."

I drew in a breath and forced my voice to a permittable level, even though I longed to scream and yell. Her time would come. "I have not received my mail yet."

With an irritated shake of her head, she snapped the thick Bible closed. "I ain't your private secretary. Maybe all those fancy friends are too busy to write ya."

It wasn't that. I knew it wasn't that. Jack wouldn't leave me in here without a word. A sickening thought hit me. A ball of anxiety, thick and cold settled in my stomach. Victoria was an incredible mimic. She'd fooled staff who had known us for years at Harewood when she'd taken it on herself to pretend to be me. Caught with her hand in the cookie jar—"I'm Adelaide." The piglets released from their pens—Adelaide. The inside of Morris's precious topiary tree hacked open—Adelaide. Father's precious glass paperweight smashed on the tiles—Adelaide.

But surely Jack would know the difference? Surely? I was no longer sure of anything.

"Are my letters being withheld from me?"

My Sister's Shadow   ☞ 243

She stood, crowding me with her bulk. "I've got better things to do than worry about your letters." A pause, and then that smile I had come to know so well. She had something over me. "Ask the doctor about it next time you meet with him. Right, you girls! Into line."

I lined up with the other women, but I couldn't shake the sight of Matron's smile.

★   ★   ★

I stepped into the doctor's office as if walking into a dream. He was in the same suit he always wore, sitting at the desk, the same arrogant, indulgent expression on his face.

The same ledger.

Although on this day, several papers were spread out before him, as starkly white as bodies laid on a marble slab.

My letters.

The sight of them almost brought me to my knees. I pitched toward the bench and fell on it. A buzzing began in my head.

He smiled, a grotesque movement of his mouth, and swept the papers into his hand. "Do you know what these are?"

"My *private* letters."

They never posted them. All my words, all my waiting, had been for nothing. They had tricked me. No one knew where I was. No one was coming. The floor felt as if it had opened beneath me.

"Lady Stanley." His tone was that of a nanny scolding a child. "There is no such thing as privacy here. If I am truly to understand your illness, then I need an insight into your mind. What better way to do that than to read the words that your own hand has written?"

Liar. I looked at his face. He was nothing but a voyeur. He got a thrill from all the peeping and peering. He enjoyed laying us bare, stealing our truths from us, having us stand metaphorically naked in front of him.

244 ⟡ January Gilchrist

"Yes, you were so very adamant, assuring me your interest was not merely curiosity. Yet here we are. Reading my personal letters, the very equivalent of rummaging through my drawers." My tone was sharp.

His mouth tightened and his mask of gentle benevolence slipped. "You will speak to me with respect."

I said nothing. Panic fluttered to life in my chest.

"I have been perusing your papers." He leaned back in his chair. "Who is Jack?"

His name was like a blow, but I took the hit without flinching. "Have you not sent *any* of the letters? Not a one? Not even to my father? You have misled me."

"We have done no such thing. I am required to continue my investigations. I shall return them to you upon your discharge."

I huffed a breath. Fat lot of good a letter begging for my release would be to me after I was released. If I was ever released.

I stood. "I demand to speak with Lord Stanley. Now. I demand it."

I had imagined I would sound like Wiffy, but instead my voice was shrill, unsteady. Frighteningly unstable.

"You don't get to demand anything here. I'm in charge."

I finally saw the truth of him. These men were all the same. They wanted to tear the flesh from my bones with their teeth, simply to prove they could. That frantic fluttering in my chest spread. But it wasn't panic after all.

It was rage.

A deep, white-hot rage that pulsated within me.

He leaned back in his chair, the movement causing the buttons on his jacket to strain around his paunch. I wanted to lean forward and jab my fist into it. To show him how it felt to have the wind knocked out of you.

My Sister's Shadow   ☞ 245

Instead, I stood and swept my arm along his desk, knocking my letters, the ornate glass paperweight, and his mug of coffee to the floor. He lurched forward, arm outstretched to grab me, but I had avoided craftier men than him and I was out the door before he could touch me.

Like an oasis, the finishing line shifted and moved the nearer I thought I got to it.

CHAPTER 28

The women grew bad-tempered, complaining about their gowns, pulling and scrunching their skirts as if the fabric were responsible for the cold that had begun to hover. Outside in the garden the ladies huddled closer, tucking chilled hands into skirts and armpits.

The nights were the worst. The damp seemed to cling to the brick, and the wind tore through the open window, bringing with it sleet, rain, and the stench of rot. The rough bed linen did little to warm or protect against the damp. There was no relief.

And then there were the dreams. I fretted and tossed and turned on my pallet, wide awake, listening to the noises of the other women and the rain. This was no gentle drizzle; it smashed to earth, causing rivers to spring where no river had been, pooling and rising violently into cracks and crannies. The noise of it was terrifying, thunderous pounding that made you fear the roof would collapse at any moment. The force of it! The sky would darken and flash in silent warning as the storm moved across the sky until it broke into the evening air. The ladies would begin to shriek and yell over the din.

I would dream of Victoria. Her name chased me through the halls here.

There were no looking glasses in the asylum, for fear of them being smashed, or perhaps to discourage the sin of vanity, of which there was no chance here in our stained, worn dresses.

But I didn't need a mirror to see her.

When I thought of myself, I saw her. Not the hard face that had stared at me as the carriage had rattled down the path that dreadful day. It was her wide, delighted eyes at the taste of the first sweet summer strawberry. The way her mouth dropped open into a smile while she slept. The soft downy skin on the back of her neck.

I hated her. Oh, how I hated her!

But she was as much as part of me as my own arm. Hating her was like hating myself.

* * *

I woke one morning with Jack's name on my lips and my tears on the linen that covered the unforgiving pallet. A pale sliver of sun shone through the window, hitting the wall just below the ceiling. I rolled to my back and stared at the ceiling, trying to will myself back into the dream. The warm feeling of it was ebbing slowly, and I lay perfectly still, savoring it as it receded back into the dream realm. It wasn't unusual for me to dream of Jack—his name was never far from my lips. Like the trams that ran on their tracks around New York, my thoughts always circled back to Jack.

This morning was different, though; the strange half world between dreaming and wakefulness lingered. He had been standing beneath a tree, a book in his hand. Unread. That was important. It was if the entire purpose of the dream had been to tell me that the book was unread.

The birds began to sing their frenetic tune. The musical warbling of the territorial blackbird, the grief-stricken mourning dove, the *"oh dear me"* of the golden crown sparrow.

Oh dear me, indeed.

248 ⟋

The dream dissipated, and the concrete weight of the never-ceasing dread settled back onto my chest. I swung my legs over the pallet, staring at my feet against the filth of the cement floor. I no longer felt the cold. I no longer felt anything. I just moved through the day like a ghost.

The chorus of ladies began, informing me it was time to start the day. I squatted over my tin and then shrugged into the thick linen uniform that now fit me like a second skin. Its peaks and valleys were those of my own. My ribs and hips had appeared, sharp protuberances on a bone-white canvas. The flesh on my face felt as heavy as my heart. It was if the dream had made the reality of my situation all the worse. Like a boot pressed relentlessly on the back of my neck.

Although I had just woken, I felt exhausted, drained of life. I could have lain on that rock-hard pallet and slept for a week. The rattle of the stairs, the clomp of Matron's boots as she worked her way down our row, the clinking of the keys as she unlocked the doors before mine, the chirp of voices. The women greeted Matron enthusiastically, as it was the only time we were really permitted to speak.

I took my place on the bed. Wrists and ankles crossed over one another as I once had as a dutiful debutante. The thought brought a wave of disturbed laughter to me.

Matron unlocked the door, but instead of moving on, she hovered. Her face was flushed an unpleasant shade of red, but she didn't look angry—merely uncomfortable.

"Good morning, Matron."

Matron's bosom heaved as she sucked in a breath, almost as if steeling herself. Curious. "We have guests today. A reporter and his photographer. They work for *The Post*. They're doing an article on the new procedures the doctor is trialing."

I nodded, wary. What did this have to do with me?

She ran a reddened hand along her lantern jaw. I waited for her to continue, eyes wide, guileless.

My Sister's Shadow ❧ 249

"They'll want to hear about how things go here and the like. They'll want to talk to one of the women."

My heart leaped. This might be my opportunity to tell my story, to find someone who would believe me.

"You'll talk to them. Won't you?"

I cocked my head at the pitch of her voice. She wasn't asking me to speak to the journalist. She was asking me to speak well *of her* to the journalist.

"Is there anything in particular you'd like me to mention?" I asked, as gracious as any society lady.

Relief softened her features, and for a moment, fleetingly, she was merely a woman, showing herself to another.

"It's for funding. Be sure to mention your respect for the doctor. He will be sitting in for a morning lesson."

"Lesson?"

There were no lessons here, no opportunity for betterment. Just hours of waiting, whiling away our dreary lives with an endless desolation.

She pinkened. Not the right term—*pinkened* conjures images of blushing, plump women fluttering their fans, youthful embarrassments, the flush of desire. This color came in splotches, highlighting the sunken gray skin around it. This color was ugly, repulsive. I glanced away.

"We will be doing a lesson in the dining room."

I understood. Instead of idling, either roasting or freezing, depending on the season, in the garden, we were to be dusted off and wheeled out like overgrown dolls. I wondered how she imagined she would keep the other women under control.

"The article may help us secure more funding," she confided.

Funding for what? There was little of any value to be found within the walls of the asylum. Nothing to read but the Bible, which had been torn to a quarter of its size, the pages now lining the slop pile. That was the only use we had found for God in here.

250 ☙   January Gilchrist

I nodded, though, and thought again of Jack in my dream. Unread, he had said. The book in his hand. *Unread.*

This story was salacious enough to interest the hardest-nosed journalist, but if not, I would resort to bribery. The wire that had tightened around my chest since I'd entered this hellish place began to tighten again. This was my chance. I had to make this my chance.

Matron moved off to open the other doors, and I made my way down the rickety staircase, into the blinding sun, with dream Jack's words ringing in my ears.

★ ★ ★

And so it came to pass that Meadowleigh Insane Asylum was visited by Misters Fegan and Ruddle, two smug young men who inspected our quarters with an interest that was equal parts unseeing and unprofessional.

The iron door was pulled open, and two well-dressed men stepped into the shadow of the portico. They removed their hats and wiped their brows, exclaiming loudly.

"It's a relief to get inside. The wind is positively barbaric today."

The warden shook their hands and welcomed them in. His manner was that of the lord of the manor welcoming his hunting party.

"If I can just ask you gentleman to add your signatures here to our autograph book." His voice was booming, cheerful.

"Oh, ho, I hope we aren't signing our lives away," said one, taking up the pen.

"Be sure to let us out after our visit," joked the other.

How they laughed. As if being locked in here, day after day, was merely a joke.

Neither man was a day over twenty-five. One's face was red and pocked with acne. The other was slender, healthy looking,

MY SISTER'S SHADOW 251

and tanned, as if he might enjoy a jolly game of cricket in the park with his pals on the weekend. They had the laughing, jeering faces of young boys often found huddled in groups around the entrances to parks and alleys. The spotty one ran his gaze over the ladies boldly, winking at Mary as he met her eye. The other one carried a leather satchel that bulged in a particular way. A camera. Like the reporter at Wiffy's party the first night we had met. The difference between the two events struck me like a blade to the ribs.

They stood in the portico, eyes squinting as their blameless fingers pointed out something of interest to the other. We were queued up in a row at the front of the building, like horses lined up at the starting gate, anticipating the gun.

It rankled, the shininess of these men's shoes, the money evident in the cut of their warm woolen trousers, the rosy apples of their cheeks. It infuriated me to be laid bare to these men, without payment for the pound of flesh they would surely take.

The handsome one stared in our direction longer than was polite before adjusting his hair and turning back to the warden.

"If you're going to boff me, you'd better pay," Mary muttered in the line.

"Them don't boff the likes of you, Mary. Prefer each other I'd mind."

A wave of silent laughter moved along our line, nothing more than energy, a gold thread binding us neatly to each other. Sisters we were in that moment. Sisters united against these men. Perhaps all men, should the occasion have required it.

There is nothing like the fierce kinship of women. When petty jealousies and squabbles are put aside, when no power play exists. Just kinship. Pure and true.

Perhaps it was the two strangers who stood among us after weeks of seeing only the same faces; perhaps it was the sharp edge of derision in their eyes, the curl of their lips, the fresh powder on

Matron's face—agonizing in its hopefulness. But whatever it was, without word we reached, one by one, for one another's hands.

We stood, heads bowed, expressions hidden by our bonnets, hands clasped tightly, in unity with each other.

"Not today," those clasped hands said. *"You will not break us today."*

I watched as the visitors chatted easily to Matron. Only the slender one had removed his hat. His hair was long and greased back but a lock had fallen over his brow in a highly practiced manner. He looked over at us and flicked his head to encourage it back into its position. Which it compliantly obeyed. His smile was confident and polite and utterly empty.

My fingers tingled. This young, unsuspecting man was my ticket out of here.

Matron clapped her hands twice, and it took us a bewildered moment to realize she was gesturing to us. We spread out, like stars in a pond, hands still tightly clasped.

The men walked along our line, nodding and examining while Matron prattled on about nonexistent achievements and successes. I was last in the line, and by the time the camera-less man approached, I was ready.

"How do you do?" I said, my accent sharp enough to cut glass, and Victoria's tilt to my chin. A planned attack that squarely hit its mark.

His eyes widened. He was too young to have mastered hiding his emotions, or perhaps he'd only ever been the hunter, not the prey. His gaze flicked from my eyes to my lips, then my hopeless gray dress. What was it that made his eyes linger so? The dress was barely better than a potato sack. But linger they did.

"That is not an accent I expected to hear within the hallowed halls of Meadowleigh," he said, an incredulous tilt to his lip.

He lowered his voice, but Matron angled her head toward us a fraction, her face straining with the effort of listening to both men at once.

MY SISTER'S SHADOW

"Hallowed halls? I wouldn't quite say that."

"What would you say?"

I gestured to his notebook, which hung loosely from his hand. "On the record?"

His eyebrows raised at my use of the term. "That depends."

"On?"

He smiled. It was partly amused and partly self-conscious. "On if it's newsworthy."

I darted a glance Matron. If it weren't for her stilted smile and stiff posture, she could have been at a tea party.

"I am Lady Stanley."

His eyes widened.

I continue. "Wife of Lord Stanley, the esteemed gentleman behind the proposed Belmont Racetrack. I'm being held here against my will. Inform John Carter from the *New York Herald*," I hissed urgently.

As if sensing our conversation had taken a turn, Matron gestured toward him. "Shall we move through to the laundry, sirs?"

Her tone left no room for argument, not that it was likely these two would, and they followed her gesture toward the laundry room. She hovered, turning to me with a sharp eye. I returned her look blankly. Matron moved forward, positioning herself between me and the men. Something in me quivered.

The knowledge that someone knew where I was, finally, was like a match held to tinder. I had spoken my name for the first time in months. To a reporter. A man paid to write on matters of interest. I lifted my chin to the sky as a cardinal took flight above us, flashing fire against the sky.

The men were shuttled between the big rooms, as we called them. Matron's room and the doctors' and warden's spaces.

They did not visit our rooms. Some things were best left to the imagination.

There was no further chance to speak to the reporter. He spent the remainder of his visit shooting panicked glances at me,

254 ⇌   January Gilchrist

intercepted always by Matron. But he writhed like a fish on a hook.

He vibrated with the desire to get back to his comfortable office in the city, with its view of the river perhaps. I glanced at his shoes. No, he didn't have an office, but he was ready for one.

And if Lady Luck was on our side, this would be the story that would take him there.

CHAPTER 29

My eyes were shut, and my head was against the brick of the main house, which was deliciously warm despite the cool air. The chatter of the ladies droned about me like the sweet sounds of spring. As I dozed, I imagined it was the chirping of crickets in the soft breeze or starlings calling to one another as they dipped and flew, free, in the forests of Harewood. The women's hushed laughter was the soft coo of the doves in Harewood's dovecote. The jangle of Matron's keys was the clinking of ice chips in a glass of cool, tart lemonade. Victoria was beside me, her hand brushing hair from my eyes, as if for a child by a mother.

"Stanley."

I jolted from my doze to see Matron standing in front of me, her face impassive.

"You have a visitor."

My daydream shimmered, and I blinked slowly as Harewood dissolved beyond her. One by one, the white caps turned toward me, tilting toward the sky slightly as blank eyes watched me intently.

"Well? Are you getting up, or will you sit there all day? I'll send them away, should I?" Matron said with exasperation.

"A . . . a visitor?" My heart began to thump like a drum. I daren't believe.

256 ☙   January Gilchrist

Matron tsked, then turned and strode back toward the gatehouse without a second glance.

"What are you waiting for?" Bosie hissed. "Get going. Before she changes her mind."

I scrambled to my feet, falling heavily on my knee in my haste. I ran to catch Matron, who hadn't slowed her pace nor stopped once she reached the gatehouse.

The visiting room was merely a small front section of the warden's rooms. A long table stretched the length of the room, six bare chairs along one side, six padded chairs on the opposite, for our visitors.

I walked into the room with a strange stirring in my heart. One that was almost so unfamiliar to me now, I wasn't able to recognize it. It was simply the pleasure of seeing a friendly face after seeing only strangers for so long.

Wiffy was alone in the room, perched on the edge of the stingy visitor's chair.

She looked up and our eyes met. I saw myself reflected in her horrified gaze, although she was quick to replace it with a tremulous smile. My heart thumped once, twice, painfully, and a raw dread grasped me around the throat. Wiffy was anything but tremulous.

My throat closed up, and I longed to throw myself into her arms, her nearness a pleasure I could not begin to describe. I bit the inside of my cheek to stop any thought of crying. How ridiculous, how pathetic I must seem to her. In this drab dress, this awful place, crying at the sight of her. I studied her as she sat primly at the table, her shoulders tight, her face a rictus.

She hadn't removed her coat. It was a pale green wool, with small pearls as buttons. I had forgotten about buttons like that, about fabric like that. My hands burned with the desire to run my hand along the collar, to work my thumb over the buttons, to bury my face into the soft silk lining.

My Sister's Shadow

Her hair had been wrestled into a bun, but tufts curled around the rim of her hat, which was a shock of bright yellow wool in the dreary room.

I stumbled into the chair gracelessly.

Her hands were clasped tightly, resting on the table between us, encased in bone-colored gloves so pristine that I wondered if she had another pair in her purse that she had exchanged in the doorway before entering.

She smelled clean, like ordinary soap, like clothes dried on a windblown clothesline.

Like freedom.

She sighed deeply, and the sound pierced my heart.

"I shan't ask how you are, Ducky. That haircut says it all." Her voice transported me. I didn't bother to wipe the tears when they came, just let them drip along my cheeks into my lap.

"That journalist from *The Post* called John Carter, who called me immediately. He told me everything. You clever girl." She pressed her fingertips to her eyes and breathed deeply. "My God. We have been beside ourselves."

"We?" I croaked out insensibly.

I half believed this to be a dream. Was Wiffy really here? At the asylum? I suspected that the last thread to my sanity had finally snapped, and I was still outside, back against the brick wall, dozing. Dreaming.

"I knew something had happened. I didn't know where you were, but I knew she'd done something. The way she appeared afterward. Like the cat that had got the cream, she was." Her face hardened. "Jack swore you weren't at the house. That you had been taken somewhere. Beebah was only too happy to withdraw her offer for them to stay, once I explained the situation."

I smiled. They would have hated that. The prestige of being in a Vanderbilt's house taken from them, and with it, their sense of entitlement, of otherness.

258 ~ January Gilchrist

Wiffy continued conversationally, as if it were merely weeks since we had last spoken. "Stanley found his entrée into New York's inner circles revoked. Walt's vote of confidence for his race-track also. Along with Belmont's and the Astors'. They've requested their donations back. Victoria is persona non grata and hasn't been seen in public since she was refused a table at Rector's."

Wiffy let out a sigh. That unnerved me, as she was not a woman who sighed. She was a woman who saw what needed to be done and set about making it happen. We sat in silence as she tugged the fingers of her gloves and placed them on the table between us.

"Stanley has hired the doctor here as his personal physician. There is little I can do about that. I offered to pay him more to be my doctor, but as your husband, Stanley still has the power to keep you in here. And while he's paying . . . there isn't anything I can do, I'm afraid. It's their word against yours."

I slumped against the chair. She wasn't here to take me home.

Her mouth pinched into a thin line, and for a moment she looked older, tired, angry. She narrowed her eyes at me.

"I asked Father, but anything Stanley tells the doctor is bound to the doctor–patient confidentially agreement, so we can't even sue him to have you released either. Walt is in England. He has written a letter to the governor, demanding an investigation, a change of legislation. But he can't do anything until his return. When it comes down to it, a rich woman is still just a woman. The boys' club has closed ranks around me."

Her eyelids fluttered closed, but her eyes were clear when they opened again.

"I'm sorry." She reached across the table to grasp my hand. Her eyes bored into mine, and she no longer looked sad; she was a fury, blazing with righteous anger.

"My dearest cousin, Connie." She blinked at the bare table. "Her mother had made a match for her with a duke. Technically a 'good' one, but it was one she didn't want. She was in love with

MY SISTER'S SHADOW ⌒ 259

Winty, and he with her. So very much. They decided they were going to run away together, Constance and Winthrop. But her mother got wind of it and had a doctor come to the house to diagnose her as insane. Her choice was to be committed or marry the duke. Her mother locked Connie in her room until the wedding and hired bodyguards to ensure she didn't escape."

Wiffy pressed her lips together into a thin line. "Or take her own life in despair. So, Connie married the duke. She sobbed all the way up that aisle. That's when I realized not every woman is a *sister*. Not every woman will protect other women. Some align themselves with the devil, and that is what her mother did. To further her own standing in society, she destroyed Connie's life. I told you before that some people would do anything to have our lives. To enter the orbits of the stupendously wealthy. The money, the servants, the dresses, the parties. But it's a gilded cage full of corpses."

She stopped, suddenly aware that her voice had risen and begun to shake. She swallowed. "That a mother would force her daughter to marry a man she didn't love simply to advance the family name, that a man can have you locked away for no damn reason and we can't do anything about it. It makes me so angry I could scream."

"I shouldn't have—" I started, but fell into silence as she grabbed my hand.

"Don't you dare. You did not do anything, *anything* to deserve this. This is not your fault." Her lip trembled. "I swear. I couldn't save Connie, but I will do whatever I can to save you."

Her eyes filled and my chest tightened.

I was awed by bearing witness to such a display from Wiffy.

Wiffy, of the sharp wit, quick quips, and hardened shell that nothing seemed to penetrate, was crying. Here. Had there been any feeling left in me, if I hadn't cried myself dry, it would have been enough to bring me to tears.

Instead, I smiled. "Winifred Williamson, crying in an asylum. Now there's a headline."

"If you tell anyone you saw me cry, I'll kill you myself, you hear?" Her tone was light, her gaze fixed on her purse as she rummaged through it. She dabbed at her eyes with the corner of a spotlessly clean handkerchief, sucked in a breath, and fixed a gimlet stare on me.

"I'll get you out, but you have to hang in there. Promise me."

She reached for my hand and squeezed so tightly that momentarily I feared she would break a bone.

"Promise me." She didn't release my hand.

I nodded.

"When Walt returns, he will be meeting with the governor, but you must be brave and fight. Do not give up."

I nodded again and she released my hand. She took her silver cigarette case from her purse and tapped the tip of a pre-rolled cigarette on the table.

The sound of the flint against the wheel of her lighter was the only sound in the room. I doubted that either myself or the guard stationed at the corner of room was breathing. I was suddenly aware of him at my back, his presence an ominous, thick energy. Wiffy leaned back in the chair as she inhaled her cigarette, and for a moment I was breathless by the glamor of her. Her skin, so clean and clear, her scent a veritable flower bed. She exhaled loudly, blowing a long stream of blue smoke into the air between us.

"As you know, my father worked as a solicitor."

My eyebrows puckered. I was well aware of who he was. Everyone was.

"He is a man who understands the law. Made it in many cases."

She unclipped an earring and rubbed at her ear.

"He is also a father of five daughters. All women now." Her gaze was firm on mine; her jaw set; her lips tight, as if holding back anger, although her tone was as flippant as ever.

"When I married Walt, Papa gave me a house. On the river. It's mine and is held in a trust that can only ever be amended by

MY SISTER'S SHADOW   261

me. I also receive an allowance from him. Not that I need it. Walt makes more than enough to keep me in comfort. And then some."

Her voice was loud in the still room, and I cringed at how it reverberated off the walls. I felt the hot, angry gaze of the guard, Samuels, against my neck. The walls began to close in on me. My mind was reeling, seeing her, someone from my past—a past that felt so untouchable, so far removed from the life I was living here. It felt unreal, as if it were all a dream.

Although which life was the false one, I couldn't tell.

"Some months I don't even touch my allowance. I have no need to. Papa did the same for all his girls. Gave us sanctuaries and allowances and assets in our names."

I nodded. "He's a good man. As is Walt."

"He is, but if I wanted to leave him, divorce him, I could. I would be exiled from society, of course, but it would be on my own terms. I could spend my days at Newport. Choices. My father says the difference between people like us and less fortunate people is not money, but choices. Not the ones we make, but the ones that are available to us."

My top lip began to tremble. Her words were darts, piercing my skin. I had no choices. There was nothing available to me.

Wiffy leaned back in her chair and unfastened her other earring. She discarded the second on the table next to the first, carelessly, and drew on her cigarette again.

"Do you know how much a guard here earns?"

My gaze flew to hers. Her eyes were wide, and she held my look firmly. A corner of her mouth lifted, and my heart began to pound uncomfortably. She didn't understand this place. If she embarrassed Samuels, the power he had, the things he could do. It didn't bear thinking about.

"They make less in an entire year than my monthly allowance. Astounding isn't it. Obscene, almost. Unfair, certainly."

Her look of contemplation shifted to the corner of the room. My reluctant one followed.

262 ⮜ January Gilchrist

Samuels's face was red, his small eyes narrowed in anger, his top lip curled in disgust.

She raised her voice, directing it toward Samuels. "Do you know who I am?"

He spat a stream of dirt-colored tobacco to the floor. "Nope."

"Winifred Williamson née Helmsley. You might not know me, but you know of Daddy, Alfred Helmsley, don't you?"

I released a huff of air. She was magnificent.

"If you assist this woman to leave here, unharmed, I will reward you beyond your wildest dreams."

His small eyes darted to the back wall of the room, where the windows were pushed open to the corridor that led to the main rooms. He said nothing.

"I will make you a very rich man. You'd never need to work again. Do you have a family?" she asked him, her tone light, social.

He remained silent.

She half rose from the chair and began to rummage again through her purse. Pulling out a card, she extended it between two long, thin fingers. He made no move to take it. Her hands were soft, clean, pale. Her knuckles dimpled. She stood and leaned across the table toward Samuel, and as she did so, she covered the earrings with her other hand and slid them toward me.

"Here is my card. You've heard how fabulously wealthy my family is. I will commission a payment that would take you over two years to earn to have this woman freed. Safely."

Samuel's Adams' apple bounced as he swallowed, his gaze shooting to the window. He still made no move to take the card.

While Wiffy held his gaze, I bent forward to clutch her hand, scooping the earrings into my palm as I did so. I pressed them against her arm to let her know I had them, and she dropped the card onto the table.

"Very well. Should you change your mind, you can reach me at my New York residence. But think very carefully. On my husband's return from abroad, he will have this woman released, and you will have missed your chance."

I raised my hand to my mouth and coughed, shoving the earrings into my mouth. My hands trembled. Fear burst through my skin, leaving my hands slick with sweat, my armpits damp, my heart racing. I stared at the table blindly. I had to keep myself together. Samuels was suspicious and mean, and he would tear me apart if he suspected she had given me anything.

Using my tongue, I tucked the earrings into the space between gum and teeth in the fleshiest part of my cheek. The metal tore at the delicate flesh, but I did not flinch.

Wiffy stood and collected her gloves.

"Father is meeting with the governor regarding Walt's letter. But until then, please be assured I am doing what I can. Lord Stanley has underestimated the power of women here. I run society," she said without a shred of humility. There was a power in her voice that set something alight in me. A tiny flicker of heat that I thought had been extinguished flickered back to life.

I parted my lips to speak, but my mouth was too dry for the words to escape, and panic closed my throat. Thoughts were falling over themselves, wild untethered things.

Wiffy raised an eyebrow at me, as scathing and sardonic as she had ever been.

She draped her coat over her shoulders, and I couldn't help but smile at the image of her. Backlit by the sharp sun at the windows, she was a goddess. Both impossibly young and ancient at the same time.

"My grandfather was one of the world's wealthiest men. He made that money himself. Through sheer grit and determination. And as they say, the apple never falls far from the tree." She winked at me. "Chin up, Ducky."

Cocking an elbow at Samuels, she said, "Come on, handsome, walk me to the door."

Her hips swayed in a languorous manner. Not the scuttling, shuffling gait of the women here, as if we want to become invisible; Wiffy was a reminder that women could take up space.

Even in her heels Wiffy was inches shorter than the guard, but there was something about the way she held herself, shoulders back, chin raised, that made her seem taller, larger than him. His eyes narrowed at her, and she smiled her mocking society smile.

She was magnificent. Powerful. Brave. Strong.

She was a reminder that if I wanted something, I had to do everything in my power to make sure I got it. I could do this. I would do this if it was the last thing I ever did. That fire that had sparked in my chest flared back to life.

"Wait," I called when she reached the door. "Will you . . . tell Jack where I am?" Just saying his name was a lightning strike.

Her face softened. "He already knows, sweetheart. I had to stop him from laying into the place with a hammer. He would've knocked the walls down to get to you. But as I explained, that's not the way to play this game. *This* game needs a feather-light touch." She brushed her hand against the feather in her hat. "Before we smash it all to pieces."

* * *

That night I woke in the dark, my heart pounding in my ears. Rain thundered on the roof, filling the gutters with water, sending rivers along the wall. The water seeped through my blanket.

Victoria's name echoed in the room around me. I threw off the damp blankets and sat, staring blankly into the dark. Fear gripped me tightly, my hands were shaking, and my breath came in short, ragged gasps.

Visions of my dream flicked through my head. Iron, cold and heavy, and blood. So much blood.

My Sister's Shadow   ⌒ 265

I shoved the blanket between the cot and wall in the hopes of mopping up some of the water. The rain thundered and lightning flashed.

Merely a bad dream, I told myself, as my tongue worried over the diamond stashed in my gum until I tasted blood.

CHAPTER 30

That week was the worst of them all. I was twitchy, impossibly on edge. The bread stuck in my throat, impossible to wash down. I went through my chores with one eye on the door, my heart leaping into my throat every time the figure of the matron or warden appeared in the shadowed doorways.

Every morning I woke with a growing sense of desperation and dread. Perhaps I was mad after all? Perhaps I had dreamed Wiffy's visit. All I had to prove it was real were the earrings. In my last shift at the laundry, washing, mending, and ironing linens that arrived by truck, in huge bags, every Monday morning, I had stolen a needle and carefully stitched one earring into the bodice of my shift and the other in the hem. I checked them compulsively, unable to bear the idea of one of them slipping out, of losing my only chance to be free.

Then Wednesday came.

I woke to birdsong and a damp stream of sun through the window. I lay on the cot, my hand pressed to my heart. The clanking and jangling of Matron's keys began. The calls and whistles of the women as they started another day. An overwhelming feeling of dread overcame me.

MY SISTER'S SHADOW ⁓ 267

I stood and whipped my nightdress from my head, replacing it quickly with the now soft linen of the drab gray uniform. The blanket was sopping wet and smelled like wet wool. I cringed.

Today had to be the day.

* * *

We circled each other warily, Samuels and I.

He had to have been thinking about what Wiffy said, the money, the opportunity for him, the risk.

I could feel his eyes following me, watching, waiting for a moment to find me alone.

While the ladies lolled mindlessly in the garden, I edged toward him.

"Have you any thoughts?" I didn't need to say about what those thoughts could be. I imagined that, like me, it was all he had been thinking about.

"I reckon your pal gave you something," he muttered, his voice low and angry.

He'd been thinking about Wiffy's jabs. He'd lain in his mean bed, perhaps the bed he shared with an unhappy wife, pregnant again, asking for money, trying to make what little they had work. Perhaps his youngest was sick; they'd lost one already, age two; the happy loving woman he married had turned into an uncommunicative seething monster who made him feel like he should be doing more, being more.

His breath, stale and tobacco scented, was everywhere; his eyes bored into mine.

No, I reconsidered. There is no loving woman or wailing bairns. His eyes are too unkind. There is nothing in them but greed and anger.

"She did and you can have it all. If you help me," I said.

I dug my nails into my palms and focused my gaze on the white crescents they left behind.

268 ～ January Gilchrist

Don't breathe, not even a little, lest he hear the rattle of fear in it.

He stepped toward me, pressed against me. "Why don't I just take it from you?"

I raised my eyes and released that breath. "Because you know who she is. Because, one day, I will get out of here, and Winifred's father will know where to find you. You will be charged to the full extent of the law, and you will find yourself in my position, but I will not be in *your* position. I will be a woman with money. With influence. With power."

Our gazes locked. The truth of my words settled between us like dust.

"This is an opportunity. One you won't see again."

Please, God, let him be brave enough to take this chance.

The tip of his tongue worried at a weeping sore at the corner of his mouth. I averted my gaze. This wasn't the just the last opportunity for him. It was the last for me too.

"Take it or leave it. I'm sure someone else will be interested in hearing about it."

I gazed around the yard as if looking for the next person to talk to, but truthfully I was scanning to see who was looking at us. Who was watching.

Perhaps I really was mad—it certainly was madness to try this. To even stand here talking to this man. Let alone making an offer I couldn't have dreamed up even in my maddest moments. To make that offer in a voice that didn't tremble or waver.

If I showed this man the tiniest amount of weakness, of fear, then it was over. There was no reason for him not tell the warden or matron that I had tried to bribe him and that he believed I had something valuable on my person. They would strip me naked without a second thought. He might have been thinking about this ever since Wiffy had made her offer in the visiting room, but so had I.

He had turned it over and over like a stone in his palm, and he had come to the same conclusion that I had.

MY SISTER'S SHADOW   269

There was nothing else. No other option.

"What if you double-cross me?"

My eyebrow twitched. "Why would I? You're far more likely to double-cross me."

He would, this man with his black teeth and callous eyes. There was not an ounce of humanity in him. He would take whatever he could from me and destroy me afterward simply because he could.

"As unlikely as it seems, we will just have to trust each other," I said in a voice that was not my own.

He spat on the ground and took a step backward. With his backward step I felt my shoulders relax. I had him.

"Of course, there is the matter of Winifred's husband. Passionate supporter of women. Of me." Lies upon lies. "You will go to jail yourself if anyone gets wind of this. So, the way I see it, we both need to keep our mouths shut. I won't dob you in, and as you say, you won't rat me out."

He hadn't said anything of the sort. We both knew that.

"And in case you have any ideas, Winifred knows exactly what is planned and should I be found coshed on the head, lying in a ditch somewhere, she'll know who to have hung for murder."

He scoffed. "What is it? What you got from her."

I couldn't tell him what he was looking for. It wouldn't take much for him to come to my room and take it from me. Then I would be left with nothing, No, not nothing. Wiffy and Jack knew I was here now. I eyed Samuels, considering. He needed to know it was of enough value that it was worth the risk that we were both taking.

In for a penny, in for a pound. I closed my eyes and leaped.

"A diamond."

His chin lifted and his mouth tightened, his eyes aflame with greed.

"It needs to be tonight."

He shook his head. "Tomorrow. I'm on with Jenkins, that lazy shit. He sleeps most of the night shift."

"What will we do?" I had done nothing but think about this. I needed to get my door unlocked; go out the main door to the building, which was locked, but not staffed; and then out of the main door to the asylum, which was both locked and staffed. No matter which way I turned it, it would be impossible without him. Very nearly impossible *with* him.

He eyed me, a wicked tilt to his lip. "Don't go to sleep tomorrow night. I'll come get you."

I nodded, blinking as I turned back toward the hulking brick building that had been my home for all these months. My stomach rolled and I clutched it, sucking in deep breaths to stop the bile that rose, hot and sour, in my throat.

The asylum hunched against the vast blue sky, its windows like eyes, watching me. A light flashed in the top window. Just the sun of course, but it felt like a message.

The ladies stared at me with their hard eyes, their mad eyes as I returned to them. Only I knew now that most of them weren't mad.

Outrageous, funny, unusual, damaged.

Repressed, abused, powerless.

But not mad. Not truly.

Out of nowhere the wind whipped up around us, lifting our skirts around our knees. The linen in the drying yard flipped and dipped as if waving me farewell.

I blinked and the women's gazes had returned to the blank wall of the exercise yards.

My throat tightened.

Although I had hated this place, had done nothing but dream of the day I would leave its walls and never return, I had the strangest sense that it was not me leaving. The young, terrified woman with no voice that had entered was no longer, but had been forged into a harder, stronger version of herself.

My Sister's Shadow   ⌒ 271

Like a snake shedding its skin, I had outgrown the dutiful, kind, obedient Adelaide I had been. I was angry and ready to set the world on fire.

I was going to get those boots off my neck, even if it killed me.

★   ★   ★

Samuels held true to his word and came for me far earlier than I had expected. I sat on the edge of the metal cot, staring sightlessly at the stained floor. The sound of the key striking the lock sounded like a gunshot in the still evening. I cried out softly, and a burst of sweat broke out along my neck.

The door creaked open, and he peered at me through the crack. His eyes were black holes in the dim light. We stared at each other for a long moment, each of us weighing up just what we were about to attempt. Could we go through with it? He disappeared back into the black of the hallway, and I lurched to my feet to follow him.

Once I was in the hallway, he grasped my upper arm, his fingers biting into the soft skin painfully. But I dared not gasp, I dared not even breathe. The door was closed, locked, and we were out into the night air.

"To the back of the laundry," he muttered. "Quick now."

I ducked my head and ran toward the low building that steamed and hummed all day.

I didn't look back. I didn't think about the women inside. I didn't think of the shabby trick that had kept me trapped inside those damp, dark, steaming walls.

I thought only of reaching Jack, closer than he'd been for months. I was willing to risk it all to get back to him.

This would either take me to him or end in disaster. Either way, I knew I wasn't coming back here.

In the shadows Samuels held open a canvas laundry bag, and I climbed inside. He closed the top of it, and I plunged into darkness, and then he dragged me across the gravel of the courtyard.

272 January Gilchrist

Terror clawed at my throat, and how my stomach roiled. My heart beat so fast, so painfully, that I thought I might pass out from the sheer panic of it all.

Here we go, I thought. *He will kill me. This will be my last breath.*

I was thrown through the air and thumped to the wooden bed of the truck. I leaned into the agony in my hip. I wanted to feel every single moment of it, so convinced that he would kill me after it.

I lay in the stifling darkness and listened as the men shouted orders and commands, shared jovial asides, and made plans for their futures. How hopeful they were. I listened to my breath. The rasp of it against the rough canvas. I folded in on myself, willed myself to be invisible, to disappear. I prayed in the black stillness of that canvas bag, as black as a mother's womb, that I would be reborn at the end of the journey.

The truck grumbled to life and bounced and wove for what felt like hours.

My tongue worked at the diamond that I'd lodged in my cheek earlier that evening. The idea that I would accidentally swallow it was a compulsion. I needed it, and the fear that it would suddenly be taken away from me was one that I couldn't fight.

The rumble and roar of the engine, the whine as Samuels shifted gears, the bump and crash as the truck traversed potholes.

It was hell.

The day of my arrest, the realization that it was not a joke, the first night in that mean, humid cell—none of it compared to how terrifying that trip in the truck was. Because this time I knew. If I didn't escape, if I didn't get out of the truck, away from him, the asylum, all of it, then I wasn't going to make it.

I couldn't bear to live out my days at the asylum, the powerlessness, the dreary repetitive tasks, the looks, the fear, the bloody pointlessness of it all. I would rather be dead.

When the truck finally heaved to a stop, I almost cried out. With every agonizing moment that passed, the fear that had

MY SISTER'S SHADOW 273

clawed at me dissipated, and a burning anger arrived in its place. If this man with his black teeth and filthy fingers had betrayed me, then I would fight. I would rage. I would not go quietly this time. A tingle started in my fingers and flowed through my arms, filling my body with energy. My hip no longer hurt, my breathing became shallow, I lay still but my muscles hummed with blood, ready to spring at a moment's notice.

I thought of Stanley, how he had ripped me from my home for no reason other than that he desired to. But meek and mild Adelaide was dead. This girl would fight until the death for her freedom.

The rasp of the bolt, the groan of the door, a shuffling noise I couldn't decipher.

Then nothing.

He dragged me across the floor of the truck. "Out," he barked. He pulled at the rope that closed the bag, taking some of my hair with it. The pain was sharp, but I didn't cry out.

Yanking, tugging, pulling—and finally a rush of fresh air that told me the bag was open. In a tangle of arms, legs, and fabric, I gracelessly found myself half in and half out of the bag.

He stood at the back of the truck, a hand on the edge of both doors. His gaze darted from me to something outside my view. The fear it was the warden, the police, doctors who would send me somewhere worse gripped me by the throat.

"Give it to me."

"Once I am out of the truck."

He fixed me with that dark stare of his and lifted his head in affirmation. He enclosed my wrist in his rough hand and yanked me from the truck. I was flying, sliding, falling. I landed violently on the ground, my ankle twisting painfully.

"Give it to me."

"My things first."

I wouldn't get far in this dress. It wouldn't take much for them to find me and put me straight back in. He would keep the

274 ☙ January Gilchrist

diamond, his part of the agreement fulfilled, but I was not safe. I needed to blend in, to disappear.

"Give it to me. Now." His voice was low, and a muscle pulsed violently along his jaw. He wanted to hit me, I could tell, but I wouldn't give him what he wanted until I was sure I was safe. It was the only thing I had left to bargain with.

I would not be giving another man a single thing until I had gotten what I wanted. I lifted my chin. "My things."

We stared at each. A fox shrieked, and I was transported back to the misery of Greycliffe House. How far ago that seemed. It was another girl who had taken fright at noises in the night. This girl merely adjusted her weight onto her heels and stared hard at the man in the darkness. *Just try,* my hot gaze said as it bored into his. *Just. You. Try.*

After what felt like a century, Samuels leaned into the truck and reached for a bag at the open door. He shoved the bag against my chest but didn't release it.

There wasn't time to look in the bag. And I didn't really care if it was my things he had brought or someone else's. I just needed something that wasn't a sign on my back announcing "asylum escapee."

My fingers fished in my mouth for the earring, and I held it out toward him. The stone burned at my fingertips, making them feel light, too light, like they might fall open, dropping the stone into the long grass at our feet. He released a long fetid breath, and I saw then that he was scared too.

He snatched the stone from my fingers and pushed me to the ground. I scrambled backward, out of his reach.

"Get." He kicked at me.

I clambered to my feet, clutching at that drab canvas bag and ran. Stones scraped at the worn soles of my boots; I stumbled in my haste, but I ran. I ran for all the times I hadn't.

When Father told me I was marrying Stanley; as the veil was being placed on my head; the moments Victoria's attention had

My Sister's Shadow   ☞ 275

been diverted as we boarded the ship; the endless plunge to the cool ocean I didn't take; that still moment just after Victoria's small smile; the carriage looming up the driveway with the doctors inside.

My legs pumped; my arms clutched that bag so tight I would have strangled it were it alive. Blood roared furiously in my ears, and my breath came so loud that it sounded like three or four men puffed furiously behind me.

I didn't look back to see what Samuels did or where he went.

Keeping to small dark roads, I wove in and out of laneways, circling back on myself, until I was utterly, exhaustingly lost. A small alley between two large houses appeared. The windows of both houses were black, the inhabitants away or asleep. The laneway split along the back of the properties, and once I was hidden from the street, I collapsed to my knees and vomited the contents of my stomach up. I retched and retched until the convulsions shook me dry.

I placed my head on the dirt, running my fingers through it. I dug my fingers into the soft, silty soil until they hurt. That soil hadn't been tramped rock-hard by endless circles of inmates with nowhere to go.

Thirty breaths, I promised myself. Thirty breaths of that sweet, mossy soil. Thirty breaths out until I would stand, dress myself, and begin the rest of my journey.

The enormity of what I had done, and not yet done, was too much for me, so I listened to those breaths and counted slowly. Nothing else existed.

When I reached thirty, I sucked in a breath, opened the plain canvas bag, stripped to my undergarments, and replaced that filthy, worn canvas dress with a cotton and lace dress.

It had been mine the day I entered the gaol but now felt foreign to me.

The soft kid leather gloves were gone—sold to a pawnbroker, I imagined—and the small row of decorative pearls that had once

276 ∾ January Gilchrist

lined the front panel of the dress had been yanked from their spots. Sad wisps of thread hung limply where they had once been. The dress now hung from my asylum-withered frame like I was a scarecrow, but it was passable. A woman down on her luck perhaps, someone you might avert your eyes from pityingly, but not too unlike all the other down-on-their-luck women. No cause for a second look, no cause for alarm.

I tore at the fabric of the asylum-issued dress with my teeth, freeing the second earring from its hiding place and scrubbed at my face with the skirt before shoving it back into the bag.

Lumbering to my feet, I set out toward the low rumble of activity in the distance. Eventually I came across a brightly lit, squat red brick building—the railway station. A cry of relief escaped my lips, and I clutched at the wall lest I fall to my knees. It was so close.

The road leading to the station was industrious, and despite the late hour, trams rumbled along the road, bells dinging in warning to pedestrians.

People milled about, waiting for collection or lugging suitcases and unwieldy boxes, stacking and unstacking sacks of unknown things.

The entrance to the station was crowded as people paused to check they had all their belongings or attempted to wrangle their wailing children. A policeman stood idly at the entrance, his gaze on his shoes.

I watched with horror as the policeman pushed off the wall and strolled into the station, his long legs making short work of the distance. My blood rushed in my ears and my hands shook.

This task was beyond me. Stuck like glue to the wall, my chest shook as sobs heaved. Victoria was the forthright, brave one. This escape, this risk was something she would do, not me.

My dreams of escape were close enough to touch, but as far as they had ever been, for I had no money. I had an earring made of gold and its diamond, a worn and torn dress, and prison-issued

MY SISTER'S SHADOW   ☞ 277

boots. No hat to hide my bright shock of pale hair, with its asylum cut, and should a description be sent out to search for me, no chance, no luck.

I had nothing.

Time passed and eventually my sobs became whimpers. Eventually I regained my breathing, stilled my frantic heart. This didn't end here, me against the wall, crying. No, it wouldn't end here. I didn't have nothing: I had hope. And I had a fire that stormed inside me.

The chime of a clock announcing a half hour sounded like a starter's gun in my ears. I lifted my skirts and ran across the now-empty street, my twisted ankle crying painfully in my urgency. The solitary stationmaster sat in the window of the ticket booth, not raising his eyes toward me until I placed my hand on the stand between us.

"When is the next train to New York?" My voice was little more than a desperate rasp.

I swallowed to calm myself, to at least give the impression of calmness. That it was perfectly normal for me to stand in a darkened station requesting a ticket at this time of night, looking like this. But this man, with his reddened jowl and heavy jacket announcing him the ticket manager, had encountered people like me before. His disinterested gaze flicked up but did not rest before moving back to the newspaper on his desk.

"Two a day to New York. Six AM and PM."

My teeth began to ache, and a pain shot up to my temple. I blinked against the shame that swirled, ugly and hot, inside me.

I couldn't care what other people thought of me.

"How much is a ticket?

"Two dollars."

"And"—I licked my lips and cast about for the lone policeman I had watched wander into the station—"could you tell me if there is a pawnbroker nearby?"

He still didn't lift his eyes from the newspaper.

278 ֜   January Gilchrist

"Ann Burt, up the road on the corner of North Street. She opens before the first train goes." His tone was brisk, businesslike.

"Please. W-w-where is North Street?"

"Three streets to your left."

He flicked the newspaper and raised it so it hid his face. I was dismissed.

I pushed my fears down; there would be more of them to come—and plenty of time to give them the attention they would demand—and thanked him. I couldn't think of the dangers of what lay ahead of me, of how tenuous my freedom was, or I finally would go mad.

A large, white-faced clock hung above the entrance. Its chime had spurred me into action, but I hadn't been able to see it from my position across the road. It was now eleven forty-five.

There were six painfully long hours in which everything could fall in a heap.

I could not let it happen. I would not.

A train pulled into the station with a scream of brakes, wheels, and couplings. The smell of smut, smoke, steam, and bodies too long in one place filled the air.

Fingering the earring that I had pinned to the neckline of my dress, to reassure myself there was still hope, I walked out of the station into the balmy air, avoiding the cold gaze of a dirty-coated man, and trudged the four blocks to Ann Burt's pawnshop.

CHAPTER 31

Ann Burt was a short, round lady, with a bosom like a shelf and small round spectacles that reflected the light, making it impossible to see her eyes.

She held a jeweler's loupe to her eye, and the earring to the window.

A woman of few words, her small, hidden eyes had appraised my shoes, dress, hatless head, gloveless hand, and air of terror and desperation that a night lurking in the cramped, smelly alleyway behind her shop had given me, and she had formed her professional opinion. One, I imagined, that had determined that I had found myself in trouble that required a desperate meeting at five o'clock in the morning and was willing to accept any offer, regardless of how pitiful it was.

She had not even blinked as I approached her but simply nodded as she'd pulled a bloated ring of keys from her bag.

Now, she pursed her lips and pulled her lips back into a smile that showed crooked gray teeth.

"Worthless, if it ain't a pair."

I pressed my lips together to stop them trembling.

"The other one?"

I shook my head. "Gone."

She tsked. "Pity. Could've fetched a pretty price if there were two of 'em. Now, useless. No good to me."

She didn't attempt to hand it back. This was a well-worn game she played with every desperate person that landed on her doorstep before the morning train—to anywhere—departed.

I held my hand out between us. It was raw in parts, stained by dirt in others. Certainly not lady's hands. "It's of no concern. I am certain there will be someone else willing to reset a stone that size, not to mention the gold's worth."

She stared at me with a narrowed eye. "But you need the money now, don't you, pet."

She had me and she knew it.

"I do. My mother is sick, and I must . . ." I trailed off.

As soon as I had agreed, she'd walked to the counter. There was no story she hadn't heard before, and none she was interested in. What got her excited was the deal, driving the bargain, the win. I almost smiled. Let her have it. All I needed was two dollars for the train ticket. It mattered not to me if I was paid what that stone was worth. What it was worth to me was my freedom.

I gazed about the shop while she fussed at something behind the counter.

"Perhaps we can strike some sort of deal. I need a hat, gloves. A coat. Enough to buy my ticket too." I paused. I wasn't telling her anything she didn't already know.

The night had felt endless, stretching and lengthened in a way that undermined my resolve. The shadows mocked me, threatening to retreat and expose both the warden and the guards, and sometimes Stanley too. The rattle of trams spoke of the clip-clop of horses pulling carriages whispered of guards on their way, hidden in the shadowy depths. But as the shadows lightened, turning gray, then lilac, and finally disappearing, they brought nothing with it. Nothing but Ann Burt.

She lifted her chin and gazed at me through the specs hanging low on her nose. I smiled back, my gaze hard. I knew what I

MY SISTER'S SHADOW 281

needed, and I wasn't leaving here without it. Something had broken during the long night. Perhaps it was the last of my humanity. Or maybe it was the final string weaving me into a tapestry that others had woven.

I was finally free. And I would do whatever it took to stay that way.

There was a hardness to my voice. "I don't care what else you give me. As long as you give me those things and promise not to share my details should anyone come asking."

Ann Burt said nothing for a long moment, and whether she was considering my request or merely thinking about what she desired for breakfast was not clear to me.

"Aye," she said finally. "Lucky for you, I can rustle up some clothing. And as for telling anyone anything, as far as I'm concerned, the minute that door closes behind you"—she jerked her head to the door in question—"I never saw you."

In the end, the clothing she managed to dig up had been a presentable enough dress, too short at the hem and too wide at the waist but well enough to pass. She had assisted me into it in the backroom. The hat was her own, a serviceable felt number that I pulled low on my head. Ann found stockings, undergarments, and a small, worn bag. I dressed and she ran a practiced gaze over me.

The way her eyes roved over me transported me back to my bedroom in Harewood the night of the dinner, when it was Victoria's expert eye that had run over my dress, studying, considering, critiquing. But now wasn't then, of course.

Now it was the wary, brown gaze of Ann Burt. A sister. More a sister to me than my own.

★ ★ ★

People were gathering outside the train station for no reason other than it seemed to be what people did at stations. It was simply travelers and their companions, I reassured myself. The comfort

282 ☙   January Gilchrist

I'd found under Ann Burt's assessing gaze and strong hands, dissipated into the cool morning air. What I had done, and was hoping to do, pressed down on me like a weight. Again, I wondered if I were up to the task.

A man strode through the throng of people, buttoning his coat, his head swinging from side to side as he searched the crowd. The sheen of his boots flashed as he marched through the foyer. There was a sense of purpose about him that chilled me. I pressed myself into the shadows of the entrance and fumbled with Ann's little bag, pretending to search within it. Risking another glance at him, I watched as he stopped dead, causing another man to bump into him. Apologies were offered and received, but he remained still, his eyebrows drawn together as he stared at me. After a moment's hesitation he took a step toward me, then another.

Footsteps behind me increased in sound and speed. I closed my eyes. My heart hammered in my chest, and I was certain I would lose the contents of my stomach. I slumped against the wall, and my previous commitment drained from me. My chance was gone.

"Darling." A voice at my ear, and my eyes shot open.

The man was in front of me, smiling now, his hand outstretched. A woman brushed past me to clutch at him, kissing him on the cheek.

"Hello, darling," she said breathlessly. "Did you think I was not coming?"

He laughed, "I expect you to be late. I'm only surprised you're quite so early."

They linked arms and as they brushed past me, her gaze rested on me for a moment. "I say, are you feeling all right?"

I was slouched against the wall, my forehead against the hand resting on the cool brick, the other at my chest in prayer.

I nodded, pushing off the wall and lurching toward the crowd that surged and swelled at the ticket booth.

MY SISTER'S SHADOW 283

"How very odd." Her voice floated back to me.

I hurried on with my head down. I couldn't afford to draw any more attention to myself. Until I was on that train, I needed to hold myself together.

The line for tickets was orderly and moved fairly quickly, two windows open now. One displayed the man I had spoken to last night, and in the other, a younger man, who smiled and wished each passenger a jolly trip. Would the man from last night remember me? Would he think there was something strange about a woman with no luggage boarding a train? I didn't know and couldn't second-guess, but I joined the line for the younger man. The line moved briskly and within moments I was standing at the window, my voice requesting a one-way ticket, tense, waiting for a question I couldn't answer. I went through the motions, counting out the money with a trembling hand and blind eyes.

"Platform two. You have twenty minutes until departure."

I nodded, keeping my gaze on the ticket he had placed on the counter between us. The ill-fitting gloves and my nerves made me clumsy, and I fumbled with my change, which felt like lead in my hand. The heels of my boots tapped out a staccato rhythm on the stone floor.

"Miss! Excuse me, miss! Someone stop that lady."

I charged forward, increasing my pace to a trot. There were people everywhere, and faces turned toward me as I pushed through the crowd, connecting with shoulders, bags.

A hand closed around my arm, pulling me to a stop and I shrieked.

"Miss. You forgot your ticket."

It was the boy from the ticket booth.

I stared at him, open mouthed, panting.

His expression was kind. "Are you all right?" he asked softly, releasing my arm. "I didn't mean to startle you."

How extraordinarily I had revealed myself. I sucked in a breath and steadied myself. I was set to my course, and I must not

284 ⮒   January Gilchrist

falter. If I were to succeed, then I needed to gain control of myself, muster my thoughts, and forge onward.

"I have had some bad news, and it has rather unsettled me. My apologies. I am not myself." I fluttered my trembling hand to my chest, "My mother is gravely ill, and I must return to New York to attend to her."

The boy's expression cleared, and the crowd that had gathered around us moved on, disinterested in a poorly dressed woman and her ailments.

"Do you know which platform you need?" His tone was solicitous, gentle, and he remained next to me, awaiting my reply.

I nodded at his hand, gesturing toward the platform I sought. The platform that held the train that would take me to my destiny. All I had thought of was boarding this train. What lay beyond me once I disembarked, I had not considered.

"Can I assist you with your luggage?"

"Oh no, no. Truly, I am fine. Thank you for your concern." I moved off toward the platform, not daring to look back.

When I was certain I was hidden from sight, I picked up my skirts and ran toward the platforms, past the slow-moving crowd. I made my way around piles of luggage, and men with their newspapers, until I reached the very end of the platform. It was dim and solitary, most passengers congregating beneath the hurricane lamps or sitting on the bench seats. I stood, fearful that my lack of luggage made me conspicuous. The soft mewling of a baby began, and its mother paced along the platform, jiggling the bundle in her arms, making shushing and soothing noises. I watched blankly.

People gathered, lugging trunks and bags, large boxes, and wailing children. A porter hurried by, his hat pulled low and head bent, avoiding the pleading eyes in the crowd and calls for his attention. He was finishing his shift and had no interest in the needs of the customers.

The baby's wailing increased, as did the mother's urges for it to settle down. She pressed her finger into the baby's mouth, and it sucked furiously. A clock chimed, six tones.

And finally, the platform began to tremble, and the noise and heat increased as the train pulled to a stop.

CHAPTER 32

It took me a moment or two to disentangle myself from the confines of the carriage. my legs seemed unable to manage the task of negotiating the step down.

I tumbled from the cab, landing heavily on my hands and knees, the gravel cutting into my palms. A sharp pain shot through my leg, but I scrambled upright and tumbled forward, lurching toward the gleaming front door. I banged against the thick wood once, twice, three times before collapsing onto the cool brick step.

The vague shouts of the carriage driver demanding payment buzzed in the air, but I cared not. I had done all I could.

One of the arched oak doors opened, and the butler appeared, a curse on his lips. He stepped back, alarmed at the sight of me.

"Madam." His voice held caution, fear, surprise even, but no compassion, no kindness. Even to servants, women were disposable things unless a man's name protected them and positioned them in society.

"I am . . ." My voice was a rasp. I swallowed hard and tried again. "Fetch Wiffy. Tell her Adelaide made it."

He regarded me aloofly for a long moment. How perfectly trained he was. His gaze flicked to the still shouting cab driver.

He adjusted the lapels of his black suit and whistled, short and sharp.

"Quit your hollering. You'll get what you're owed. Jacob," he directed over his shoulder into the dim of the house, "find some coins for the cab driver."

A young man strode out from behind the door, toward the driver. I marveled at his unhurried step, his lack of urgency. The freedom he took for granted was unbelievable to me.

"You'd better come in." The butler took a step back and glanced along the street before closing and locking the door behind us.

He took me straight through to the waiting room, not her study as he used to. I suppose he feared me mad; servants talked just as much as their employers. The whole of New York would know of my madness and my imprisonment for it. I found I didn't care as I once might have.

"I'll arrange for a pot of tea." He stared down at me for a long moment until I clutched at the fabric of my ill-fitting dress to still the trembling of my hands. "And perhaps some brandy?"

I nodded, tears gathering. I pushed them down. *Not yet,* I told myself. *Not just yet.*

The room shifted and pulsed before my eyes. The opulence of the room served only to highlight how stained and worn my dress was. A large, curved mirror took up most of one wall. In it stood a disheveled, wild-eyed woman. I bared my teeth at her. There was an energy that thrummed about that lady, a wild kind of energy like the strange green light that electrified the air before a storm.

My hip began to ache, from when I had fallen heavily out of the truck. A great trembling began, first in my hands, then my arms, until I watched as if outside myself as my legs began. They shook and jigged like some mad sort of puppet show. A shrill noise sounded, loud in the still room, and it took me a moment to realize I'd made it. A laugh of some sorts. I had finally gone mad. Now, at the midnight hour, I had finally broken.

A small, redheaded maid appeared with a tray. I startled when she spoke to me, I hadn't heard her enter.

"Would you like me to pour, miss?"

I nodded mutely. My shuddering hands were not up to the task of tea.

She filled a little fluted glass with sticky brown liquid and held it toward me. The scent transported me. Father. Stanley. The doctor. Victoria. My hand itched to dash it from her hand, to send it crashing to the floor, but I forced myself to take it gently. I gulped at it, coughing as the sharp pungent liquid warmed my throat and chest. I closed my eyes and focused on my breath. The maid lifted the glass from my hand and placed it on the table with a soft clink. She left as noiselessly as she had entered.

I clutched the arm of the chair. Rubbed my hand along it. Reminded myself that I was here. In Wiffy's house. Not safe— not quite. Not yet. But so close.

A sudden fear came on me, and I jolted in the chair as if I had been pricked. What if she refused to see me? What if the disgrace and humiliation this scandal had brought upon me was abhorrent to her, and she turned me away? Or worse: perhaps all this waiting was a delay tactic while they fetched law enforcement.

I couldn't go back to the asylum. I couldn't. And I wouldn't. I lurched to my feet and yanked open the door, coming face to face with Wiffy.

Pink lace traced her neck, the bodice of her dress made from a fabric that looked like a striped confection one might purchase at a fair. She looked clean. Rich. Fresh. Untouched. Unmarred by the ugliness of life.

Her eyes shifted slowly along my dress, skirt, boots before closing tightly. She pressed her lips together and inhaled a deep, wavering breath. Ever the unflappable hostess, when she opened her eyes, they were clear.

My Sister's Shadow ⌒ 289

"Make up the guest suite please," she directed to the butler hovering at her shoulder.

She took my elbow and steered me back into the reception room. Her eyes searched mine. "Are you . . . ?"

My lip began to tremble. I understood why she didn't finish her question. I was clearly not all right. My hair had begun to grow back but it was not long enough to stay in a plait, and I had no pins. It clung to my face damply.

She took two faltering steps toward me, her arms outstretched. I flinched, uncertain as to what she intended.

"Oh, Ducky." Her arms were around my neck, and she was sobbing into my hair. "Adelaide. You brave, clever darling. I'm here. I will keep you safe. They won't take you away again. I promise you."

I stood as stiff as a board in her arms while she sobbed and murmured into my hair. She pulled away and studied me. Her show of emotion had a curious effect on me. It was as if she had consumed any feeling I might have felt. The floor beneath me felt unsteady, as if I were back on the *Orient*. I was emptied of all thought and feeling. I fancied that if I were to look in the mirror, I would see the flinty expression of Victoria staring back.

Wiffy nodded, in communication with herself over whatever it was she saw in my eyes. "Come upstairs. Sarah will run you a bath. You'll feel better after a decent night's sleep.

$$\star \quad \star \quad \star$$

"I've burned your dress," Wiffy announced to the curtains as she yanked them open. A shaft of light, far brighter than it ought to be, highlighted dancing dust motes. I rolled over, jerking the bed sheets with me.

"Thank you."

"I thought that for the best."

I said nothing. I felt nothing.

290 ☞   January Gilchrist

Silence thickened, but I could tell from the energy in the room that she hadn't left. The bed depressed as she perched on the side of it. I rolled toward her, and she took my hands in hers.

"Do you know how to shoot?"

The question startled me. I lifted up onto my elbow.

She patted the bed. Between us lay a small pearl-handled revolver. "I want you to take this. But . . . only after you promise me something."

She said nothing more, but I didn't look up. My gaze was on the gun. There was something hypnotic about it. The chill of it seemed to seep through the bed covers. A fancy I'm sure, but when I rested my hand on it, my fingers began to tingle.

"Look at me." Wiffy ordered. Her face was hard. "I will leave this gun with you. It isn't loaded. The bullets are here." She rattled a small brown box. "Do you know how to shoot?"

I nodded again. Father didn't hunt, but Morris had often taken us out with him to the veggie patch and set us to work snapping rabbits.

"A woman should always know how to shoot," he had said with a strangely serious look in his eyes. Darling Morris.

"Only a shotgun."

Wiffy raised her eyebrows, impressed. She smiled tightly, without humor. "It's not terribly powerful, but it's easy to use."

We sat without speaking for a spell. The stillness of the house was thick and dense, strange after the noises of the asylum. Padded footsteps sounded in the wall behind me as the servants moved along their hidden staircase.

"Walt will phone the warden today, if you wish. An escapee is career limiting, to say the least, so he will wish to keep it under wraps, we are certain; and if not, then money will keep him schtum."

My fingers pick relentlessly at a seam on the bedspread.

"Adelaide. Our world isn't fair. I know that. But I want you to know that you have my full and utter support. I promised you I

MY SISTER'S SHADOW   ⌒ 291

won't let them take you again, and I won't. I will do whatever you need."

Her voice was clear, true, and earnest. This woman was the truest and dearest friend I could have ever found. I fumbled for her hand and squeezed it. *Will she forgive me?* I wondered? Or would what I planned to do be a step too far, even for her?

"Who else knows you're here, Ducky?"

I shake my head. "Only your servants."

A loaded pause. I knew what she was going to say before she said it. "Your sister?"

I said nothing. There was a time when we knew where the other was, always. My mind reached for hers along the invisible ribbon that connected us.

Like the handset of a telephone that lay abandoned on a table, there was now nothing but silence.

"Would you like me to let someone know you're here?

Jack, I longed to say, but I said nothing.

I turn away from her, afraid that everything I was feeling was shown as vividly as a mark on my face. The less she knew, the better.

She placed a warm hand on my arm and rested it there. Her touch was so gentle, so loving that I wanted to weep. But not just yet. There was still final business for me to conduct.

"Invite my sister to dinner," I said finally. "This Sunday."

Wiffy made a disbelieving sound. I kept my face averted.

"If that is what you want," she said, confusion coloring her tone.

"It is. Keep her here until it's dark. Send her home at nine and not a minute before."

CHAPTER 33

Sunday arrived without fanfare, the days passing in a blur of damp sheets, meals on trays, and dreamless sleep.

Sunday evening. The same routine, like clockwork. The bookmakers spend Sunday afternoon collecting their debts. They give the men that owe them the morning, but come five o'clock, Sabbath or not, payment is due. Stanley spent every Sunday afternoon at the racecourse, not planning his own racecourse, as I had once imagined, but gambling. Depending on his luck, he would either return to Greycliffe at twilight, morose and short tempered, or he would not return until the early hours of tomorrow morning, full of booze, food, and his own self-importance.

I had crept through the eerily silent house into Stanley's office. At first, my search was noiseless and careful, but when the letters from the good doctors of Meadowleigh did not present themselves, I swept everything from the desk in frustration. It had all hit the floor with a satisfying crash and now lay in chaos on the floor. Shattered inkpots spilled their guts along the carpet, ink blooming among crushed and crumpled papers.

There was nothing. Not a single notation or communication. It must all be stored in the single locked drawer at the bottom of the desk. Which, no matter how I forced or kicked at it, remained firmly shut. The need for knowledge burned within me. What he had said, what she had said, the lies, the agreement. I needed those papers to free myself, to prove their deceit. Without them it was merely my words against theirs. I would not go back to the asylum. I could not.

So I waited.

Inch by inch, the panel of sunlight crept toward the window until it glowed orange, aging to the sick gray twilight that was unique to New York. My feet were numb; I wiggled my toes to wake them. But like a lizard on a rock, I waited.

A trick I had mastered at the asylum. Perhaps one I had been practicing my whole life. How to sit so still as to become invisible.

A snip, a clunk, the rasp of wood on wood as the front door opened and closed. She had arrived. I could feel her. My skin vibrated with her nearness.

I averted my gaze from the vein that jumped in my wrist and unfolded my skirts. The trigger was cool, the gun heavy in my clammy hand.

Gooseflesh scuttled along my skin, and I closed my eyes, listening for sounds of others. There was nothing but a single pair of shoes along the hallway. Panic rose up inside me. Except it was not panic, it was harder, sharper than that. It was something hot and furious, desperate to get out.

Rage.

The door opened, moving on the hinges soundlessly, revealing Victoria. She did not enter the room, but instead remained in the doorway, as still as the marble angel of Fairview Court. It appeared I was not the only one who still knew where her twin was, like sensing a phantom limb. She ran her tongue over her teeth, considering her next move.

"Addy," she said, her face in shadow.

"Vivi."

Our gazes met and locked. The months had hardened her, as if she were one of Father's bugs encased in resin. Lines bracketed her mouth, giving her face the hinged appearance of a puppeteer's dummy. Her hair was braided, long and thick, and coiled like a snake over her shoulder. Her expression blank.

She moved into the room, three slow steps toward me.

I raised my eyebrows. "Not even a how-do-you-do for your long-departed sister?"

Her eyes narrowed at the venom in my voice. *Oh yes,* I wanted to tell her, *it is to be an evenly matched fight tonight.*

"I do not need to ask how you do. You look terrible."

Something cracked inside me. The last vestige of hope died that she would have an excuse. A reason. An assurance that it had all been some kind of mistake. In our conception, the mold had cracked, leaving two halves of the same piece. But we were not. We were two images, one the shadow of the other. Her face was half lit by the gas lamp out the window, but it was the shadowed side I watched.

We were not the same, she and I. Perhaps we never had been.

"What do you want?" She was belligerent.

My heart knocked against my ribs. She took a step toward me, and I stood on shaking legs. Unfolding the gun from my skirt, I lifted it and held it between us.

"Don't come any closer," I warned, scuffing the chair behind me farther away.

Blond hair flashed as she threw her head back and laughed. It was maniacal, grating, like fingers along a slate. "Or what? You'll shoot me? They'll cart you back off to the asylum, and you'll never see the light of day." She smiled as if the idea amused her.

"You are going to admit what you've done. What you did. You are going to tell them the truth."

She pursed her lips and gazed at her fingernails. "No, I'm not. It's clear from just looking at you, you are not well."

Suddenly, I was overcome, exhaustedly overcome with sadness. Victoria was the storm that had battered my windows all my life. I had become accustomed to the noise, to the deluge, the

MY SISTER'S SHADOW   295

chaos she brought. The rages, the pain inflicted, the extremes she required in her life, just to feel alive.

But then other images came too. Laughing until we collapsed, conversations conducted only with the merest raise of an eyebrow, a twitch of a lip, the comforting touch of fingertips. Her milky breath against my cheek.

Still, I loved her.

"I love you," I said. And I did. "But I also hate you."

Her lip curled with derision, and her eyes, those hateful, wretched eyes, were narrowed as they ran along my body. "Hate me? You can't live without me. You are nothing without me. You can't do anything without me. Always following me around, waiting for me to have an idea, tell you what to do. Whom to marry." Her face tightened. "Whom to love."

A thread inside me snapped. "It's you that cannot live without me. Who will you have to blame? When loneliness shrieks through the windows at you, when it hovers at the crack of your door at night. When the truth scratches at the window, begging to be let in? Who will you have? Who will listen to your excuses, your lies?"

"You want truth?" Her gaze searched the room for a weapon, I could tell by the way her eyes knocked from item to item. "You don't know what is true and what is not. Poor little Adelaide, pathetic little Adelaide. Always waiting for someone to come and save her. You would be nothing without me. This is mine. I deserve this." She thumped her fist against her chest.

Her eyes were dark, wretched, filled with hatred, and it was as if I had never seen her before.

She stabbed toward me with a finger. "You never wanted any of this, but you took it from me anyway."

I shook my head. "I didn't take it. You are right: I never wanted it. But I didn't take it from you. I asked you to help me. Told you I didn't want it. Any of it. You could have had it all."

296 ⟫ January Gilchrist

"I don't want your castoffs," she screamed. Her face was twisted with rage. "I wanted it to be *me* that he chose. For it to be *me* that he wanted. I wanted my name to be on the invitations, not as an afterthought. I wanted to be the lady, not the lady's sister."

A sadness so dark, so deep overcame me. My sister had done this to me simply because she hadn't gotten what she wanted.

"Do you really believe he chose me over you because he preferred me?" I asked. "He is a bad man, a cruel man. I would never have wished him on you, Vivi. Why would you wish him on me?"

I lowered the gun.

"Look around you," I said, gesturing to the shabby room. "He is afflicted with the gambling disease. This is all about money. Not me. Not you."

"This *is* about me. And it's about you. You thought you could leave me?" she screamed, spittle flying across the room and landing on my cheek. "You thought you could replace me with Wiffy? With Jack?"

She closed the distance between us swiftly, her hand closing around my neck. I gulped for air.

"You thought you could leave me behind and start a life without me in it?"

Her hand tightened against my throat, squeezing, crushing. My hand scratched uselessly at hers, searching for a way to release some of the pressure building in my head.

Panic screwed through my belly, as familiar as my own name. She was mad. I must have known it, but I hadn't admitted it, even to myself. She wasn't just selfish; she truly was not sane. I wanted to scream, to shout, but I couldn't breathe. Colors sparked and popped in the room, becoming both brighter and dimmer. Victoria's face was almost pressed against mine. I could see the gray flecks in our irises that appeared silver in sunlight, the red veins that tracked through the whites of her eyes, and her breath hot against my lips.

My Sister's Shadow ⬥ 297

I thought of the cell I'd spent the last two months in, the fetid stench of unwashed bodies, damp linen, and misery. How she had left me there to rot because she couldn't stand the idea of me living a life without her. She would rather me dead, my own sister.

My lungs burned without oxygen, and my eyes closed as darkness washed over me.

"You are nothing without me," she said again, louder.

Flashes of long-forgotten memories overcame me, rolling over me like the waves that had crashed along the shoreline at Newport.

Victoria in a rage, pulling things from shelves, mirrors thrown to floors, shards shattering across the floor, windows smashed, animal scat on clean shoes, dead birds in my bed.

The black kitten I'd favored as a child, neck broken, discarded where she knew I would find it. The glass in my soap. Digging in the garden, talking to herself.

I was not nothing without her. I was Adelaide Wisteria Windlass. Not just Lord Radcliffe's daughter, Lord Stanley's wife, Victoria's sister, not her other half . . . not Victoria's scapegoat nor a doll to be moved around at whim. I was myself and I refused to die here, like this. Rage turned my spine to iron. I was done with being controlled by her.

The gun fell to the floor as I reached for her with my left hand. Blindly I reached for anything to grasp. My fingers skimmed across her skin until my thumb landed on the soft pad of her eye. I gathered every last piece of energy I had, all of my cells fighting, making one last effort to live. My thumb sank into her flesh. Her grip loosened, just slightly but I felt it.

Now.

I shoved against her, stamped on her foot, shifted my hands to her hair and pulled her to the floor as I collapsed, desperately sucking in much-needed oxygen.

My lungs burned as air filled them, and my ears were full like I was underwater. I was vaguely aware of movement, a flash of color as Victoria scooted backward away from me.

298 ✣   January Gilchrist

The gun lay on the floor between us. I should grab it, take it out of Victoria's reach, but my legs were stiff, motionless. My heart thrashed in my throat. I couldn't catch my breath.

A snip, a clunk. The sound of the door opening and closing downstairs.

Victoria smirked at me.

"In here. Help me!" she called, her gaze never shifting from mine. An ugly smile tilted the corners of her mouth.

It was impossible for me to imagine a world that bent to your every whim, your every desire, where any story you told became the truth simply because you did whatever it took to make it so.

The walls pressed in on me, and the floor thinned beneath me. She would win. Victoria would win this fight, like she had won every fight. No one would listen to me with my ragged nails and dirty hands, my asylum-shorn head. I looked mad. I felt mad. No one was going to save me. I would be sent back to the asylum—Stanley and Victoria would ensure it.

But I would take her down to the depths of hell with me.

Summoning every ounce of strength I had left, I lurched forward and grabbed the gun. I lifted it in the air between us, Morris's voice in my head: breathe in, aim, pull the trigger, exhale.

My finger twitched on the trigger.

"Adelaide."

Victoria's gaze flew to the doorway, but I didn't shift my eyes from her. I couldn't despite my shock. I hadn't heard Jack on the stairs. He moved like a cat; I'd quite forgotten that.

"Hello, Jack," Victoria said, her voice like honey. "Just in time. Adelaide appears to have escaped. We'd better call the police, call the asylum, have her sent back. You can see how dangerous she is."

Jack didn't respond to her jibes. "Adelaide. Adelaide. Put that down. You don't want to do that."

MY SISTER'S SHADOW   ⌒ 299

My hand quivered at the sound of his voice, but I kept the
gun trained on Victoria. I would not put it down. Not even for
him.

"Yes. Put the gun down. It seems too heavy for you." Her
tone was contemptuous. She clearly didn't believe I'd do it.

I swallowed hard. "I'll put it down. After I settle my score."

Victoria laughed again. It was not the light jingle of crystal it
used to be, but sharp, brittle. She shuffled closer to the desk. "Are
you going to shoot me? Your own sister? We all know you won't.
You are useless, pathetic."

I hadn't planned to. Didn't believe it would be required. I
thought when I saw her, all our old feelings would return. That
she would have an explanation for me. That she could tell me
how she hadn't had anything to do with it. But now, I saw it in
her eyes. She had planned this. She had spent days, evenings,
months planning how she would destroy me. I lifted the gun
higher, leveling it at her chest.

Wiffy's words rang in my ears. Some people would do anything to be part of this life.

Victoria sneered, but her eyes were dead. There would be no
winners here.

I inhaled, my finger tightening against the trigger.

The thump of the street door opening pounded in my head.
Stanley was back. Too early. He was never usually back until the
gray hour of morning. Had someone told him? I glanced at Jack.
How had he known I was there? A sick feeling swirled in me.
Was he in cahoots with Stanley and Victoria? Was it all just a
trick? A trap?

I tried to still the tremor that shook through me. Whom
could I trust? My breath was as loud as a river in my ears. I
couldn't think. The gun shook. Words battered me. Jack and Victoria were speaking, but I couldn't hear anything except Stanley's
footsteps pounding up the stairs.

300 ⤳ January Gilchrist

Stanley threw open the door with a rattle.

His face was beige and shiny, like wax. He was in what was obviously yesterday's clothes—crumpled, sweat stained, and sour smelling. "What the bloody hell is going on here?"

The three of us straightened, like children found by a parent doing something they knew they shouldn't. Jack reached for the gun. Catching sight of him out of the corner of my eye, I instinctively lurched backward. His hand knocked the weapon from my hand and sent it skittling along the floor between Victoria and me.

Stanley loomed in the doorway. He was smaller than I remembered, although heavier. In my memories, he was Zeus or Ares, but in reality he was a slightly portly man, with too-small eyes and a face split by a beak of a nose. A man so desperate for money and renown that he would do anything to get it.

His beady gaze flicked between us all, lingering longest on the mess of his desk lying on the floor. "Anyone care to enlighten me?" His voice was frigid.

Jack cleared his throat, but Victoria jumped in, her voice a gruesome parody of my own.

"Stanley, thank God you're here! Call the police! Adelaide has escaped the asylum and attacked me. She's threatening to kill us all. Take her wrists!"

Stanley narrowed his gaze on me, but he didn't take a step. "You," he ordered Jack. "Go call for Doctor Mortimer. No need for the police to get involved."

"No." Jack's voice was an iron club. "I will call the police, and I'll tell them what you and she have been up to."

Stanley's eyes widened as a look of dumb surprise slackened his face, as if he couldn't believe someone would say such a thing to him. "I beg your pardon?"

"You ought to be strung up for what you've done. I won't let you get away with it. Adelaide"—he gestured to me with a fist so tightly closed his knuckles were white—"and I are leaving, and you won't be stopping us."

MY SISTER'S SHADOW   301

He stepped between Stanley and me, so close that I could smell the stable on him. "Get your affairs in order, because you're both going away for a long time."

"Who do you think you're speaking to?" Stanley spluttered.

"Believe me, I know exactly who I'm speaking to," Jack answered.

Stanley raised his nose in the air and glared down it at Jack. "I'll have your job. You'll never work in this town again."

"Ha." Jack spat the sound. "You'll never be able to show your face in this town or any other once everyone hears about what you've done. The papers will love this story. Lord Stanley, liar, cheat, thief, has his wife committed to a lunatic asylum so he can consort with her sister? Whispers will follow you both like flies."

Stanley sucked his teeth, his mustache quivering like a caterpillar. "I'm certain I don't know what you're referring to. If her sister has misled me, using trickery, or that certain type of female sorcery women are known for, well, it's surely not me to blame." He inhales. Clearly, he has thought on his excuse for some time.

"They can both go to the asylum—both sisters. Tainted blood perhaps. People might talk, but only with pity for me. I won't be the first man to have been disappointed by the weaker sex. They are so prone to hysterics."

Victoria made a stifled sound of rage. "You are lying! You knew! You knew and you agreed to make me Lady Stanley. You promised me!" She was screeching, eyes wide in a way I recognized too well. Fury had its hold on her.

Stanley looked at her with such distaste. "I'm afraid I don't know what you're talking about."

Her gaze slithered around the room before stopping on the gun. A chill skated along my skin. Still, I knew her well enough to know what she was thinking.

We lunged for the gun at the same time.

There was an explosion of noise and color, brighter than I had expected. My ears popped and began to ring, and then—

Nothing but silence.

EPILOGUE

"I have left the newspaper here for you, Ducky. It holds some surprising news, I'm afraid. Lord Stanley has been shot and killed."

We were in Wiffy's house, in the drawing room. I had been staring at the wall, blindly reliving the moments of that night two evenings ago. Her words brought me back to myself with a horrible jolt.

The man who decimated my life, who had come into my life and picked me up by my ankles and shaken, as hard as he could, was no longer. I release a sigh.

"It says here they suspect he was murdered by a *business associate*. Stanley was in debt, Adelaide. A lot of debt. To some unsavory characters. Far more unsavory than we could imagine."

Jack is beside me, his hand over mine, warm, strong.

"His debts leave you in a precarious position, Adelaide." Wiffy continued. "I will speak plainly. He has defrauded the gentlemen of the raceway. The money they have invested is gone, and the men contracted to build it are striking, reporting they have not received a penny from him. The house will be sold to cover the debts, but as his widow, you will be shamed and destitute. I'm afraid the scandal will be immense. Even I could not help you weather it."

304 ⮑ January Gilchrist

I say nothing. Her eyes wrinkle at the corners.

"Adelaide dear, we think it would be for the best if you were to return home. To England. I took the liberty of purchasing you passage on a ship departing in two weeks' time.

Wiffy's fingers tremble lightly on my arm, like the touch of a butterfly. I lift her hand from my arm and press her fingers to my lips. "What would I have done without you?"

She smiles. "Lucky for you, we need never find out."

⋆ ⋆ ⋆

The smell of the port transports me to our arrival in New York. It's impossible to conjure up the feelings of that day now, and for that I am grateful.

The sky has been low and ominous all morning, and it rumbles as I dodge a lifted cobble on the footpath. A newspaper wheels past. I don't need to see the headline to know what it says; they've all be repeating the same thing since the story broke. Lord Stanley, murdered by some unknown criminal mastermind, had stolen obscene amounts of money from New York's greatest men. His wife, recently released from an insane asylum, is returning to England, destitute and disgraced. I clutch Jack's hand, which is clasped in mine, a little tighter.

"All right?" Jack's eyes search mine.

I nod as a thrill jolts through me, I will never tire of staring into his eyes, in the middle of the street, for anyone to see. I release his hand, link my arm through his, and smile, leaning my head briefly against his shoulder.

"I am, indeed."

And I am.

We weave through the bustling crowd, dodging men with crates, trunks, and bags, and the children that tear through the crowd, coats trailing behind him.

The ship looms above us like Goliath, sending the dock below into shadow.

MY SISTER'S SHADOW ⟡ 305

A black suited, broad-shouldered man stands at the edge of the gangway. There is something of a coiled snake about him. His hat is tipped back, his eyes dart along the faces of the crowd, and his hand hovers in the air between him and the woman next to him. Close enough to touch quickly, should he need to. The woman says something and gestures to the sky, and he nods, as if conserving his energy. He lifts a hand and summons a porter. They speak, heads close together, but he doesn't shift his gaze from the woman beside him.

Suddenly I can't breathe. I press my hand to my chest, gulping for air that won't come. I suck in a desperate breath and press my fist to my mouth to stop myself from crying out.

Wait, I want to call. *Turn around. I love you. I forgive you.*

I do not speak.

She doesn't turn.

The sky has been low and ominous all morning, and as lightning rips it apart, images fall through my mind like a deck of cards drifting to the ground.

The feeling of that cold hard trigger under the soft flesh of my fingertip, how the light fell on Victoria in such a way that I could see myself reflected in the shimmering silver of the eyes we shared. How soft her hand had been as it covered mine. She didn't pull or pinch, just rested it there. You wouldn't dare, her touch seemed to say.

Breathe in, aim, pull the trigger, exhale.

One's happiness should not be dependent on another person, but for my whole life it had been. I had clung to memories of Mother and lived my life for Victoria, never forming an independent identity outside of the one I shared with my sister. The asylum had taught me that much at least. Now I was free to start anew in a life completely of my own choosing. Finally free.

The wind swirls and eddies around us, carrying the porter's words down to us.

"Welcome aboard, Lady Stanley. Robbins here will see you to your quarters." A porter speaks to the woman.

306 ⌇ January Gilchrist

The man in black shepherds her to the gangplank, his body a wall, a shield, a vise, squeezing her onto the gangway. Wiffy engaged this man to guard Victoria after delivering to her an ultimatum as sharp as a blow. *Leave America as Lady Stanley or hang for the murder of Lord Stanley.* Even Victoria's acrobatics could not free her from the binds that she herself had created, so she'd signed the agreement Wiffy's father had drawn up, a legally binding document we all hoped would never see the light of day.

Her foot hangs in the air, for the briefest moment, as if she is considering her options, and I see myself, right here in this port on the day of our arrival, foot extended in the air, visions of escape tearing through me.

"My lady?" the shipman queries, and her boot makes contact with the wooden plank. Then she is moving, a blur of motion and memory.

When I open my eyes, she is gone. My final memory of my other half is the back of her swirling hair, mist surrounding her as if she were but an apparition. And perhaps she only ever was, an apparition of my heart.

Jack's hand is on my arm, and I turn my head.

"Ready, Mrs. Halloran?"

I smile. Joy bursts through me, and I placed my hand over his, the ring under the glove still evident. A joyful reminder that, even out of sight, it is there. Like flower bulbs in the dead of winter, it is unseen but still there.

"I am, my darling husband."

This morning, we stood under the dark oak paneling of the Office of the City Clerk and made our vows: Victoria Windlass—although she preferred to be called Lavender, her middle name, she assured anyone who asked—and Jack Halloran, joined in holy matrimony.

Wiffy was overjoyed when Jack accepted her offer to train her horses. She had offered us a small house of our own, close enough that we could continue our daily rides. As Victoria, I was no longer acceptable in society, but I was grateful for Wiffy's company in whatever form it took. Leaving society was no hardship for me, as I'd never found myself comfortable in its strict confines. What I longed for was a life that was of my own creation, a life with someone I loved and who loved me in return.

Who would have thought that the happiest I would ever be was when I was not myself?

ACKNOWLEDGMENTS

Until as recently as the 1950s, men could have their wives committed to asylums with no more evidence required than his 'words'. These women were subjected to unspeakable horrors with no recourse.

The bones of this story were inspired by Marie Wilmerding, a Vanderbilt heiress who liked 'men and absinthe too much.' Much like Adelaide, she was found and freed by her friends, however, her first attempt to have herself released was rejected by a judge, merely because her wealthy uncle (who had her committed so he could steal her inheritance) said so.

If you're interested in reading further about this subject then I highly recommend Kate Moore's *The Woman Who Could Not Be Silenced* and any story written about Nellie Bly, the brave journalist who went undercover in an asylum in the late 1800s to expose its injustices.

Thank you to all the twins who generously shared their stories and experiences of how being a mirror twin shaped their lives. Sometimes loving, sometimes estranged, always obsessive, some responsible for causing enormous, unimaginable pain to each other. Living (or not) with another as your mirror image can be both a gift and a curse, and I appreciate everyone who spoke so willingly to me about their experiences.

Acknowledgments

This is a book about sisters. Both those thrust upon us and the ones we choose.

The patriarchy wants us to believe female friendships are difficult, that we betray easily, that our petty power struggles over trivial matters consumes us. Thank you to my chosen sisters:

Sara J Henry - Last time I used every word I could find to thank you but this time I'm beyond words. You're a dream. The best kind of stalwart sister.

Jacqui Lipton - Thank you for helping navigate the publishing world.

Clare and Sarah - Thank you for being sisters to this book, although perhaps I should call you midwives. You held my hand, wiped my brow, and jollied me right until the final moments of birth. Although I'm sure I regularly give you reason to want to, please don't have me committed!

Nicola, Malerie, and Erin - I can count on my sister cheerleaders to, at the very least, read the acknowledgments, if not the entire book.